Literature and Cultural Criticism in the 1950s

Literature and Cultural Criticism in the 1950s

The Feeling Male Body

Susan Brook
Simon Fraser University

First published 2007 by
PALGRAVE MACMILLAN
Houndmills, Basingstoke, Hampshire RG21 6XS and
175 Fifth Avenue, New York, N.Y. 10010
Companies and representatives throughout the world

PALGRAVE MACMILLAN is the global academic imprint of the Palgrave
Macmillan division of St. Martin's Press, LLC and of Palgrave Macmillan Ltd.
Macmillan® is a registered trademark in the United States, United Kingdom
and other countries. Palgrave is a registered trademark in the European
Union and other countries.

ISBN-13: 978-1-4039-4106-0   hardback
ISBN-10: 1-4039-4106-8   hardback

This book is printed on paper suitable for recycling and made from fully
managed and sustained forest sources.

A catalogue record for this book is available from the British Library.

A catalog record for this book is available from the Library of Congress.

10   9   8   7   6   5   4   3   2   1
16   15   14   13   12   11   10   09   08   07

Printed and bound in Great Britain by
Antony Rowe Ltd, Chippenham and Eastbourne

In memory of John Bernard Brook (1946–1992) and Matthew John Brook (1979–2004)

Contents

Acknowledgements

My thanks go to the following people for their feedback on versions of the material presented in this book: Sandra Courtman, Jon Beasley-Murray, John Brannigan, Andrew Lawson, Ken Hirschkop, Patience Schell, Natalie Zacek, Peter Wade, and Berthold Schoene. I would like to thank Ian Baucom, Barbara Herrnstein Smith, and Janice Radway for their help and feedback on a much earlier and very different version of this project. Thanks also to students from Staffordshire University and Simon Fraser University, whose questions and insights helped me to develop and clarify my own thoughts, especially Simon Fraser students from English 342 (Fall 2004) and English 378 (Spring 2006). An earlier version of part of Chapter 2 was published as 'Engendering Rebellion: Angry Young Men, the New Left and Masculinity' in *Posting the Male: Masculinities in Post-war and Contemporary British Literature* (Amsterdam: Rodopi, 2003). A version of Chapter 4 is forthcoming in *Women: A Cultural Review*.

This book was written during a period of upheaval – geographical and emotional – in my own life, and I would like to thank the following people for their friendship, support, and love over that time, when I often felt like George Eliot's Casaubon, 'toiling in the morass of authorship without seeming nearer to the goal': Jon Beasley-Murray, Matthew Parry, Clancy Lyon, Jenny Cooper, Andrew Geddis, Louise Sinclair, Jeremy Lane, Chris Bongie, Sue McPherson, Sandra Courtman, Patience Schell, Lucy Burke, Alan Girvin, Freya Schiwy, Alessandro Fornazzari, Ryan Long, Tracy Devine Guzmàn, the Beasley-Murray family Peter Dickinson, Richard Cavell, Jeff Derksen, Dana Symons, Sophie McCall, and David Chariandy. My special thanks to the following members of my family for their encouragement, patience, and tolerance, particularly in the latter stages of writing: Jonathan Brook, Rosie Fleming, Theresa Novin, and, above all, my mother, Lynette Brook.

My greatest debts cannot be repaid here, although I can at least mention them. Toril Moi has been an exemplary reader, teacher, and mentor over the last decade. Her own brilliance and intellectual verve have inspired me; her unique combination of devastating criticism and warm encouragement has supported and challenged me when I needed it most. This book is dedicated to the memory of my father, John Brook, and my brother, Matthew Brook. My father's passion and integrity and my brother's grace and humour remain with me every day.

Introduction: The Feeling Male Body

The 1950s and early 1960s are often recycled in British popular imagination as an era of cosy consensus, and as the last gasp of a more innocent and more stable – or more rigid – society. Sometimes the invocation of the postwar period is tinged with a rosy glow, as in the long-running ITV television series *Heartbeat*, all bicycles and village fetes; elsewhere, it is grey and grim, as in Mike Leigh's *Vera Drake* (2004), a film which plunges us into a world of sexual naivety and social censoriousness in order to reveal its dark underside in the form of the illegal abortion trade. Yet these versions of postwar Britain overlook the fact that this was a period of flux and of transition between modernity – with its utopian faith in progress – and postmodernity – characterized by radical pluralism and the proliferation of decentred, multiple identities, as well as by the post-Fordist, globalized economy of the later twentieth century. As Doris Lessing described in 1957, the experience of living in the postwar world was the experience of being 'caught up in a great whirlwind of change' (Lessing, 'Small Personal Voice' 27). This book argues that a key figure emerges in the literature and cultural criticism of the 1950s and early 1960s as a response to this sense of change: the 'feeling male body', which is both the symptom of cultural crisis and its cure. It concentrates on the appearance of this figure in the work of the generation of writers and critics who came to prominence in the 1950s, and who are associated either with the New Left or with the label of 'Angry Young Men'. Anger, however, is only one of a range of intense affects, emotions, and sensations that these texts attribute to men and to male bodies. These bodies are rugged, virile, robust, and aggressively heterosexual, though they are frequently also wounded, marked, and suffering. Whether they are in pain or blissfully doing the jive, men are linked with life, vitality, and feeling.

1

The feeling male body of the mid-twentieth century takes on different forms, but it is always associated with transformation, whether nostalgic or utopian, social or individual. Frequently, the feeling male body
is metonymically aligned with the social body. At times it is a metaphor
for wholeness, the symbol of an organic community that stands
in opposition to a society divided and fragmented by class divisions.
In other manifestations, it embodies the disruptive and unruly energies
of modernity that have the capacity to transform a society perceived as
moribund and static. Yet the feeling male body is also an individual
body, and in several of the texts I discuss, the authentic individual's
capacity for life and vitality enables him to transcend and escape social
divisions, rather than to resolve them. In these texts it is the social elite
that is transformed: the new elite are marked by their capacity for feeling, in contrast to the traditional elite who are withered, cerebral, and
feminized. Frequently the male body is wounded and in pain, often as
protagonists masochistically choose the injuries that are inflicted upon
them. Here the social and economic shifts of the postwar era are represented as a loss that is marked on the body. Paradoxically, however, the
protagonists' suffering also revitalizes them, so that the feeling male
body is simultaneously a site for social and individual renewal.

The book is not a survey of 1950s literature. Instead I use sustained close
readings of selected texts, combined with analysis of their reception
(including, in some cases, their film adaptations), to illustrate my larger
argument that gender, and the discourse of masculine affect focused on
the 'feeling male body', is central to understanding the literature and
cultural criticism of this period. The first three chapters of this book trace
the contours of this discourse as it emerged across cultural criticism, literature, and film, using as case studies Richard Hoggart's *The Uses of Literacy*
(1957), Raymond Williams's *Border Country* (1960), a range of articles from
Universities and Left Review, Kingsley Amis's *Lucky Jim* (1954), John
Osborne's *Look Back in Anger* (1956), John Braine's *Room at the Top* (1957),
and Alan Sillitoe's *Saturday Night and Sunday Morning* (1958). The final two
chapters explore the effects of this discourse, both on women writers of the
immediate postwar period, and on the cultural criticism and literature of
the later twentieth century. The dominant discourse of affect was both reit-
erated and rewritten by women writers of the period, in Shelagh Delaney's
A Taste of Honey (1958), Lynne Reid Banks's *The L-Shaped Room* (1960), and
Doris Lessing's *The Golden Notebook* (1962). The feeling male body continued to have a powerful hold over the British cultural imaginary in the
1970s, 1980s, and 1990s, appearing in cultural criticism, literature, and
film from Paul Willis's *Profane Culture* (1978) and Dick Hebdige's *Subculture*
(1979), to Martin Amis's *Money* (1984), Irvine Welsh's *Trainspotting* (1993),

and *The Full Monty* (dir. Peter Cattaneo; 1997) – all of which represent the feeling male body as the symptom of social crisis and as its cure.

From sentiment to vitality: historical contexts

While the feeling male body of the 1950s and early 1960s has descendants, it also has a number of antecedents. In a 1952 letter, Kingsley Amis tells Philip Larkin that the working title of his novel (published in 1954 as *Lucky Jim*) is 'The Man of Feeling', a reference to Henry McKenzie's 1771 novel of that name (*Letters* 289).[1] The eighteenth-century novel of sensibility, from McKenzie to Laurence Sterne to Samuel Richardson, celebrated the faculty of refined feeling, which was displayed above all through the protagonist's body – sighs, tears, and wordless gestures.[2] Although sentimentality was primarily associated with femininity, the 'man of feeling' took on the qualities of femininity, including helplessness and weakness, so that he became 'a male body feminized by affect, a sort of emotional cross-dresser' (Chapman and Hendler 3). The protagonist in these novels illustrates the plight of the virtuous individual in a hostile world, whose benevolent sympathy dooms him to impotence. In the 1950s and early 1960s the feeling male, such as Amis's protagonist Jim Dixon, is also pitted against a hostile world, and in the literary texts associated with the Angry Young Men, as in the novel of sensibility, misery is similarly alleviated by sensibility rather than by political action. But in his twentieth-century incarnation, the feeling male is not distinguished by his capacity for benevolence or sympathy, although he forms connections with others who share his capacity for life and vitality. Moreover, feeling in these novels is muscular, associated with masculine vitality and sexuality, in contrast to the impotent eighteenth-century man of feeling. While in some cases the feeling male's pain and suffering temporarily feminizes him, his ability to feel ultimately helps to revitalize and prove his masculinity.

How and why is feeling linked with virile masculinity in this period, and to what end? We can begin to answer this question by turning to key literary and intellectual currents of the first half of the twentieth century. By the nineteenth century, according to Janet Todd, sentimentality had come to be seen as a lapse of masculine rigor and moral seriousness, and its descendant, melodrama, was a feminized mode and genre. But by the end of the nineteenth century, a new account of 'muscular' feeling emerges in the work of Friedrich Nietzsche, who links masculine energy with life force and with the will to power, in contrast to decadent, feminized sentimentality and benevolence. For Nietzsche, the capacities and energies of the vital body are bulwarks against the dehumanizing effects of industrialization and of the mass-produced culture associated with industrialism, and this is also the case for two early twentieth-century champions of life and vitality, T. S. Eliot and Cambridge literary critic F. R. Leavis. Eliot famously identifies and laments the 'dissociation of sensibility', the gap between thought and feeling that set in after the Metaphysical poets; like Leavis, he longs for an organic, pre-industrial agrarian community in which mind and body are united, and feeling and vitality flourish, safe from the dulling, anaesthetizing effects of capitalism and mass culture.[3] D. H. Lawrence, Leavis's favourite twentieth-century novelist, depicts a version of this organic community in *The Rainbow* (1915), which emphasizes the unity between nature and the bodies of the Brangwen men: 'The young corn waved and was silken, and the lustre slid along the limbs of the men who saw it. They took the udder of the cows, the cows yielded milk and pulse against the hands of the men, the pulse of the blood of the teats of the cows beat into the pulse of the hands of the men' (8).

The sensations and the natural rhythms of the body that Lawrence celebrates are frequently represented in this period as the casualties of capitalism. Across a range of texts and films in the 1920s and 1930s, the labouring body is the site that registers the wounds inflicted by industrial capitalism on the individual and on society. Charlie Chaplin's *Modern Times* (1936) portrays the effects of industrialization on the body: working at an assembly line, the gestures of Charlie Chaplin's tramp become more and more jerky and machine-like, until his body is literally swallowed up by the cogs and wheels of the machinery. Similarly, Fritz Lang's *Metropolis* (1927) shows the body as a casualty of the factory, depicting the shuffling gait and bowed bodies of the labourers who toil in the underground city, and who are fed to a machine that is shown – literally – as a monster. But if workers' bodies are wounded by industrial capitalism, in other interwar texts they are icons of strength and vitality in contrast to the alienating forces of the machine and of mass production. Most famously, George Orwell admires the miners in *The Road to Wigan Pier*, celebrating their 'arms and belly muscles of steel' (31) and the 'splendour of their bodies' (32) which transcend the harsh conditions in which they work. As Leavis and Lawrence romanticized the body of the agrarian labourer, so Orwell romanticizes the body of the industrial labourer.

In certain respects the feeling male of the 1950s is a descendant of these earlier figures, as both the symptom of social crisis and its potential cure, but he also differs from them in key respects. Both Lang's robotic workers and Orwell's ennobled ones are distinguished and defined by their class, and by their capacity for labour; workers' bodies – working-class bodies – register the pain of industrialization and also potentially resist its anaesthetizing and alienating effects. In contrast, the feeling male body in the literature of the Angry Young Men, the films of the New Wave, and the criticism of the New Left is not primarily a labouring body. The feeling male of the postwar period is as likely to be an accountant, a university lecturer, a scholarship boy, or a smartly dressed mod, as he is to work in a factory. In all cases, the feeling men in the texts I examine are associated with class transition, rather than with an easily identified or stable class position. Richard Hoggart's nameless scholarship boy and Matthew from Raymond Williams's *Border Country* are from working-class backgrounds, but have become socially mobile through education. Similarly, Jim Dixon and Jimmy Porter, both from lower-middle-class backgrounds, find themselves mixing with the traditional middle classes because of education (for Dixon) and marriage (for Porter). Education and marriage both play a part in Joe Lampton's social mobility, enabling the protagonist of *Room at the Top* to make his way from working-class Dufton to the highest point, both socially and geographically, of middle-class Warley.

Other feeling male bodies are more clearly working-class, such as the youths whose pictures and presence dominate the pages of *Universities and Left Review*, but these also signify transition. The transition embodied by such figures is social rather than individual. They mediate between an older working-class identity based on manual labour and relative material deprivation, and a new social formation in which the decline of traditional working-class occupations, the rise of youth culture, and postwar affluence all help to blur and complicate traditional class identities and class distinctions. This is illustrated in the character of Arthur Seaton in *Saturday Night and Sunday Morning*, a factory labourer and the figure perhaps closest to Orwell's 'noble bodies', who is associated with social transitions rather than individual class mobility. He marks a shift between the 1930s working-class community of his parents, found in traditional terraced housing, and the new 'consumerist' culture of working-class affluence associated with his fiancée Doreen, who wants to move with Arthur to the suburbs.

The feeling male body of the postwar period is therefore not congruent with working-class identity, as it was in its interwar manifestations. Instead, the postwar feeling male body responds to the waves of social change rippling through British society, and his unstable or indecipherable class position indicates such change. Rather than registering the shock of the industrial revolution, these feeling men are marked by the shock of the social upheavals of the postwar period. Masculinity becomes the defining characteristic of the feeling male in this period, referencing the iconography of working-class identity – rugged, robust, and aggressively heterosexual – but also substituting for class identity.

Postcolonialism and postmodernity

While this book focuses on postwar Britain, the trope of the feeling male body responds to broader global geopolitical shifts: in particular, post-colonialism and postmodernity. The postwar period heralded a major shift in national identity with the final unravelling of Empire; 1945 marked the beginning of preparations for Indian independence as well as the end of the war, and throughout the late 1940s and the 1950s, independence movements in Africa, Asia, and the Caribbean signalled the imminent end of Britain's role as the centre of a global empire, made spectacularly visible in the Suez crisis of 1956, as I discuss in Chapter 1. The *Empire Windrush* docked at Tilbury Harbour in 1948, symbolically marking the end of an old British imperial order and the beginning of a new era of more diffuse global and transnational flows of people and products. During the 1950s the after-effects of Empire made their presence felt in new ways in the former metropolitan centre, as flows of immigrants from former colonies replaced the earlier flows of raw materials. As Bill Schwartz has argued, this transformed racial and national identity in ways which were profoundly modern, if also conservative, as the notion of the colonial frontier was 'relocated onto the domestic terrain' of the nation (191). Meanwhile, attempts were made to redefine Britishness after the loss of Empire: for example the 1951 Festival of Britain defined Britishness as modernity, con-necting modern design and technology to national identity; similarly, while the 1953 coronation of Elizabeth II celebrated tradition, it also 'strove to project an image of the future' (Conekin, Mort and Waters 1), as the televised ceremony was projected across the globe, emphasizing a modern Commonwealth in place of the traditional Empire.

The feeling male body responds to Britain's demise as a global power and the postwar crisis in national identity by simultaneously expressing this loss and compensating for it. This is clearly seen in Ian Fleming's James Bond novels, from *Casino Royale* (1953) onwards, which are satu-rated with images of the tortured Bond. One context for understanding Bond's pain is that of Empire, and more specifically postimperial melancholy or postcolonial melancholy, concepts intro-duced by Ian Baucom in *Out of Place* and Paul Gilroy in *Postcolonial Melancholia*. Bond's torture at the hands of Doctor No in the epony-mous novel (1958) extends for pages, and his wounded vulnerability can be seen as the expression of postimperial melancholy – melancho-lia, in Freud's terms, being the condition in which an external loss is internalized. Bond feels the loss of Empire keenly, agreeing with the view of postcolonial Jamaica expressed by the colonial administrator

Pleydell-Smith: 'Self determination indeed! They can't even run a bus service' (46). But Bond's melancholic pain is also a way of repairing this loss, as pain and feeling are the means through which masculinity is revitalized. By the end of *Doctor No*, Bond's wounds are fetishized as a key component of his masculinity and of his sexual magnetism: in the masochistic fantasy of the final chapter, 'Slave-Time', Bond takes up the position of colonial slave in relation to Honeychile, his lover, who kisses him and splashes his 'battered body' with antiseptic until 'the tears of pain [ran] out of his eyes and down his cheeks' (185). This passage links Bond's victimhood with revitalized masculine sexuality rather than postimperial impotence, and national identity is displaced onto masculinity through the vitality of the feeling male body, which both expresses and compensates for the loss of Empire. James Bond, despite his wounded, tortured nature, is nonetheless an iconic figure of postwar British masculinity. And although the texts I discuss in this book engage with the loss of Empire in less obvious ways than the Bond novels, their anxieties about masculine power are linked to anxieties about national identity in a postcolonial era.

However, postcolonial melancholy is not the only framework for understanding the significance of the feeling male body in this period. It must also be seen as a response to the social and economic shifts of postmodernity. Fredric Jameson points out that 'the economic preparation of postmodernism or late capitalism began in the 1950s, after the wartime shortages of consumer goods and spare parts had been made up, and new products and new technologies (not least those of the media) could be pioneered'. Although the 1960s bring about the psychic break that characterizes postmodernism, Jameson emphasizes that it is the larger period of 1945–73 that emerges as 'the hothouse, or forcing ground, of the new system' (*Postmodernism* xx). In Britain as in America, the 1950s heralded the beginning of a shift from a production-based economy to one built around the service sector, and a concomitant shift in both the relative size and character of the working classes and of the middle classes. The changes in British life were not just economic, but also cultural. The welfare state was consolidated, and changes in education policy and the establishment of new cultural institutions were designed to redistribute cultural capital.[4] Attitudes to sexuality were beginning to change: the Wolfenden Report of 1957 suggested that homosexuality be decriminalized. The period predates the Women's Movement, but gender roles were by no means as fixed or stable as some might therefore assume. Critics such as Lynne Segal have argued that in Britain, as in the US, the 1950s are marked by a tension between the new emphasis on domesticity urged on returning servicemen – 'Men too, in popular consciousness, were being domesticated. They had returned from battlefield to bungalow with new expectations of the comforts and pleasures of home' (*Slow Motion* 3) – and an older narrative of masculinity based on action and glory: the best-selling books of the 1950s were stirring novels about the Second World War. It is no coincidence that superheroes such as Superman – alternately mild and bespectacled, then heroic and all-powerful – became popular during this decade, as conflicting versions of masculinity jostled for position.[5]

In this book, I explore the way in which the feeling male body negotiates the cultural and social changes linked with the rise of postmodernity: it embodies and celebrates change but also – sometimes simultaneously – protests against it. Although I concentrate primarily on texts associated with the Angry Young Men and the New Left, and on issues around class and consumption, the figure of the feeling male body appears in other texts as well. It is striking how many images of tortured male bodies can be found in postwar British fiction, from Winston in Orwell's *Nineteen Eighty-Four* (1948), to Alex in Anthony Burgess's *A Clockwork Orange* (1962); in both these texts the feeling male body is certainly the symptom of social crisis, as the protagonists' pain indicts the loss of agency in the new decentralized forms of social order which Gilles Deleuze termed 'societies of control'.

The turn to feeling as a way of combating the social and cultural effects of late capitalism was not confined to Britain, and across postwar Europe and America, left-wing cultural critics championed feeling as a safeguard against fascism and as the solution to capitalist anomie. Wilhelm Reich analysed fascism in terms of social and sexual repression, suggesting in *Listen, Little Man!* (1948) that affect was anti-fascist: 'There is but one anti-dote to the average man's predisposition to [emotional] plague: his own feeling for true life' (xi). Writing in 1947, the Frankfurt School theorists Theodor Adorno and Max Horkheimer link feelings to cultural health, lamenting the rise of the culture industry because even '[t]he most inti-mate reactions of human beings have been so entirely reified' that per-sonality 'hardly means more than dazzling white teeth and freedom from body odour and emotions' (136); they imply that real emotions and the authentic, imperfect body can somehow resist the blandishments of mass culture which requires responses that are no more than automatic. In *Eros and Civilization* (1955), another Frankfurt School critic, Herbert Marcuse, called for the end of a sexually and emotionally repressed society that he identified with capitalism, arguing that the rise of a technico-managerial culture was inseparable from lack of feeling.

Although from different political positions than the Frankfurt School critics, Beat writers such as Jack Kerouac, William Burroughs, and Allen Ginsberg also asserted the power of feeling and authenticity to counteract what they saw as the feminizing managerial conformism of mainstream American life. Unlike their Angry Young Man contemporaries in Britain, the Beats paid comparatively little attention to class in their iconography of masculinity, instead appropriating signs of blackness and black culture as a means of accessing feeling and claiming authenticity. Yet in its romantic celebration of the feeling male body as both disruptive and healing, Beat writing displays similarities to both New Left and angry writing. Ginsberg's 'Howl' depicts the body of the 'angel-headed hipster' (line 3) wounded by postwar America, yet this wounded body also has a two-fold transformative potential: it disrupts the conformism of Madison Avenue, and it holds out the possibility of reconciling language and the body. Beat writing constantly links language to the body – the outsiders in 'Howl' 'were dragged off the roof waving genitals and manuscripts' (line 35) – and the emphasis on performance and poetry reading within the Beats similarly emphasized the corporeal qualities of language and the link between the body and the word.[6] An account of Ginsberg's famous first reading of 'Howl' in the Six Gallery in San Francisco testifies to the way in which the audience thrilled to the affective quality of the poem's delivery as well as of its content:

> Ginsberg read on to the end of the poem, which left us standing in wonder, or cheering and wondering, but knowing at the deepest level that a barrier had been broken, that a human voice and body had been hurled against the harsh wall of America and its supporting armies and navies and academies and institutions and ownership systems and power-support bases.
>
> (McClure 15)

From Bond to the Beats, the feeling male body can therefore be understood not only as a response to anxieties about class and consumerism in mid-twentieth-century Britain – an important focus of this book – but also in the context of broader narratives about Empire and post-colonialism, and modernity and postmodernity.

Affect, emotion, and feeling

I use the term 'feeling male body', along with the phrase 'masculine affect', as a way to describe the perceived connections between bodies and feelings in the texts I discuss, rather than to endorse these connections. Specifically, the term describes the way in which literary and critical texts of the 1950s link three different but interrelated properties. The first is an individual's capacity for specific emotions: anger, joy, fear, boredom, and pain. However, the particular emotion is less important than the intensity with which it is felt. The second is the individual's capacity for feeling or affect in the broadest sense, signalled by terms such as 'vitality', 'life', or 'openness'. These terms are invariably positive, and are associated with freedom, change, and renewal. I argue that in the literature and cultural criticism of the period, these emotional capacities are also associated with particular bodies that embody the freedom traditionally associated with the category of the aesthetic. The third property is, therefore, the masculinity of these bodies. The feeling male body not only literalizes the corporeality of emotion, but also literalizes it within a particular physical form – the rugged male body. These male bodies are virile, and aggressively heterosexual; yet, perhaps surprisingly, they are also frequently wounded and hurt.

Throughout the book, I employ the terms 'feeling', 'emotion', and 'affect' interchangeably, although I tend to use 'affect' to refer to the more general qualities of vitality and sensation, as opposed to the specific emotions of pity, anger, and so on. The turn to affect in contemporary cultural theory since the late 1990s is striking, though equally striking is the extent to which the very term 'affect' is contested: most notably, certain critics seek to distinguish between affect and emotion, while others use them as synonyms. At the time of writing (2005) the wave of studies on affect has not yet peaked, and it is perhaps too early to analyse with any clarity what is at stake in the contemporary fascination with the affective.[7] Yet certain shared concerns emerge across the work of critics such as Brian Massumi, Eve Sedgwick, and Teresa Brennan, for whom affect refers to sensations or intensities that escape, bypass, or short-circuit the cognitive or the discursive; and to feelings or intensities that are nonsubjective rather than the properties of individuals. Eve Sedgwick has praised the way in which the work of the psychologist Silvan Tomkins challenges the notion that affect is a 'discursive social construction' (*Shame* 7), instead positing affect as autonomous of the processes of cognition and interpretation.[8] However, to complicate matters, Tomkins and Sedgwick use affect and emotion as synonyms. In contrast, critics such as Brian Massumi and Larry Grossberg – who draw a Deleuzian concept of affect that has its roots in a philosophical rather than a psychological tradition – insist on distinguishing the two. Massumi explains the distinction between emotion and affect, as he sees it: 'Affect is autonomous to the degree to which it escapes confinement in the particular body whose vitality, or potential for interaction, it is … emotion is the intensest (most contracted) expression of that capture [of affect]' (96). Here Massumi employs a distinction between emotion, understood as interpretive and psychological, and affect, understood as noncognitive and as nonsubjective – escaping the individual body. The work of Teresa Brennan similarly explores the notion that affect is a social rather than an individual phenomenon, and that affects are primarily transmitted and experienced in and through groups.

The affective turn – or some versions of it – can be understood in the context of a broader reaction against the linguistic turn of the 1970s and 1980s, also found, for example, in the rise of trauma theory, or in Robert Young's 2001 criticism of postcolonial theory's emphasis on 'colonial discourse's predominantly textual nature' (394), and his call for a return to a more properly materialist notion of discourse. Perhaps as a result, certain contemporary accounts of affect, particularly that of Massumi, tend to assume and reinforce a polarizing distinction between representation, discourse, and mediation, on the one hand, and a romanticized notion of the immediacy and disruptive capacities of the bodily and the affective and their potential for creating new forms of solidarity, on the other. Many of the critical and literary texts I examine do articulate a sense of affective frustration with the status quo along the lines that Massumi describes; moreover, they might be seen as a protest against the rise of new social and economic order based on the needs of a service sector economy that sought to minimize and to manage emotion.[9] However, I remain suspicious of the romantic assumptions about the body's capacities that underlie the distinction between affect and discourse, and hence affect and emotion – a romanticism also found in much New Left and angry writing – and for this reason I use the terms 'affect' and 'emotion' interchangeably, along with the term 'feeling'. For similar reasons, I use an interpretive methodology, questioned by critics such as Massumi, as I seek to analyse and understand the significance of a cultural and literary *discourse* of affect centred on the feeling male body, and the way it encodes and embodies ambivalent and contradictory desires.

Therefore, while this book examines the relationship between language and affect, its argument is literary historical rather than theoretical. It suggests that the discourse of affect in the literary texts is also a discourse about the power and the limits of language and aesthetic form, whether such a discourse is self-conscious or implicit. 'Angry' writers rely on an aesthetic I describe as 'expressive realism', in which the language of emotions and feeling is linked to realist form.

This aesthetic dreams of a correspondence between word and feeling; angry texts self-consciously reject performance and theatricality, although the distinctions they seek to draw between the natural or transparent and the performative frequently break down. The angry writers' rejection of metaphor in favour of metonymy, and of experi-mental modernist form in favour of verisimilitude, is mirrored by the New Left's rejection of the abstraction of standard political language in favour of the language of literature and film – of culture – which they in turn associate with the immediacy of experience and feeling. New Wave directors are less wavy of imagery than their angry counterparts, but their 'poetic realism' still relied on the metonymic image – such as the lingering shot of the railway viaduct to express the desire for escape – rather than the metaphorical image, remaining within the aesthetics of realism.

However, another conception of the relation between affect and lan-guage underlies the literary texts I examine from Doris Lessing's *The Golden Notebook* (1962) onwards. These texts are increasingly sceptical of language's ability to capture the chaos and complexity of the world, including the slippery nature of feeling, and they often mark moments of heightened emotion through the failure or the inadequacy of lan-guage. Emotion or affect is frequently registered through linguistic blockage and fractured syntax, rather than through the spontaneous outburst of speech celebrated in the earlier realist texts. Yet I suggest that these texts – postmodern in their form – share with realist texts a desire for the immediacy of the real, although this real is elusive, absent, or inaccessible, and they emphasize their awareness of the ironic gap between language and feeling, or language and the world. The story of the desire for feeling, and of the feeling male body, is therefore a story about postwar aesthetics as well as postwar society.

The feeling male body from the New Left to New Labour

The first three chapters of the book explore the way in which the trope of the feeling male body in the 1950s and early 1960s displaces social and cultural anxieties onto the individual body, and onto a particular aesthetic style associated with expressiveness and transparency. My first chapter draws on the New Left journals *Universities and Left Review* and *New Left Review*, Richard Hoggart's *The Uses of Literacy* (1957), and Raymond Williams's *Border Country* (1960), to argue that the feeling male body in these texts expresses – often simultaneously – two very different desires: on the one hand, the desire for organic wholeness and social reconciliation; and on the other hand, the desire for rupture and transformation. The ambivalence of the feeling male body therefore reflects contradictory strands and desires within New Left thought, and the New Left's ambivalent relationship to modernity, which it both embraced and rejected. The chapter ends by contrasting the New Left's feeling male body to previous left romantic visions of working-class men, arguing that its distinctive quality is the way it detaches masculinity from class, so that it both expresses and displaces class identity.

The second chapter analyses the discourse of feeling, masculinity, and realism in Kingsley Amis's *Lucky Jim* (1954) and John Osborne's *Look Back in Anger* (1956), and the way in which these texts were read by the New Left and by contemporary reviewers. It argues that these texts imagine a new social elite characterized by its capacity for feeling. However, while these texts celebrate authenticity – understood as the correspondence between feeling and expression – in their content and in their realist form, they are also drawn to the parodic energy of performance and to the instability of figural and metaphorical language. Similarly, while these texts contrast vital, authentic masculinity to inauthentic femininity, they also depict authentic masculinity as victimized and metaphorically feminized; these qualities, paradoxically, characterize the new elite. Reviewers, however, overlooked the ambivalence of these texts and their celebration of a new elite, interpreting their emphasis on feeling as an expression of left-wing radicality and romanticizing the feeling male body as the source of political resistance.

My third chapter focuses on the fears and desires associated with consumerism in John Braine's *Room at the Top* (1957) and Alan Sillitoe's *Saturday Night and Sunday Morning* (1958). Both texts are critical of consumerism, but at the same time suggest that the market might open up new possibilities for self-expression and creativity. This tension is displaced onto the feeling male bodies of Joe Lampton and Arthur Seaton, which register the deleterious effects of affluence, but also celebrate consumption's invigorating potential. The chapter argues that the anxieties around the figure of the consumer, who is both masculine and feminized, are also expressed through the figure of the masochist. The masochism of the protagonists invokes powerlessness and the fear of feminization, but also turns vulnerability into strength, offering a path for revitalizing masculinity.

Together, the first three chapters show that the feeling male body expresses contradictory impulses and desires and is an unstable trope; moreover, they explain how a shared fascination with the feeling male body yoked together writers, filmmakers, and critics whose political views differed significantly, from the socialist Raymond Williams to the increasingly libertarian John Osborne. The instability of the feeling body helps to explain how and why it was taken up and reworked by women authors such as Shelagh Delaney, Lynne Reid Banks, and Doris Lessing. In the Angry Young Man texts I examine, authors grant their male protagonists the possibility of freedom, rebellion, and authenticity, while representing women as fetishes either of class mobility or of domesticity and containment. My fourth chapter argues that Banks's *The L-Shaped Room*, Delaney's *A Taste of Honey*, and Lessing's *The Golden Notebook* rewrite the standard 'angry' narrative by using and mimicking the aesthetics, narrative conventions, and thematics of angry literature to explore the positions of middle-class and working-class women. Through a reading of Banks's treatment of shame, Delaney's sceptical attitude to 'life', and Lessing's refusal of the distinction between performance and authenticity, I show the way in which these texts reject some of the problematic features of angry and New Left writing, while reiterating others.

My final chapter examines the persistence of the trope of the feeling male body in the cultural criticism, literature, and film of the later twentieth century. In the cultural studies analyses of Paul Willis's *Profane Culture* (1978) and Dick Hebdige's *Subculture* (1979), this body expresses the wounds of a fractured society, but holds out the possibility of transforming that society. In Martin Amis's *Money* (1984), Irvine Welsh's *Trainspotting* (1993), and *The Full Monty* (1997), the feeling male body is associated with three different transitional or liminal identities that emerge under Thatcherism: the entrepreneur, the underclass, and the unemployed manual labourer, respectively. The excessive body of entrepreneur John Self in *Money* registers the cost of 1980s consumerism; *Trainspotting*'s underclass (and subcultural) junkie bodies parody and mirror Thatcherite consumption; whereas *The Full Monty*'s Gaz and Dave – tearful, vulnerable, respectively too skinny and too fat – illustrate the effects of Thatcher's decimation of traditional industries. Yet John Self emerges symbolically purified by the end of *Money*, free from the control of consumerism as well as from the control of author/character Martin Amis; *Trainspotting*'s Renton is poised on the beginning of a new life, in which he may or may not escape the problems of his old life; and, at the end of *The Full Monty*, Gaz and Dave transform their vulnerability into a means of comic reconciliation and personal renewal by stripping. In all three texts, the feeling male body embodies some possibility for renewal and revitalization, however fleeting or ironic. In this respect, these postmodern feeling male bodies are unexpectedly similar to the feeling male bodies of the 1950s and early 1960s. Yet it is with these earlier manifestations of the feeling male body that this book is chiefly concerned, and with which I begin my analysis.

1
From Dream Boy to Scholarship Boy: The New Left, Richard Hoggart, and Raymond Williams

A 1960 issue of the journal *New Left Review* includes an article entitled, simply, 'Dream Boy'. Its subheading describes the author, Ray Gosling, as 'a young signalman writing a manifesto for youth venture clubs' (30), but the article contains no mention of the putative clubs. Instead, Gosling gives a lyrical description of young, working-class masculinity in the postwar period: the Dream Boy. This boy, working class in background, is a symptom of postwar social change: 'a new youth in a new world' (34). His heterosexual, virile masculinity symbolizes resistance to conservatism, as he 'stands up in his sexual and phallic dress, rebel against a sexless world of fear.... his dress, his whole way of life becomes a rebellion against them' (30). Gosling emphasizes both the boy's corporeality and his capacity for feeling: his qualities are 'physical in looks and voice' (34), and his motto 'you've got to keep alive' (30). The singer Cliff Richard – who has since become a leathery establishment institution – is Gosling's prime example of the Dream Boy, the boy who is 'sizzling, sexy, poetic' (33). This boy is a source of vitality and energy, a 'catalyst' for a generation which 'throngs to Violent Playground, Room at the Top, Expresso Bongo, to Roots, to Look Back in Anger [*sic*] (34) – plays, novels, and films which had all appeared in the late 1950s.

This chapter traces the appearance of different versions of this 'dream boy' in the criticism of the cultural and political movement known as the New Left in the late 1950s and early 1960s. It argues that New Left criticism is permeated by an image of the feeling male body as the symptom of cultural crisis and as its cure. On the one hand, the New Left criticized the dehumanizing effects of consumption and mass culture, and the superficiality of a postwar society focused on affluence. The feeling body, in pain or bruised, registered the negative effects of these developments as wounds, and it also offered an alternative to superficiality and dehumanization, acting as a symbol of wholeness and authenticity. On the other hand, the New Left identified Britain's crisis as its stagnation, and its failure to modernize. The New Left's feeling body also expressed a sense of deep frustration with a hierarchical, static society, and became the embodiment of the diffuse energies and flux of a changing society – the 'new youth in a new world'. While the New Left mounted a critique of aspects of contemporary culture, it also saw an alternative to Britain's moribund, hidebound hierarchies in the vitality and energy of postwar youth culture, and in the new novels, plays, and films of the late 1950s and early 1960s.

The recurring trope of the feeling body both expressed and resolved these tensions and contradictions in the New Left's cultural and political criticism. This body was a symptom in two different ways: it registered the ill effects of postwar social change, but it was also the casualty of a world in which not enough had changed. Similarly, it embodied two different models of social 'cure': wholeness and unity, or disruption and upheaval. Moreover, it drew on the iconography of a traditional political subject – the working-class male – while reworking this subject for a postwar world. For the New Left's feeling body, as I will show through readings of Hoggart, Williams, and other New Left critics, was invariably coded as male, and had many of the capacities associated with rugged, muscular, working-class masculinity, such as force, vitality, and energy. The 'feeling male body' therefore referenced a familiar notion of the working classes as the vanguard of social change, and as the class that embodied the desire for solidarity – a desire that Raymond Williams romantically associates with working-class life in the final chapter of *Culture and Society* (1958). However, in its dynamism and flux, the feeling male body also signalled the breakdown of traditional class identities and political blocs in a manner that heralded postmodernism.

In the first section of the chapter, I discuss the formation of the New Left, arguing that it was poised between modernist universalism and postmodern pluralism, and between the desire for wholeness and the desire for rupture and change. I then analyse the way in which these tensions are expressed through the 'feeling male body' in the work of Richard Hoggart, in articles in the journal *Universities and Left Review* (*ULR*) and *New Left Review*, and in the fiction and criticism of Raymond Williams. The chapter ends by situating this feeling male body in relation to discourses of the body in the work of F. R. Leavis, and also in a left literary tradition that includes George Orwell and D. H. Lawrence. However, as I shall argue, the criticism of the 1950s reworks these earlier discourses in significant ways, drawing on the iconography of working-class masculinity while detaching this iconography from labour.

The New Left: the milieu and its context

The term 'New Left' describes a grouping of left intellectuals and activists who were associated with two journals, *ULR* and the *New Reasoner*, both founded in 1957. The former was edited by Stuart Hall, Gabriel Pearson, Raphael (also known as Ralph) Samuel, and Charles Taylor, four Oxford graduates whose average age was 24, and published the work of 'independent socialists'; the latter was edited by the historians John Saville and E. P. Thompson, and appealed to 'dissident communists' (Chun 10) who had left the Communist Party after the 1956 Soviet invasion of Hungary.[1] The two journals fused in 1960 to re-emerge as *New Left Review* under the editorship of Stuart Hall.[2] All three New Left journals were characterized by their conviction that *culture*, however understood, was the means both of understanding and transforming contemporary society. Stuart Hall explained, retrospectively, why the question of culture seemed so important to the New Left:

> First, because it was in the ideological and cultural domain that social change seemed to be making itself most dramatically visible. Second, because the cultural dimension seemed to us not a secondary, but a constitutive dimension of society .... Third, because the discourse of culture seemed to us fundamentally necessary to any language in which socialism could be redescribed.
>
> ('The "First" New Left' 25–26)

The journals and the subculture around them attracted a range of people who were dissatisfied with the Labour Party and the Communist Party, and looking for new modes of left social and political analysis.[3] Although the New Left largely comprised intellectuals and political activists, it deliberately sought to establish a space beyond the university or traditional political parties in which political and cultural criticism could take place. As Michael Kenny writes, it was 'inspired by the Left Book Club of the 1930s, a project which fused cultural and political activity and fought to retain its independence from the Labour and Communist Parties' (13). Like the Left Book Club, the New Left set up a series of clubs in London and around the country, 'holding weekly public meetings as well as having a series of discussion groups based on education, literature, new theatre, race relations and science' (Davies 11). The first of these, in 1957, attracted over seven hundred people, which greatly surpassed the organisers' expectations (Hall, '"First" New Left' 28). These ongoing meetings (24 a year) were designed to encourage 'readers' discussion and criticism' based on articles from the current issue of *ULR*.[4]

The New Left's influence extended even further as the result of three significant books published in the late 1950s and early 1960s by writers associated with the movement: Richard Hoggart's *The Uses of Literacy* (1957), Raymond Williams's *Culture and Society* (1958), and E. P. Thompson's *The Making of the English Working Class* (1963).[5] All three books politicized the idea of culture by looking at culture in relation to larger social and economic changes, and culturalized politics, suggesting that lived experience, culture, and human agency, as well as economic structures, needed to be taken into account in any analysis of social change. The work of Hoggart and Williams bears the imprint of F. R. Leavis, whose particular style of literary criticism as cultural criticism and moral commentary provided a model for both critics. Leavis held that society was under threat from industrialization and mass culture, and could only be redeemed by a classless intellectual minority who would safeguard a cultural tradition and work towards extending this tradition into a truly common culture through the study of literature, which at its best embodied the key values of life and humanity, and through the critical exercise of discrimination. However, both Hoggart and Williams, 'scholarship boys' from working-class backgrounds, opened up Leavis's definition of culture to include previously denigrated cultural forms and practices. In their rejection of the superior taste and wisdom of the intellectual elite, as well as in their interest in non-literary cultural production and cultural practices, Hoggart and Williams paved the way for cultural studies.

These works, and the New Left subculture more generally, are both responses to and indicative of a nation in transition. The New Left was founded in the wake of the 1956 Suez crisis, the abortive British attempt to repatriate the Suez Canal after the Egyptian President Nasser had nationalized it. Britain's place in the world was profoundly different than it had been before the Second World War, though its new role was unclear. The Suez incident provoked both disgust that the government would still want to carry out an imperial mission, but also dismay that British complacency had led to its decline as a world power (Jefferys 53–55). The Suez debacle was merely one sign of the way in which Britain's place in the world had changed; it was also signalled by the new waves of immigration from former colonies, reversing the direction of earlier waves of colonizing immigration. In many respects members of the New Left exemplified the new global flows of postcolonialism: several of its members had come to Britain from the Commonwealth (for example, Stuart Hall from Jamaica, Charles Taylor from Canada, and Doris Lessing from Rhodesia), and many of them stayed in Britain rather than returning to their home countries as colonial intellectuals had done in the 1930s.

The postwar period opened up opportunities for social movement as well as geographical movement. With the establishment of the welfare state, the 1944 Butler Education Act, and the expansion of higher education, increasing numbers of men (fewer women) from working-class backgrounds went to grammar schools and entered higher education, and these 'scholarship boys' often experienced a profound sense of being caught 'between two worlds', as Richard Hoggart (appropriating Matthew Arnold) described in his discussion of the scholarship boy in *The Uses of Literacy* (300).[6] At the same time, class distinctions were being redrawn because of a global shift from a production-based economy to a service-based economy. As Ross McKibbin argues, the British class structure had undergone a gradual but significant shift between the period of 1918 and 1951, as the gap between middle class and working class narrowed and in some cases blurred, with an expanding new category of 'lower middle class' composed primarily of people from a working-class background filling new jobs in the service industry.[7] The working class rejected domestic employment for new service jobs, and the middle class were no longer distinguished as the servant-owning class. Although these changes had been taking place since the end of the World War I, their full extent was obvious only after World War II.

The New Left emerged out of this broader context of a transition between modernity and postmodernity, colonialism and postcolonialism, and imperialism and globalization. On the one hand, the New Left can be seen as an early version or a precursor of postmodern social movements based on multiple and shifting identity categories. It was, as Grant Farred has argued, 'deeply influenced by the radicalism of the Third World' (628), particularly in its sympathy for Nasser during the Suez crisis, and it attracted a range of participants who, though largely Oxbridge educated, were marginal to the Establishment whether because of class, ethnicity, or nationality – including many scholarship boys and émigrés. Although socialist, it rejected monolithic notions of the class identity, recognizing that the category of 'working class' was itself in flux. As Raymond Williams put it in a discussion with Richard Hoggart, 'there's no automatic kind of correspondence between being working class, objectively, feeling working class, and voting for a working class party' (Hoggart and Williams 28). Like later postmodern theorists such as Michel de Certeau, the New Left looked more to everyday life and popular culture for evidence of resistance and transformation and less to grand theoretical metanarratives. The New Left's cultural agenda can also be seen as the precursor of postmodern cultural pluralism, insofar as it embraced a more relativist and anthropological notion of culture, defined plurally and democratically, in contrast to a more rarefied, aesthetic notion of culture authorized by elite intellectuals and mandarins.

On the other hand, aspects of the New Left's vision can be seen as modernist, rather than postmodern: it remained committed to a vision of commonality and wholeness rather than flux and fragmentation, and to notions of totality, whether understood as a lost and mourned social cohesion under threat from new cultural developments – in the case of Richard Hoggart – or as a utopian possibility yet to be realized – in the case of Raymond Williams. Although Williams's notion of common culture was pluralist, extending beyond the literary to include other creative activities such as gardening and carpentry, it was nonetheless based on the ideals of universalism and equality which 'would require the shaping of a new common experience' (*Culture and Society* 319), and would be formed as the result of democratic participation in the construction and selection of meaning. Jed Esty argues that this goal of commonality is implicitly linked to the notion of a whole, bounded, national culture, suggesting that the work of Hoggart, Williams, and the New Left can be seen as part of a larger trajectory within 'late modernism' in which national identity is reworked in the wake of Empire. In this trajectory, which Esty also traces through the later work of Virginia Woolf and T. S. Eliot, the anthropological eye, formerly extended to the periphery, is turned inwards, so that Englishness is both relativized as one national culture among many, and simultaneously reinscribed as a unified identity.[8] As a result, the New Left produced Englishness not as the unmarked universal, as it was during the height of Empire, but as a new marked universal, whereby Englishness came to represent 'the very archetype of modern nationalism, of deep and integral shared traditions emanating from within the prototypical industrial class society' (14). The New Left, or 'early Cultural Studies', therefore occupies a curious and unstable position between postmodern relativism and modernist universalism. As Esty points out, while it 'relativizes England as one particular national culture among many in a global system and relativizes the high aesthetic as one specialized element among many in a national culture' (197), it also promises 'to restore some hope for a reconnection between high art and a socially deeper, but politically narrower, culture' (198). In other words, the work of the New Left offered the possibility of the reconciliation between high culture and culture as everyday life, and in so doing it remained committed to the ideals of wholeness and totality.

The New Left's cultural and political project therefore encompassed various conflicting desires: writers like Hoggart criticized the dehumanizing and destructive effects of certain forms of mass culture, while others like Stuart Hall embraced popular cultural forms such as film and jazz; the New Left asserted the specificity of working-class culture and values, yet it called for the withering of class cultures in the name of an inclusive common culture; its members saw the opportunities for transformation in the flux and transition of postwar culture, while longing for a whole society characterized by unity rather than flux; and they aligned themselves with a modern aesthetic, but also with an aesthetic based on notions of organic Englishness and organic working-class culture. In what follows, I argue that these contradictory impulses within the New Left are expressed through the language and imagery of the feeling body, a body that is frequently gendered as masculine. Building from Esty's argument that Englishness becomes a marked universal in postwar Britain, I argue that the feeling male body reinscribes masculinity not as an unmarked universal, but as a marked universal, whose universality lies not in its invisibility but in the way in which it visibly registers the social changes of postwar Britain and symbolizes national renewal.[9] The criticism of the New Left helps to produce a discourse in which the feeling male body emerges both as the symptom of cultural crisis, whether this crisis is understood as moribund stasis or destructive fragmentation, and as its cure, whether this in turn lies in disruption or wholeness.

Here my argument differs from that of Dan Rebellato, who also observes the New Left's investment in the corporeal and the somatic, and the way in which both the language and aesthetics of New Left critics expresses a fascination with the power of the body and with sensation. Rebellato points out that '"Life" is .... part of a cluster of terms that are distributed equally through the works of the New Left and the New Wave: the variant forms, "life," "living," "alive," the antonyms, "dead," "death," the synonyms "vital" and "vitality," and the related term "feeling"' (21), and concludes that these terms, drawn from critics such as Leavis and Eliot, express the fear of a fragmented society that threatened both the possibility of a common culture and the inner life of the individuals. In contrast, however, I suggest that the New Left relied so heavily on a critical vocabulary suffused with corporeal imagery because this imagery was able to express the conflicting and potentially contradictory political and aesthetic impulses that characterized the movement: not only its nostalgia for wholeness, but also its desire to embrace the flux of the new. Similarly, its fascination with representations of feeling bodies at times expressed the desire for a unified society and for whole individuals, yet elsewhere signified the desire for change, disruption, and transformation. As Martin Francis has pointed out, the post-war Labour government used the language of restraint and emotional self-control to present itself as modern, aligning itself with the traditional rhetoric of middle-class masculinity in order to legitimate its authority. Yet by the mid-1950s, with the rise of affluence, the rhetoric of restraint 'was archaic and redundant in a world which prioritized personal choice' (154), and the Labour Party adopted the language of authenticity and release, as modernity was redefined as 'immediacy, impact, and sensation' (168).[10] Similarly, the New Left, in embracing sensation and emotion, defined themselves as modern and contemporary.

Mass culture, the scholarship boy, and *The Uses of Literacy*

In the New Left spectrum between universalism and pluralism, Richard Hoggart's *The Uses of Literacy* is closer to universalism. Hoggart rejects a pluralist conception of cultural value, arguing instead that certain universal values are to be found in the previously denigrated category of working-class culture. *The Uses of Literacy* both analyses working-class attitudes and also revalues working-class cultural practices, arguing that the everyday speech and popular culture of working-class people reveals similar values and qualities to those of 'high culture': irony, criticism, compassion, and responsibility. Hoggart thus extends the notion of culture to encompass activities and practices previously considered beyond the pale, arguing that 'to live in the working-classes is even now to belong to an all-pervading culture, one in some ways as formal and stylized as any that is attributed to, say, the upper-classes' (*The Uses of Literacy* 32). While much of the book focuses on traditional working-class culture, Hoggart is also interested in cultural change; indeed the ostensible purpose of *The Uses of Literacy* is to describe the impact of the growth of literacy on working-class life. Mass literacy, according to Hoggart, affects social structures and traditional class identities. This change is potentially positive, as it paves the way for a shared culture that would be impossible without shared literature, but Hoggart also warns that certain popular publications jeopardize the possibility of a true 'classlessness', as their tawdry values threatened the establishment of true community. Hoggart's defence of working-class culture is therefore partly elegiac, and stems from his fear of its imminent disintegration in the face of mass culture.

The Uses of Literacy clearly falls into the strand of New Left thought that is broadly critical of postwar cultural change, particularly of developments in mass culture. This aspect of the New Left appealed to a left-leaning constituency who associated the rise in living standards and full employment, often referred to as 'affluence', and the development of mass cultural forms such as television, advertising, and popular music, with the break-up and decline of traditional working-class communities and identity, and therefore with the potential decline of socialism. In 1959 the leader of the opposition Labour Party, Hugh Gaitskell, admitted that postwar economic and cultural changes had appeared to erode or at least change the character of the working class whose votes Labour relied on: 'The changing character of labour, full employment, new housing, the new way of life based on the telly, the fridge, the car, and the glossy magazines – all have had their effect on our political strength' (qtd. in Hall, *Policing* 230). A Tory policy report of 1960 suggested that 'the divisions between the classes have narrowed ... The rise in the number of white-collar workers and the fall in the number of manual workers has favoured us' (qtd. in Jefferys 175). Increasingly, traditional assumptions by both left and right about the relation between employment, class position, class consciousness, cultural preferences and tastes, and voting patterns could no longer be relied on. The New Left offered the chance to 'redescribe' socialism, in Hall's terms, or as Raymond Williams explained, 'to analyse this society, not to come to terms with it, but to offer some deep and real alternative' (Hoggart and Williams 30).

Hoggart laments such changes, particularly the depredations of mass culture, which he often characterizes in terms of its effects on the body. One of these effects is the dulling of the senses, described as anaesthesia or death. He writes: 'Most mass-entertainments are in the end what D. H. Lawrence described as "anti-life" .... These productions belong to a vicarious, spectators' world; they offer nothing which can really grip the brain or heart' (340). Mass culture is here associated with passivity, mediation, and distancing, and with the disengaged or even dead bodies of the 'spectators'. Hoggart's discussion of gangster-fiction also uses the image of the inanimate body as a signal of this literature's poor quality: 'Gangster-fiction writing is in large measure dead', since it has only 'in parts a kind of life' (267). Implicit in this claim is its corollary: that true art is pro-life, a quality which can be judged by its visceral effects on the body of the reader or viewer, and its capacity to revivify or animate this body. Indeed, Hoggart contrasts an imaginary pulp fiction novel with Faulkner's novel *Sanctuary*, praising Faulkner for the way in which he is 'seeing, smelling, hearing, responding round and through the experience. And his language stretches and strains to meet the demands of the emotional situation; words and images become alive as they explore its nature' (268).[11] The body of the text is linked to the body of the author, whose talent is indicated by his own capacity for intense sensation, as well as his ability to animate language. Hoggart's invocation of corporeality and vitality therefore moves between the metaphorical – Hoggart says of Faulkner's prose that it has 'more "body"' than that of gangster-fiction (268) – and the literal, as the real bodies of both readers and authors display the qualities of vitality or of death.

For Hoggart, the negative effects of mass culture also fragment the body. This is a common trope in other criticisms of mass culture, especially those which emerged out of the Frankfurt School in the 1930s: Siegfried Kracauer, for example, uses the image of the disembodied legs of the Tiller Girls (a dancing troop) to denounce the fragmenting and alienating effects of mass culture more generally.[12] Hoggart's body in pieces, like Kracauer's, is also female. He describes the increasing explicitness of new magazines who suggestively represent 'the turn of a leg or the bend of a shoulder', 'the cleft between the breasts', 'the little bump of the nipples under opaque material', or even 'the dark shading of the nipples' aureoles' under transparent nylon (214). In its fragmentation, this body shares the failings of these magazines, which Hoggart denounces as being 'extremely fragmentary in their approach' (215) and as exhibiting 'bittiness run riot' (216). It is important to point out that Hoggart does not object to the physicality of the images, but instead to what he sees as their lack of vitality: 'this sex-interest is largely "in the head" and eye, a removed, vicarious thing. It thinks of itself as a smart and sophisticated interest, but it is really bloodless and reduced to a very narrow range of responses' (222). However, the mixture of prurience and distaste in Hoggart's description of these images suggests he is both disgusted and fascinated by the feminized, sexual body as it is itemized and broken down into body parts.

As we have seen, to an eviscerated or fragmented body that is the casualty of mass culture, Hoggart counterposes the body fully alive with intense sensory responses. Vital bodies, which are both metaphorical and literal, textual bodies and the real bodies of readers and authors, resist the dulling effects of what Hoggart describes as 'the candy-floss world' of contemporary mass culture (*The Uses of Literacy* 206). These bodies are found in the world as well as in texts, and Hoggart concentrates on two specific examples of resistant bodies: the body of the working-class mother, and the wounded body of the scholarship boy. He discusses the former in a chapter in which he praises the resistance of working-class people to the new rhythms and blandishments of mass culture: 'this is not simply a power of passive resistance, but something which, though not articulate, is positive. The working-classes have a strong natural ability to survive change by adapting or assimilating what they want in the new and ignoring the rest' (32). Working-class people, Hoggart claims, resist the superficiality of mass culture to the extent that they live 'intuitively, habitually, verbally, drawing on myth, aphorism and ritual' (33). The figure of the mother is a central image of such resistance, and of the continuity of older traditions in the face of new forms of culture. The mother's body, whose description Hoggart sets up as anti-romantic ('We should not try to add glamour to such a face' [49]), is in fact deeply romanticized through its associated with continuity, ritual, and habit – all qualities which Hoggart associates with the best of working-class culture. The mother's face bears evidence of an ongoing way of life: dirt engrained by 'years of snatched washes' and lines produced by 'years of "calculating"' (49). Older working-class women often have 'an habitual gesture which illuminates the years of their life behind'; which can be 'a rhythmic smoothing of the hand … a working of the lips or a steady rocking' (49). The images of dirt and the face's 'scaly texture' (49) might seem negative, but this description connotes depth and authenticity when it is contrasted with the adjectives Hoggart uses to describe mass culture, such as 'hollow' (232) and 'shiny' (246). In contrast to the tawdry, fragmented sexuality represented in the popular press, this mother 'will have lost most of her sexual attraction' by thirty, and soon thereafter she becomes 'shapeless' (46). In her asexuality, she is virtually defeminized, presiding over a home that is 'not chintzy or kittenish or whimsical or "feminized"' (40). Sexualized femininity is, by implication, associated with mass culture and the fragmented depiction of breasts, nipples, and legs.

Hoggart depicts the mother through her appearance and her unconscious characteristics (such as habitual gestures) rather than any emotional life. As Carolyn Steedman has pointed out, Hoggart's depiction of working-class mothers is characterized both by emotional passivity and by the 'attribution of sameness' (11) to working-class lives, in a way which downplays the existence of emotions such as the sharp desire and envy which motivated Steedman's own (working-class) mother. Although the mother's body resists mass culture, she is not granted the capacity for intense sensory perception and inner life that Hoggart prizes in a writer like Faulkner. Here she contrasts with the scholarship boy, a semi-autobiographical figure Hoggart describes with ambivalence, who is characterized by his intense feelings and emotions. The scholarship boy, able to proceed to grammar school through government funding, is subsequently 'uprooted and anxious', stranded in a no-man's land between the working class and the middle class, fully at home in neither. During his childhood, this boy is feminized; he 'sits in the women's world' (295) doing his homework, rather than playing outside with other boys. The cost of the scholarship boy's trajectory is marked on his body, according to Hoggart: he loses his spontaneity, and 'some of the resilience and vitality of his cousins ... He plays little on the streets ... his sexual growth is perhaps delayed' (298). In a passage strangely reminiscent of nineteenth-century physiognomy, Hoggart suggests the scholarship boy's face registers his difficult history: 'some feature of the face is illuminating – a crinkled forehead, eyebrows drawn together, a "shaded eye": most of all, the mouth, with the lower half only prevented from slackening unhappily by the tightened upper. The upper half provides a front to disguise the deeper discontents, gives a suggestion of loss-cutting quasi-stoicism' (315).

Whereas the mother's face was marked by the cycle of the years, by continuity and habit, the scholarship boy's face reveals his inner torment – his 'bruised consciousness', 'submerged idealism', and 'pervasive indecisiveness' – and it is this inner life which distinguishes him from the mother and gives him a cultural significance that the mother lacks. Scholarship boys 'care', and their capacity for feeling gives them a 'special value' (316). In contrast to those who have been lulled by 'television sets, pin-ups, and cinema screens' into a state of 'obediently receptive passivity' (316), the scholarship boy is a 'more sensitive, though now bruised, [tentacle] of society' (317). With his capacity for feeling, he also offers a mode of revitalization and awareness that might combat the dull passivity that threatens to dominate postwar society, according to Hoggart. He both encompasses and transcends the two kinds of female bodies Hoggart describes: the sexualised body in bits, a symptom of cultural change, and the maternal, timeless body, an image of resistance to this change. The feeling, bruised bodies of scholarship boys exemplify broader social wounds, such as the problem of rootlessness, but they also offer the possibility of healing society through their capacity for feeling. Hoggart concludes: 'the main body on the whole ignores them; but the symptoms they show refer in some degree to all. Bishop Wilson's conclusion of two hundred years ago is just as true today: "The number of those who need to be awakened is far greater than that of those who need comfort"' (317). We see, therefore, that the feeling male body of the scholarship boy becomes both the symptom of cultural crisis and, potentially, its cure. In quite literal ways he embodies cultural change, but through his capacity for feeling and caring, he also offers a way of combating the ill effects of consumer culture and rootlessness, and opens up to a way of redeeming or 'awakening' the broader social body.

'The power and the capacity to feel': *Universities and Left Review*

The Uses of Literacy delineates a traditional working-class life that Hoggart sought to defend against the rise of mass culture and other postwar cultural change. In contrast, many of the contributors of *ULR* and the *New Left Review* explored and responded to the cultural and political changes of the period by embracing the new mood of postwar Britain. As Raphael Samuel points out, 'in our own self-perception we were forward-looking and iconoclastic' (41). For a younger generation whose problem was not so much the disturbing social changes of the postwar era, but rather the sense that not *enough* had changed. For this constituency, Britain was a moribund and sterile society in need of galvanization and transformation. By the late 1950s, debates about culture, as well as the new novels, films and plays, often criticized the failure of the welfare state to have changed the British class system, and the perceived failure of politics itself in dealing with the pressing issues in peoples' lives. One sign of the growing dissatisfaction with British society was the rise of the term 'the Establishment', which started to be used to refer to a governing class who were still as firmly in power in political, cultural, and educational institutions as they had been before the war (Jefferys 117). The Establishment was increasingly characterized as lifeless and stagnant (as in the title of Michael Shanks's 1961 book *The Stagnant Society*), and was the target of satirical attacks such as the 1960 revue show *Beyond the Fringe*, featuring Alan Bennett, Dudley Moore, Peter Cook, and Jonathan Miller, who later told Michael Billington that they were attacking 'the complacency of Macmillan's England' (Carpenter 2).

The New Left presented itself as modern and radical, and spoke to this restless, discontent generation, its influence extending beyond a narrowly intellectual or political circle, as illustrated by two collections of essays, *Declaration* (1957), edited by Tom Maschler, and *Conviction* (1958), edited by Norman Mackenzie. Both collections included 'non-aligned' creative writers as well as critics and writers associated with the New Left: *Declaration* brought together the emerging writers John Osborne, Colin Wilson, and John Wain alongside Lindsay Anderson, filmmaker and contributor to *ULR*, and Doris Lessing, who was on the board of *New Left*

Review, while *Conviction* included essays by critics Raymond Williams and Richard Hoggart alongside Iris Murdoch. The close connection between New Left criticism and creative practice was further exemplified in the Free Cinema movement, a left-wing group of filmmakers and directors including Lindsay Anderson and Karel Reisz. Both Anderson and Reisz contributed to *ULR*, and both of them went on to direct both critically and commercially acclaimed films such as *Saturday Night and Sunday Morning* (dir. Reisz, 1960), and *This Sporting Life* (dir. Anderson, 1963). These films themselves were adaptations of novels by the young working-class writers Alan Sillitoe and David Storey, respectively; Sillitoe's novel and the film adaptation were reviewed in *ULR* and *New Left Review*, and he wrote a piece for *New Left Review* on the process of writing the film script. Other creative writers also contributed to *New Left Review* in its first two years, including Arnold Wesker and John Braine. For the New Left, contemporary cultural production was not just the object of criticism, but also the source of criticism itself, exemplified by Michael Kaye's comment that Arnold Wesker's play *Roots* 'tells us the truth about ourselves in the New Left' (65), and Gabriel Pearson's observation that John Braine's *Room at the Top* was 'an exploration of the dilemmas of our age in contemporary terms' (72).

In other ways, too, the New Left allied itself with new cultural forms and styles: the covers of *ULR* were modern in design, using bold blocks of bright monochrome colour and geometric designs (such as bright red circles for volume three, and rectangles in yellow, green, and magenta for volumes four to seven respectively). *ULR* and *New Left Review* reviewed films as well as plays, used modernist sanserif typography, and included many articles on aspects of youth culture. Nor were these just written from the perspective of the fusty outsider, insofar as those associated with the *ULR* themselves 'dressed sharply and danced coolly' (Samuel 44). The journal also funded a coffee house in Soho, tapping into one of the hippest London trends of the 1950s.[13]

Many contributors to the *ULR* and the early *New Left Review* embraced the contemporary world, and as a result, the discourse of feeling in the journal is not predominantly linked to the fear of cultural and social decline, or to the anaesthetizing and dulling effects of mass culture. In contrast to Hoggart's emphasis on feeling and corporeal habit as a mode of continuity, feeling and the body instead tend to be represented in *ULR* and *New Left Review* as the source of rupture and change. Feeling opens up the way for change partly because, for many contributors, it is associated with the fluidity of the contemporary world. It is an index of contemporary life because it registers and indicates experience in a way that language can strive for but cannot always achieve: feeling and experience are aligned with immediacy, in contrast to language's mediated quality, which leaves it following in the wake of experience. Stuart Hall, for example, states 'Everyone can *feel* and *smell* the concentrations and arbitrary exercise of power in our society. But who can name them? The intellectuals founder about ...' ('Politics' 2). In a review of the volume *Declaration* he argues 'we need new ways of looking at, new ways of speaking together about the deep, immobilising contradictions of our culture' that appear 'in our ways of feeling and response, in the manners and postures of our moral life. They are beyond the language of politics – at least the language of the political pamphlet and the hustings' ('In the No Man's Land' 86). The diction – 'smell', 'manner', 'posture' – links the ideas of feeling and morality to bodily dispositions, and the feeling body is shown to be a more accurate register of modern life than language, which implicitly lags behind social change. However, the caveat in the sentence suggests that traditional political language is the problem rather than language itself, and Hall implies that literary language is an alternative political language because it is more closely connected to feeling. Indeed, he calls for a socialism which would mirror literature itself: 'What we need above all, as Leavis once remarked of the nineteenth century novel, is "a vital capacity for experience, a kind of reverent openness before life, and a marked moral intensity"' (87). Throughout the article he quotes Donne and Arnold, both with and without quotation marks, in an apparent attempt to incorporate some of the intensity and feeling he associates with literary language into his own critical discourse. Literary language, and art more generally, are models for cultural criticism and political activism because of their capacity to register and articulate feeling, and therefore to register – and produce – social and political change.

For Hall and other *ULR* contributors, feeling is a political virtue as well as an aesthetic one, insofar as intensity and vitality are associated with political change as well as with art. Lindsay Anderson writes that 'artists whose convictions are progressively [*sic*]' should produce art which is 'neither exclusive or snobbish, nor stereotyped and propagandist – but vital, illuminating, personal and refreshing' ('Free Cinema' 52). In a discussion of 'committed' art, Michael Armstrong claims 'it is the artist's intensity of feeling for life which is his important contribution' (65). W. I. Carr insists that the work of new writers has potentially political effects in challenging the apathy and indifference of contemporary society: 'Mr Osborne (and one or two others) are a salutary reminder to the effect that we are, after all, alive' (33). Feeling is important not just because it opens up a window onto the contemporary world, offering access to the new experience of the postwar world, but also because it is as a way to break through what Hall describes as 'the apathy of our political life, the narrowness of our economic theories' ('In the No Man's Land' 86). Elsewhere Hall complains 'Our politics has no emotional relevance, resonance, and no humanity: it is stiff, and dry and colourless and conciliatory' ('Politics' 3), and he claims that socialism should aim not only for the goal of equality, but also for 'the justification of the power and capacity to feel' ('In the No Man's Land' 87). Hall and others therefore link feeling with modernity, newness, change, and dynamism. For example, in the editorial of *ULR* 7, the claim is made that the New Left 'represents a new current of feeling' (1). In a discussion of Beat writing and Jack Kerouac's *On the Road*, Clancy Sigal (an American novelist and Doris Lessing's lover) notes that the hipster, 'isolated in a sea of imposed togetherness, fighting in the only way he knows how .... will do anything in order to *feel*' (59–60; emphasis in the original). He writes: 'Hip is ... our brother and our extension ... the ... image of our reflected selves' (59), showing the identification between the non-conformism of the Beats and the modernity of the New Left (a link confirmed by Raphael Samuel, who later described the Beat magazine *Dissent* as 'our sister publication' [44]).[14]

Sigal's article indicates that the New Left associates feeling not just with aesthetics and art, but also with particular figures who are seen to embody – quite literally – the contemporary world, such as the hipster. Most commonly, feeling, whether seen as a symptom of cultural change or as a tool for political radicalism, is associated with working-class bodies. Indeed, there is a tendency throughout *ULR* to romanticize the working classes as corporeal, and therefore as more truly authentic than political intellectuals, distanced from the world of immediacy in their prison-house of language. This can be seen quite clearly in Stuart Hall's article 'The Politics of Adolescence', in which he extols the political potential of feeling and associates this with working-class teenagers: 'Instinctively, young working-class people are radical' (2). In this article Hall slips between the claim of instinctive radicality and the assumption that instinct *is itself* radical, as his evidence for the radicality of young working-class people is their capacity to feel rather than evidence that this feeling is explicitly or consciously political. These people 'may understand superficially; but they *feel* in depth' (2; emphasis in the original), and when they dance 'the absence of feeling in their faces and eyes betrays the depth of feeling they have. They *care*, though they may not care *about* much' (3; emphasis in the original). Feeling may not be evident on the face, but it is expressed through the body and through movement, as these youths have made 'an expressive language of their own: a language of rhythm, in jazz and skiffle, a language of movement in jive .... a language of colour and variety in their dress' (3). We can see Hall's receptiveness to the new forms of cultural expression that emerge in the postwar period, in contrast to Hoggart; rather than denouncing commercial music and fashion as mass culture and consumerism and deeming them anti-life, he associates them with the 'youthful energy' of the working-class body (3). More explicitly, in 'Absolute Beginnings', he states: 'If post-war prosperity have [sic] raised this working-class generation up out of poverty, and raised their cultural experiences and their social contacts – that is an unqualified gain' (25). In their capacity for feeling and in their vitality, these young people embody the possibility of social change – 'they know, from the inside, what conservatism feels like. It is anti-life .... What young people want is the taste of life itself' ('Politics' 3) – and Hall expresses the hope that 'the cool young men of today' might become the 'social conscience of tomorrow' (25).

Although in 'The Politics of Adolescence' Hall talks in gender-neutral terms about 'working class people', the photographs that accompany 'Absolute Beginnings' (taken by Roger Mayne) reveal the extent to which the journal associates youthful vitality with the male body in particular. The article is illustrated throughout with action photographs of males in their late teens and early twenties. The first photograph shows two teenagers casually dressed in jumpers leaping for a ball, caught in mid-air with their legs splayed, while the sense of movement and energy is emphasized by the blurred focus on their hands and the ball itself (16). The second photo shows two men crouching down, perhaps looking for something on the pavement, perhaps in the midst of some game (18). Again the pose emphasizes kinetic dynamism, as the men are caught with their heels raised and their knees bent, the figure in the foreground with his hands spread wide as though he is about to scoop something up. Out of six photographs, there is just one of a teenage girl in Capri pants, flats and cropped hair, along with one of a young couple, the male in the foreground. A photo of the same couple is featured on the cover, again with the man in the foreground, shot from the knees up, accompanied by the girl who stands behind him, smaller in the picture space.

The way in which men are literally as well as figuratively the default image of 'working-class people' and of youth culture can also be seen in the fourth volume of *ULR*, whose cover features the shoulders and head of a young teddy boy staring straight at the camera with a woman (presumably his girlfriend) looking over his shoulder, her head notice-ably smaller than his. It illustrates a collection of articles jointly titled 'The Face of Youth', including Clancy Sigal's article on the Beats, an article by Derek Allcorn on suburban working-class men, and 'The Anti-Culture Born of Despair', an article by Michael Kullman discussing students in a secondary modern school, who remain unidentified by gender at any point in the article except for the hint that to the answer 'What gives you the most satisfaction in day-to-day life' they reply 'girls' or 'sex' (53). The latter two articles prefigure the ethnographic studies of working-class life that came out of the Centre for Contemporary Cultural Studies at Birmingham in the 1970s, and like these studies, they focus on men. In terms reminiscent of Hoggart, Kullman's article discusses educational segregation as an illness in a larger social body: 'The violent teddy boy, the pathologically shy northern chemist, and the blasé public school boy, each in his way a victim, are all symptoms of the same disease. They will not speak to each other for they cannot' (54). The emotionally damaged or wounded boy becomes a symptom of a social crisis, and points to the need for wholeness, or 'a complete human life for all' (54). Allcorn associates working-class men with a sim-ilar kind of wholeness in his discussion of male peer groups. Interestingly, he notices that 'The short-comings, limitations, and neg-ative qualities of the kind of "equality" implicit in peer-group behaviour are only too apparent. Half the human race, womanhood in its entire-ty, is excluded .... The notion of equality tends to be merged with that of identity' (58), but despite this qualification, he concludes by praising such peer groups for 'indoctrinating new generations in those values which ... constitute a key component in working class solidarity' (58).

We can see here an indication of the variety of conceptual work per-formed by images of working-class men and of the feeling male body in the pages of *ULR* and *New Left Review*. For Kullman, the feeling male body indicates a wound in the social body; for Allcorn, working-class men display a particular kind of feeling – solidarity – that could pro-vide the means of resolving the wound identified by Kullman. Yet Hall, who also optimistically associates the youth of the late 1950s and early 1960s with the possibility of a future socialist utopia, ascribes to the feeling body the capacity for social renewal not through wholeness but through rupture: he links the 'revolt and iconoclasm of youth today' with their exploration of 'the frontiers of experience in search of the *feel of living*' ('Absolute Beginnings' 21), and sees in this refusal and revolt the possibility of 'revolution' (25). In *ULR* and the early *New Left Review*, the feeling body therefore acts not only as a symptomatic wound indicating a lost wholeness but also as a demand for change and a rejection of the status quo.

Structures of feeling: Raymond Williams and *Border Country*

Raymond Williams produced the New Left's most sophisticated and self-conscious discussion of the political and social import of feeling, but his work also displays the characteristic tension of the New Left: on the one hand, feeling is a vanguard force for change which opposes received ideas and the status quo, and on the other hand, feeling leads to reconciliation and wholeness. The former position is found in his theoretical work, whereas, I will argue, the latter account of feeling emerges in his first novel, *Border Country* (1960). Williams provides a more nuanced account of feeling than other critics associated with the New Left in his concept of 'structure of feeling', a term he first uses in *Preface to Film* (1954), which then later appears in *Culture and Society*, and is discussed at greater length in *The Long Revolution* (1961).[15] As we have seen, Hoggart and *ULR* contributors such as Hall tend to see feeling and caring as absolute virtues, and as inherently positive forces: feeling indicates a social crisis, but always at the same time provides some kind of solution to this crisis, acting as an alternative to a status quo seen either as fragmented or as stultifying. Williams, by contrast, offers a less romanticized description of a 'structure of feeling' as a response to broader social conditions. He writes: 'I use the phrase *structure of feeling* because it seems to me more accurate ... than *ideas* or *general life*' ('Film' 33; emphasis in the original). His discussion of Carlyle in *Culture and Society* uses the term – 'that structure of contemporary feeling' (72) – to refer to Carlyle's description of the sense of isolation produced by the Industrial Revolution. In *The Long Revolution*, Williams illustrates 'structures of feeling' through a pattern in the novel of the 1840s, in which an underlying anxiety about debt and ruin belies the belief articulated by politicians and in newspapers of the time that the decade was one of prosperity and optimism. This anxiety is expressed in the novels but also resolved by 'magic' solutions such as emigration and inheritance (48–71). Some years later he describes the structure of feeling of the 1840s as 'an anxious oscillation between sympathy for the oppressed and fear of their violence' (*Politics and Letters* 166).

In these examples, Williams does not invest a 'structure of feeling' with any inherent disruptive or resistant force. Insofar as it describes cultural and literary narratives that emerge in response to social conditions, 'structure of feeling' instead seems related to Althusser's notion of ideology as 'the lived relation to real conditions of existence', or to Fredric Jameson's concept of the 'political unconscious', the buried and hidden narratives in literary texts that respond to particular social conditions.[16] But while Williams uses the term to discuss what he describes as an 'ordinary structure of feeling' (*Long Revolution* 68), he also associates it with the notion of an emergent response to a broader social context which has not yet been articulated explicitly: 'we find some art expressing feelings which the society, in its general character, could not express' (*Long Revolution* 70). Even a dominant structure of feeling is for Williams somehow at odds with or opposed to an official account of the period; for example, the novels of the 1840s express a response to social conditions not found in other records of the period, and they thereby offer some kind of unofficial, unsanctioned knowledge which Williams sees as a more authentic record of experience. Discussing the concept in the late 1970s with reviewers from *New Left Review*, Williams states: 'I did want to insist very sharply on the true presence of a structure of feeling, as distinct from the official or received thought of a time, which always succeeds it' (*Politics and Letters* 163). He described his own account of the late 1950s and early 1960s in *The Long Revolution* as an attempt to outline the 'structure of feeling of working class people, rather than the political doctrines or arguments of the time' (174). Feeling therefore captures for Williams some kind of truth about experience, which itself is associated with immediacy and truth, in contrast to the mediation of ideology: as he explains, 'experience necessarily exceeds articulation ... always containing more than ideology can remit' (170).[17]

Moreover, Williams distinguishes between dominant structures of feeling and those that he later names 'pre-emergent' (*Politics and Letters* 164), which he identifies even more clearly as forms of resistance to the sanctioned status quo. He identifies certain literary works as articulating a new or emergent structure of feeling through new kinds of form as well as new kinds of content, and gives the naturalist drama of Ibsen and Strindberg as examples of work which articulate 'fundamental changes of feeling ... changes in the whole conception of a human being and of his relation with what is non-human' ('Film' 34). A structure of feeling, then, often expresses a new emergent kind of consciousness that cannot be explicitly articulated. Instead, it is felt, or expressed obliquely through literature – hence the privileged status of creative work for Williams (like Hall) as both the symptom and vanguard of change: 'the new work will not only make explicit the changes in feeling, but will in itself promote and affect them' (35). It is thus clear that while Williams provides a more careful and qualified account of the relation between feeling and social structures than others in the New Left, recognizing the way that 'feeling' is shaped by social structures rather than necessarily opposing such structures, he nonetheless frequently links feeling to change, modernity, rupture, and with an unofficial or emergent response to a social situation that has a privileged epistemological status.

Williams's semi-autobiographical *Border Country* treats feeling even more romantically. Throughout the novel feeling is associated less with rupture, change, and resistance, and more with community and wholeness. The novel interweaves the story of Matthew Price, an academic living in London who is called home to Wales because of the illness of his father Harry, with a flashback narrative about Harry's life as a young signalman and Matthew's boyhood. Feeling offers a superior kind of knowledge, associated with Wales and with Harry, which is frequently contrasted to the knowledge imparted by language, especially written language. Matthew, an economic historian studying emigration from the Welsh valleys to London in the nineteenth century, is 'trained to detachment: the language itself, consistently abstracting and generalizing, supported him in this' (79), but as a result feels that he lacks the means of understanding and measuring the changes experienced by those early emigrants, whose path of course mirrors his. A recurrent theme of the novel is the failure of language to capture and express feeling (a failure Williams's own straining and portentous style often seems to enact): so the phone call informing Matthew of Harry's stroke is symptomatic, as he tells his wife: 'It was a bad line. They can talk endlessly but they couldn't make it clear' (12).

The adult Matthew (called Will at home, exemplifying the scholarship boy's split between two worlds) encounters feeling not in the spoken word or in academic language, but in song, when he attends an eisteddfod during his visit home. Here the choirmaster identifies all the children singing in terms of their relationship to other members in the family, and this sense of communal connection is embodied in the voice of the massed choir: 'the entry and rising of an extraordinary power, and everyone singing; the faces straining and the voices rising around them, in the hushed silence that held all the potency of these sounds, until you listening were the singing, and the border had been crossed' (199). The singing acts as a means of reconciliation for Matthew between his present and his past, as he, the split subject living on a cultural border, crosses the border from 'listening' to 'singing' and erases that border, as 'you listening were the singing'. This idea of commonality and reconciliation is expressed in terms of corporeal intensity as well as feeling, as the singing of the anthem has 'a direct effect on the body: on the skin, on the hair, on the hands' (199).

Feeling is associated with community, and with Matthew's gradual reconnection to the local community, but it is also associated with Harry, from whom Matthew feels distanced. His father's friend Morgan tells Matthew/Will that Harry 'took his own feelings and he built from them. He lived direct, never by any other standard at all …. What we talk about, Will, he's lived' (276–77). Matthew's triumph by the end of the novel is his ability to feel and his revitalization, a process that is expressed in terms of a corporeal identification between Matthew, his father, and the community, as the individual bodies merge into one. Standing on a railway platform, about to return to London, Matthew moves away from the thronging crowd, then realises:

> over the years he had gradually been steadily moving away, avoiding contact …. The sources of denial, the small real denials like this moving away, seemed to glow again in his body, in an overwhelming rush of feeling …. Closing his eyes, he saw Harry's heavy body, and the crowd moved in it, the crowd in its constant pressures. Through his whole body he would hear the deep, strong voice, and the rhythms went out into all the voices around him, until he heard his own voice, differently pitched.
>
> (301)

At this point a railway inspector who sees Matthew's physical likeness to Harry approaches him, and tells him that Harry has had a second stroke. Having been recognized as Harry's son, Matthew is subsequently able to recognize himself as part of the community, and this process of reconnection and reconciliation is expressed in terms of physical revitalization: 'he went slowly down the steps, watching the people who passed him. It was as if, for the first time, he was able to know them as himself, and this was like a change in the weight of his body, a deep flowing-back of energy' (302). Matthew's renewal is complete after his father's death, at which point he seems to inherit Harry's capacity for feeling. Williams's prose emphasizes the heft and bulk of the (masculine) feeling body that is paradoxically more articulate than language: 'the weight seemed to shift suddenly. All the words went, and he stood and wept as he had not wept since childhood, beyond the possibility of control' (324). Matthew is no longer isolated but is connected to the experience of others through his body, which registers feelings beyond his own: on the day of Harry's burial, he 'felt a sudden wrench in his body, that seemed to come from outside him, as if it were not his own pain' (328). He is also physically revitalized and renewed, as his wife

Susan (a shadowy character) notes after his return to London: 'he was evidently stronger ... certain energies were released. There was a difference of physical presence, that she had felt at once before anything was said' (333).[18]

In *Border Country* we see the bruised and wounded body of the scholarship boy described by Hoggart revivified and healed as the energies of the father are passed down to the son. Matthew/Will, the scholarship boy, is reunited with his community and with Harry, the political activist of an earlier generation, a connection expressed through the image of the male body that can once again feel. Williams's concept of 'structure of feeling' is the least romanticized account of feeling we see in the work of the New Left, although it does tend to associate feeling with resistance to official histories and to the received ideas of the political status quo. However, Williams the novelist depicts a fantasy that Williams the theorist would probably have baulked at, bluntly identifying the feeling male body with reconciliation, wholeness, and community, or to use Williams's own terms, with a 'common culture'. This depiction has a markedly nostalgic element to it as the metropolitan intellectual comes to embody in a very literal manner the energy and feeling associated with his father, the worker and union activist from an earlier generation. The man Matthew is reconciled with the child, the past with the present, England with Wales, and the city with the country.[19] The feeling male body is the bridge that crosses the border between these divided categories, and unites them in its strength and energy.

Left Leavisites: rewriting the feeling male body

I have argued that the feeling male body emerges throughout the work of the New Left as an image that is both highly charged and ambiguous. It signifies wholeness and totality, but also rupture and revolution, and while it is an alternative to the fragmentation and alienation of modernity, it also embodies the energies of the modern in the face of the conservatism of the status quo. In its multivalency, it reflects the divergent political goals within the New Left, from the desire to modernize both an out-of-date socialism and a conservative society, to the concern with maintaining the integrity of traditional working-class culture in the face of the destructive effects of modern mass culture. In their use of the feeling male body to express such potentially conflicting desires, the New Left both inherit and rework other representations of the body in early twentieth-century Britain and Europe. The final section of this chapter seeks to show that New Left's feeling male body is the offspring of various versions of the feeling body in circulation in twentieth-century Britain, in particular the discourse of feeling in the literary criticism of F. R. Leavis, and the body as it had been represented in a tradition of left criticism from William Morris to George Orwell. The New Left articulate the Leavisite feeling body to masculinity, drawing on the iconography of working-class masculinity, yet at the same time detaching such masculinity from labouring bodies.

As I discussed in the introduction, throughout industrialized Europe in the early twentieth century the body is imagined as a site of resistance to industrialized capitalism and urbanization, an image of organic unity in the face of technological fragmentation. The turn to the body was not just textual or representational, but could be quite literal. In Germany, from the late nineteenth century when 'improved personal hygiene, dietary reform, sunbathing and gymnastics promised to free the body from the restrictions of modern industrialization and city living' (Jay, Kaes, and Dimendberg 673) to the 1920s and 1930s, the body became the focus of various leisure activities and 'lifestyles', including nudism, hiking, and vegetarianism. The body was seen as a means of revitalizing a country crushed by defeat in the First World War. A founder of nudism, Adolf Koch, wrote: 'The urgency of the times in which we live, the monotony of work, and the world war and its results have caused a disturbance in our spiritual and physical dispositions', which nudism promised to address: 'We strive for the unity of body and soul' (675). The socialist Fritz Wildung claimed that 'Sport is a rebellion against the threat of decay, an expression of the will to live' (682). Valentine Cunningham argues that in Britain, too, 'the 30s was emphatically the era of the body', with a rise in leisure pursuits associated with the body such as gymnastics, rambling, hiking, and youth hostelling, as well as vegetarianism and nudism (162).

A similar focus on the body is found in the work of F. R. Leavis in the 1930s. Leavis sees an alternative to the dehumanization of capitalist society in the return to an organic society, which he associates with images of physicality and affective immediacy, and with the terms 'life', 'vitality', and 'experience'. Leavis criticizes twentieth-century society for its failure to integrate thought and feeling, calling for an educated public to fight against the dehumanized, 'technologico-Benthamite world' whose growth accompanied the Industrial Revolution. Leavis terms this world 'civilization', associating it with the mass-produced, the machinic and the inhuman, with gross, material concerns, and with productivity and profit; civilization produces alienated individuals, a fragmented, atomized society, and mass culture such as film which offers merely a 'vivid illusion of actual life' (*Mass Civilization* 21). To this 'civilization', Leavis counterposes 'culture', the sphere not only of spiritual values but also, as Terry Eagleton describes, of the 'verbally rich, complex, sensuous and particular' (*Literary Theory* 36). True culture, appreciated only by a minority in the industrialized age of the twentieth century, is characterized by its immediacy and its capacity to revivify a reader or spectator, by its 'concrete livingness, the immediacy of sensuous and life charged presentation' (*English Literature* 97).

Leavis's bodily metaphors draw heavily on the notion of wholeness and on the integration of consciousness and corporeality. Like T. S. Eliot, he looks back nostalgically to the organic, pre-industrial community of the sixteenth and seventeenth centuries in which thought and feeling were united – an image of society based on the body, as Gary Day points out (64). This helps to account for the particular significance of emotion for Leavis, as emotion is the category that reintegrates thought and feeling in an organic unity, in contrast to the 'debasement of emotional life' (*Leavis and Thompson* 48) in the industrial age. In the organic society, thought and feeling are joined in words that 'render their meanings in terms of bodily sensation. They are formed from simple verbs which express the act, notions, and attitudes of the body and its members' (qtd. in Pease 170).[20] But as well as indicating wholeness and unity, Leavis's body also has potentially disruptive capacities. As Allison Pease has argued, Leavis, along with Eliot and I. A. Richards, was concerned not just with a notion of sensibility, 'the connection between sensations, emotions, and cognition', but also with what Pease describes as 'invigorating shock', a kind of feeling that hitherto had been primarily associated with devalued forms of culture such as the sensation novel and pornography (167). By the 1920s, shock – previously associated with emotional exploitation – had become a positive term which contrasted with the passivity and dulling of the senses seen as the effect of mass culture. Pease suggests that the incorporation of shock into modernist critical discourse was a potentially democratic aesthetic practice that subverted modernism's elitist tendencies, as well as a means of controlling potentially subversive cultural forms. Certainly Leavis's emphasis on the sensuous body can be seen as disrupting the dominant cultural order as well as acquiescing to it. Despite his nostalgia, Leavis criticizes an aristocratic, aestheticized view of culture which he associates with metropolitan literary culture, particularly Bloomsbury – those '*milieux* of which the frequenters cultivate quickness in the uptake, knowingness about the latest market-quotations, and an impressive range of reference' (*English Literature* 8). That is, the merely cerebral, the overly knowing culture of the Establishment inheritors is a poor second to the richly sensuous culture appreciated by a classless minority.

The disruptive, levelling qualities of the body partly accounts for the appeal of Leavis to the New Left, as it valued a critical response which (at least in theory) was independent of class and background. As Francis Mulhern argues of Leavis's journal, '*Scrutiny* seemed in some obvious respects a "natural" ally of the Left ... resolutely opposed to a "civilization" which was, in truth, that of capitalism' (330).[21] Chris Baldick explains that Leavis was opposed to Establishment culture as well as to mass culture: 'the conformity imposed by the public school and by the cinema have one and the same root. Resistance comes only from the sensitive minority' (181). In valuing the outsider, Leavis emphasizes the importance of individual experience in validating critical judgements, so what Baldick describes as Leavis's 'cult of "experience"' (204) also opened the way for Williams and Hoggart to challenge aspects of the Leavisite world-view that did not fit with their own experience. For example, Williams criticizes Leavis's utopian organic community for ignoring 'the penury, the petty tyranny, the disease and mortality, the ignorance and frustrated intelligence which were also among its ingredients' (*Culture and Society* 260). But Williams and the New Left also retain from Leavis the notion of the feeling body as an index of cultural health and wholeness and a means to such wholeness, although they imagine a 'healthy society' as a socialist society based on a common culture, rather than Leavis's prelapsarian, pre-industrial, organic community. Like Leavis, they oscillate between a notion of the body as wholeness, a notion that circulates widely in early twentieth-century Europe, and a sense of the body's disruptive capacities.

However, the New Left depart from Leavis in their continual and often explicit identification of the feeling, sensuous body as male and working class. Gary Day makes the useful observation that Leavis privileges a body whose capacity for pleasure is tempered by the effort associated with work, whether this is manual labour or the labour of criticism (51). While the labouring body is implicitly male, for Leavis this body is associated with the traditional organic community rather than with contemporary working-class males. Indeed, Day argues that when Leavis attempts to police a distinction between good, productive bodies, and dangerous bodies that are associated purely with consumption and with mass culture (84), the latter category includes both female bodies and working-class bodies (196). In contrast, the New Left make the masculinity of this body explicit, and link it to the figure of the working-class man, as we have seen in the photographs and articles in *ULR*, and in *The Uses of Literacy* and *Border Country*.

Part of the reason for this was doubtless the ongoing struggle of the many former literary critics in the New Left to distance themselves from the feminizing associations of literary study, a struggle begun by Leavis in his attempt to inject rigour and 'force' into a discipline at that time dominated by women students and belle-lettrism. The masculinity of the feeling body combats any perceived feminizing effects of literary study. Intriguingly, during the 1950s Williams taught in continuing education at Oxford and also worked for the Workers' Educational Association (WEA), which had been founded in order to educate a target audience of working-class men, but by the 1950s enrolled a majority of middle-class women in its classes. Fred Inglis points out that Williams's classes were no exception; over three-quarters of the students in his WEA literature courses were women (Inglis 119), whom Williams later described dismissively as 'commuter housewives … who wanted to read some literature' (qtd. in Inglis 120).[22] Yet in *The Long Revolution* Williams presents quite a different picture of his work in adult education. He writes: 'In recent years I have discussed D. H. Lawrence with working miners; discussed methods of argument with building workers; discussed newspapers with young trade unionists; discussed television with apprentices' (qtd. in Inglis 119). This may well have been true. But by any stretch of the imagination, Williams's account of his work is selective, as he brings together masculinity, the working classes, and an expanded notion of culture – one that extends beyond the literary to include newspapers, television, and 'methods of argument'.

The New Left were also influenced by a long tradition of representing class by left-leaning writers from William Morris to George Orwell which romanticized masculinity. Lisa Jardine and Julia Swindells argue that the intellectual left in Britain has always 'allowed nineteenth-century paternalistic fiction to mediate its class history' (3), as it has tended to rely on literature and fiction to provide evidence of class-consciousness, and on a particular literary tradition which produced a version of authentic class-consciousness in which women are erased, and in which English working men are romanticized. They trace such narratives into the twentieth century, giving as an example Orwell's *The Road to Wigan Pier* (1937). By reading the section of Orwell's diary in whichhe records his visit to Wigan Pier alongside the published text, theyshow some of the transformations that take place between the initial journal observations and the finished literary text. They point to the way in which the male working class body is aestheticized and given moral value in the literary text, in which Orwell refers to men's 'noble bodies: wide shoulders tapering to slender supple waists, and small pronounced buttocks, with not an ounce of waste flesh anywhere' (qtd. in Jardine and Swindells 11). Yet at the same time, they argue, in this 'literary idyll of equatable masculinity and work, the literary text erases the graphic evidence of women which there is in the diary' (16). The run-down and unhappy women Orwell describes in the diary are meta-morphosed into women who make a comfortable home for their men. Jardine and Swindells claim that Orwell is continuing a left literary tradition of 'moral realism', in which the moral burden is carried both by art and by the family: women are associated with an aestheticized version of the family, which upholds moral values rather than being seen as a terrain for politics.[23] Similarly, in William Morris's *News From Nowhere* (1890), a seminal text for the left, the representation of a socia-list utopia involves, among other things, handsome serving wenches bringing the narrator sweet smelling herbs and roses – an aestheticized domesticity in which the women serve only to fulfil male desires.

The New Left brings together the feeling body from Leavis and the romanticization of the male body from the literary left, and mixes these two together into a potent cocktail, the 'feeling male body', which becomes both the symptom of cultural crisis and its cure. This feeling body draws on but marks a shift from the heroic, noble bodies celebrated by an earlier generation of left writers such as Orwell and D. H. Lawrence. The vital bodies celebrated by the New Left are often implicitly rugged, virile, and manly, but they are not the bodies of the labourers celebrated by Orwell and Lawrence. Their authenticity and radicality is signalled by their masculinity and their aptitude for feeling, rather than by their capacity for labour. In *Border Country*, the capacity for feeling and ener-gy links the bodies of socially mobile scholarship boys and their fore-bears; feeling and vitality does not just signal working-class identity, but it also substitutes or compensates for the loss of such identity. In addi-tion, the emergence of a wounded, feeling body, such as the bruised body of Hoggart's scholarship boy, marks the departure from the heroic bodies of the thirties – 'the big, the tough, the butch' as Cunningham describes them (170) – worshipped by Orwell, Lawrence, and the leftists of the Auden generation.

In the writing of New Left, the feeling male body therefore marks a key moment in the transition from a class-based politics to a 'cultural studies' model of a politics of resistance through style, in this case through mas-culinity as style. It refers back to the 'noble bodies' of an older model of working-class masculinity, and forward to the new youth culture based on style. The romanticization of the feeling male body indicates the desire for wholeness and the healing of the social body linked with the utopian spirit of modernity, but also the desire for rupture and the break-down of fixed certainties that could be described as postmodern. Masculinity becomes a new marked universal in the form of the feeling male body, which both represents the wounds to the social body and offers the possibility of healing those wounds. As we will see, the New Left helped to produce the trope of the feeling male body, but it also responded to its emergence in other texts. The next chapter explores some of the anxieties and desires connected with other manifestations of this body in two key 1950s texts: Kingsley Amis's *Lucky Jim* and John Osborne's *Look Back in Anger.*

2
Affect and Politics in *Lucky Jim* and *Look Back in Anger*

In the mid-1950s, two literary events provoked widespread debate about their political significance: the publication of Kingsley Amis's first novel, *Lucky Jim* (1954), and the performance of John Osborne's play *Look Back in Anger* at the Royal Court Theatre (1956). Most contemporary commentators saw *Lucky Jim* and *Look Back in Anger* as challenging Establishment values and embodying the new egalitarian cultural and political attitudes of the postwar era, whether for good or for ill. Osborne and Amis themselves became iconic figures, representative both of a new generation of postwar writers (who would in time be described as 'Angry Young Men') and of the postwar generation more broadly. *Lucky Jim* and *Look Back in Anger* seemed to capture the voice of their generation: a voice which was rebellious, radical, striking out both against the inability of the Welfare State to deliver its promises, and against the cultural complacency and consumerism of the Macmillan era.

Claims that the novel and the play were associated with left-wing rebellion and with the reforms of the postwar welfare state came from both the antagonistic right and the enthusiastic left. Evelyn Waugh, writing after the publication of *Lucky Jim*, sweepingly characterized the new generation of postwar authors as 'a new wave of philistinism', and as 'Mr Butler's protégés' (11), seeing them as the boorish products of the 1944 Education Act.[1] Somerset Maugham drew on Amis's novel to paint a picture of postwar decline, and of all that was wrong with a new generation of university students and faculty:

They do not go to university to acquire culture, but to get a job, and when they have got one, scamp it. They have no manners, and are woefully unable to deal with any social predicament. Their idea of celebration is to go to a pub and drink six beers. They are mean, malicious and envious. They will write anonymous letters to harass a fellow under-graduate and listen in to a telephone conversation that is no business of theirs .... They are scum.

$$(4)^2$$

Similarly, an antagonistic review of *Look Back in Anger* in the *Times Literary Supplement* described the protagonist, Jimmy Porter, as 'racked with uncertainty and rotten with self-pity', but the review grudgingly concluded that 'there is something about this nagging young man which audiences recognize as giving him some vital connection with the social system' (qtd. in Anderson, 'Commitment' 47).

But if Amis and Osborne were dismissed by some as symptomatic of all that was wrong with British society, for others they were exciting new voices. David Marquand's article in the first issue of *ULR*, 'Lucky Jim and the Labour Party', describes Jim Dixon as an example of the new kind of 1950s intellectual, the scholarship boy alienated both from the world in which he grew up and the world in which he finds himself at university. Marquand praises Jim's critical stance in relation to con-temporary society, seeing such criticism as a necessary bulwark against a 'Complacent State' in which social change is assumed to be unneces-sary: 'some at least of Lucky Jim's attitudes are shared by the over-whelming majority of those who think at all .... Lucky Jim is forced by his own history to be an outsider and a critic: until this country becomes wholly egalitarian he can be nothing else' ('Lucky Jim' 57–58). Like Marquand, who sees Jim Dixon as embodying a postwar problem, the influential critic Kenneth Tynan in his famous review of *Look Back in Anger* discusses Jimmy Porter as an iconic figure for contemporary Britain:

All the qualities are there, qualities one had despaired of ever seeing on the stage – the drift towards anarchy, the instinctive leftishness, the automatic rejection of 'official attitudes', the surrealist sense of humour ... the casual promiscuity, the sense of lacking a crusade worth fighting for .... The Porters of our time deplore the tyranny of 'good taste' and refuse to accept 'emotional' as a term of abuse; they are classless and they are also leaderless.

(178)

Tynan's praise for the play was mirrored by other left critics: in *ULR* 7, Graham Martin praised Osborne's 'authentic voice' (40), while in the

Guardian Marquand described the way that the play had become a political statement and a resource for young left-wing intellectuals:

> Oxford socialists ... are scarcely concerned at all with politics as usually understood. What are they concerned with instead? The short, superficial answer is, culture. '*Look Back in Anger*', one prominent university left winger shouted at me recently, his voice almost shaking with passion, 'is a more important political document than anything the Labour Party has said since 1951.'
>
> ('The New Left' 4)

The degree of attention the play and novel attracted meant that even antagonistic commentary confirmed their social and political significance. Robert Hewison contests the notion that the left's view of new writers was predominantly positive, arguing that the new writers were 'sniped at for their lack of commitment' by the New Left (*In Anger* 140). Yet while such criticism can be seen at times – in David Marquand's review of *Lucky Jim*, for example – it was nonetheless always tempered with the assumption that these texts were identifying political problems and representing authentic experience, while the texts' rejection of conventional politics also reinforced their status as documents of 'instinctive leftishness'.

However, in retrospect, the political claims made on behalf of both *Lucky Jim* and *Look Back in Anger* are bemusing. *Lucky Jim*, for example, reveals all kinds of tensions and contradictions in its representation of class and culture, as it alternates between critique and neutrality, rebellion and accommodation. The novel's utopian, comic structure minimizes Jim's contradictory opinions and trajectories as luck frequently intervenes to ensure Jim triumphs over the social system without having to change it. By the end of the novel, Jim Dixon is no longer David Marquand's alienated intellectual, if he ever was; he has vanquished his enemies and is happily employed, on his way to London, with a rich and beautiful girlfriend. In Osborne's play, Jimmy Porter identifies the problems of contemporary society as inauthenticity, a lack of feeling, and apathy, qualities he associates with the upper middle classes and with women; however, Osborne, like Amis, does not represent these problems as the result of social structures that should be transformed. Rather, *Look Back in Anger* implies that the problems have an appealingly simple solution: they can be resisted and transcended by feeling male body, whose authenticity and emotional honesty contrast with the dominant culture, and whose masculinity is superior to inauthentic femininity.

Even at the time, John Osborne rejected the attempts of critics such as David Marquand to analyse the protagonists of 'angry' texts as indicative of the failure of conventional politics to address the concerns of a new generation.[3] Instead, Osborne favoured an interpretation of *Look Back in Anger* that saw the play as a reflection on the human condition, and on the difficulty of facing up to that condition. He continually disputed interpretations that the play depicted the state of Britain, or even the state of a generation, arguing in a foreword to the play that it was simply about 'two people in love'.[4] More recently, critics have responded in different ways to the lack of political coherence in these texts, and in those of other authors associated with the 'Angry Young Men', such as John Braine, Alan Sillitoe, Colin Wilson, and Arnold Wesker. For some, the texts' ambiguous politics confirms their ephemeral nature, as they are redeemed neither by formal experimentation nor by political radicalism. Others conclude that the very notion of a category of writers called 'Angry Young Men' is flawed, given the lack of any ideological coherence could provide some justification for such a grouping. Robert Hewison and Stuart Laing, for example, both point out that the writers included under this rubric were not part of a movement in the conventional sense: they did not know each other personally, they had no consciously shared project, and the similarities in their work seem to have emerged in spite of the differences in their backgrounds rather than as the result of a shared social situation.[5] Hewison argues that the 'Angry Young Men' were constructed as a movement in the wake of the crises in Suez and Hungary as a literary focus for political frustrations:

> The timing of Suez and Hungary was coincidental, but their combined effect was to exacerbate disaffections and tensions. Some of these disaffections had been voiced in the novels of Amis and Wain, but there was nothing that gave them particular focus. What was needed was a myth, and in 1956 there appeared the myth of the Angry Young Man.
>
> (*In Anger* 129)

However, the construction of the Angry Young Man cannot simply be understood as the result of a generalized desire for a political focus that arbitrarily yoked together a number of disparate texts, as Hewison suggests. Through an analysis of *Look Back in Anger* and *Lucky Jim*, I show that while these texts lack a coherent analysis of class and culture, they do share a common emphasis on feeling and vitality, and link these affects to masculine and working-class or lower-middle-class bodies.

As I discussed in the previous chapter, the New Left attributed a revolutionary force to bodies, cultural production, and criticism that emphasized life and vitality, qualities which could signify either wholeness or disruption. Seeing both a similar discourse of affect and a familiar representation of the feeling male body in the 'angry' texts, they understood these texts to be offering a criticism of dominant society that was broadly leftist. But when we turn to these texts, we discover that their emphasis on vitality differs in key respects from the New Left's, as does their representation of the 'working-class body': the affective discourse of these texts does not express the desire for social change, but rather the desire for individual escape. In *Lucky Jim* and *Look Back in Anger*, the traditional tastes and bodily dispositions (what Bourdieu calls the habitus) of the working classes magically become the attributes of a classless elite, despite their wealth and class background.[6] The texts associate this body – marked by class, but paradoxically classless – with freedom and vitality, as well as with victimhood and woundedness: both vitality and pain indicate the protagonist's capacity to feel and hence his superiority. In *Lucky Jim* and *Look Back in Anger* the affective and the bodily are not associated with class warfare or political protest, but are instead the means through which feeling individuals can transcend the social world and escape class hierarchies.

The appeal of the feeling male body helps to explain the construction of the category of 'angry young man', and to tease out the identifications and misidentifications between left cultural critics and the new generation of writers and dramatists. Both the New Left's critical discourse and 'angry' texts associate affect with transformation and freedom, whether social or individual; but these texts and the critical discourse that surrounded them show that feeling and the body can powerfully reinforce social distinctions by naturalizing them. We see this particularly in the way that *Look Back in Anger* and *Lucky Jim* organize affect in gendered terms: men are feeling, authentic individuals, whereas women are inauthentic, either unfeeling or hysterical. Lawrence Grossberg has argued that it is 'affective investment which enables ideological relations to be internalized and, consequently, naturalized' (83). These texts not only make use of pre-existing, recognisable versions of class and masculine embodiment, but also help to forge new connections between feeling and vitality, the male body, and authenticity. This chapter examines these connections but also shows their tenuousness, as the distinctions between immediacy and distance, authenticity and performance, and masculinity and femininity constantly break down even as they are being reasserted. Ultimately, however, I argue that this breakdown is recuperated into the revitalization of masculinity despite – and even because of – its wounded vulnerability.

A new elite: *Look Back in Anger*

Both *Look Back in Anger* and *Lucky Jim* attack the privilege of the traditional middle classes and the way in which class distinctions are reinforced and expressed through cultural distinctions. Even more than they target the habits or tastes of the upper middle class, they target their supposed values – superficiality, hypocrisy, selfishness, pretentiousness, and inauthenticity. *Look Back in Anger* launches the attack on the traditional middle classes through its very setting. Kenneth Tynan welcomed its distance from the typical play of the time, set in 'a country house in what used to be called Loamshire but is now, as a heroic tribute to realism, sometimes called Berkshire', whose characters 'belong to a social class derived partly from romantic novels and partly from the playwright's vision of the leisured life he will lead after the play is a success' (148). In contrast to country house luxury, *Look Back in Anger* is set in a small attic flat somewhere in the Midlands, and its central character is Jimmy Porter, a scholarship boy who has graduated from a university which was 'not even red brick, but white tile' (42), and who runs a sweet stall. The play's content confirmed for many its challenge to 'the Establishment', particularly the way in which Jimmy Porter's anger is directed against Alison, his upper-middle-class wife, and against her friends and relatives, but more generally against the upper middle classes and their cultural institutions. Jimmy reads the 'posh papers' (13) on Sunday, but criticizes them; he says to his friend, Cliff, 'I've just read three whole columns on the English Novel. Half of it's in French. Do the Sunday papers make *you* feel ignorant?' When Cliff agrees, Jimmy takes the opportunity to insult him, at the same time pointing out the class distinctions the papers help produce: 'Well, you *are* ignorant. You're just a peasant.' He then turns to Alison and adds: 'You're not a peasant, are you?' (11). Jimmy here reveals the symbolic violence of the system of cultural distinction – as when later in the play he says: 'There's a particularly savage correspondence going on in there about whether Milton wore braces or not. I just want to see who gets shot down this week' (77). He turns this violence against the upper classes when he describes the way in which he and his friend Hugh used to turn up uninvited at the houses of wealthy friends of his parents-in-law, eating their food and drinking them dry in an apparent act of class warfare. Jimmy despises the weakness of his targets: 'I used to hope that one day, somebody would have the guts to slam the door in our faces, but they didn't. They were too well-bred, and probably sorry for me as well. So we went on plundering them, wolfing their food and cigarettes, and smoking their cigars like ruffians' (44).

But rather than criticizing elitism, *Look Back in Anger* proposes a new elite, characterized by a capacity for feeling and emotional honesty. As this quote reveals, what frustrates Jimmy about his wife Alison's family friends is their inability to say or express what they feel – here, their own anger with Jimmy – rather than their social privilege. Although Alison says that during these sorties Jimmy 'revelled in the role of the barbarian invader' (44), he is also trying to prevent a different kind of alien invasion, the invasion of superficiality and inauthentic feeling. What upsets Jimmy is not the economic and social privilege of the upper middle classes, but their desiccated emotional lives. This can also be seen in the reasons Jimmy gives for criticizing Alison's brother Nigel the 'straightbacked, chinless wonder from Sandhurst .... He'll end up in the Cabinet one day, make no mistake' (20). Jimmy objects to Nigel not primarily because of his class privilege, but because he and the people like him who will govern the country do not know how or what ordinary people feel: Nigel's 'knowledge of life and ordinary human beings is so hazy, he really deserves some sort of decoration for it – a medal inscribed "For Vaguery in the Field" (20).

The play therefore mounts a social critique. But this critique is not, as many seemed to think, an indictment of social and cultural inequality motivated by the desire for a more democratic society. Jimmy's goal is not a more equal and democratic society, but one in which the sensitive minority, comprised of people like himself, are no longer under threat from superficial, inauthentic people such as Alison's family and their friends. Although Jimmy is an alienated sweet-stall owner who mocks cultural and social pretension, his views, endorsed by the play, are very similar to those of F. R. Leavis: the problem with society is cultural decline, which can only be halted by the sensitive, feeling minority, who defend or keep alive values in the face of an indifferent majority.[7] A meritocratic elite – in Leavis's case, his students; in Jimmy's, the emotionally authentic – will safeguard the values that really matter, preserving what made Britain great – for Leavis, the organic community; for Jimmy, passionate conviction. For both men, the minority is marked by its capacity for feeling and its capacity for life. The idea that Jimmy is the defender of culture appears to contradict his role as the barbarian storming the gates of the Establishment. But *Look Back in Anger* implies that the truly valuable aspects of culture – feeling and passion – will only be kept alive by the minority constituted by Jimmy and by people like him who can transcend class culture. Jimmy charges himself and Alison with this task: 'Let's pretend that we're human beings, and that we're actually alive. Just for a while' (15). The authentic minority is characterized by feeling and by honesty, and for Jimmy these qualities are displayed through particular cultural choices. He declares: 'Anybody who doesn't like real jazz, hasn't any feeling either for music or people' (48).[8] Jimmy therefore gives us a view of the world in which affect and feeling are much more important than class, and indeed transcend class. The play's emphasis on feeling was picked up, if not analysed, by some critics at the time: one wrote: 'if you are young it will speak for you. If you are middle-aged, it will tell you what the young are *feeling*' (qtd. in Taylor, *Look Back* 53; my emphasis).[9]

Voice, performance, and authenticity in *Lucky Jim*

In *Lucky Jim*, affect is also an important touchstone and a means of distinguishing the true elite, characterized by emotional authenticity and honesty, from the false elite. This novel follows Jim Dixon's escape from the university in which he works, which is mirrored by Jim's growing emotional freedom and authenticity, so that by the end of the novel Jim is able to express openly the thoughts and feelings he spends much of the narrative trying to hide. This novel is sometimes seen as distinct from 'angry' literature, and instead as part of 'The Movement', along with the work of poets like Thom Gunn and Philip Larkin; Blake Morrison contrasts the Movement's mode of reconciliation with the rebelliousness of the later 'Angry Young Men' (247).[10] However, *Lucky Jim* shares with other 'angry' texts a central concern with feeling, as shown by its early working title 'The Man of Feeling', although it depicts a somewhat different version of the feeling male body than *Look Back in Anger*. *Look Back in Anger* values the capacity for feeling in general, whereas in *Lucky Jim* not all feelings or affects are equal, as Jim's progress is an escape from the negative emotions of fear and pity which are shown to hamper honesty and openness. The novel also places more emphasis on the body than *Look Back in Anger*, so that Jim's increasing emotional authenticity is linked to physical processes, particularly the ability to speak in his own voice.

The novel counterposes Jim's own appreciation of the sensory and the physical to a Kantian notion of the aesthetic as reflective and intellectual, represented by the false elite of the Welch family, and especially by the upper-middle-class cultural airs and the anaemic aesthetics of Jim Dixon's boss, Professor 'Neddy' Welch. Much of the novel's rebellious, critical energy is directed against Welch, in whose milieu Jim feels distinctly uncomfortable. Jim is a scholarship boy with vaguely lower-middle or working-class origins, who went to a 'local grammar school', a provincial university (Leicester), and has a mild Northern accent. His academic appointment as a medieval historian is probationary, and since he is dependent on Welch for its renewal, he is torn between his utter disgust at Welch's notion of 'culture', and the need to ingratiate himself with Welch. But there is little evidence that Amis's satirical portrayal of Welch stems from the desire for a more democratic society, or that Jim Dixon is David Marquand's alienated, left-leaning intellectual. Jim's trajectory means that it is implausible to see him as mounting a serious attack against upper-middle-class privilege. By the end of the novel, Jim is well on the road to social mobility, as he obtains a job working for a wealthy patron of the arts, Julius Gore-Urquhart – which will entail moving from the provinces to London – and wins the hand of Gore-Urquhart's rich and beautiful niece, Christine.

The novel's endorsement of Jim's social mobility makes more sense if we see that the novel's own primary category of analysis is not class but affect and feeling, qualities which for Amis are only indirectly related to class. Early in the novel, Jim is invited to one of Welch's 'arty weekends', which provides an opportunity for Amis to counterpose Welch's notion of the aesthetic with Jim's much more visceral tastes and pleasures. For Jim, the weekend is as painful as he had feared: madrigals, recorder recitals and an Anouilh play. Welch's notion of culture and his cultural responses are presented as non-affective, ascetic, refined, and disinterested. As a corollary, Welch is shown to be more generally remote and eccentric, backward looking and academic, detached from the real world and from the responses and concerns of ordinary people. Welch is notorious for not listening to the world. He is isolated and unable to communicate properly with those around him; Jim continually has to repeat himself, or finds Welch repeating questions he has just answered. This isolation in the present is also portrayed as an isolation *from* the present, as Welch glorifies a utopian medievalism, and describes his main interest as 'the English social and cultural scene, with a kind of backward-looking bias in a sense, popular crafts and so on, traditional pastimes' (176).

In contrast to Welch's version of culture, characterized and caricatured as remote and non-affective, Jim's tastes are earthy and 'natural', as we see after the first day of the arty weekend, when Jim finally can stand it no longer and runs off to the pub. As he staggers drunkenly back to the Welch's house, he sings a drinking song rather than a madrigal. He also, defiantly and mockingly, claims the vocabulary of aesthetics to describe the moment during the evening when he found out that the village pub closed half an hour later than usual: 'It had been like a first authentic experience of art or human goodness, a stern, rapt, almost devotional exultation' (54). In using the language of aesthetics to describe the joy of drinking beer, Jim is rejecting a cultural system that legislates a distinction between abstract and visceral tastes, the taste for art and the taste for food and drink. His attack on the distanced aesthetic can be compared with Pierre Bourdieu's desire to 'abolish the sacred frontier which makes legitimate culture a separate universe', and to refuse Kant's opposition 'between the "taste of sense" and the "taste of reflection", and between facile pleasure, pleasure reduced to a pleasure of the senses, and pure pleasure, pleasure purified of pleasure, which is predisposed to become a symbol of moral excellence' (*Distinction* 6).[11] Jim also wants to overturn this opposition; his touchstone, 'nice things are nicer than nasty ones' (140), rejects the distanced aesthetic attitude for the more directly visceral.

Throughout, the novel distinguishes between an unworthy elite – notably the Welch family – whose tastes are overly refined and full of artifice, and a more worthy minority – Jim, Gore-Urquhart, and Christine – who are characterized by their capacity for visceral pleasure, and whose tastes are natural, earthy, and vigorous. Welch is not the only member of his family whose taste is portrayed as both detached and stylized; Bertrand, his son, prides himself on his paintings' form rather than their content, describing his own self-portrait as 'more wall than Welch .... The real idea is the pallor and sort of crumpledness of the clothing against the great, red, smooth wall. A painter's picture' (101). In contrast, Gore-Urquhart and Christine are associated with the immediate and the visceral rather than the formal and the abstract. When Jim first meets Gore-Urquhart, the latter offers him beer in large glasses, whereas Welch had earlier poured Jim a glass of port that is 'the smallest drink he'd ever seriously been offered' (59). Jim is even more impressed when Gore-Urquhart, meeting him in the men's toilets before he is about to deliver his 'Merrie England' lecture, offers him several swigs from a hip flask of whisky. While Jim literally has different tastes from the Welch family – even the Welches' cornflakes have an unpleasant malty taste – he admires Christine's appreciation for hearty breakfast food in large quantities: 'he noted with surprise how much and how quickly she was eating' (67). Christine's proper appearance and social manner mask a kind of raw physicality that is shown by her prodigious appetite, which contrasts with his current, quasi-girlfriend Margaret, who disdains anything so mundane as food: '[Christine] took two biscuits when he offered them, which reminded him of how

Margaret would never eat on this sort of occasion, as if making an easy claim to individuality' (149). Christine's physicality is also shown by her spontaneous, unaffected 'unmusical laugh', as opposed to Margaret's laughter which is like 'the tinkle of tiny silver bells' (23).

Unlike Bourdieu, however, Amis detaches taste and feeling from social background. Bourdieu argues that the pure, detached Kantian aesthetic is a bourgeois aesthetic, or the aesthetic of the dominated fraction of the dominant class – of upper-middle-class intellectuals. He suggests that 'the unique capacity of the pure gaze … sets the aesthete apart from the common herd by a radical difference which seems to be inscribed in "persons" …. The pure gaze implies a break with the ordinary attitude towards the world which, as such, is a social break' (31). In other words, the bargeor's aesthete's cultural distinctions serve to reinforce and per-petuate social distinctions. Bourdieu claims that the popular or working-class aesthetic rejects the distanced gaze of the Kantian aesthetic along with its emphasis on form for form's sake, tending instead to relate representations back to the reality that is being represented, and to 'norms of morality or agreeableness' (41). But in this novel taste bears only an arbitrary relation to class background. Welch and Jim may fall on different sides of a traditional class divide, but this does not adequately explain Jim's antipathy to Welch. Jim is equally antagonistic towards his fellow-lodger, Johns, an accounts clerk who cannot afford a proper hair-cut, but who plays the oboe and subscribes to magazines with modern composers on the cover. Johns's taste for classical music here indicates his detachment and lack of capacity for visceral enjoyment; his lack of feeling and of honesty is also seen in his tendency to report Jim's failings to the Welches. In another novel, Johns might have been portrayed as a kind of Leonard Bast, attempting to educate himself in cultural matters. But in *Lucky Jim* Johns is read unsympathetically because the novel detaches taste from class position, so that Johns's taste signifies his inauthenticity and lack of feeling.

Similarly, while the tastes shared between Gore-Urquhart, Christine, and Jim might seem to illustrate what Bourdieu describes as the popu-lar or working-class aesthetic, Gore-Urquhart and Christine belong to the same class as the Welches. Gore-Urquhart is not only a man of the people but also 'a rich devotee of the arts' (47) who contributes to arts reviews, donates pictures to galleries, has a house in London and anoth-er in the country, and is wined and dined by the local dignitaries, including Jim's Principal. The novel therefore depicts an arbitrary rela-tionship between taste and class, at the same time as it draws on class-based semiotics of taste to distinguish between its characters. A (rather caricatured) working-class aesthetic is evoked, but also transcended or disavowed, as the novel represents an elite characterized by shared tastes rather than shared class position. These shared tastes are sensual and hearty, primarily visceral rather than primarily intellectual. The novel suggests that the true elite deserve money, fame and privilege, instead of the traditional elite represented by Welch and his sons. In the novel's own terms, there is no conflict between Jim's dislike of Welch's version of upper-middle-class culture, and his own social mobility, as Jim is merely rewarded for his taste and his capacity for affect, here characterized as visceral feeling and enjoyment, rather than *Look Back in Anger*'s more abstract endorsement of 'feeling' and 'life'.

Although Bourdieu could be marshalled to criticize the novel's fantasy world in which taste and class bear little relation to each other, the novel equally challenges Bourdieu's own romanticized distinction between the distanced aesthetic of the intellectual and the immediacy of the popular aesthetic. It does so by suggesting that Jim's preference for the visceral and the immediate actually enables him to distance and detach himself from the banality of academic conventions in which Welch is myopically entrenched. For example, Jim's distaste for the stylized nature of academic language, which elevates form over content – a key characteristic of the legitimate aesthetic, according to Bourdieu – is shown by his capacity to distance himself from such language, even when he is the author. Jim wearily starts to read his own article on medieval ship-building techniques between 1450 and 1485: '"In considering this strangely neglected topic," it began. This what neglected topic? This strangely what topic? This strangely neglected what? His thinking all this without having defiled and set fire to the manuscript only made him appear to himself as more of a hypocrite and fool' (14–15). What differentiates Jim from Welch, whose own academic publications are undistinguished, is his preference for immediacy and directness over abstruse evasion. This, however, allows him to distance himself from the abstraction and empty formalism of his own writing. Moreover, Jim uses the visceral reactions of his body to distance himself from academic writing, describing his own article's 'funereal parade of yawn-enforcing facts' (14), and later telling Gore-Urquhart: 'I'm the boredom-detector. I'm a finely tuned instrument' (215). Jim's boredom indicates his desire for sensation and stimulation, and it enables him to detect the emptiness of the academic world in which he finds himself. Most importantly, it illustrates his own distance and detachment from the pretentiousness and mediocrity of Welch and Bertrand, and his superiority to the cultural gatekeepers who have rewarded such mediocrity. Jim's preference for the earthy and the

visceral therefore collapses the distinction between working-class immediacy and bourgeois distance on which Bourdieu depends: his desire for
immediacy is both a criticism of the detached, distanced aesthetic of
Welch and Bertrand, and the means by which he in turn distances and
distinguishes himself from second-rate academics and artists.

A similar tension or paradox can be found in *Lucky Jim's* distinction
between authenticity and performance, a distinction it both invokes and
unwittingly complicates. We know that Jim belongs to an affective elite
not only because of his taste, but also because of the intensity and violent
strength of his feelings – Christopher Hitchens suggests that 'his disasters
and triumphs are rendered in such a way as to put us in mind of manic-
depressive mood swings' (107). However, for much of the novel, Jim does
not articulate these feelings openly. Not until the end of the novel is Jim's
physical, slapstick resistance to Welch and to Margaret – such as his constant face pulling – transformed into openly articulated resistance. On the
one hand, the novel depicts Jim's development as a fully authentic character who moves from imposture and disguise to openness and honesty.
David Lodge has argued that Jim's path to success and freedom begins in
earnest after he wins a fight with Bertrand and is able to speak his mind
aloud: 'The bloody old towser-faced boot-faced totem-pole on a crap reservation, Dixon thought. "You bloody old towser-faced boot-faced totem-
pole on a crap reservation," he said' (209, qtd. in Lodge, xii). On the other
hand, the novel delights in Jim's performance – his face-pulling and role-
playing – as the source of parodic, creative energy through which Jim out-
wits the fools with which he is surrounded.

The novel's ambivalent treatment of the relationship between imposture and authenticity can be traced through the representation of Jim's
voice. For much of the novel, Jim is either struck dumb or described
as a ventriloquist. He is unable to voice his true feelings about Welch,
or about Margaret and her emotional blackmail: 'He'd never be able to
tell Welch what he wanted to tell him, any more than he'd ever be able
to do the same with Margaret' (86). When Welch tells him to write a
public talk on 'Merrie England', his impulse is to finish it with
'Something along the lines of "Thank God for the twentieth century"'
(195). Writing the draft, however, he reproduces Welch's line of thought
in order to fill blank pages and keep Welch happy:

What, finally, is the practical application of all this? .... Each of us
can resolve to do something, every day, to resist the application of
manufactured standards, to protest against ugly articles of furniture
and table-ware, to speak out against sham architecture, to resist the

importation into more and more public places of loudspeakers relay-
ing the Light Programme, to say one word against the Yellow Press,
against the best-seller, against the theatre-organ, to say one word for
the instinctive culture of the integrated village-type community. In
that way we shall be saying a word ... for our native tradition, for our
common heritage, in short, for what we once had and may, some
day, have again – Merrie England.

(204–205)

After writing this paragraph, he belches and does 'his ape imitation all
round the room' (205). This incident illustrates the way in which, for
much of the novel, Jim's rebellion against Welch's notion of culture is
muted, or at least that it is physical and private rather than verbal and
public; Jim is publicly respectful and even deferential towards Welch,
while privately rebellious.

Up until his fight with Bertrand, Jim is continually stopped from saying
what he wants to say by the negative affects of pity and fear. Fear strips Jim
of his voice. He kicks a stone that hits the Professor of English: 'As always
on such occasions, he'd wanted to apologize but had found, when it came
to it, that he was too frightened to' (16). At times his fear leads him to
ridiculous lengths to avoid telling the truth: after Margaret discovers him
trying to hide the damage he has done to Welch's bedclothes and furniture after an accidental cigarette fire, she says sarcastically:

'You couldn't have gone to Mrs Welch and explained, of course.'
'No, of course is right, I couldn't have. I'd have been out of my job
in five minutes.'

(75)

After this, fear causes him to hide his real voice quite literally. He makes
two phone calls to the Welch household where he gets through to Mrs
Welch; fearing her wrath over the burnt bedclothes incident, he dis-
guises his voice, passing himself off the first time as Alfred Beesley and
the second time as 'Farteskyaw'. Jim's fear is evident not only in his attitude towards Welch, but also in his relationship with Margaret, rendering him unable to express his true feelings to her. His relationship with
Margaret is sustained by pity as well: 'If he was going to eat that meal
with any female it would not be Christine but Margaret. He remembered a character in a modern novel Beesley had lent him who was
always feeling pity moving in him like sickness, or some such jargon.
The parallel was apt; he felt very ill' (185). During a conversation

towards the end of his relationship with Margaret, Jim thinks: 'what he said and did arose not out of any willing on his part, nor even out of boredom, but out of a kind of sense of situation .... With disquiet, he found that words were forming in his mind, words which, because he could think of no others, he'd very soon hear himself uttering' (186). Both these passages show that Jim's difficulty in expressing himself is linked to the fact that he quotes words that are not his own, whether literally or metaphorically.

Much of the textual evidence therefore seems to support an interpretation of Jim's gradual passage from inauthenticity to authenticity, in which Jim manages to throw off the shackles of pity and fear and to speak in his own voice. His 'Merrie England' lecture provides the most magnificent, exaggerated example of inauthentic voice, but it is also the first time that Jim articulates his feelings and opinions in public. In the first part of his lecture, fear and a large dram of Gore-Urquhart's whisky cause him to unwittingly emphasize its imitative, inauthentic nature. He first realizes that he has added various expressions reminiscent of Welch which are recognized by the audience, then he '[hears] Welch's intonation clinging tightly round his voice, powerless for the moment to stop it' (223). This is just the beginning; later he realizes he is imitating the Principal, then 'an unusually fanatical Nazi trooper in charge of a book-burning reading out to the crowd excerpts from a pamphlet written by a pacifist, Jewish, literate Communist', then that he is speaking in 'an unnameable foreign accent' (226). Finally, however, he has the drunken courage to leave aside his prepared conclusion and substitute for it his real thoughts: '"What, finally, is the practical application of all this?" Dixon said in his normal voice .... "Listen and I'll tell you. The point about Merrie England is that it was about the most un-Merrie point in our history. It's only the home-made pottery crowd, the organic husbandry crowd, the recorder-playing crowd, the Esperanto ..."' (227).

At this point Jim's drunkenness overwhelms him and he breaks off the lecture. But he has made his point, and finally said what he really thinks: Welch's dream of 'Merrie England' is nonsense. From this point on, Jim is increasingly able to speak in his own voice. When he returns a phone call from an unidentified caller, he is confident enough to maintain his own voice despite a hostile reception. The caller is Gore-Urquhart, and Jim is rewarded for his honesty and openness by the offer of a job. In the utopian world of this novel, Jim is also rewarded by romantic success. When he is (relatively) honest to Margaret about his lack of love for her, he is rewarded by the discovery that she had dishonestly faked a suicide attempt, and he therefore legitimately escapes from her thrall and turns to Christine. The final line of the novel emphasizes Jim's newly acquired authentic voice, as he walks along the street with Christine: 'The whinnying and clanging of Welch's self-starter began behind them, growing fainter and fainter as they walked on until it was altogether overlaid by the other noises of the town and *by their own voices*' (251; my emphasis).

Yet the representation of Jim's voice also complicates the argument that Jim moves from inauthenticity to authenticity. Immediately before Jim and Christine walk away speaking in 'their own voices', Jim greets the Welches by saying 'excuse me' in a 'fruity comic-butler voice' (251), using a parodic, performative voice to mock the Welches' own pretentious performances (indicated, in this final scene as throughout the novel, by their affected headgear: a fishing-hat and a beret). Jim's performance and his role-playing are therefore not simply shackles he is forced into by his dependence on Welch's approval; even after he need no longer ingratiate himself with Welch, he uses imposture and mimicry to mock authority. The novel elsewhere associates performance and imposture with fakeness and inauthenticity: the crooked academic Caton, for example, passes Jim's academic article off as his own; Bertrand's irritating description of his own art is made worse because it 'had clearly been delivered before' (41); the untrustworthy, hysterical Margaret is described as 'actress and as script-writer' (76); while Welch is not only a performer, but is mocked for poorly impersonating himself: 'it was as if some entirely different man, some imposter who couldn't copy his voice, had momentarily taken his place' (7). However, Jim himself uses imposture in his final drunken speech – as well as in his performances on the telephone – for parodic ends, destabilizing the content of his speech through his mimicry. The novel, in fact, is torn between the denunciation of performance in favour of authenticity and honesty, and its own representation of the parodic, creative energy of Jim's own role-playing.

It is therefore difficult to decide whether Jim's social mobility is a reward for his outrageous parody of authority figures or his authenticity. This mobility is depicted metaphorically as well as literally, as the novel ends with him walking away freely while the Welch family are bound to an unreliable car – a fitting image, since the social exclusion he feels in the Welch household is often figured in terms of physical confinement or immobility. For example, during the arty weekend he is given a room that he can enter only through a bathroom; coming back from the pub, he finds himself barred from his room by someone in the bathroom. Later, locked into his room from the inside while Welch sings in the bathroom,

Jim utters one of the most quoted lines of the book, 'Filthy Mozart!' (63). Welch's taste excludes Jim, and this is literalized and mirrored in the way Welch physically excludes Jim from the rest of the house. Jim's initial fear of moving down the social system and losing his job is accompanied by a series of frightening rides in Welch's car (Welch is a terrible driver). But in the penultimate chapter of the novel, Jim takes a bus to the station in the hope of catching Christine before her train leaves, and despite his fears, he is successful (fittingly, Welch has made a mistake about the time of its departure and also has failed to get her there on time). Jim's final social mobility is therefore linked to his physical freedom: he can move free from the obstacles – both literal and metaphorical – that Welch has placed in his way. Yet, as I have argued, it is unclear whether this freedom stems from for his newfound ability to speak in his own voice, or from the destabilizing effects of his verbal mimicry and slapstick performances.

Throughout *Lucky Jim*, then, the distinction between performance and authenticity is both asserted as the ground for distinguishing between the true and the false elite and constantly destabilized. What is clear, however, is that in this novel, as in *Look Back in Anger*, affect defines the true elite, an elite defined not by class background but by their capacity for deep feeling and for enjoying visceral pleasures, and for expressing such feelings and admitting to such tastes (whether through parody or sincerity). In *Look Back in Anger*, Jimmy Porter asserts himself as the model of an affective individual, whose authenticity is guaranteed by his feeling and his honesty; in *Lucky Jim*, Jim Dixon is rewarded for his emotional intensity – whether this is expressed through ape impressions or through the assertion of his own voice – with social mobility. But the anxieties around performance in Amis's novel point to a broader tension that also haunts *Look Back in Anger*, which is above all aesthetic. Both texts endorse an aesthetic of realism based on the desire for the immediate rather than the mediated, on the self-present rather than the re-presented, and also on a notion of language in which words communicate feelings directly and transparently, yet both texts simultaneously undermine such an aesthetic. The final section of this chapter will explore this problem. First, however, I will return to the political claims made for the play and the novel, and reconsider the political implications of the texts in light of their emphases on the class body, and on feeling and vitality.

Gender and the politics of affect

Lynne Segal has argued that 'it is clear that the scorn which the Angry Young Men hurled at "the Establishment" was a class resentment, but one devoid of any collective class consciousness' (*Slow Motion* 15). However, Segal's claim needs to be more carefully nuanced. *Lucky Jim* and *Look Back in Anger* set up affective divisions that can be mapped along class lines to some extent, and that certainly appeal to understandings of the working-class or upper-middle-class habitus. *Lucky Jim* contrasts the squat bodies of Jim and Gore-Urquhart with the aristocratic languor of the Welches, and the earthy tastes of the former with the visceral tastes of the latter. Jimmy criticizes upper-middle-class detachment and remoteness in *Look Back in Anger*, and contrasts this with his own affective investments and capacities. Yet what is striking about the texts is the way in which they conflate the class-inflected bodies of Jim and Jimmy with the protagonists' capacity for feeling and vitality, which is then linked to the possibility of transcending class and class divisions. Although *Look Back in Anger* and *Lucky Jim* privilege the immediacy and directness of feeling in a way that implicitly criticizes the distanced, detached aesthetic associated with 'the Establishment', in the end they also represent feeling as a category or quality which bypasses or ignores the grubby world of class distinction, creating bonds between feeling individuals from a range of class backgrounds. To argue, as Segal does, that the texts demonstrate class resentment is to over-simplify. The protagonists, who at times appeal to a recognizably class-based structure of affect, also imagine themselves as classless individuals who transcend class cultures. The expression of class resentment becomes the means through which class is transcended, as the feeling body becomes a means of both evoking and denying class.

Both texts therefore set up a potential contradiction. On the one hand, they criticize remoteness and detachment, represented by the Welches, or by Alison's family, and champion the immediacy of affect, the body, and the senses. On the other hand, life, feeling, and sensation are the means by which the protagonists detach *themselves* from the world around them, and transcend their circumstances, as Jim's earthy tastes enable his escape to London, and Jimmy's reverence for feeling and life prove his superiority to those around him. Feeling, life, and sensation, these apparently immanent and immediate qualities, themselves become transcendent, and the means through which the protagonists are able to detach themselves from their social situation. Feeling is transcendent in *Look Back in Anger* insofar as it becomes valuable in itself, regardless of what provokes the feeling or the consequences it has. The important thing is that Jimmy *cares*; it does not matter, really, what he cares about. So, in the play's terms, when Jimmy mourns his father – '*I* was the only one who cared!' (58) – and when he tells Alison he wishes that she 'could have a child and that it would die', in order to provoke some passion from her, he is doing the same thing: asserting his passion and feeling. It has frequently been noted that anger in *Look Back in Anger* is a statement in itself, rather than being 'about' anything. While this is usually seen as a sign of the play's incoherence, it in fact draws our attention to the fact that within the play, the cause or the object of anger is irrelevant, because the important thing is the assertion of feeling, any feeling – just as, more generally, the anger of the 'Angry Young Men' was important only insofar as it showed the protagonists' capacity for strong feeling. Throughout *Look Back in Anger* 'feeling' is more important than specific feelings: whether thrilling to jazz or raging against Alison's family, Jimmy is proving his capacity for emotion.

In *Look Back in Anger* and *Lucky Jim*, feeling and 'the taste of sense' are an end in themselves as they display the protagonists' inner life and physical vitality. The emphasis on individual affect replaces a concern with the wider world, as neither the novel nor the play are particularly interested in the world beyond their protagonists. The entire action of *Look Back in Anger* takes place in a bed-sit, and has little action beyond the conflict generated by characters' emotions. *Lucky Jim's* narrative style is limited omniscience, with the action is narrated in the third person but from Jim's perspective. The form of these texts, as well as their thematic emphasis on the individual, emphasizes the personal and the subjective over the external world. Affect, in the texts' own terms, is an escape from and an alternative to political engagement. It is significant that the only politician in *Look Back in Anger* is Nigel, who is too busy trying to get into Parliament to find time to talk to his sister (43).

Both texts use affect to mark out a 'classless' elite who can either assert their superiority over others, as in the case of Jimmy Porter, or miraculously achieve wealth and success without having to change or compromise, like Jim Dixon. Inevitably, though, this elite is male: virile, heterosexual men have the capacity for life, sensation and feeling, while women and effeminate men help to mark out the limits and excesses of affect and feeling. These texts and their reception by the New Left therefore show – contrary to the texts' own claims – the interconnectedness of affect and hegemonic social relations, as both embodiment and feeling are articulated to very conventional discourses of gender, and as they help to shape and are shaped by such discourses. These texts link feeling, vitality, and sensation to *male* bodies, so that gender difference is inscribed in the difference between feeling bodies and either unfeeling or hysterical bodies. The potentially threatening or disruptive force of affect, which we see in the violent energy of *Look Back in Anger* and the slapstick humour of *Lucky Jim*, is neutralized as affect reinforces conventional gender relations.

This is shown through the very different portrayals of Margaret and Jim Dixon. Margaret's habitus is closest to Jim's – Jim describes her as belonging to the 'huge class ... that was destined to provide his own womenfolk' (39) – yet she is portrayed as neurotic and emotionally manipulative. While Jim is attracted to Gore-Urquhart's lack of grooming, he is repelled by the same thing in Margaret, who is damned for her ordinariness, her propensity to wear 'a too-tight skirt, a wrong-coloured, or no, lipstick', as opposed to the 'premeditated simplicity' of Christine's clothes (39). Margaret's physicality is not authentically unpolished, but distasteful and excessive; moreover, her emotional life is represented as fake and inauthentic rather than authentic and internal. She twice attempts suicide, but these suicide attempts are represented as ways of manipulating her boyfriends, as are her hysterical outbursts – her emotions are as excessive as her lipstick. Her inauthentic affect does, however, provide an opportunity for male bonding, when Jim and Catchpole (Margaret's previous boyfriend) meet up and discover that each has experienced the same kind of emotional manipulation at her hands, at which point Catchpole remarks: 'I can see that you and I have more in common than we thought at first' (236).[12]

Margaret's role is therefore to illustrate inauthentic feminine affect against which authentic male affect can be judged. She also functions as part of a system of exchange between men, marking out the authentic elite, such as Jim and Catchpole, who recognize inauthenticity when they see it. This is very similar to the pattern that Eve Sedgwick sees in nineteenth-century English literature, where women's primary role is to mediate relationships between men; Sedgwick observes: 'in the presence of a woman who can be seen as pitiable or contemptible, men are able ... to confirm each other's value' (*Between Men* 160). More broadly, Sedgwick argues that women often have 'a kind of ultimate importance in the schema of men's gender construction – representing an absolute of exchange value, of representation itself, and also being the ultimate victims of the painful contradictions in the gender system that regulates men' (134). This notion not only illuminates Margaret's role in *Lucky Jim*, but also Christine's. To some extent, Christine shares tastes and bodily qualities with Gore-Urquhart and Jim, namely earthy, raw tastes, and an accent that is not entirely upper –middle class. Yet the novel also suggests that she is a woman without qualities, whose characteristics are absolutely exchangeable according to the man she is with; for example, Jim notices how much nicer Christine is when she is with him rather than with Bertrand, concluding 'It was queer how much colour women seemed to absorb from their men-friends, or even from the man they were with for the time being' (142). By this logic, we might even see

Christine's earthy tastes as the result of her friendship with Jim, rather than the cause of it. Overall, the novel focuses much less on Christine's affective qualities than on the way in which she is exchanged between men and illuminates the affective capacities of these men.

Christine is the object of the rivalry between Jim and Bertrand, and as she is exchanged between the two men, power is also exchanged between the two men. Just as Jim wants a better job, he wants a better woman: Bertrand is his rival for both goals. Christine's virtue lies largely in her beauty, as she has been 'lucky with her face and figure' (242), but also in the way that she helps Jim to establish a crucial relationship with another man, Gore-Urquhart. When Jim wins Christine, he also wins a closer relationship with Gore-Urquhart, who in the absence of any mention of Christine's parents functions as her father-figure; Jim thus moves into the position of the son, a familial bond that strengthens their affective connection. The relationship between Jim and Gore-Urquhart is further strengthened by the way in which they both win women from Bertrand, since by the end of the novel Gore-Urquhart has begun a relationship with Bertrand's former mistress, Carol Goldsmith. The exchange of women in *Lucky Jim* thus helps to confirm which men belong to the affective elite. Women in the novel can be inauthentic in their own right, as we see with Margaret, but their authenticity is always the result of their relationship with men. Conversely, the inauthenticity of male characters is indicated by their feminization. Jim's red-blooded heterosexual virility is in direct contrast to the representation of the Welches' effeminacy, as Alan Sinfield has pointed out (80). For example, when Jim sees the Welches for the last time, he describes Welch and Bertrand as looking like 'Gide and Lytton Strachey', thus tarring them at one stroke with the brush of foreignness, Bloomsbury, and homosexuality. James F. English notes that Welch is also feminized by the qualities he shares with Margaret: both characters are evasive, pretentious, irrational, and impractical (138).

If women in *Lucky Jim* either confirm men's affect, or illustrate the dangers of inauthenticity, *Look Back in Anger* similarly shows men who feel more deeply than women. In Osborne's play, women are unfeeling and violent, and female characters lack interiority. The tragedy for Jimmy is that Alison, as a woman, cannot be alive inside in the way that Jimmy wants and in the way he believes himself to be. Nonetheless, she is capable of violence. Jimmy tells Cliff:

> Do you know I have never known the great pleasure of lovemaking when I didn't desire it myself. Oh, it's not that she hasn't her own

kind of passion. She has the passion of a python. She just devours me whole every time, as if I were some over-large rabbit. That's me. That bulge around her navel – if you're wondering what it is – it's me. Me, buried alive down there, and going mad, smothered in that peaceful looking coil.

(37–38)

The animal imagery dehumanizes Alison, as Jimmy suggests she lacks both sexual desire and the capacity for feeling more broadly – he elsewhere describes her as 'a monument to non-attachment' (21). In the image of the victim swallowed by the python, Jimmy constructs himself as Alison's interiority; Jimmy, because of his capacity to feel, literally embodies inner life, whereas Alison lacks interiority, and therefore authenticity. Jimmy's feeling displaces and is the supplement for Alison's lack of feeling. Equally, however, Alison functions as Jimmy's supplement in a Derridean sense: Jimmy, supposedly complete in himself, relies on Alison's lack of feeling to construct himself as a feeling being.

This speech links Jimmy's capacity for feeling with his status as victim and his woundedness. A similar picture of wounded masculinity emerges in the play's most famous speech, Jimmy's proclamation that there are no longer any 'good, brave causes' to die for, an observation which is sandwiched between the two images of wounded men victimized by violent, powerful women:

Why, why, why, why do we let these women bleed us to death? Have you ever had a letter, and on it is franked 'Please Give Your Blood Generously'? Well, the Postmaster-General does that, on behalf of all the women in the world. I suppose people of our generation aren't able to die for good causes any longer .... There aren't any good, brave causes left. If the big bang does come, and we all get killed off, it won't be in aid of the old-fashioned, grand design. It'll just be for the Brave New nothing-very-much-thank-you. About as pointless and inglorious as stepping in front of a bus .... No, there's nothing left for it, me boy, but to let yourself be butchered by the women.

(85)

Wounded masculinity is both a symptom of male powerlessness and a potential source of power, because if men are feminized through their victimhood, their pain and suffering – their capacity for feeling – nonetheless confirms their superiority over women. The feeling male body is therefore the site where masculinity breaks down, as this body is feminized and powerless, but also the site where masculinity and male power are reasserted.

We see this tension further illustrated in the play's treatment of male–male relationships. On the one hand, the play links homosexuality to feminized inauthenticity – Webster, Alison's gay friend, is dismissed as a 'banjo player' rather than being a jazz fan like Jimmy (48). On the other hand, affective relationships between men cement the superiority of feeling masculinity over unfeeling femininity, so the homosocial bond between Jimmy and Cliff reinforces masculinity, as Jimmy proclaims that Cliff is worth two of Helena, Jimmy's lover. However, the play's celebration of wounded, feeling masculinity, simultaneously masculine and feminized, threatens its distinction between masculine homosociality and feminized homosexuality, as Jimmy reveals: 'Sometimes I almost envy old Gide and the Greek Chorus boys ... they do seem to have a cause – not a particularly good one, it's true. But plenty of them do seem to have a revolutionary fire about them, which is more than you can say for the rest of us' (35). Moreover, Jimmy says of Alison's gay friend, Webster: 'He's not only got guts, but sensitivity as well' (21) – a quality which, in the play's taxonomy, proves his masculinity. If masculinity is asserted as feeling and as woundedness, then the homosexual, through his feminized and wounded status, becomes the most masculine of men. The play's treatment of homosexuality destabilizes yet simultaneously reasserts masculinity, as authentic feeling masculinity trumps inauthentic femininity.

The relationship between Jimmy and Alison further illustrates the way in which male wounding is asserted as male power, even as such wounding breaks down the distinctions between heterosexual and homosexual, and masculinity and femininity. Alison's pregnancy ends in miscarriage at the end of the play, and it is only after this event that she can experience deep emotions. In a sense, she is metaphorically defeminized – in the play's terms – as feelings replace her baby, and she occupies the position of victim. Her most impassioned moment comes when she returns to Jimmy after her miscarriage and cries: 'Don't you see! I'm in the mud at last! I'm grovelling!' (95). She thus fulfils Jimmy's earlier desire: 'I want to stand up in your tears, and splash about in them, and sing. I want to be there when you grovel ... I want to see your face rubbed in the mud' (59–60). Yet while Alison's emotional plea breaks down the distinction between feeling male bodies and unfeeling female bodies, this is also the moment of Jimmy's greatest triumph, as his feminized masochism is transformed into traditional masculine sadism, and he gains pleasure from Alison's pain and her vulnerability.[13]

Lucky Jim similarly draws on imagery of wounded masculinity and uses male powerlessness as a way of reasserting male power. Throughout the novel Jim is frequently portrayed as powerless: his academic probation makes him vulnerable to the whims of Welch and Welch's family, and he is forced to carry out menial tasks for Welch, from carrying his bag to completing his library research. He is equally helpless in his relationship with Margaret, thinking 'I haven't got the guts to turn her loose and let her look after herself' (201), and even his dealings with Christine are characterized by her relative power and his relative powerlessness: 'A pang of helpless desire made Dixon feel heavy and immovable, as if he were being talked to by Welch' (218). This powerlessness is frequently described in terms of physical injury. At the arty weekend, for example, Jim is depicted as the passive victim of a violent hangover which leaves him feeling as though he had 'been expertly beaten up by the secret police' (61).

Yet just as Jimmy Porter's wounded masculinity helps him gain power over Alison, the wounds that Jim Dixon suffers strangely help him to gain power over Welch and Bertrand. Wounding and power come together in Jim's fight with Bertrand; Jim both wins the fight and receives a black eye, which serves as the catalyst for a key conversation with Gore-Urquhart. Similarly, at the end of his drunken speech Jim stumbles and falls to the ground, and this moment is also important in cementing his relationship with Gore-Urquhart. Jim's final triumph over the Welches on the novel's final page is also described in terms of a wound: 'his body sagged as if he'd been knifed' (251). Jim's wounding is therefore linked to his newly found social power; it enables his transformation from helpless anti-hero to the successful victor who gets the girl, escapes the world of 'yawn-enforcing facts' (15), and – like Jimmy Porter – is granted the power of redefining the standards of cultural and aesthetic value. *Lucky Jim*, like *Look Back in Anger*, ultimately uses wounded masculinity – which potentially undoes the distinction between femininity and masculinity – to reassert masculine power and the superiority of the feeling male.

Affect, embodiment, and the critical response

Critics at the time recognized the centrality of gender relations in *Look Back in Anger*, but puzzled over their connection to the play's anti-Establishment content. In *ULR* 3, Stuart Hall wrote:

> The personal emotions we generate or stifle eat their way into our words and our actions and alter their character. The public and personal life are deeply interrelated, and we must learn to comprehend

them as a totality. That is why it is nonsense to argue whether *Look Back in Anger* is about sex or politics. Each is an analogue of the other: it is surprising that, after D. H. Lawrence, socialists should have to learn that lesson all over again.

('No Man's' 87)

However, the analogue Hall sees between one and the other is not clear: 'personal emotions' in *Look Back in Anger* are not to be found in the upper middle classes, nor in women. Kenneth Tynan, in contrast, saw a disjuncture between the play's treatment of class and of gender: 'Social plays are traditionally sexless, and plays about sex are mostly non-social. Jimmy Porter is politically liberal and sexually a despot .... Others may solve Jimmy's problem: Mr Osborne is the first to state it' (199). This is a problem for Tynan as he assumes, like Hall, that affect necessarily has a political force; but if we see that in *Look Back in Anger*, as in *Lucky Jim*, affect is a means of individual escape rather than social transformation, it makes no difference whether feeling is expressed through railing against upper-middle-class privilege or hitting a woman.

The broader critical response to 'angry' writing suggests that the perceived political force of these texts had, in fact, relatively little to do with their ideological content, or with any consistent anti-Establishment position. Instead, it was at least partly a result of visceral responses to the emphasis on feeling in these texts, and to the way in which feeling was connected to virile male bodies – both textually and on stage. The New Left, for example, continually emphasized the emotional veracity and the affective appeal of 'angry texts' which mirrored their own conception of a new kind of socialism that would take account of 'the justification of the power and capacity to feel' (Hall, 'No Man's' 87). Stuart Hall wrote that Colin MacInnes's novel *Absolute Beginners* had 'a flow and authenticity .... The book asks to be tested against 'life' – and that is no mean accomplishment' ('Absolute' 23), while Graham Martin praised Osborne's 'authentic voice' (40). Raymond Williams, who criticized the novels of the 1950s for their failure to adequately take into account or represent the outside world, nonetheless praised their emotional force: 'The paradox of these novels is that on the one hand they seem the most real kind of contemporary writing – they were welcomed because they recorded so many actual feelings – and yet on the other hand their final version of reality is parodic and farcical' (*Long Revolution* 284).

The representation of feeling in these texts had a particularly strong effect when critics identified with the habitus of the male protagonists. David Lodge saw *Look Back in Anger* while doing National Service, and remembers 'the delight and exhilaration its anti-establishment rhetoric afforded me, and the exactness with which it matched my own mood at that juncture in my life' (qtd. in Segal, *Slow Motion* 14). The *Guardian* drama critic Michael Billington recalls the significance the play had for him as a sixth-former in 1956: 'I solemnly gave a talk on Angry Young Men to my classmates and, when I finally got to London to see the play, I waited outside the theatre to scan the faces of the audience to see if they had been changed by the event' (5). When such gendered, affective identification was absent, the response to 'angry' literature was often less rapturous. Doris Lessing, also a member of the New Left, writes in her autobiography that: 'Jimmy Porter, with whom so many young men identified, I thought was infantile and ... self-pitying' (207). In *Still Life*, A. S. Byatt's 1985 novel, the central character of Frederica (who is at Cambridge in the late 1950s, as was Byatt) reads *Lucky Jim* to find out what her male friends see in it. Although lower middle class, like her friends, she fails to identify with Jim: 'Frederica felt a very simple sexual distaste for *Lucky Jim*. There was a nice girl, whose niceness consisted of big breasts and a surprising readiness to find the lunatic Dixon attractive and valuable, and a nasty woman, who was judged for bad makeup and arty skirts as well as for hysteria and emotional blackmail' (132).

Bourdieu has argued that the 'affinities of the habitus' play an important role in shaping political identifications, and we can see in the reception of these texts the importance of such affinities.[14] Equally, however, it could be argued that the dynamic is at times affinity and at others desire. When Alison describes her first sight of Jimmy, she says: 'Everything about him seemed to burn, his face, the edges of his hair glistened and seemed to spring off his head, and his eyes were so blue and full of the sun' (45). Similarly, Raphael Samuel admitted in 1989 that '*Universities and Left Review* was plainly fascinated by the phenomenon, even the glamour, of masculinity' (52). This romanticization of the feeling male body can also be seen in the films made by directors sympathetic to the New Left, and associated with the 'Free Cinema' movement of the early and mid-1950s, such as Lindsay Anderson, Karel Reisz, and Tony Richardson, who directed the film version of *Look Back in Anger*.[15] For example, Anderson's 1957 documentary *Every Day But Christmas* portrayed male working class experience through depicting workers in Covent Garden, focusing on their muscled bodies as the sound of their work is replaced by music, lending the images a poetic, romanticized quality: in these films, as well as in the performance of plays, the feeling male body was a physical presence.

The combination of identification and desire helps explain why many critics and commentators improved on the politics of both *Lucky Jim* and *Look Back in Anger*, assuming these texts and their authors shared not only their habitus and affective investments but also their political views. Kenneth Tynan wrote: 'One cannot imagine Jimmy Porter listening with a straight face to speeches about our inalienable right to flog Cypriot schoolboys. You could never mobilise him and his kind into a lynching mob, since the art he lives for, jazz, was invented by Negroes' (178). As Alan Sinfield points out, 'This credits the play with more than it says: Jimmy doesn't talk about Civil Rights or the British invasion of Cyprus, but in Tynan's view he could have' (261). Tynan, like the New Left critics, assumed a political force inhered in the feeling male (working-class) body, and therefore read these bodies as political. In the intersection between text and reception, discourses of feeling and vitality, affinities of the habitus, and emotional identifications work together with discourses of gender and representations of the male body to establish the political charge of the feeling male body.[16]

Writing and realism

I have discussed the way in which *Lucky Jim* and *Look Back in Anger* both invoke and disavow a classed body. But the feeling male body in Amis and Osborne can also be seen as a response to two conflicting versions of postwar masculinity identified by Lynne Segal: the 'new family man, content with house and garden' and the 'old wartime hero, who put "freedom" before family and loved ones' ('Look Back' 88). Jimmy Porter negotiates both versions by asserting his emotional freedom and vigour within the domestic space (the setting of the flat) and contrasting this with unfeeling femininity. Similarly, in burning Mrs Welch's sheets with his cigarette, Jim Dixon attacks not just Welch's arty weekend, but also domesticity. In both cases the freedom fighter attacks domesticity, but from within the domestic space.

Another important context for the feeling male body in these texts is the loss of empire, although I differ from critics such as Berthold Schoene-Harwood, who suggests that 'Jimmy Porter's temper tantrums foreshadow, or are in fact analogous to, the death throes of patriarchal imperialism' (88). Alison, according to this line of argument, is the colonial other, a figure of mysterious alterity whose inscrutable impassiveness Jimmy tries to pierce and conquer. As David Cairns and Shaun Richards put it, woman, in the form of Alison, is 'one of the terrains on to which the discourse of metropolitan superiority vis-à-vis the colonial [is] transposed in decolonising and "postcolonial" Britain' (194). However, the loss of empire is expressed less through anger or nostalgia and more through identification with the figure of the displaced victim. This includes identification with the colonized other: Osborne's film adaptation of the play represents an Indian shopkeeper and fellow stallholder as Jimmy's fellow outsider. Yet it also includes Alison's father, Colonel Redfern, who Jimmy identifies with despite his Establishment credentials because of their shared vulnerability and sense of loss: 'I think I can understand how her Daddy must have felt when he came back from India, after all those years away' (17). Alison describes the connection between them as a shared wound, saying to her father: 'You're hurt because everything is changed. Jimmy is hurt because everything is the same' (68). Being hurt or wounded here becomes a fetish of authenticity, and Jimmy seizes on wounded, displaced subjects – whether the former colonizer or the former colonized – as his kinsmen. We see Jimmy not so much asserting imperial power, as luxuriating in postimperial melancholy, in Ian Baucom's phrase, or postcolonial melancholia, in Paul Gilroy's, which is expressed through and displaced onto male victimhood regardless of class or race.[17] The loss of empire is expressed through Jimmy's wounded masculinity, yet his woundedness – as in Ian Fleming's Bond novels – is linked with virile masculinity rather than impotence, and with the revitalization of English masculinity. A similar logic is at work in *Lucky Jim*. Jim is identified with England and Englishness, in contrast to Michel and Bertrand, who are condemned for their foreign names as well as for their taste for nasty foreign food like spaghetti. Jim's relationship with Welch is frequently described in terms of military metaphors and imagery, and his fight with Bertrand could be seen in terms of the triumph of Jim's version of contemporary Englishness over Bertrand's foreignness, as well as over Welch's archaic, outdated notion of Merrie England. If we understand the novel in this sense, Jim represents wounded English masculinity which is nonetheless revitalized and empowered by the end of the novel, as Jim prepares to move from the (provincial) periphery to the heart of the nation, London.

But perhaps the most significant context for understanding masculine affect in these texts is literary or aesthetic: the rise of realism. Dan Rebellato argues that the aggressive masculinity of the realist drama ushered in by *Look Back in Anger* was a conservative heterosexual reaction to a previous 'queer' theatre: 'the whole revolution in British theatre can be seen as responding to the linguistic perversity of a homosexuality which seemed on the point of constituting itself as an oppositional subculture' (190–91). He contends that pre-1956 British theatre was a largely camp institution in which gay men (such as Noel Coward and Terence Rattigan) had prominent and important roles, and that the emotional honesty that struck the first audiences of *Look Back in Anger* was a reaction against the decorative subversiveness of the theatre it replaced. In Rebellato's view, a new emphasis on realism, feeling, identity, and honesty replaced a previous theatrical culture of subversion, destabilization, and camp.

But the emphasis on masculinity cannot solely be explained within a theatrical context, not least because we see the same phenomenon in novels as well as plays. As Alan Sinfield points out in *Literature, Politics and Culture in Postwar Britain*, the assertion of realism as masculine style goes beyond the theatre: postwar novelists also reacted against a prewar modernism which was associated not so much with camp, but with femininity, effeminacy, and the upper classes. The charges of artifice and femininity were laid at the door of any literature seen as remote or inauthentic, whether because of its poetic qualities or its linguistic experimentation. Such an association can be seen in *Look Back in Anger* when Jimmy says: 'I may write a book about us .... Written in flames a mile high. And it won't be recollected in tranquility either, picking daffodils with Aunty Wordsworth' (54). The authenticity and feeling of the realist form is here implicitly contrasted with poetic remoteness and effeminacy.

Rebellato's argument can therefore be modified and extended by suggesting that 'angry' novels and plays privilege an expressive aesthetic in contrast to an aesthetic that places more emphasis on form or on representation than on (emotional) content.[18] *Look Back in Anger* and *Lucky Jim* are examples of what we might call 'expressive realism', realism which is more concerned with the subjective world of feeling than the external world of social relations, and which sees language as the transparent expression of such feelings. Writing in 1957, Amis praised George Orwell for 'passionately believing what he has to say and ... being passionately determined to say it as forcefully and simply as possible' ('Socialism' 8). *Lucky Jim*, like *Look Back in Anger*, takes pot shots at aesthetic forms which emphasize form and representation, including theatricality, camp, and modernism. When Amis describes Welch and Bertrand as looking like 'Gide and Lytton Strachey', they are damned not only by their effeminacy, but also by their association with modernism; similarly, Catchpole's unprepossessing appearance – 'like an intellectual trying to pass himself off as a bank clerk' (235) – is indicated by a comparison to Eliot. In contrast to modernism's linguistic experimentation, Amis and Osborne both privilege linguistic transparency, as the expression of inner feeling is seen to depend on the direct correspondence between language and feeling, and more generally between words and things. *Lucky Jim* satirizes the inability of certain characters to connect words and things through their failure to correctly name Jim: Welch sometimes calls him 'Faulkner' (16), the name of his predecessor (and another jibe at modernist writers); Bertrand addresses him as 'Dickinson or whatever your name is' (42); the journal editor, Caton, calls him 'Mr Dickerson' (193); Margaret refers to him as 'James'. In contrast, Christine uses 'Jim', and Gore-Urquhart refers to Jim as Dixon from their first meeting; Jim is 'pleased that Gore-Urquhart had caught his name' (110).

But the goal of correspondence between word and thing starts to undo itself in both texts. Jim Dixon questions Welch's evasive idioms – 'my word' – by interpreting his dead metaphors and rhetorical flourishes literally – 'Quickly deciding on his own word, Dixon said it to himself' (8) – but *Lucky Jim* itself relies on densely metaphorical language. The long description of Jim's hangover, for example, does not mention the word once, instead relying on a series of metaphors drawn from the natural world to describe his condition; perhaps most memorably, the comment that 'His mouth had been used as a latrine by some small creature of the night' (61). For all its celebration of the immediate and the literal, the novel is repeatedly drawn to the metaphorical, which introduces a gap between word and thing, just as it is drawn to the destabilizing energy of imposture and performance. Even more surprisingly, it is drawn to the linguistic experimentation of modernism. The example David Lodge uses to illustrate Jim's authenticity as his words and thoughts coincide – 'The bloody old towser-faced boot-faced totem-pole on a crap reservation, Dixon thought. "You bloody old towser-faced boot-faced totem-pole on a crap reservation", he said' (209) – actually incorporates a quotation from James Joyce's *Ulysses* that Jim has recalled earlier (without naming the source): 'And with that he picked up the bloody old towser by the scruff of the neck, and, by Jesus, he near throttled him' (*Lucky Jim* 50).[19] Strangely, therefore, the moment when Jim speaks in his own voice is also the moment he speaks in Joyce's voice, undermining the distinctions between realism and modernism, and between authenticity and inauthenticity, that the novel elsewhere relies on. Linguistic transparency is similarly frustrated in *Look Back in Anger* through the game of squirrels and bears which Alison and Jimmy play at the end of the play. Alison describes the game as a retreat into pure feeling: 'we could become little furry creatures with little furry brains. Full of dumb, uncomplicated affection for each other .... They were all love, and no brains' (47). Yet this attempt to escape the intellectual and discursive and to retreat into a world of pure feeling is achieved through acting and performance. Elsewhere in the play, feeling is associated with honesty and openness, with a refusal to dissemble or to perform; paradoxically, at the end of the play it is expressed through role-playing. The game of squirrels and bears is therefore an aporia where the play's aesthetic of transparency, always an impossible dream, begins to undo itself.

The question of representation brings us back to the relationship between gender and affect. *Look Back in Anger* and *Lucky Jim* attempt to *masculinize* literature, and to wrest the literary from its associations with femininity and effeminacy by connecting it to feeling and to realism. Both texts prize the unity of inner and outer, whether this is found in authentic individuals who express their feelings openly, or in an aesthetic of realism which is associated with honesty and openness, and is implicitly masculine. They use the rhetoric of feminization to criticize 'dishonest' art, namely art that foregrounds representation, from modernism (Gide and Lytton Strachey) to the poetic more generally ('Aunty Wordsworth'). Moreover, both texts translate a distinction between feminized performance and masculine honesty onto the bodies of women and men. In both texts, women come to embody, quite literally, a disturbing lack of correspondence between inner and outer: Margaret's 'arty get-up' (77) is linked with her more general tendency to cover up the truth and to speak and act falsely; and Alison's lack of interiority means that she is opaque and unknowable, in contrast to Jimmy's own apparent transparency. The gendering of affect is a powerful way of reinforcing sexual difference, so that masculinity becomes inscribed in the body as pure feeling and sensation, and inscribed textually through the aesthetics of realism.

However, this chapter has argued that the distinctions set up in both texts between authenticity and performance, immediacy and distance, and realism and modernism, are also continually undermined through the texts' own ambivalent attraction to their occluded other. The distinction between masculinity and femininity is also complicated, most obviously in the texts' depiction of wounded masculinity, where the powerless, feminized male victim is also the most honest and authentic character. The language of feminization is used to signal inauthenticity and evasiveness ('effeminate writing Michel'), and yet both texts also rely on a subject position traditionally associated with femininity – victimization, powerlessness, and passivity – to signal their protagonists' authenticity and their capacity to feel. These traits complicate Lynne Segal's argument that scholarship boys in the 1950s were characterized by 'a particularly pugnacious manliness and heterosexual aggressiveness' ('Look Back' 83); rather, Jim and Jimmy are split between aggression and victimhood. Despite the potentially unstable subject position of the feeling male body, however, wounded masculinity becomes the means through which male power is reasserted: Jimmy triumphs over Alison, and Jim wins a well-paying, prestigious job, as well as the girl. Perhaps most importantly, both protagonists are granted the power to redefine aesthetic and cultural values, at least within the world of the texts.

I have suggested that the centrality of feeling in these texts is overdetermined by a series of causes, including anxieties around postwar masculinity, postimperial melancholy, and a literary history in which modernist experimental form is associated (however reductively) with class privilege, as well a stage history in which theatricality is linked to homosexuality. The feeling male body, moreover, expresses a number of conflicting subject positions simultaneously – subaltern class identity and classlessness; powerlessness and power; femininization and masculinity; authenticity and performance. It is partly this ambiguity that enabled so many critics to identify the feeling male body as a political rebel – an identification which owed much to the bodily identification between critics, protagonists, and authors. Terry Lovell has criticized Bourdieu's notion of habitus for the way it suggests that gender and class are embedded and naturalized in bodies in fixed ways such that these identities can be read off particular bodies; she argues instead that '*habitus,* body language, is as polysemic as speech, has to be interpreted and may be ambivalent' ('Resisting' 13). This is precisely what so many contemporary critics failed to recognize, associating the feeling male body of the Angry Young Man with class resistance and with an inherently disruptive and revolutionary force, and overlooking the clear class differences between junior university lecturers like Jim Dixon and factory workers like Arthur Seaton in *Saturday Night and Sunday Morning. Look Back in Anger* and *Lucky Jim,* and the critical discourses around their reception, reveal the way in which a particular version of masculinity emerges at the intersection of the affective and the discursive, which, despite its contradictions and ambiguities, is nonetheless recuperated into a celebration of male power and vitality.

3
Consumption and Masochism in *Saturday Night and Sunday Morning* and *Room at the Top*

Arthur Seaton, the protagonist of Alan Sillitoe's 1958 novel *Saturday Night and Sunday Morning*, prides himself on his masculine physical prowess, which he displays in his work at the Raleigh factory in Nottingham, with his skill with the capstan lathe, and in his leisure pursuits, with his capacity for enormous quantities of alcohol and his sexual exploits with married women. Arthur's prowess seems threatened when he encounters two soldiers or 'swaddies', one of whom is the husband of Arthur's lover Winnie, who proceed to beat him up. Yet the description of this fight suggests that Arthur willingly and even masochistically accepts the position of victim, choosing not to escape when he has the opportunity: 'The way was open to run, but for some reason that he could never bring himself to understand, he did not run' (174). Moreover, rather than emerge from this fight weakened and emasculated, Arthur is paradoxically invigorated, as his individuality is enhanced in contrast with the nameless collectivity of the soldiers, and his capacity for feeling and life is enhanced by the beating he suffers: 'They were undifferentiated and without identity, which put a sense of exaltation into Arthur's attacks ... Rage helped him to get up ... Pain leapt into his head ... His fingertips had a will to live' (174–75).

In this incident, Arthur adopts the role of the masochistic victim, which leaves him wounded and potentially feminized, but also helps to revitalize his masculinity. He simultaneously occupies two subject positions: the powerful masculine aggressor, inflicting pain upon himself, and the feminized victim, experiencing pain. This chapter identifies the split subjectivity of the protagonist as an important feature both of *Saturday Night and Sunday Morning* and of John Braine's *Room at the Top* (1957). It argues that this subjectivity can be read as an ambivalent response to perceived changes in class identity in the postwar period, and to the mutation of traditional working-class masculinity. On the one hand, both novels mourn the loss of such masculinity, and portray post-war males as feminized and wounded, yet on the other hand, they also imagine the possibility of a new, reinvigorated masculinity. I explore the way in which the protagonist's split between masculine power and feminine weakness is displayed when they occupy two different roles: the role of consumer, and the role of masochistic victim. The possibilities of new forms of consumption available to Joe Lampton, through social mobility, and to Arthur Seaton, through an increased standard of living, both invigorate and enervate masculinity. Similarly, as victims Joe and Arthur suffer pain and injuries that signify the wounds dealt to working-class masculinity, but their capacity for pain and for withstanding pain also regenerates masculinity. The positions of consumer and of victim, both usually associated with femininity, are redescribed as masculine and as powerful; simultaneously, however, these roles invoke feminized power-lessness.

In the first part of the chapter I look at the ambivalent treatment of consumption and of the consumer in both novels. I disagree with those critics who see these texts as warnings about the dangers of consumer society, and as elegies for or celebrations of the authentic values of tra-ditional working-class culture.[1] Ian Haywood argues that *Room at the Top* is a critique of the new affluence in postwar Britain, a 'left-cultural jeremiad' against the consumerism that is eroding 'authentic working-class identity' and suggests that Joe is conducting a 'personal class war' (98), while Stuart Laing has described the novel as a 'critical assessment of the morality of affluence' ('*Room*' 167). Similarly, John Kirk argues that the novel 'represents the new tokens of mass commercialization as life-denying, or inauthentic' (68). Critics acknowledge the contradicto-ry treatment of consumption in *Saturday Night and Sunday Morning*, but usually emphasize the novel's critical stance towards affluence.[2] However, I argue that both these novels associate consumption with possibilities as well as with pitfalls for their protagonists. Cultural his-torians propose that the 1950s mark the emergence of style-based expressions of masculinity that begin to replace class-based masculini-ties such as the gentleman or the worker. I suggest that we see early examples of style-based masculinity in these texts, and that for Joe Lampton and Arthur Seaton, style enables the assertion of a masculini-ty whose power rests in performance rather than occupation and inher-itance. Both novels represent consumption positively insofar as it is articulated to masculinity.[3] Nonetheless, another narrative in both nov-els suggests that consumption feminizes and traps the protagonists: the protagonist as consumer is therefore alternately empowered and emasculated, as he is split between a masculine subject position and a feminized one. The treatment of consumption in both novels expresses in gendered terms the fears as well as the possibilities associated with postwar affluence. The male consumer remains a deeply ambivalent and contradictory figure in both novels, and the tension between the powerful masculine consumer and the vulnerably feminized consumer is unresolved.

The second part of the chapter turns to the figure of the masochistic victim in both texts. I argue that the masochistic victim, like the consumer, also expresses the tension between the assertion of masculinity and the fear of feminization, and between power and weakness. However, in the figure of the masochistic victim this tension is not only expressed but also *resolved*, as a position of weakness becomes at the same time a means of displaying strength. The masochist therefore represents a solution to the problem expressed through the representation of the consumer, split between male power and feminine powerlessness. Both novels consistently align their protagonists with other victim or outsider figures, and use the position of the victim and imagery of the wounded male body to express the protagonists' sense of powerlessness and their fear of feminization. Yet in their ability to feel pain and to withstand pain, the protagonists' masculinity is also revitalized. The masochistic victim therefore provides a means of resolving the crisis in the split subject, as a position of weakness is transformed into a position of power: the feeling male body as victim expresses a crisis in male identity, but also helps to revitalize the masculine subject.

Affluence, class, and style-based masculinity

Prime Minister Harold Macmillan famously claimed in 1957 'Most of our people have never had it so good.'[4] While such a statement is certainly debatable, it is true that the 1950s saw a national rise in affluence, measured both by increased incomes and a sharp rise in the ownership of consumer goods. Between 1951 and 1964, the average income increased by 110 per cent; the number of cars rose from 2 million to 8 million, and television sets from 1 million to 13 million (Lacey 10). By 1960, most working-class families owned televisions, and a third had washing machines (though only one family in five owned a car) (Jefferys 156). The significance of this rise in affluence with respect to class structure was the subject of much discussion at the time and is still a topic of debate amongst historians of the period.[5] After winning the

1959 election, Macmillan declared 'The class war is over.' Kevin Jefferys argues, however, that while overall affluence had increased, there were still widespread inequalities between classes, with the relative gap in average incomes between the middle classes and working classes unchanged. In addition, wealth was distributed unevenly over the country, with the North of England and Scotland less well off (157–58).

While some of the changes brought about by affluence may have been exaggerated, others are beyond doubt. First, the percentage of the population classified as working class was shrinking, if only gradually, in relation to the population as a whole; and second, affluence was changing what it meant to be working class. The working class had already declined as a proportion of the whole population, from 78.29 per cent in 1921 to 72.19 per cent in 1951, a decline that continued in the 1950s (McKibbin 106). Jefferys points out that at the same time, a 'sizable minority of skilled workers began to describe themselves as middle-class', and while class distinctions were being shaken rather than fundamentally stirred, the period 'witnessed new ways – in changing circumstances – of being working-class' (158–59). Even amongst those who were deeply suspicious of the rhetoric of classlessness associated with the growth in affluence, there was a recognition that the category of 'working-class' was changing qualitatively as well as quantitatively: E.P. Thompson, for example, agreed that 'a new "working-class consciousness"' had emerged over the decade ('Long Revolution' 29).

The shift in class identity associated with affluence was often expressed in terms of gender, as Stephen Brooke points out: 'If being working class was gradually being detached from established social, economic and political nodes (such as the experience of insecurity, tenement housing, antagonism to employers, or voting Labour), it was also being detached from established understandings of sexual order, in which women and men were clearly separated' (786). As a result, anxieties about social change, including the fear that affluence was eroding traditional working-class culture and its political institutions, such as trade unions and the Labour Party, were often expressed as a fear of the feminizing effects of affluence on working-class men.

But while the shifts in the established order raised gender anxieties, they also opened up possibilities for new articulations of gender identity. The cultural historian Frank Mort argues that the 1950s mark the beginning of an important shift in the relationship between masculinity and consumption, as a style-based masculinity begins to replace older class-based versions of masculinity. Mort explores the emergence of style-based masculinity through the case study of Burton's tailors, a menswear store (still a staple of the British High Street) whose clientele were mainly lower middle class and 'respectable' working class men. From the 1930s until the mid-1950s, Burton's advertisements for suits featured 'the gentleman', 'indeterminate in age but secure in position' (137). The purchase of a suit was a sign of male status, and was mapped onto class. Although Mort points out that it is not until the 1980s that commercial images of masculinity break substantially with class-based roots, he identifies the start of this change in Burton's advertising campaign of 1955, including television ads on the new ITV channel, in which the older image of the gentleman was replaced by a young man in a sports car, wearing a suit, about to meet his girlfriend. As Mort explains: 'Here was a new script from the tailor of taste, which spoke about leisure, affluence and a different type of masculinity', and with these images, Burton's moved from the depiction of class-based masculinity to a masculinity that was 'more fluid and ambiguous' (140). Affluence and consumption opened up new models of masculinity, in which money and power were no longer the property of the gentleman alone.

However, the development and promotion of a new style-based masculinity brought with it old anxieties in new forms. With the class ambiguity of the male style bunny came the danger of sexual ambiguity, and the new images of style-based masculinity also provoked a fear of feminization. Certain commentators thought that Burton's campaigns 'bordered on the feminine' (Mort 140), although the inclusion of the figure of the girlfriend in ads attempted to combat such fears and 'normalize' stylish masculinity by linking it clearly and emphatically to heterosexuality. The association between consumption and masculinity in the advertising campaign was not stable or without anxieties. Nonetheless, Mort makes a convincing case for the emergence of style-based masculinity in this period, an emergence that is not just reflected but also produced in the work of writers like Braine and Sillitoe, as well as others such as Colin McInnes. Peter Hitchcock has argued in relation to Sillitoe, 'The structural changes in the working class are not simply reflected in [working-class literature] ... working-class literary expression is part of the process of class reconstruction' (22). I suggest that the process of class reconstruction in these novels includes the assertion and production of masculinity as style. At the same time, masculinity as *style* emerges in these texts alongside an invocation and revitalization of virile masculinity as *feeling*, as figures of the consumer and the masochist articulate fears of feminization but also offer new ways of empowering men.

The trajectory of Joe Lampton, the protagonist of *Room at the Top*, mirrors a national shift from austerity to affluence. The novel is narrated retrospectively by Joe, who looks back on his first year as a young municipal civil servant in the affluent Northern town of Warley, to which he has moved from the much less affluent Dufton, where he grew up in a working-class home. Joe has a 'room at the top' after finding lodgings with a wealthy middle-class couple, the Thompsons, who live in one of the richest areas in Warley, near the brow of a hill. During this time he joins a local theatrical society, where he meets Alice Aisgill, the wife of a local industrialist, and Susan Brown, the young daughter of another local businessman. He pursues relationships with both women, and although he is in love with Alice, he chooses to marry Susan, a decision that guarantees his future and his rise in social status, but that has a disastrous effect on Alice and on Joe himself. The older narrator despises what he has become, a wealthy businessman with no soul or emotions, one of the 'zombies' he mocked as a young man.

Although at times critical of consumerism and materialism, the novel also metonymically links affluence and consumption with vitality. Joe consistently describes wealthy Warley in terms of life and vitality. Compared to Dufton's river, which runs 'sluggish as pus' (25), and in which people often drown (26), Warley's river is life-giving: Joe observes in the free-flowing river something 'more important than clarity; that pale green film of algae which means that water's clean enough for fish to live in' (25). Joe associates Warley with authenticity, openness and feeling, saying of his surroundings: 'everything seemed intensely real … Not one inch, one shade, one decibel was false; I felt as if I were using all my senses for the first time' (26–27). In contrast, Dufton is 'too small, too dingy, too working-class' (85–86), and associated with inhumanity and death. Joe refers to the town as 'dead Dufton' and goes on to explain: 'the councillors and chief officials and anyone we didn't approve of were called zombies' (16).

To read this as a class judgment against the social elite of Dufton would be an over-simplification: Warley is a middle-class town, yet Joe's friend Charles tells him 'When you go to Warley, Joe, there'll be no more zombies.' (17) Instead, Joe observes the qualities of life and openness amongst Warley's middle-class residents, such as his landlady, Mrs Thompson. Joe notices a photograph of the Thompsons' dead son on display, and comments: 'Mrs Thompson wasn't a zombie; she'd been able to look at her dead son without hysteria. The room hadn't the necessary atmosphere for hysteria anyway. It was a drawing room furnished in what seemed to me to be very good taste ….' (19). The Thompsons' affluent good taste is therefore seen as a mark of life and openness, rather than its opposite. Joe describes the Thompsons' house and its contents in loving detail, from the flowers in the hall – 'a large copper vase of mimosa on a small oak table' (10) – to the chromium towel rails in the bathroom and the expensive enamelled coffee set (13–15), and these tasteful commodities are linked metonymically with the authenticity and vitality of their owners.[6]

The novel associates affluence and consumption not only with vitality, but also, quite explicitly, with masculinity. When Joe meets Susan's father in the Leddersford Conservative Club, in the centre of an even wealthier town than Warley, he comments on the powerful bodies of its affluent members: 'What marked the users of the bar as being rich was their size. In Dufton or even Warley I was thought of as being a big man; but here there were at least two dozen men as big as me, and two dozen more who were both taller and broader' (204). One of these men happens to be Jack Wales, Joe's nemesis and his rival both in relation to Susan and to Alice. In this novel, as in *Lucky Jim*, women also mediate relationships between men, and Joe's relationships with both women primarily enable him to prove his masculinity in relation to Jack, the Oxford-educated former RAF officer and inheritor of a business empire. Unlike *Lucky Jim*'s Bertrand and Michel or *Look Back in Anger*'s Nigel, Jack is no effeminate upper-class twit. He is instead resolutely masculine as well as wealthy and middle class, as Joe notices frustratedly: 'What annoyed me the most about him was that he stood four inches above me and was broader across the shoulders' (40).

Both class and masculinity are therefore inscribed physically on bodies, yet Joe's great revelation, towards the beginning of the novel, is that masculinity and class are also prosthetic. That is, virile masculinity and middle-class privilege are linked with particular kinds of goods and commodities, rather than simply being physical qualities, and this potentially puts them within Joe's reach. Joe learns that masculinity is not an organic essence, but a role to be performed with the help of commodities as costumes and props. Joe's epiphany recalls Mort's description of Burton's 1955 advertisement campaign, as he sees a man of about his age with a green Aston Martin sports car and a beautiful girlfriend with a 'Riviera suntan' (29) and an expensive haircut, and he realizes 'The ownership of the Aston-Martin automatically placed the young man in a social class far above mine; but that ownership was simply a question of money' (28). Throughout the novel, cars are, unsurprisingly, a key prosthesis or prop for masculinity: for instance, when driving Alice's Fiat, Joe notes 'the masculinity of steel and oil and warm leather' (79).

Like the car, the girl who confirms the other man's wealth and masculine prowess is also a commodity to be acquired: 'her ownership, too, was simply a question of money, of the price of the diamond ring on her left hand' (28). Joe notices the man's 'olive linen shirt and bright silk neckerchief … he wore the rather theatrical ensemble with a matter-of-fact nonchalance' (28), and he identifies performance and props as the source of the man's ease and power, which he immediately determines to win for himself, proclaiming: 'General Joe Lampton … had opened hostilities' (30). The connections between performance, masculinity, and consumption are further underlined when Joe waits for Susan at the theatre, and smugly imagines himself with a box of chocolates, using the metaphor of consumption to represent his virility: 'I was undecided as to which to taste first; the plain dark chocolate of going out with a pretty girl, the Turkish Delight of vanity, the sweet smooth milk of love, the flavour of power, of being one up on Jack Wales, perhaps the most attractive of all, strong as rum' (70).[7]

Joe, a socially mobile civil servant, expresses his masculinity through his relationship to consumption, rather than through his labour or his relationship to production as his father who worked in the mills might have done. Joe's story of individual social mobility is symptomatic of a broader economic and social transition, with the increasing decline of industries which traditionally employed working-class men, such as textiles, coal, ship-building and heavy-engineering (McKibbin 107), and the growth of the service sector employing clerical workers (McKibbin 44–46). The novel registers this transition through the descriptions of the ruined buildings that Joe encounters during trysts with his girlfriends. Seeking a secluded spot to have sex with Alice, Joe passes a boarded-up brickworks, and faced with this image of industrial decline, he feels 'a not unpleasant melancholy' (82). The double negative reinforces the building as a site of absence, and the phrase invokes pleasure and its opposite, suggesting Joe's ambivalence towards the building and the vanishing world of industrial production it symbolizes. Joe's ambivalent nostalgia contrasts with his response to the ruined St Clair house, the seat of Susan's ancestors, which he visits with Susan. The male St Clair line has died off, leaving only 'Mummy', and Joe celebrates the decline of aristocratic male privilege as he looks at the ruins and thinks 'The man who built it was dead, all the St Clairs were dead; I was alive, and I felt that the mere fact of my survival was in itself a victory over them; and her parents … and Jack Wales; they were all zombies, all of them, and only I was real' (156). Joe thus both welcomes and mourns the social changes in twentieth-century Britain, in which the advantages gained by the decline of hegemonic aristocratic masculinity are tempered by the decline of traditional working-class masculinity. In these vignettes the novel suggests that the traditional class identities of aristocrat and worker are in ruins. In staging sexual encounters by both sets of ruins, the novel represents Joe's virile masculinity as a new form of power that replaces the power formerly held by aristocratic men, and that compensates for the decline of traditional working-class masculinity.

Saturday Night and Sunday Morning differs from the texts discussed previously in this book in that its protagonist, Arthur Seaton, is working class, with a job in a factory, and has neither the opportunity nor the desire for the upward social mobility of Joe Lampton or Jimmy Porter.[8] But Arthur's life is also marked by postwar affluence, and like *Room at the Top*, *Saturday Night and Sunday Morning* links consumption and affluence with masculinity. The novel frequently contrasts the situation of workers before and after the war – 'The difference between before the war and after the war didn't bear thinking about' (27) – suggesting that the rise in wages and the full employment of the postwar period gives workers like Arthur a certain power over their employers: 'No more short-time like before the war … if the gaffer got on to you now you could always tell him where to put the job and go somewhere else' (27). This power is specifically associated with the power to spend: 'With the wages you got you could save up for a motor-bike or even an old car, or you could go on a ten-day binge and get rid of all you'd saved' (27).

Arthur himself spends most of his money on clothes and alcohol, and both these forms of consumption are associated, directly or indirectly, with masculinity. Arthur's expensive wardrobe signifies his capacity to earn high wages, but also shows the extent to which his identity is bound up as much in his stylish suits as in his work: 'These were his riches, and he told himself that money paid-out on clothes was a sensible investment because it made him feel good as well as look good' (66). His clothes illustrate the transition between working-class masculinity based on manual work and masculinity based on style, as they link labour to style: 'Up in his bedroom he surveyed his rows of suits, trousers, sports jackets, shirts, all suspended in colourful drapes and designs, good quality tailor-mades, a couple of hundred quids' worth, a fabulous wardrobe of which he was proud because it had cost him so much labour' (169).

Arthur also spends much of his wages on a commodity that is literally consumed, namely alcohol. Alcohol is associated with sexualized images of release and flow, as its consumption leads to the expulsion of various bodily fluids (vomit and piss) or more directly to violence and sex, all of which figure as expressions of Arthur's anarchic sexuality and virile masculinity. The novel opens with Arthur falling down a flight of stairs, drunk, with the comment: 'Piled-up passions were exploded on Saturday night, and the effect of a week's monotonous graft in the factory was swilled out of your system in a burst of goodwill. You followed the motto of "be drunk and be happy", kept your crafty arms around female waists, and felt the beer going beneficially down into the elastic capacity of your guts' (9). The aggressive language of explosion is repeated when Arthur twice vomits over fellow drinkers: he 'emitted a belching roar' (15), and 'the beast inside Arthur's stomach ... leapt out of his mouth with an appalling growl' (16). This opening chapter connects Arthur's consumption of alcohol with his masculinity, emphasizing the fact that Arthur is with his married lover, Brenda, and 'drinking the share of her absent husband' (9), and ending with Arthur going home to sleep with Brenda. He is seemingly unaffected by the large quantities of alcohol he has drunk, and cheekily leaves the following morning out the back door as he hears Jack coming in the front door.

These images of release and expulsion are clearly sexualized, and associated with Arthur's emotional openness and his virile masculinity, which contrasts with Jack's closed or even blocked masculinity.[9] Arthur is expressive and emotional, judging the people around him not 'on their knowledge or achievement' but instead 'by a blind and passionate method which weighed their more basic worth. It was an emotional gauge, always accurate when set by him' (42). In contrast, Jack is 'timid in many ways, a self-contained man' who seems not to consume or expel: he 'never shouted or swore or boozed like a fish, or even got mad no matter how much the gaffers got on his nerves' (43). Significantly, Arthur also perceives Jack to be less masculine, the kind of man who is unable to satisfy his wife: 'There was something lacking in them, not like a man with one leg that could in no way be put right, but something that they, the slow husbands, could easily rectify if they became less selfish, brightened up their ideas, and looked after their wives a bit better' (44). The novel therefore links physical consumption as well as metaphorical consumption with the expression and assertion of masculine power. Masculine style here involves physical performance as much as it depends on the display of fine suits.

The fear of femininity

Both *Saturday Night and Sunday Morning* and *Room at the Top* link consumption with virile masculinity, and with opportunities to express masculine power through style, commodities, and physical prowess. Yet alongside this narrative, the novels also associate consumption and affluence with femininity and effeminacy. This contradiction is figured through two different kinds of consuming body. Alongside the virile, vital body, whose power is increased by ability to consume both literally and metaphorically, both novels imagine a different kind of body, one that is trapped or deadened. Often these two bodies belong to the same subject, and indicate a split in the subject: so Arthur is both empowered and potentially trapped by consumption, just as Joe is both invigorated and enervated by the possibilities and the dangers of performing masculinity through style.

In *Saturday Night and Sunday Morning*, Arthur imagines the effects of television on his father as effects on his father's body. Arthur clearly associates television with the affluence of postwar Britain, comparing his father's ability to buy a television set with his newfound opportunity to go on holiday, and buy 'all the Woodbines he could smoke' (27). But television leads to a weakened body, whose movement and vision are impeded: 'You stick to it like glue from six till eleven every night … You'll go blind one day. You're bound to' (25). Arthur here links his father's domestic confinement to a classic image of castration, denouncing the television through its feminizing effects on his father.

But Arthur is also threatened by the negative effects of consumption and affluence on the male body, and this is shown through the depiction of the suburban housing estates at the edge of Nottingham in which Doreen, Arthur's girlfriend, lives with her mother. As Peter Kalliney points out, 'the proliferation of material goods such as vacuum cleaners, refrigerators, televisions, and cars coincided with the massive suburban housing projects of the 1950s' (106). The suburban estates in the novel can therefore be seen to have a metonymic relationship to consumption more generally, as Terry Lovell has also argued.[10] After his engagement to Doreen, her mother invites Arthur to live with them in her suburban house which Arthur sees as 'crowded' (210): Arthur's impending conformity and domesticity are linked with spaces that restrict his movement. Arthur associates physical entrapment with the suburban estate as well as the suburban house, describing Doreen's estate as 'a giant web of roads, avenues, and crescents, with a school like a black spider lurking in the middle' (157). Suburbs also bring the destruction of nature, and with this the potential destruction of the (natural and organic) body: Arthur, who is 'happy in the country', remembers that his grandfather's rural house had 'long ago been destroyed to make room for advancing armies of new pink houses, flowing over the fields like red ink on green blotting paper' (205). The martial imagery and the suggestion of blood associate suburban development with threats to the body. Arthur therefore faces the prospect of being feminized by consumption, at the same time as his increased affluence and his expensive suits allow him to assert and to display his masculinity.

Room at the Top also demonstrates unease about the effects of consumption and affluence on the male body. In linking masculine power with style, with the display of commodities, and with performance, the novel destabilizes a class hierarchy based on inherited wealth and demonstrated through inherited physical characteristics. For instance, Joe notes that middle-class Bob's speech mannerisms are copied from the actor Ronald Coleman, and 'felt a little less impressed – it put him on the same level as the millhand with the Alan Ladd deadpan' (31). Performativity brings new possibilities for masculine power, quite literally when Joe joins an amateur theatre group in Warley, and his performances on stage lead to his relationship with Alice. But by suggesting masculinity is performative, the novel also denaturalizes and unwittingly destabilizes masculinity. If masculinity can be performed, then perhaps the distinction between masculinity and femininity itself is unstable. As a result, the novel also associates performance with inauthenticity and with effeminacy. Famous actors are described as 'pansies' (30), and Joe himself is feminized by the insincere role he plays with Susan:

> 'Oh God, I'm sick of myself. I'm afraid you've mixed yourself up with a very queer type.'
> As the word came from my lips I felt that they had nothing to do with me.
>
> (139)

Here Joe is a split subject, and his role-playing is linked with linguistic instability, as words are detached from any source that might ground them; the floating, ambivalent meaning of 'queer' enacts this instability, as well as linking Joe's performance with effeminacy.[11]

The connection between performativity and an unstable subject position is further exemplified through episodes in the novel that link consumption with theatricality and suggest these both have emasculating effects. Joe notes the décor of the flat in which he has sex with Alice: 'It was furnished in a middle-class, *démodé*, vaguely theatrical kind of way .... The white carpet was very thick, and the chairs gilt and spindly-legged .... It was a boudoir, faintly naughty, rather too feminine. I felt not quite in place there, as if I'd got into the wrong room by mistake'

(101). The description of the room suggests that both performance and consumption are feminine and inauthentic. Commodities are also linked with feminization through the image of the dressing-gown. Joe remembers the pleasure his first dressing-gown gave him, the 'sensation of leisure and opulence and sophistication', but he tells us that his Aunt had thought the purchase extravagant, and had denounced dressing-gowns in terms that evoked both feminization and inauthentic performance: 'Working people look daft in dressing-gowns, like street-women lounging about the house too idle to wash their faces' (13). The implication here is that Joe is feminized by his dressing-gown, just as he is potentially feminized by his relationship to theatricality.

The novel's ambivalent treatment of affluence and of commodities, which both invigorate and enervate masculinity, is perhaps best seen in the image of the car. As I have discussed, cars are linked to masculinity, in the Aston Martin driven by the successful young man with the beautiful girlfriend, or Alice's Fiat with 'the masculinity of steel' (79). But the car, a prosthetic extension of masculinity, also becomes a symbol of Joe's feminization. The older narrator Joe paints himself as a 'brand-new Cadillac in a poor industrial area, insulated by steel and glass and air-conditioning from the people outside', and he compares his fate to that of a car in an assembly line: 'What has happened to my emotions is as fantastic as what happens to steel in an American car; steel should always be true to its own nature, should always have a certain angularity and heaviness and not be plastic and lacquered; and the basic feelings should be angular and heavy too' (124). This description aligns Joe, steel, and intense feeling, suggesting that all three of these have become weakened and distorted by plastic and lacquer – surely here feminized products in contrast to steel's masculinity. The shifting image of the car illustrates the novel's ambivalence about the association between masculinity and the props through which it is performed. The feminized and feminizing American Cadillac is implicitly contrasted with the masculine English Aston Martin: one weakens masculinity, while the other enhances it.

This split between inauthentic feminine affluence and authentic masculine affluence is dramatized in the depiction of Susan Brown's parents in the successful 1959 film adaptation of the novel, directed by Jack Clayton and starring Simone Signoret and Laurence Harvey.[12] Mrs Brown, who has a middle-class accent, is soignée, impeccably dressed, but distinctly frosty towards Joe, taking every opportunity to put him down ('Curious names some of these people have', she comments when introduced to him). She is affluent, inauthentic, and snobbish, asking her husband: 'Don't you mind [Susan] getting mixed up with a small town nobody?' Mr Brown, in contrast, has a Yorkshire accent, and reminds his wife that he too was once such a nobody. His affluence is clearly coded as masculine, as he tells his draughtsmen that a planned administration building looks too much like a ladies' lavatory, declaring 'We make machine tools, not silk stockings.' Throughout the film, he is a symbol of affluent masculinity (one of the first things Joe sees in Warley, during the film's title sequence, is a phallic factory chimney with the word 'Browns' written on it, the white letters standing out clearly against the dull mise-en-scene). In these two characters, the film attempts to distinguish between affluent masculine authenticity and affluent feminine inauthenticity. However, both the film and the novel display a continual anxiety that this distinction between masculine authenticity and feminine inauthenticity cannot be maintained. Joe is split between these two subject positions, and his trajectory suggests that clear and stable distinctions between male and female bodies are potentially undercut by performance.

Masculinity, masochism, and class

The deep ambivalence around the effects of affluence and of consumption is thus expressed in gendered terms throughout *Room at the Top* and *Saturday Night and Sunday Morning*. Affluence opens up the possibility for the assertion of masculinity as style, an assertion that potentially disrupts traditional class hierarchies. However, as masculinity begins to be defined and asserted through consumption and style, it is also destabilized and haunted by the spectre of feminization. In both novels, affluence is associated with new possibilities but also with new dangers, as the broader economic and cultural shifts of the postwar period are shown to bring gains as well as losses. Affluence produces male subjects who are split between masculine power and feminized entrapment, between masculine performativity and effeminate inauthenticity.

If consumption enervates and invigorates the novels' protagonists, so does pain. The figure of the masochistic victim is another way in which these novels express their ambivalent response of these novels to the social and economic changes of the postwar period. On the one hand, the figure of the victim registers these changes as a wound; on the other hand, the experience of pain and of wounding opens the way for masculinity to be revitalized. In both novels, the protagonists align and identify themselves with other victimized characters; they also willingly choose to put themselves in positions where they are subject to violent physical attacks or where they experience intense psychic pain. In willingly embracing the position of victim, the protagonists both express their sense of feminization, but also transform their weakness into strength, reasserting and revitalizing their masculinity. The masochist, like the consumer, is split between feminized victim and masculine power, but unlike the consumer, the masochist also provides a way for this split to be resolved, as his ability to feel and to withstand pain is transformed into a sign of masculine strength rather than of feminized weakness.

A number of critics have recently addressed the relationship between masculinity and masochism, suggesting that masochism can be seen not just as a psychoanalytic sexual category but also as an historically situated set of cultural and political discourses and practices (Mansfield 72). One of the most influential accounts of this relationship is David Savran's *Taking It Like A Man*, in which he discusses the representation of white man as victim in postwar American literature, film, and popular culture. Savran argues that the trope of white man as victim and masochist emerges in response to the perceived loss of white male privilege in the wake of the civil rights movement and feminism, and of the postwar shift from a production-based economy to a service-based economy. He suggests that this 'fantasy of the white male as victim' is an attempt to recoup the perceived losses suffered by white men (4). I differ from Savran in my interpretation of the particular cultural significance of the figure of the victim as it emerges in postwar Britain, and its relation to hegemonic masculinity, as I explain below. Yet Savran's claim that the masochistic victim both expresses the male subject's fear of feminization, and simultaneously enables him to be remasculinized, is extremely helpful for understanding the way in which both *Room at the Top* and *Saturday Night and Sunday Morning* use the figure of the masochistic victim to represent and to resolve the gendered crisis provoked by postwar social and economic change.

Central to Savran's thesis is Freud's concept of 'reflexive sadomasochism', in which 'the ego is ingeniously split between a sadistic (or masculinized) half and a masochistic (or feminized) half, so that the subject, torturing himself, can prove himself a man' (33). The masochistic subject, for Savran as well as for Freud, is split and potentially unstable, what Savran calls a 'hybridized subject' (52), since the masochistic fantasy 'allows the white male subject to take up the position of victim, to feminize and/or blacken himself fantasmatically ... all the while asserting his unimpeachable virility' (33). This last point is crucial for Savran, who argues that the masochistic fantasy does not fundamentally dislodge or destabilize hegemonic masculinity, but instead attempts to revitalize it, positing that 'the cultural texts constructing masculinities characteristically conclude with an almost magical restitution of phallic power' (37). Here Savran differs from other critics who discuss the relationship between masculinity and masochism, and who suggest that masochism undermines or redefines hegemonic masculinity rather than revitalizing it.[13] These include Sally Robinson, who provides a somewhat different analysis of the white male as victim in postwar America, as she argues that masochism does not necessarily lead to 'remasculinization': 'the masochistic male subjects I consider do not use their ability to withstand pain as a sign of their masculinity; instead, they use the pain itself to reimagine a new conceptualization of masculinity' (197). For Robinson, who situates the rise of the white male as victim in the context of the rise of identity politics, part of the appeal of masochism is the avenue it opens up for men to become 'attractively vulnerable in a culture that is so taken with the dynamics of victimization' (197). Yet another position is taken by Kaja Silverman, who argues that the figure of the masochist in Freud is no longer identified with a masculine subject position, as he 'not only prefers the masquerade of womanliness to the parade of virility, he also articulates both his conscious and unconscious desires from a feminine position' (60). Silverman therefore reads masochism as a dissident phenomenon, potentially destabilizing masculinity.

Drawing on both Savran and Robinson, I argue that masochism in *Saturday Night and Sunday Morning* and in *Room at the Top* is a means of revitalizing masculinity, and that such revitalization comes through the protagonists' capacity to experience pain as well as to withstand it. While I agree with Silverman that the figure of the masochist opens up fissures in male subjectivity, in these texts masochism also offers a way of resolving such fissures, and of healing the very gendered crisis it also expresses. However, this revitalization responds not just to a crisis in masculinity, but also to a crisis in class identity. Most discussions of male masochism, including Savran's and Robinson's, concentrate on 'normative, white middle-class masculinity' (Savran 48): they therefore assume that the position of victim is a *disavowal* of actual privilege, a claim to victimhood on the part of the powerful white male which is above all fantasmatic. While both Savran and Robinson gesture towards class as a complicating factor, in their analyses of texts the issue of class tends to drop out, particularly for Savran, who sweepingly describes 'white men' as a 'powerful and wealthy constituency' (97). In the case of *Saturday Night and Sunday Morning* and *Room at the Top*, however, both the protagonists and their authors are either working class or from working-class backgrounds, which complicates the equation of white men with power and privilege.[14] As R. W. Connell points out, different kinds of hegemonic masculinity can be in conflict with each other; in the example Connell gives, a clash between policeman and bikers can be understood as a clash of competing forms of hegemonic masculinity (215). Not all white men are powerful in the same way, even if they all participate to some extent in hegemonic masculinity, and class complicates masculine power.

The interesting problem that these angry texts raise, then, is how to analyse or understand the masochism of the working-class man, for whom occupying the position of victim is not a simple disavowal of privilege. Working-class men may be associated with a romanticized powerful virile masculinity, but they are also in a relatively disempowered position in relation to middle-class or aristocratic men. I suggest that in Braine and Sillitoe the masochistic subject, split between a masculine, sadistic self, and a feminized, masochistic self, expresses two different kinds of injury. The wounds of the masochistic victim represent the fear of the wounds dealt to traditional working-class masculinity by postwar social changes such as affluence. But the masochist's pain also reveals class as injury, and makes visible 'the hidden injuries of class', in Richard Sennett's phrase. The masochist therefore not only articulates the fear of the feminizing effects of affluence and postwar social change more broadly, but he also expresses his sense of being feminized in contrast to men with more economic and symbolic power than he has. At the same time, however, he combats this feminization through the remasculinizing effects of feeling and withstanding pain. Both *Saturday Night and Sunday Morning* and *Room at the Top* use the position of the victim as the foundation of a new, revitalized masculinity, and both texts imagine this revitalized masculinity as the means of healing the injuries of class, as well as the injuries dealt to traditional working-class masculinity in the postwar period.

The reflexive sado-masochist is a fundamentally split subject, identifying with victims as well aggressors and I will show that the formal qualities of each novel, in particular their narrative voices, further illustrate this split. Yet masochism not only dramatizes the split subject, but also offers the possibility of healing the split, as the feminized victim position is recuperated as powerful and, paradoxically, remasculinizing, providing some kind of resolution to the split between victor and aggressor. The experience of pain is linked to vitality, as feeling – any feeling – provides proof of virile masculinity, and helps to revitalize masculinity. Stephen Brooke suggests: 'If changes in gender identities were identified with the emergence of a new working class in the fifties, gender also provided a language with which to register the discomfort provoked by this transformation' (775). Extending Brooke's argument, I suggest that through the figure of the masochistic victim, gender also provides the language for resolving such discomfort fantasmatically.

'Maybe some of us will want to starve': the masochistic victim in *Saturday Night and Sunday Morning*

Arthur Seaton in *Saturday Night and Sunday Morning* is usually seen not as a victim, but as an anti-authoritarian, anarchic rebel. He declares 'I'll never let anybody grind me down because I'm worth as much as any other man in the world' (40), and kicks against almost any institution with which he comes in contact:

> Factories sweat you to death, labour exchanges talk you to death, insurance and income tax offices milk money from your wage packets and rob you to death. And if you're still left with a tiny bit of life in your guts after all this boggering about, the army calls you up and you get shot to death .... Ay, by God, it's a hard life if you don't weaken, if you don't stop that bastard government from grinding your face in the muck ...
>
> (202)

Yet even in this defiant credo, we see the extent to which Arthur situates himself as a victim, as the repeated metaphor of being sweated, talked or robbed, constructs him as physically wounded or weakened by the 'bastard government' and the bosses, to the point of being literally 'shot to death' in the army. Here Arthur's class position is expressed as an injury inflicted on him by the state and by bosses. Throughout the novel, Arthur not only takes up the position of aggressor – shooting Mrs Bull with an airgun, for example, or provoking pub fights – but he also identifies with victims. He votes for the Communist candidate because of the candidate's underdog status, telling Jack that he 'thought the poor bloke wouldn't get any votes. I 'allus like to 'elp the losing side' (36). Arthur also identifies with a drunken man trying to steal a headstone from a funeral parlour, who is then caught by an officious woman in khaki and turned over to the police. Hearing the sound of breaking glass, Arthur is 'stirred ... it synthesized all the anarchism within him' (108). Arthur encourages the man to break free, but his escape attempt is unsuccessful. After this incident, Arthur castigates the woman, who becomes a symbol of the repressive authorities: 'she's a bitch and a whore .... She's no heart in her. She's a stone, a slab o' granite, a bastard, a Blood-tub, a potato face, a swivel-eyed gett, a Rat-clock', adding 'But the man was a spineless bastard, as well' (113). Arthur's identification is clear, but ambivalent, as the man is earlier described as 'bewildered' and 'trembling'; he is a victim, but seems to lack the true masochist's ability for flinty endurance that Arthur displays, as I discuss below. This victim is only effeminized – 'spineless' – and not remasculinized as Arthur is.

Arthur identifies with another outsider figure, a postcolonial figure marginalized and displaced through race and nationality: Doreen's mother's Indian boyfriend, known as Chumley, 'because that's what [his name] sounded like when we asked him what it was' (211), according to Doreen. Chumley, like Arthur, seeks the liberation of affluence: he is in Britain to earn money, so that he can 'go back to Bombay with a thousand pounds saved', because in Bombay 'you could be a millionaire with a thousand pounds' (210). Although we discover that 'Arthur did not like him', Arthur nevertheless has some sympathetic identification with Chumley, as another male isolated and alienated within this suburban, feminized household. Arthur tells Doreen 'He's a lost soul ... He looks lonely ... I can tell when a bloke's lonely. He don't say owt, see? And that means he misses his pal' (211–12). Doreen replies 'He's got mam', but Arthur says 'It's not the same ... not by a long way' (212). Like the drunken man, Chumley's status as a victim is signalled by his dependence on women (whether the woman in khaki or Doreen's mother), and his own subsequent feminization. In his identification with Chumley, Arthur therefore also takes up the position of the feminized other as well as the racial other.[15]

Arthur's identification with the feminized victim is also revealed in his response to his cousin Jane's assault on her husband, Jim. Jane throws a glass at Jim, who bleeds from a head wound, which Arthur treats. This incident revivifies Arthur, as he aligns himself with Jim, and feels himself revitalized by this imaginative identification with victimhood: 'He pressed the cold wet handkerchief to Jim's head, feeling strangely and joyfully alive, as if he had been living in a soulless vacuum since his fight with the swaddies .... The crack of the glass on Jim's forehead echoed and re-echoed through his mind' (201). In this incident we see the paradoxically revitalizing and remasculinizing effect of victimhood and pain, an effect that is shown throughout the novel.

Arthur takes up the position of victim not just through psychic identification, but through various incidents in which pain is inflicted on him. He not only endures the position of victim but seems to enjoy it, insofar as it affords him the opportunity to show his ability to 'take it like a man', in David Savran's phrase, or in Arthur's constant refrain, 'not to weaken' (100). When Arthur reluctantly goes to do his two weeks of military service, he awakens one morning after a drunken night out to find himself tied to the bed, a prank played on him by his fellow soldiers. Arthur is frustrated, but then almost revels in his position, turning his weakness into pleasure and advantage like a true masochist:

> Arthur was tied to his bed and couldn't move. Yet it wasn't disagreeable to him, for he was tired and worn out: he closed his eyes and went back to sleep …. Arthur stayed in bed till teatime, obliviously sleeping, forgetting that he was tied up, the hours passing with such pleasant speed that he remarked to Ambergate later that they should leave him be, that he could think of no better way to spend his fifteen days.
>
> (141–42)

Arthur's victimhood here provides a way of regaining the power that he lacks in his subordinate position in the army, and can also be seen as a way in which he resists his relative lack of power as a working-class man. Elsewhere the novel suggests that victimhood and pain are a means not only of expressing individual resistance to the status quo, but also of revitalizing masculinity through creating new bonds between men. Arthur remembers lines from Olivier's film version of *Henry V*: 'For any man this day that shed his blood with me shall be my brother … shall in their flowing cups be freshly remembered' (152). Here it is not just warfare that enables male bonding, but specifically the experience of being wounded together. Such bonding is illustrated towards the end of the novel, when Arthur meets by chance Doreen's husband, one of the swaddies who had beaten him up at Goose Fair. They have a drink together, uneasily, as Arthur tells him (falsely, as it happens) that he is getting married next week. This curious incident suggests that both Arthur and the swaddie are, or will be, victims of domesticity, as the distinction between the swaddie as aggressor and Arthur as victim is blurred: Arthur thinks 'If he worn't a sowjer he'd be on my side' (209). Mutual victimhood creates a common bond between men, and this (uneasy) solidarity is a way in which the working-class man's relative lack of power is both expressed and resisted.

In key moments in the final 'Sunday Morning' section of the novel, when Arthur seems to be settling into respectability and domesticity with Doreen, he explicitly testifies to the revitalizing possibilities of masochism, and the strength of the apparently feminized position of the victim. He thinks to himself:

> One day they'll bark and we won't run into a pen like sheep. One day they'll flash their lamps and clap their hands and say: 'Come on, lads. Line-up and get your money. We won't let you starve.' But maybe some of us will want to starve, and that'll be where the trouble'll start .... Blokes with suits and bowler hats will say: 'These chaps have got their television sets, enough to live on, council houses, beer and pools .... We've made them happy. What's wrong? Is that a machine gun I hear or a car back-firing?
>
> (202–203)

This passage illustrates anxieties about affluence turning men into sheep, but it also shows the way in which masochism is constructed as a resistant, remasculinizing strategy: it is precisely the *choice* to starve, the choice of pain and victimhood, that will invigorate the soft, conformist consumer. Similarly, Arthur depicts marriage as a masochistic choice that opens up possibilities for resistance precisely in the opportunities it provides for Arthur to kick against its imposition of limits. Fishing on a Sunday morning, he begins to philosophize, identifying with the fish as victim as well as seeing himself as the fisherman-aggressor:

> Whenever you caught a fish, the fish caught you, in a way of speaking, and it was the same with anything else you caught, like measles or a woman .... Arthur knew he had not yet bitten, that he had really only licked the bait and found it tasty, that he could still disengage his mouth from the nibbled morsel. *But he did not want to do so.* If you went through life refusing all the bait dangled before you, that would be no life at all. No changes would be made and you would have nothing to fight against.
>
> (217; my emphasis)

Here again we have Arthur as masochist, choosing to submit himself to the bait and become a victim in order to display his power: if he is not a victim he cannot fight. It is precisely the willed submission to the position of victim (especially, for Arthur, the victimhood of domesticity, 'hooked up by the arse with a wife' (217)) that opens up the opportunities for new forms of resistance. Paradoxically, it is only by embracing the pain of the hook and the potentially feminized position of victim that Arthur can be revitalized.

Arthur is a fundamentally split subject, identifying alternately and simultaneously with the positions of feminine masochist and masculine sadist, victim and aggressor, even of white and nonwhite. These internal splits are expressed in the novel's narrative voice, which shifts constantly from third person to first person to second person. Arthur is split as a narrated and narrating subject between 'he', 'you', and 'I', and this split is unresolved in the text, as the final page is narrated from all three perspectives. Yet while Arthur remains a split, proto-postmodern subject throughout the text, the novel also ends in the same way as postwar American texts which construct 'masochistic masculinities', according to David Savran: that is, with 'an almost magical restitution of phallic power' (37). The final sentence of the novel shows Arthur with (phallic) fishing rod in hand, the catcher, not just the caught: 'The float bobbed more violently than before and, with a grin on his face, he began to wind in the reel' (219). Arthur, wielding his fishing rod, is the Fisher King rejuvenated, and the wounded male revitalized. Masochistic pain and affect constitute the subject as alive and vital, and the end of the novel reinforces his vital masculinity.

The film (whose screenplay was written by Sillitoe) also emphasizes the renewal of masculinity through victimhood in its final scene. Here Doreen and Arthur are on the outskirts of the town looking out over a new housing estate. Arthur tells Doreen that he would be happy with an old house, whereas Doreen insists she wants a new one, with a bathroom. Arthur throws a stone against the advertising hoarding, a gesture which could be seen as either rebellious or futile.[16] Peter Hitchcock points out that Sillitoe's original screenplay emphasized Arthur's revitalization by the end of the film, with a final scene at the factory in which Arthur explicitly details his commitment to keep on fighting (88). But even with the more ambiguous ending, Arthur's potential entrapment by the forces of conformity enables him to display his rebellious masculinity. Far from seeming cowed or beaten down, Arthur remains powerful, as the camera emphasizes the strength and size of Albert Finney's upper torso, shot from below, and Arthur tells Doreen that 'It won't be the last stone I'll throw either'.

Here I disagree with Christine Geraghty's interpretation of the film. Geraghty argues that the film denies Arthur the opportunity of demonstrating his masculinity through action, noting Arthur's passivity in relation to Doreen, the fight scene where he is beaten up, and his failure to help the man escape from the woman in khaki. In this last incident, Geraghty comments on the film's 'aggressive dialogue' and the way in which Albert Finney's face 'dominates the image', but she argues that his representation as a victim in terms of the narrative implies that 'he is powerless to dominate his world' (68), and concludes 'the masculinity embodied in Finney/Seaton is experienced outside the narrative action and is based on what we see and hear' (70). She thus sees a tension between the iconography of powerful masculinity, and the weakening of the character within the narrative – 'a narrative which, using realism as its alibi but class fear as its rationale, denies the audience the full measure of a working-class hero' (71). I argue, in contrast, that the narrative and imagery work together to construct Arthur's masculinity, as the position of masochistic victim enables Arthur to demonstrate his virile rebellion all the more.

Sacrifice, redemption, and masochism in *Room at the Top*

Sadism and masochism are also central to *Room at the Top*, and structure Joe Lampton's relationships with both Susan and Alice. At first it seems as though these qualities are mapped conventionally along gendered lines, with Joe as the sadist and his girlfriends as masochists, as seen in exchanges that now seem both shocking and slightly ridiculous. In apparently playful mode, Joe tells Susan, 'Don't argue. Or I'll beat you black and blue', to which she responds, 'I'd like that' (140). Joe's first sexual encounter with Susan is described in violent terms: 'I shook her as hard as I could. I'd done it in play before, when she'd asked me to hurt her, please hurt her; but this time I was in brutal earnest, and when I'd finished she was breathless and half-fainting. Then I kissed her, biting her lip till I tasted blood.' After sex Susan responds 'you hurt me .... – look, I'm bleeding here – and here – and here. Oh Joe, I love you with all of me now, every bit of me is yours' (198–99). Alice also embraces pain with pleasure: she tells Joe he should have been a navvy, when 'I'd let you beat me every Saturday night' (98); she declares 'I'm so happy with you I wish I could die now' (169), and even more dramatically, 'I wish you'd kill me' (185). Alice's orgasmic cries indicate, at least according to Joe, 'the last extremity of a pleasure almost indistinguishable from pain' (101).

Alice's masochism is also illustrated in the novel's disturbing conclusion, in which she dies in a car crash after having been out drinking, after hearing the news that Joe has left her for Susan. We are given gruesome descriptions of the way in which she is scalped and crawls around bleeding all night, the text almost revelling in her physical degradation (219). This ending, along with Alice's other masochistic tendencies, could be seen as the novel's attempt to manage Alice's independence: Alice is vital, sexual, and cannot be easily controlled – as illustrated in her refusal to apologize to Joe for once having posed naked for an artist.[17] Her death is a way of expelling the potentially dangerous independence and sexual desire which threaten Joe – it is significant that she is killed off immediately after admitting that she has slept with Jack Wales – and transforming it into a kind of masochistic death-drive.

Yet Joe is also represented as a victim, and he identifies with Alice's capacity for pain throughout the novel. But while Alice's masochism leads to her death, Joe's leads to his revitalization through intense feeling. He is not just a sadist but also a masochist, as he takes up a feminized subject position through his identification with Alice. Joe identifies with Alice because she, like him, is socially mobile, rather than having been born into the middle classes: they both have bad teeth, and Joe tells us 'this fact gave me a kind of shabby kinship, as if we'd both had the same illness' (78). An important basis for Joe's identification with Alice is their similar class position, and Joe's sense of victimhood can be seen as an expression of his sense of class injury, figured throughout by his sense of inferiority in relation to the broad-shouldered, middle-class Jack Wales. Like Alice, he sees himself as wounded, and identifies with her pain when she is ill, saying that he knew: 'in a flash what it was to *be* Alice; it was as if I myself had that pain in my belly, as if, by an effort of will, we'd changed bodies' (172). Joe invites pain as proof of his bond with Alice, and throughout the novel his identification with Alice as victim places him alongside her in the position of masochist.

It is significant that Joe's most intense identification with Alice takes place after his engagement to Susan, the point at which his relationship to his working-class background is most dramatically severed. His masochism expresses his fear of feminization, but it also redeems him, as he displays his capacity for feeling. After hearing the news of Alice's death, Joe heads off on a drinking spree, mimicking Alice's actions on the night of her death. After provoking the jealousy of a woman's ex-lover in a pub, he is beaten up, the literal wounds on his body linking him with Alice: 'My hands and face were bleeding ... I saw from my reflection in the lighted window that my suit had big blotches of dirt and blood on the jacket' (233). Again identifying with Alice, he imagines himself as the victim of a road accident, saying: 'I was nearly run over twice, and I was just as frightened of the people as I was of the traffic. It seemed to me as if they too were made of metal and rubber, as if they too were capable of mangling me in a second and speeding away not knowing and not caring that they'd killed me' (233). At this point Joe begins to sing a hymn, '*the old rugged cross the old rugged cross I will CLING to the old rugged cross*' (233), the lyrics illustrating both his masochistic desire for suffering and his hope that this suffering will prove redemptive and revivifying. He similarly expresses his hope in the redemptive qualities of masochism when, watching trams go by, he says 'I saw Alice under the wheels, bloody and screaming, and I wanted to be there with her, to have the guilt slashed away' (224).

In occupying the position of the masochistic victim, Joe is also feminized and emasculated. The girl he picks up tells him 'You've lovely soft hands .... Like a woman's' (231), whereas Alice had described his hands as 'Big and red and brutal' (83). During this drunken spree, Joe enters a 'pansy bar', where someone tries to hit on him; he also runs into Alice's friend Elspeth by accident, who calls him a 'murdering little ... ponce' (224), to which he replies, 'I'll punish myself' (224). Throughout the final pages of the novel, Joe is split between masculine and feminine subject positions, and the narrative emphasizes his status as a split subject. When the news of Alice's death is broken to him, 'Joe Lampton' is calm: '"I expected it," Joe Lampton said soberly. "She drove like a maniac ..." I didn't like Joe Lampton .... He always did and said the correct thing and never embarrassed anyone with an unseemly display of emotion' (219). The split between the unfeeling Joe and 'I', the feeling, wounded subject, is mirrored throughout the novel by the split between the older narrator, who laments his capacity for feeling and intensity, and the younger Joe, who experiences pain but thereby proves his vitality.

It might be argued that Joe's status as wounded, masochistic victim leads not to the revitalization of his masculinity, but to its opposite, as Joe's decision to marry Susan rather than Alice marks the beginning of his long, slow mutation into the 'successful zombie' the anaesthetized older narrator feels he has become. Does Joe's identification with Alice ('I was the better-looking corpse; they wouldn't need to bury me for a long time yet' (224)) symbolize the death of his masculinity and his vitality, rather than its renewal? While this is the outcome of the narrative's story or *histoire*, its discourse or *récit*, to use the terms Gerard Genette introduces in *Narrative Discourse*, ends with the invocation of the feeling, wounded, younger Joe, and with his voice, as he replies to the assurance that no one would blame him: '"Oh my God," I said, "that's the trouble"' (235). The older Joe may be a zombie, but this narrative brings back to life the younger Joe, who is most fully alive when feeling pain. In ending with Joe's response to Alice's death, the novel asserts his capacity for feeling and affective intensity, qualities which here, as throughout 'angry' literature, are associated with masculinity. In fact, we could see the entire narrative itself a masochistic, self-flagellating act through which the older narrator achieves some form of penance and redemption. Joe's diegetic fall into unfeeling authenticity is redeemed by the narrative's *récit*, which ends with the assertion of feeling masculinity.

Similarly, the film (which does away with the novel's analeptic flashback structure and therefore with the doubled narrator) also ends with images of the feeling, wounded, male body. Throughout the film the camera lingers on Laurence Harvey's body and his face, with many extreme close-ups. In the opening sequence we see every woman in the treasury office stop to gaze at Joe as he enters, as Joe becomes the object of the gaze both diegetically and extradiegetically. In the novel's closing sequences, we see close-ups of his face being punched and bloodied by the men he has annoyed in the pub, and the camera takes Joe's perspective as we look up into the angry faces of the men as they kick Joe on the ground. We are shown his wounded body lying in the gutter the following morning. The action then cuts to Joe's wedding day, and finishes with Joe and Susan driving off together; we are given a close-up of Laurence Harvey's face with tears glistening in his eyes, so that the final image we see of him is a man in pain. But again, within the film we are to understand this intense feeling as preferable to the unfeeling, calculating persona that Joe takes on with Susan. Joe may be wounded, but his capacity for feeling proves his capacity for vitality and life.

In *Saturday Night and Sunday Morning* and *Room at the Top*, the protagonists, as consumers and as masochistic victims, are mobile and unstable subjects, split between masculine power and feminine powerlessness and between gain and loss. The ambivalent representation of the consumer in both novels heralds the potential opportunities afforded by style-based masculinity, which challenges or bypasses the hierarchies of class-based masculinity, but also expresses the fear of feminization associated with postwar social change. The figure of the masochistic victim expresses a similar ambivalence, but at the same time resolves this ambivalence by recuperating feminized powerlessness as masculine strength. It is precisely in their desire for pain and victimhood, and in their capacity for pain as well as in their capacity to withstand it, that the protagonists of these texts are able to show their ability to 'take it like a man', and to revitalize masculinity.

Sally Robinson suggests that the figure of masochist or victim in postwar American culture transfers a social loss or wound onto the individual, and that 'individualizing a more properly social wound is a way to evade, forget, deny the very marking that has produced those wounds in the first place' (8). In *Saturday Night and Sunday Morning* and in *Room at the Top*, the social wound marked on the body of the victim is two-fold: it indicates the injuries of class, and the decline or mutation of traditional working-class masculinity. As in *Look Back in Anger* and *Lucky Jim*, the feeling male body, here the male body in pain, invokes class but also substitutes for it. The revitalized masculinity we see in these texts expresses not just the desire for lost male privilege, but also the claim to power on the part of a class traditionally associated with physical power but not granted intellectual or social power. The feeling male body in these texts registers and resolves the contradictions around class and masculinity in the postwar period, as the male body expresses a sense of powerlessness, but paradoxically leads to strength and to revitalization.

4
Angry Young Women?: *The L-Shaped Room, A Taste of Honey,* and *The Golden Notebook*

In the discourse of authenticity and affect that I have outlined in the previous three chapters, femininity and women play a paradoxical role. On the one hand, femininity is a temporary subject position for men, who express their sense of vulnerability and woundedness through taking up the position of the feminized victim, which enables a form of emotional release that revitalizes masculinity. On the other hand, femininity is opposed to the feeling male body, and is associated with the limits of feeling: with the hysterical excess of feeling that is linked to performance rather than authenticity – Margaret in *Lucky Jim*; or with the absence of feeling – Alison in *Look Back in Anger*. Women can enable the bonding between two feeling men and become the means through which the superiority of the feeling man is asserted over the inauthentic man – Christine performs both these functions in *Lucky Jim* – but they can also trap and domesticate men's affect, as we see with Doreen in *Saturday Night and Sunday Morning*, and Susan in *Room at the Top*.

In a further paradox, women are both everywhere and nowhere in the literary and cultural field of the 1950s and early 1960s: endlessly present in 'angry' texts in the form of ciphers and fetishes, but absent or overlooked as writers and subjects, since novels and plays which departed from the dominant discourse of male affect, and which lacked a male protagonist, were invariably ignored by opinion-forming critics and by the New Left. This absence persists in standard critical accounts of the period. In contrast to women writers of the interwar period, whose relationship to modernity and modernism has been much discussed, few women writers of the postwar period have received serious critical attention. There are notable exceptions: Muriel Spark, Iris Murdoch, and Doris Lessing all began writing in the 1950s. However, criticism on Spark and Murdoch tends to be formalist, and to treat them as 'great writers' who transcend their context, whereas criticism on Lessing tends to focus on her significance for the women's movement in the wake of *The Golden Notebook* (1962).[1] Other writers from this period remain notably under-read, falling as they do between the Angry Young Men and the feminist writers of the 1960s.[2]

This chapter turns to the impact of the 'angry' paradigm and the discourse of masculine affect on selected women writers of this period, looking at the way in which this discourse shaped the production and the reception of this work. It concentrates on case studies of three texts which engage with the dominant discourse of male affect: Lynne Reid Banks's *The L-Shaped Room* (1960), Shelagh Delaney's *A Taste of Honey* (1958), and Doris Lessing's *The Golden Notebook* (1962). I argue that the film adaptations of *The L-Shaped Room* and *A Taste of Honey*, and the New Left's reception of *The Golden Notebook*, reveal the extent to which these texts disturbed the dominant discourse of masculine affect. These texts reproduce or mimic aspects of this discourse but simultaneously rewrite it: *The L-Shaped Room* and *The Golden Notebook* explore and critique the social norms and structures that produce shame and unhappiness, respectively; and *A Taste of Honey* emphasizes the negative aspects of 'life', the category much celebrated by angry writers and by the New Left. Moreover, all three texts explore the possibilities of affective alliances between individuals across lines of race, class, sexuality, and gender, rather than depicting feeling as the means through which the solitary individual either embodies or resolves a social crisis. The unstable subject positions implicit in 'angry' texts are made explicit, as bonds on the basis of feeling not only cross identity categories but also – in the case of Lessing – begin to radically undo the nature of identity and subjectivity.

Women writers and Angry Young Men

The angry narrative, and its stated and unstated concerns – feeling, life, rebellion, masculinity – set the agenda for literature that mattered during this period, and therefore helped to confirm the kind of literature which would seem irrelevant or unimportant. This led to some comical misappropriations of texts, such as Iris Murdoch's first novel *Under the Net* (1954), which – largely because of its disaffected young protagonist, Jake – was hailed as the work of an angry young man, a categorization Murdoch strenuously resisted. She argued in a 1963 interview with Frank Kermode that the novel's concerns were primarily philosophical, and that 'the social detail of the novel ... was just self indulgence. It hadn't any particular significance' (qtd. in Bradbury 330).[3] More often, however, women's writing was ignored or criticized for the extent to which it departed from the angry paradigm: Malcolm Bradbury notes that Muriel Spark's first novel, *The Comforters*, published in 1957, was greeted by one reviewer with the disappointed cry: 'No Angry Young Woman?' (355).[4]

The dominance of the angry narrative affected not only the reception of women's writing but also its production. For some young women writers, angry writing created an anxiety of influence. This anxiety is both made visible and resisted in A. S. Byatt's first novel, *The Shadow of the Sun*, written in 1950s and published in 1964, which spends much of its energy challenging the power of the 'Angry Young Man' narrative over a generation of young women. The central character in the novel is Anna Severell, an aspiring writer struggling to free herself from the influence of two men: her father Henry, a famous novelist, and Oliver, a working-class academic with whom she has an affair. Lurking on the edge of this text is a typical angry narrative – Oliver, upwardly mobile through education and his marriage to an upper-middle-class woman, is dependent on the patronage of Henry Severell, but dislikes his influence and his Bohemian tastes, and by sleeping with Henry's daughter exacts some revenge over him. Yet Byatt deliberately contains the character of Oliver and actively resists the narrative concerns of the 1950s by focusing on Anna, and by a critical portrayal of Oliver, one of the few characters whose consciousness is not revealed by the (limited) omniscient narrative voice.[5]

Yet the premise of this chapter is that the angry narrative was productive as well as frustrating for women writers. Not all women writers, or all women readers and spectators, shared Byatt's anxiously critical attitude to angry fiction and plays. The effects of the angry narrative could be more ambivalent: it was not just a carapace from which the authentic woman writer had to free herself (the model suggested by Gilbert and Gubar's famous account of the nineteenth-century woman writer's anxiety of influence), but also a provocative and potentially enabling narrative, despite its gendered distinctions. The historian Carolyn Steedman testifies to the contradictory effects of these narratives in her seminal autobiography, *Landscape for a Good Woman* (1986). She writes:

> At the University of Sussex in 1965 ... we could not have talked of escape except within a literary framework that we had learned from the working-class novels of the early sixties (some of which, like *Room at the Top*, were set books on certain courses); and that framework was itself ignorant of the material stepping stones of our escape: clothes, shoes, make-up. We could not be heroines of the conventional narratives of escape.
>
> (15)

Steedman here indicates the way in which such narratives simultaneously excluded her, as a woman, and interpellated her, as working class
and socially mobile. Her failure to successfully imagine herself as a hero-
ine testifies to her desire to insert herself into this story as well as to her
sense of exclusion when such imaginative identifications are thwarted.
The relation of a reader like Steedman to 'angry' narratives is above all
ambivalent.

Landscape for a Good Woman is Steedman's attempt to resolve this
ambivalence, to rewrite *Room at the Top* and to expand the narrative of
working-class life to take account of the position of working-class
women through the case study of her working-class, Tory-voting, defiantly materialistic mother, who, she points out, 'was a woman who
finds no place in the iconography of working-class motherhood' (6).
The influence of angry narratives on Steedman can be seen in the way
in which she focuses on aspects of working-class life which do not fit
the acceptable face of socialist analysis: just as Joe Lampton wanted a
green MG, and Arthur Seaton rejoiced in his wardrobe, Steedman's
mother wanted 'a New Look skirt, a timbered country cottage, to marry
a prince' (9). Yet Steedman also criticizes the bland treatment of
women's emotions by male novelists and left critics, arguing that they
'[delineate] a background of uniformity and passivity, in which pain,
loss, love, anxiety and desire are washed over with a patina of stolid
emotional sameness' (12). In contrast, she focuses on the affective qualities of her mother's life, on her desires and emotions, which challenge
such traditional representations of female affect.

Steedman rewrites the angry narrative explicitly and consciously from
the perspective of the mid-1980s; however, certain women writers of the
1950s and early 1960s were also engaging with this narrative and rewriting it. Two of the examples I discuss, Shelagh Delaney's 1959 play *A Taste
of Honey*, and Lynne Reid Banks's first novel *The L-Shaped Room* (1962),
share both thematic preoccupations and formal strategies with male
'angry' texts: besides their realist styles and gritty settings, both texts
emphasize the importance of emotional honesty and authenticity, and
Delaney also asserts the importance of 'life'. The protagonists of both texts
are assertive and rebellious, refusing to accept the advice or dictates of
authority figures. Yet both *The L-Shaped Room* and *A Taste of Honey* depart
from the 'angry' narrative in one obvious respect: their protagonists – middle-class Jane and working-class Jo – are not alienated scholarship boys or
factory workers, but pregnant women. My third example, Doris Lessing's
The Golden Notebook, is seldom discussed in the context of angry writing,
perhaps because its formal structure and self-conscious engagement with

questions of literary and cultural production is more sophisticated and self-reflexive than the straightforward realism of the angry plays and novels. Yet Lessing was a central figure in the New Left, and her novel self-consciously engages with both angry and New Left concerns, both in its content, through its representation of Saul (a thinly-disguised portrayal of Lessing's lover and New Left activist Clancy Sigal) and its emphasis on emotion, and in its formal structure, which uses the aesthetics of parody and fragmentation to incorporate and to question Saul's narrative.

All three texts, whether through content or form, 'mimic' the angry narrative with the effects that Homi Bhabha describes in relation to colonial mimicry. Bhabha famously uses the concept of mimicry to describe the reproduction of English culture in India, a project which would always exceed its intended effects, by producing subjects who are *'almost the same but not quite'* (86). The result of colonial mimicry, Bhabha suggests, is a 'hybrid object ... [which] retains the actual semblance of the authoritative symbol but revalues its presence' (115). Bhabha claims that the imitation or mimicry of colonial culture is destabilizing, since by repeating English cultural practices, Indians 'problematize the signs of racial and cultural priority, so that the 'national' is no longer naturalizable' (87). Bhabha's account of mimicry overstates the disruptive potential of mimicry, assuming an inherent force in mimicry regardless of the context in which it takes place, but it is nonetheless helpful in thinking about the way in which these three texts both mirror aspects of angry texts and simultaneously destabilize them.[6] *The L-Shaped Room* and *A Taste of Honey*, by focusing on a *female protagonist* as the feeling individual, disrupt the naturalized link between feeling, authentic masculinity, and inauthentic femininity, for example. It would be a mistake to approach these texts looking for a thoroughgoing critique of angry concerns, but equally a mistake to assume they are derivative and completely accepting of the gendered discourse of 'angry' literature. Rather, they are hybrid texts, both repeating and dislodging the familiar narrative concerns that emerge from the focus on the male protagonist. The texts show a similar tension between accommodation and rebellion, for example, as other angry texts, but insofar as they focus on *women* both struggling against and accepting their positions in society, they implicitly critique the way in which angry texts fail to treat women as agents. Lessing uses mimicry in the form of parody in a much more explicit and self-conscious way than Banks and Delaney, self-consciously drawing attention to its own textual hybridity. Yet *The Golden Notebook* also endorses many aspects of the discourse about feeling and emotion that

saturated the New Left, and both its form and content reveal a complicated relationship to male affect. For Lessing, as for so many male writers and critics, the feeling body is both a symptom of social crisis and the
solution to that crisis; where Lessing differs is in the way in which she
posits female and male bodies as equally bound up in this crisis, and as
equally part of any solution. The rest of this chapter explores the nature
and the effects of these 'mimic texts', as they both conform to and
reshape the affective concerns of angry literature.

Class and sex: *The L-Shaped Room* on film

The destabilizing, disturbing effects of *The L-Shaped Room*'s mimicry of
an angry text can be seen in its reception. Lynne Reid Banks's novel
became associated with angry literature primarily through its film adaptation, which changes the novel in an attempt to make it fit back into
a recognizable narrative of class, rebellion, and masculinity. Yet even
with the changes in adaptation, the film's repetition of familiar themes
in an unfamiliar context had an unsettling effect on critics, who dismissed or criticized aspects of the narrative – sexual frankness, an
emphasis on feeling rather than ideas – that they had championed in
relation to texts like *Saturday Night and Sunday Morning*.

Both the novel and the film of *The L-Shaped Room* follow the experience of Jane, a young middle-class woman who, pregnant and unmarried, takes a room in a seedy Fulham boarding house. On its publication
in 1960, the novel had little serious critical attention, but the film version, written and directed in 1962 by Bryan Forbes, was a success, with
an Oscar nomination for the actress Leslie Caron.[7] The director Bryan
Forbes was a member of the Allied Film Makers group, whose members
included Richard Attenborough and Ealing director Basil Dearden; yet
the film he made clearly owes a great deal to Free Cinema, and to directors associated with the New Wave such as Tony Richardson, Lindsay
Anderson, and Karel Reisz, who turned again and again to angry novels
and plays for their material. The influence of the angry paradigm on the
film meant that its focus is noticeably different from the novel's.

This is shown, for instance, in a key segment of the film just after Jane
and Toby, a young writer who also lives in the boarding house, have had
sex for the first time. After showing the two kissing late at night on
Jane's bed, the film cuts to Toby who sits up in the bed, contemplative-
ly smoking a post-coital cigarette, his torso, seen from one side and
below, dominating the frame. He turns and the camera pans to Jane,
lying by his side. He promises her 'The first thing you'll hear when you

wake up will be me telling you I love you.' They kiss, and the action cuts
to the following day, where Jane is shown at the café where she works.
She is unable to concentrate, anxiously hoping that the next customer
to arrive will be Toby, who never appears. This scene's frank treatment
of sex between two unmarried people was one of the things that marked
the film out as part of the British New Wave. Yet in Lynne Reid Banks's
novel, the first sexual encounter between Jane and Toby is played out
very differently. Here Jane is the narrator, and we are given her perspective in an interior monologue.

> I dreamt no dreams, and in the morning the first thing I knew was
> his hand, still in mine; I opened my eyes and there was his face, with
> the shadows deep on it, but awake and smiling; and before I had
> even moved he leaned over me and said, 'Jane, I love you.'
> I closed my eyes and said to myself, Oh God, now what have I done?
> As with drinking, so with love – it's the morning after that counts,
> often more than the night before ... [Toby] pushed his face awk-
> wardly into my hand, nuzzling it like a puppy, and then suddenly
> grabbed it in both his and kissed it. 'I wish you weren't going out
> now' he mumbled into the palm. 'I wish not too' I said, not know-
> ing what I wished ....
> Sitting in the train ... I felt a sense of relief at being away from him.
> (Banks 97–99)

Jane is deeply ambivalent about what has just happened, responding to
Toby's declaration of love with regret and confusion. In the morning it
is she rather than Toby who takes the initiative, leaving the bed early to
go to work, finally relieved to achieve some distance from him rather
than anxious at their separation.

This brief sequence points to a persistent difference between Jane's representation in the novel and in the film. In the novel she is an agent
whose responses and decisions motivate the narrative, whereas in the
film, she is a passive victim of romance, dependent on the whims of her
new lover. In a notable departure from the novel, the cinematic Jane
becomes a Frenchwoman, just as the character of Alice became French in
the film adaptation of *Room at the Top*. The effect of this change is both
to exoticize and to normalize Jane's sexuality (she becomes the familiar
sexy Frenchwoman), and to help to erase a central concern of the novel –
the vexed place of the middle-class woman in the postwar British social
order. One of the striking features of the novel is the way in which it
implicitly compares Jane's position with that of Joe Lampton or Jim

Dixon: she suffers at the hands of a hypocritical Establishment which marginalizes or ignores anyone who challenges the status quo, or at least who does so openly and honestly. The challenge to the status quo is found not in the protagonist's accent or taste, but her sexuality, as Jane protests against the sexual double standard, and refuses to accept that she needs to be hidden away or married off. As a result, the novel suggests, she becomes declassed, as I discuss below.

But instead of exploring the issues of class and sexuality in Banks's novel, which draws on and rewrites the angry paradigm through its focus on Jane, the film turns from Jane to the character of Toby, who becomes an anti-authoritarian rebel. The film manifestly grafts a different narrative onto the original: Toby is romanticized as a broody, headstrong 'angry young man', and his character, his contradictions and his vacillations, drive the film's narrative. In the sex scene with Jane, the camera focuses on his naked body, constructing him as an object of desire as well as encouraging identification with him. The film adds an episode in which Toby objects to an interfering and officious park warden who thinks he and Jane are about to start kissing; he cries 'between her and the bomb we don't stand a chance'. Toby here becomes the subject of a political discourse involving the Campaign for Nuclear Disarmament (CND) and anti-authoritarian young men that is completely absent from the novel. Indeed, the novel explicitly satirizes the radicality of such men: the father of Jane's child operates with a sexual double standard about girls who do and girls who don't, despite the fact that he is 'a leading light in a go-ahead new publishing house specializing in novels by Angry Young Men' (125). In another change to the novel, the film strikingly presents Toby as the author of the narrative rather than Jane, who becomes a muse: towards the end of the film Toby gives Jane a copy of a short story he has written called 'The L-Shaped Room', which implicitly will become the story of the film itself. Needless to say, the other writer in the novel, Jane's unmarried Aunt Addy, is absent from the film. The differences between Banks's novel and Forbes's film illustrate the power that the discourse of affect, authenticity, and masculinity had at this time: Jane's story becomes the tale of a sexy Frenchwoman, written by Toby as the Angry Young Man, rather than Banks's more complicated narrative in which Jane learns to resist society's hypocrisy and affirm her honesty and authenticity, symbolized by a refusal to hide her pregnancy, rather than (as for Joe Dixon or Joe Lampton) a refusal to hide her class origins. We can attribute the changes Forbes made to the original as a signal of the way in which the novel disturbed the affective connections between masculinity, rebellion, and authenticity, which Forbes tries to reinstate in his depiction of Toby.

However, even with Jane's displacement and Toby's new centrality, the film nonetheless unsettled critics. One critic described it as 'the last nail in the social realist coffin' (Hill 215); another objected to its 'unmarried mothers, abortions, prostitutes, homosexuals, lesbians' (Hill 215). The sexual frankness of the earlier New Wave films had been one of their selling points: an unmarried mother and a prostitute featured in *Room at the Top* and Reisz's *Saturday Night and Sunday Morning*, in which both adultery and abortion feature, was marketed with the slogan 'Makes *Room at the Top* look like a vicarage tea-party'. Yet critics implied that the representation of sexuality in *The L-Shaped Room* was gratuitous rather than gritty, or baroque and excessive. In a 1962 *New Statesman* review of the film, John Coleman congratulates himself for not having read the novel, and proceeds to criticize the film, describing his hope, when watching it, that 'some egregiously ordinary lodger might show his face and paces, say something dull and straight and – within the terms of the piece – devastating' (752). Coleman is disturbed by the film's lack of interest in the 'egregiously ordinary' male working-class characters who were deemed to be the suitable subjects of New Wave films, and by its focus on women and their sexuality – not only Jane, but also her housemates, who include two prostitutes and (in the film) a lesbian. Ordinariness for Coleman is synonymous with heterosexual, white men, of whom there are none in the house except Toby – who unfortunately for Coleman is also a Jew and a writer, and possibly not quite ordinary enough. The film, then, by dealing with 'angry' concerns – honesty, openness, rebelling against the Establishment – yet focusing on women (in spite of its attempt to place Toby at the centre of the narrative) disrupts and disturbs the 'ordinary' narrative of rebellious, feeling masculinity that critics like Coleman apparently sought.

Exposure and shame in *The L-Shaped Room*

One of the most obvious ways in which Banks's novel differs from other angry texts, being 'almost the same but not quite', is its focus on a middle-class woman who *chooses* her temporary downward social mobility.[8] At the beginning of the novel, Jane has a well-paid job in PR for an exclusive hotel, and still lives at home with her father. After she discovers that she is pregnant, and reveals the news to her father, she realises that living at home would mean enduring her father's shame and disgust. She chooses voluntarily to leave home and her middle class life and live in a boarding house in an L-shaped room. This room eventually comes to represent freedom and independence, yet the social fall Jane embraces by moving there is also a visible, outward sign of her sexual 'fall'. She admits that the boarding house is uglier and shabbier than others she could have afforded: 'In some obscure way I wanted to punish myself, I wanted to put myself in the setting that seemed proper to my situation' (36).

This is a masochistic perspective – and this novel can be read as the revitalization of middle-class identity through the temporary assumption of a working-class subject position, just as Braine and Sillitoe depicted the revitalization of masculinity through the assumption of feminized victimhood. However, whereas the masochism in Braine and Sillitoe renders pain and victimhood visible on the wounded body, masochism in Banks is associated with the desire for invisibility. Notions of shame, self-punishment, exposure, and covering-up recur throughout this novel. They are eventually conquered or overcome; indeed, the narrative follows Jane's gradual ability to refuse the punishment she has embraced and to move from feeling ashamed and hiding her pregnancy, to being open and unashamed about it. Jane is rewarded for her honesty by a return to the middle classes, just as Jim Dixon is rewarded for his honesty by social mobility. Yet much of the novel focuses on the dynamics of shame and its ambivalent effects.

In concentrating on shame, Banks emphasizes an affect which is found on the edges of 'angry' texts but is downplayed. Angry texts emphasize the importance of honesty and openness; yet the protagonists' strenuous assertion of these qualities invokes the possibility that honesty and openness are hard-won, and under threat from their opposites – shame and covering-up. So Jimmy Porter from *Look Back in Anger* mocks the 'posh papers', but seems to have internalized their frames of reference when he describes the university from which he graduated as 'not even red brick, but white tile' (42). If Jimmy's honesty and authenticity demonstrates his freedom from social norms, and his superiority in relation to the Establishment, his shame demonstrates the opposite. In *Class Fictions*, Pamela Fox writes that 'those most likely to feel shame are those made to feel "inappropriate" by dominant cultural norms' (13), pointing out that shame is above all a social emotion, caused by a failure to fit or live up to social expectations or norms that one has internalized – in Jimmy's case, the notion that only an Oxbridge education is worthwhile.

Similarly, while Jim Dixon in *Lucky Jim* attributes his motivation for avoiding exposure and covering up mishaps somewhat pragmatically as 'fear, pity and economic necessity', one might also analyse him in terms of shame. Beyond losing his job, Jim seems afraid of exposure and social ridicule; the novel alternates between Jim's contempt for Gore-Urquhart's world, and his desire to fit in and not be exposed. *Room at the Top*'s Joe Lampton also alternates between self-exposure and self-assertion on the one hand, and shame and the desire to avoid exposure on the other hand. He is both contemptuous of the middle classes and haunted by the fear of exposure as he enters their world: 'The rich were my enemies, I felt; they were watching me for the first false move' (81). Interestingly, Joe himself identifies exposure and openness as a middle-class quality in contrast to the furtiveness of aspirational working-class or lower-middle-class 'zombies', who, for example, surround death with euphemisms in contrast to Mrs Thompson who was 'able to look at her dead son without hysteria' (20). Fear of exposure and shame are condemned in the texts' own terms as inauthentic, in contrast to emotional intensity and openness. The emphasis on openness and visibility also lies behind the texts' realist aesthetics and their distrust of artifice, and also, in the way in which masculinity is marked and made visible through wounded bodies. Shame is therefore itself a shameful affect in angry texts, which try to cover-up or minimize its role.

Pamela Fox argues that shame has a central place in British working-class novels in the first half of the twentieth century. Resisting the desire to look only for evidence of resistance and subversion in working-class texts and culture (a desire she identifies as a class romanticism that has dogged both literary criticism and cultural studies), she focuses instead on the ambivalent role of shame in these texts. Fox draws on the work of Helen Merrell Lynd, an American sociologist best known as the co-author of the classic study *Middletown* (1927), whose work *On Shame and the Search for Identity* includes an exploration of class shame.[9] Fox is interested in Lynd's perception of the emancipatory potential of shame, which Lynd sees in the way in which the subject can choose to communicate the experience of being shamed to another, thereby helping to break its power. As Fox writes, 'After suffering involuntary exposure, one can *choose* to expose that exposure, as it were, to another .... Self-awareness and confidence become possible because in the process of revealing the shame of being shamed, often one is exposing oppressive societal norms and values as well' (16).

Fox finds this a valuable notion, and yet adds the caveat that the refusal of shame is not always an unequivocally liberatory process. If Lynd associates freedom from shame with pride and self-confidence, Fox warns that the revelation of shame, and the desire to free oneself from shame, is not always counter-hegemonic, but can indicate the persistence of shame. Specifically, she notes in working-class writing of the

1920s and 1930s the recurrent trope of the rejection of working-class identity, and the desire of working-class writers to '[establish] their generic humanity ('we're just like you/them')' (17). Fox argues that this is an ambivalent gesture: on the one hand it indicates self-assertion, a refusal to accept the limitations of working-class identity; yet on the other hand, it can reveal a continued self-loathing, an internalized contempt for aspects of one's past and one's community, and a desire to cover this over.

Fox's insight about the ambivalent refusal of shame in 1920s and 1930s literature also helps to illuminate postwar 'angry' literature: she writes, 'Inscribed with a range of anxious gestures, [working-class writers] proudly claim, and just as insistently deny, their own class specificity' (2). Angry texts refuse class shame yet also, arguably, demonstrate it: the protagonists assert the validity of their (working class or lower middle class) tastes and habits, often with aggressive self-confidence, yet at the same time, they proclaim their generic humanity, their transcendence, and their membership of the feeling, classless, elite, covering over class as though it were shameful. So the texts conceal the class origins of their protagonists, leaving them vague: we hear almost nothing of Jim Dixon's parents, for example, and both Joe Lampton and Jimmy Porter's parents are dead, leaving them to forge their own way in the world, symbolically free from the ties of the past. This covering up of origins invokes shame as it seeks to deny it; shame circulates in these texts as an undercurrent coming to the surface only occasionally.

However, in *The L-Shaped Room*, Lynne Reid Banks takes the theme of shame and makes it visible: the novel is an anatomy of shame, which becomes the affect that links its major characters. Banks draws an implicit comparison between Jane's sexual shame and class shame, as Jane's downward social mobility is provoked by her pregnancy. Here the process of freeing oneself of shame seems closer to the liberatory model that Lynd describes. In communicating shame, and the shame of being shamed, as Jane chooses to do in her narrative, she gradually manages to free herself from it. But in freeing herself from the shame of being pregnant and of being a single mother, she does not seek to deny this state or to cover it up. The same but not quite: *The L-Shaped Room* reflects angry concerns, yet disrupts and destabilizes them. Like other 'angry' texts, this narrative values honesty and authenticity, and Jane is rewarded for her honesty by returning to the middle classes. Nevertheless, the novel also focuses on the way in which the feeling of shame can help to inscribe social positions and social norms, so that feeling is not just the property of an the individual pitted against a hostile, unfeeling society. By foregrounding shame, and broadening it beyond class to questions of sexuality and ethnicity, Banks also complicates and expands the 'angry' narrative, and while not challenging the notion of authenticity, she nonetheless dislodges the implicit connections between masculinity and authenticity.[10]

Jane's shame is sexual: her pregnancy reveals her sexual life as an unmarried woman, limited though it is. She spends the first part of the novel trying to hide the pregnancy, though she is angry with herself for doing so. When she reveals it, she faces belittling judgements, both from the doctor who offers her an abortion, and from her father. When the Harley Street doctor scolds her, she says that she was 'ashamed to my very soul, but I was damned if I was going to let him see it' (28). This claim reveals the complicated dynamics of Jane's shame: she covers up her shame in front of the doctor, but to the reader exposes both her shame, and the shame of being shamed, showing her desire to challenge the very social norms she is interpellated by. Jane refuses what seems to her to be the ultimate cover-up, an abortion, telling the doctor: 'Anything's better than your cheating way out' (31). For Jane, the abortion is a way of banishing shame behind the façade of respectability, just as Jane's father seeks to banish shame by telling her to 'clear out of his house, that [she] was no better than a street-woman' (36). The language of the theatre is used to underline the inauthenticity of these attempts to hide the shame of pregnancy. Jane describes the doctor as a 'stage doctor', and when she goes to her father's office to tell him she is pregnant, she sees him as an actor too: 'it was the perfect performance of the weary tycoon smiling tolerantly at the carefree daughter who knows no better than to interrupt his Atlasian labours' (34).

Even after she leaves home and moves into the L-shaped room, Jane covers up her shame to herself, refusing to think about how she got pregnant, or to reveal her pregnancy to others: 'My bogeys were chiefly questions .... What will it think of me when it's old enough to realize it hasn't a father? .... How am I going to tell people? .... Shall I wear a ring and pretend to be a widow? Have I the courage not to tell lies?' (83). At this stage she is split between her own 'inauthenticity' – her impulse to lie and cover-up – and her distaste at seeing these impulses in others, like the doctor and her father. A decision to be open about the pregnancy is forced upon her when Jane's neighbour John, who is jealous of the closeness between Toby and Jane, guesses Jane is pregnant and tells Toby, who disappears for several days.

At this point, when her shame is greatest, she goes down to meet the prostitutes in the basement, thinking: 'I had some idea that I should see what sort of creatures these whores were, so that I might find out what *I* was' (110). But rather than finding evidence to convince herself of her own degradation, Jane identifies with one of the prostitutes for reasons she had not foreseen. This prostitute, whose name is also Jane, has tried to decorate her own room as well. She tells Jane that she sees herself as less dependent on men than if she were married: 'Fancy promising to love, honour and obey – some *man*. That's what'd stick in my throat' (113). The identification here is only partial; it is undercut by the distancing when Jane later tells John, who is shocked at her affair with Toby and her pregnancy, 'I know I'm not a whore' (121). Yet the prostitute provides a kind of model for refusing sexual shame, and this meeting, combined with the fact that Toby knows about the pregnancy, is to be a turning point for Jane.

Her next step is to acknowledge and expose her initial affair to herself: 'For the first time I saw clearly that it would be impossible to go through the rest of my life with a barrier in my mind between the baby and the conception' (123). Her honesty helps her defend herself against Toby's jealousy, refusing his judgement of her and refusing to be shamed by him: 'I'm twenty-seven years old. Did you think I was a virgin? If it could happen with you, why should you think it couldn't happen with someone else? And if you accept that, why does a baby make it so much worse?' (161). Later, during a Christmas party, she tells the rest of the house that she is pregnant. By the end of the novel, just before she gives birth, Jane reflects on the move from shame to acceptance and exposure that has taken place in the L-shaped room:

> It was as if I had hated my own face and wanted to escape from the mirrors which reflected it ... only the mirrors turned into people, and it wasn't my face which was ugly, but me, as a person. Now that was changed somehow, and the L-shaped room had served its purpose – as a mirrorless house would no longer be needed by someone whose blemish had gone.
>
> (260)

This passage indicates the ambivalent role that the L-shaped room plays in Jane's journey to free herself from shame: her stay there is both escape and punishment. Her temporary class descent, and her decision to move to a boarding house in Fulham rather than a smart flat in Chelsea, provides her with a means to escape shame, to 'escape from the mirrors'. She avoids middle-class censure, the inevitable moment when 'the nice clean people in the nice clean house started to watch me out of the corner of their eyes and think nasty dirty thoughts' (59). She knows her fellow lodgers in the boarding house 'wouldn't raise their eyebrows at me. My own were pitched so near my hairline in shock at myself that I knew I couldn't endure too much of other people's opprobrium' (59). It is the place in which social norms and hierarchies are temporarily suspended, at least in certain respects – Toby still judges Jane for her pregnancy – and it allows Jane to challenge these norms around female sexuality for herself. Yet if the house first allows Jane to cover up her shame, and then helps her to free herself from her internalization of the norms which produced that shame, it also, paradoxically, continues to act as a marker of shame. Jane both challenges class hierarchies and social norms and continues to accede to them, and while the mirrorless house may not reveal her 'blemish', it indicates this blemish negatively – here lives someone with something to hide. It is simultaneously the place in which she frees herself from shame, and the outward sign of her inner shame.

The ambivalent representation of the L-shaped room indicates the novel's broader ambivalence about the relationship between class and shame. On the one hand, the (working-class) community Jane finds herself in allows her to regain her self-respect, just as she grows to have respect for her fellow lodgers. Gradually Jane loses her shame as she shares a house with others who face social opprobrium for different reasons, and who are also in some way ashamed of their identity. Jane develops close friendships with Toby, a Jew, and John, a black, gay, jazz musician: both these men are in some sense closeted, John because of his sexuality, and Toby because he has changed his last name from Cohen to Coleman. Jane does not judge them or think less of them because of their 'shameful' identities; in turn, she is able to accept herself and to free herself from her feelings of shame. Her class descent allows her to meet other marginalized figures she would not have met in Chelsea, and accept others regardless of the ways in which they transgress social norms, or are socially shunned. By implication, then, class marginality is associated with the possibility for openness, honesty, and acceptance, in contrast to the judgemental hypocrisy of middle-class life. The down-at-heel boarding house is the place where Jane reveals the shame of being shamed, and therefore challenges the moral code about female sexuality that produces this shame.

In other respects, however, working-class life remains a signifier for shame. When Jane frees herself from shame, she is rewarded by being able to leave the house. Jane's ambivalent relationship to the house, as both liberating and shameful, is expressed through a dialectic between identification and distancing. While Jane identifies with others in the house, in some ways she distances herself from them. She decorates her room in order to feel more at home, and after this the difference between Jane's L-shaped room and the rest of the house is emphasized, as her white walls are compared to the peeling brown wallpaper in the rest of the house. The residents Jane identifies with most are or have been involved with the arts – Toby the writer, John the jazz musician – so their marginality is accompanied by or invested with a certain amount of cultural capital which marks them out as potential friends for Jane. Jane and Toby, in particular, are distanced from and set apart from the others in the house.

It is significant, then, that Jane and Toby both leave the house when they free themselves from shame. At the beginning of the novel, Toby not only hides his Jewishness, but he is plagued by shame about his writing and by writer's block. This culminates in a fit of self-disgust when he storms out of the house on Christmas Day, unable to afford Jane a present. By the end of the novel, he calls himself Cohen and acknowledges his Jewishness; moreover, leaving the house enables him to write his novel, which promises to be successful. Jane earlier tells him that he should not depend on other people's judgements about his writing: 'you shouldn't need to submit your ideas to anyone else for approval. If you do, you'll get as many reactions as there are people' (83). Toby's self-respect comes when he not only exposes his real name, but also his writing, without the disabling fear of criticism that he had earlier suffered from. This move from shame to exposure and self-assertion is implicitly associated with Toby's departure from the house.

Jane's inner freedom from her feelings of shame is also associated with her departure from the house. In a fairy-tale solution, Jane is able to challenge the social norms around middle-class women's sexuality, but also to return to the middle classes. Jane's Aunt Addy dies, leaving her cottage and the rights of a novel she has written to Jane, who is then free to accept her father's invitation to return home, particularly as he has been symbolically weakened – and shamed – by the onset of a drinking problem. The legacy from Jane's aunt means she no longer has to rely on a father, husband, or employer in order to live a financially comfortable middle-class life. For Jane as for Toby, working-class life functions as a symbol of shame, and her return to the middle classes is likewise associated with her freedom from shame.

Jane's shame emerges from the intersection of class and gender – as a pregnant, unmarried woman, she has transgressed the boundaries of respectability that govern her middle-class world. Her class descent illustrates the relatively precarious position of women in the postwar middle-classes, dependent on their husbands or fathers for their financial security. Elizabeth Wilson has argued that the dependence of middle-class women on men was intensified in the postwar period, as women were increasingly discouraged from training for well-paid work in favour of a life spent in the home: as a result, she suggests, 'before as well as after marriage, middle-class women in post-war Britain became "proletarianized"' (55). It is telling that both the previous and subsequent occupants of the L-shaped room are downwardly mobile women. Jane discovers that the previous tenant was 'An old girl called Mrs Williams. Decayed gentry' (37). Her successor, whom she meets at the end of the novel, is a young middle-class woman whose husband has left her. Jane's position is thus typical, and even representative, of the class shame that could accompany the sexual shaming of women, whether through pregnancy, divorce, or widowhood. Pregnant, and without the patronage of husband, father, or employer, Jane is vulnerable. In this context, the novel's rejection of Jane's proletarianization can be seen as a protest against the way in which women's class position is determined by their relationship with men. By exposing and ultimately freeing herself from her sexual shame, Jane shows her ability to free herself from sexual mores which curb her independence. And by making Jane independently wealthy with her bequest from Addy, the novel also asserts a desire for women's independence. Jane is not only financially independent at the end of the novel; she is also emotionally independent, rejecting any straightforward romantic reconciliation with Toby. Instead Jane says: 'As our hungry need for each other diminished, and we grew stronger as individuals, we'd have more to give .... I felt so happy about him, it didn't matter too terribly that he wasn't mine yet, and might never be' (264–65).

Yet this ending leaves intact the class hierarchies, and the association of working-class life with shame, that in other ways the novel combats. Moreover, we might see the novel's emphasis on the downward social mobility of the middle classes in relation to a larger break-up of social norms and hierarchies about which the novel remains profoundly ambivalent. The boarding house is the space in which such a break-up is heightened and accelerated: for instance, when the man who owns the corner shop finds out she has taken the L-shaped room advertised in his window, Jane feels that he looks at her 'as if he were in the presence of a corpse – the corpse of the middle-classes' (10). While the novel depicts the breakdown of social norms and conventions sympathetically, insofar as these enable both Jane and Toby to challenge sexism and anti-semitism, it ultimately rejects the boarding house's utopian anarchy in favour of the social order associated with Jane's father's house. Like *Lucky Jim* (though very different in tone) *The L-Shaped Room* oscillates between rebellion and accommodation. Freeing oneself from shame is associated with rejecting internalized assumptions about social conventions, yet in rewarding their protagonists with social mobility, both novels retreat from social criticism into a fantasy of social reconciliation which upholds or endorses these conventions.

The same tension between critique and conformism can also be seen in *The L-Shaped Room*'s representation of Addy as a woman writer, which shows the way in which the novel breaks new ground but retreats back into conventionality. Just as Toby, willing to expose himself through writing, is rewarded with success, so is Aunt Addy, the other writer in the novel. Addy has written a novel which no one has seen, until Jane acts as Addy's amanuensis, typing up the novel and finding it an agent. The novel's material is intimate, consisting of love letters from a woman to a man. Addy tells Jane that the reason there are no letters back from the man is because he does not exist: 'Men like that never do. They always have to be invented' (207). Addy's act of self-exposure (the female voice in her novel is clearly based on her own) is rewarded with successful publication, like Toby's. However, her success is incompatible with femininity, and brings with it punishment. The novel associates writing with masculinity, as when Jane interprets the 'male austerity' of Toby's room as a sign that 'Toby's writing might really be a force to be reckoned with' (81–82). Addy, who is single, is described as having 'almost masculine strength' (204), and she is childless, referring to her novel as her 'only child' (208). Toby is rewarded for his writing and his self-exposure by success, whereas Addy's rewards are ambiguous, since she achieves success, but dies a lonely death in hospital before her novel is published. Her solitary life as a writer, without lover or child, is implicitly contrasted with Jane's. In the novel's form itself we find a similar ambivalence about the relationship between women and writing. Jane is the first person narrator of the novel, but she nowhere reflects upon or is self-conscious about herself as the producer of the text that is being read; she is both writer, and invisible or effaced.

The L-Shaped Room thus both conforms to and disturbs the assumptions found in 'angry' narratives. Like angry texts, it criticizes the hypocrisy of the Establishment, and advocates the virtues of visibility and openness. The open and honest individual, in flaunting the source of his or her 'shame', whether this is class, ethnicity, or sexuality, can assert his or her independence from and contempt for the standards by which others may judge him or her. *The L-Shaped Room* represents working-class life ambivalently, like other angry texts: on the one hand, it is associated with authenticity, and the path to honesty; on the other hand, it is a symbol of shame and restriction, so that escaping from working-class life is associated with freedom. The novel, like *Lucky Jim*, imagines its protagonists enjoying the benefits of middle-class life with none of the drawbacks: their wealthy benefactors free them from the expectations of others.

Yet although it shares some of the problematic assumptions and desires of other angry texts, by focusing on a middle-class woman, the novel also rewrites the angry narrative, repeating it with a difference. By concentrating on shame the novel changes the affective map of 'angry' literature. In Sillitoe, Braine, Osborne, Amis, and others, shame is visible only on the edges of the texts; the protagonists at times expose class shame, yet more often they attempt to cover over and conceal the shame of class by proclaiming their classlessness, and by turning to the life, vitality and capacity for feeling that are asserted as proof of the protagonist's authenticity, and are imbricated in masculinity. In contrast, *The L-Shaped Room* takes shame from subtext to text, looking at the way in which feelings like shame reflect and enforce social norms. In its narrative of social descent and mobility, the novel repeats 'angry' assumptions about the shame of working-class life, but it also exposes and challenges the assumptions about gendered behaviour that produce Jane's sexual shame. In Jane's revelation of the shame of being shamed, the novel ultimately refuses the sexual double standard. Subtly, by being 'the same but not quite', the novel undermines and dislodges the connections between masculinity, authenticity, feeling, and classlessness that suffuse other angry texts.

A Taste of Honey: The ambivalence of 'life'

Along with *The L-Shaped Room*, *A Taste of Honey* combines aspects of angry literature with a focus on a female protagonist Shelagh Delaney's play written in 1957 when she was 18, and was first performed in 1958.[11] Of all the texts written by women, this play was most closely associated with angry writing. Although the main character, Jo, is a woman, she is working class and Northern, and therefore more clearly similar to figures like Arthur Seaton and Joe Lampton. Jo and her mother Helen, described in the stage directions as a 'semi-whore' (7), live a peripatetic life in Salford, moving between rented accommodation, until Helen is married and Jo falls pregnant (to a black sailor). During her pregnancy, after Helen has deserted her, Jo lives with a young gay art student named Geof, who is willing to act as the baby's father. Helen, however, eventually returns to her daughter and throws Geof out, though by the end of the play it is unclear whether Helen will stay with Jo or not, as she disappears off to the pub on hearing her grandchild is going to be mixed race.

Some critics were clearly disturbed by the way in which elements of a familiar narrative – in this case, an emphasis on life, working-class characters and a desire for freedom – were combined with the unfamiliar spectacle of a female protagonist, and a teenage girl at that. The *Daily Mail* theatre critic harrumphed: 'If there is anything worse than an Angry Young Man it's an Angry Young Woman.' The *Socialist Leader* suggested that Delaney's next play could 'deal with the lives of other Lancashire workers in the mines, the mills or the factories'; implicitly, the critic desires a more properly masculine working-class subject.[12] Colin MacInnes praised the play in glowing terms, but passes over the two central characters, Jo and Helen, describing it as 'the first English play I've seen in which a coloured man, and a queer boy, are presented as natural characters, factually without a nudge or shudder' (56). Other critics sidestepped a serious engagement with the play's concerns by classifying it as formless, thoughtless, and artless. Whereas much ink was spilt speculating about the political significance of Arthur Seaton or Jim Dixon, there was almost no discussion about the comment *A Taste of Honey* was making about contemporary society. The play was praised for its documentary authenticity, rather than for its analysis or social comment. Alan Brien wrote in the *Spectator*: '*A Taste of Honey* still has the enormous advantage over any other working-class play in that it is not scholarly anthropology observed from the outside through pince-nez, but the inside story of a savage culture observed by a genuine cannibal' (qtd. in Lacey 77). Kenneth Tynan, defending the play against criticisms of its structure, ends up patronising the author, arguing that Delaney was 'recording the wonder of life as she lives it. There is plenty of time for her to worry over words like "form"' (137). John Russell Taylor, writing in the 1960s, makes the rather absurd claim that the play has 'no ideas' (*Anger* 18).

Moreover, as with *The L-Shaped Room*, many of the play's central concerns were overlooked and distorted in its film adaptation. Terry Lovell argues that the 1961 film, directed by Tony Richardson (who also directed the film of *Look Back in Anger*), brings up thematic concerns absent from the play. It grafts onto the original the nostalgia for traditional working-class community and the anxiety about the new affluence that marks the film adaptations of *Room at the Top* and *Saturday Night and Sunday Morning*, demonstrating 'the familiar concern with the quality of new working-class culture, expressed within the visual terms and references common to the New Wave' (372). Lovell suggests this happens largely through the film's mise-en-scene (rather than its script, which Delaney wrote), and pinpoints Richardson's 'use of ... children to represent the traditional community and its indigenous culture' (372). Children constantly surround Jo and Geof when they move around Manchester or take the bus to the country, and also appear in the film's final scene, a bonfire on Guy Fawkes Night.[13] They become the symbol of an authentic working-class culture, and their traditional celebrations are contrasted with the adult world of consumerism, represented in the film by Helen, Jo's mother, and Peter, the man Helen (briefly) marries, a used car salesman who owns a large new house. Richardson also adds a new scene, a visit to Blackpool with Helen, Peter and Jo, which Lovell argues is intended to show the shallow frivolity of the new mass culture. While Jo stands apart, alone and forgotten, Helen and Peter enjoy the funfair, shot in close-up angles which distort them; Lovell adds 'just in case we haven't got the point, the whole montage sequence is accompanied by raucous pop music and the loud, empty laughter of a mechanical clown' (373).

As Lovell's analysis shows, interpretations of the play tended to focus on its similarities to other 'angry' texts, and even to exaggerate these, rather than engage with the implications of the play's departure from the angry paradigm. Surprisingly, although the play is considered significant and is mentioned in every discussion of the period, it has received little sustained critical analysis. Moreover, since the play has been on the British GCSE syllabus, it has increasingly been framed as a play by a teenager for teenagers, not least by the most readily available student editions whose suggestions for analysis reinforce the notion that the play's value is in the way it reflects 'real life', and fail to analyse the particular way in which the play is structuring the real.[14]

The play is therefore a prime example of a text whose relationship to 'angry' plays and novels is 'almost the same but not quite'. In an interview with Laurence Kitchen, Delaney said that she wanted the play to show people who are 'very alive and cynical', and more generally that she thought the theatre brings the audience into contact with '*real* people, people who are *alive*' (qtd. in Speakman v). Kenneth Tynan focused on these aspects of the play in his review: 'Miss Delaney brings real people on to her stage, joking and flaring and scuffling and eventually, out of the zest for life she gives them, surviving' (137).

Colin MacInnes praised the play for its 'feeling for life that is positive, sensible, and generous' (56). Like *Look Back in Anger*, *A Taste of Honey* is notable for its emotional or affective range, moving from sadness to defiance to exhilaration in the space of a few minutes. Yet the play also depicts affect in ways that are significantly different from Osborne, Sillitoe, Amis, or Braine. Most obviously, Jo and Helen are neither hysterical nor frigid: we have feeling, emotive women on stage, who display a range of emotions. Indeed, most of the play's affective energy is between the female characters, along with feminized (and homosexual) Geof: other men come and go, the play suggests, but the mother–daughter relationship persists, despite, or perhaps because of its tensions. Delaney scratches away what Steedman describes as 'the patina of emotional sameness' found in many depictions of working-class homes and working-class mothers, and grants psychological and emotional complexity to women and to domestic life. As a result, the play shows two women who are deeply ambivalent about motherhood and fiercely independent, and who reject the confinement to the domestic sphere that motherhood entails.

However, the most striking way in which the play rewrites the angry narrative is in its treatment of the category of 'life', which complicates Delaney's own celebratory comments. Unlike other angry texts, in which 'life' is linked to affirmation, force, and power, in *A Taste of Honey*, life is not always a positive category, nor is it associated with productive energies. In this respect, it illustrates the capacities of the body described by Claire Colebrook, who argues that theorists of the body and the everyday from Nietzsche to Michel De Certeau have seen life as productivity and (phallogocentric) presence, a view which overlooks 'all the ways in which bodies embrace what is not conducive to self-expansion and recognition' (740) – from death to hunger. The play brings the unproductive aspects of life to the fore, as many of the references to life also invoke death, with the result that any assertion of vitality is quickly undercut by its opposite. The flat that Helen and Jo move into to start their new life, in which Jo also spends her pregnancy, is next to a slaughterhouse and a cemetery. At the beginning of the play, Jo unpacks some bulbs she has stolen from the park, and says: 'I hope they bloom. Always before when I've tried to fix up a window box nothin's ever grown in it' (11). In the second act, Geof finds the bulbs unplanted, and dead, behind the sofa. This provokes a conversation about life in which Geof says, 'You come, you go, it's simple.' Jo responds 'It's not, it's chaotic – a bit of love, a bit of lust and there you are. We don't ask for life, we have it thrust upon us' (71). 'Life' is not romanticized as escape and transcendence, but is instead a haphazard situation bound up with negation and absence.

'Life' is also a reminder of limits, responsibilities, and the lack of free-dom for women who are inextricably tied to the material processes of pregnancy and birth. In arguing that life is 'thrust upon us', Jo is allud-ing not just to her own birth but also to the life that has been thrust upon her with her unplanned pregnancy. Throughout the play, moth-erhood is associated with images which combine life and death: Jo tells Helen about her dream that Helen is found, dead, planted under a rose-bush; Geof tells Jo that in her pregnancy house coat she looks like she is wearing 'a badly tailored shroud' (70); the bed that Helen and Jo share is 'like a coffin only not half as comfortable' (21); and Jo describes breastfeeding as 'having a little animal nibbling away at me, it's canni-balistic. Like being eaten alive' (56). She is deeply ambivalent about her pregnancy, saying: 'I'll bash its brains out. I'll kill it. I don't want this baby, Geof. I don't want to be a mother. I don't want to be a woman' (75). We know that Helen herself has had several abortions: when she tells Jo 'I should have got rid of you before you were born,' Jo replies 'I wish you had done. You did with plenty of others, I know' (62). The play treats life as a material process inextricably entwined with limits on the individual, such as death and pregnancy, and with the body's capac-ity to refuse and to destroy as well as to affirm.

The play's ambivalent treatment of life is also seen in the ambiguous meanings attached to childhood. Images of childhood and youth are used throughout the play not as symbols of traditional community, as the film adaptation suggests, but as symbols of escape, linked to the refusal of both Helen and Jo to passively accept the circumstances that are thrust on them: Jo's precious books are largely fairy tales and children's books; Jo and Geof meet each other at a fair, and come back from it holding bal-loons like children; and Helen lyrically remembers her childhood visits to Shining Clough: 'I'd sit there all day long and nobody ever knew where I was' (86). Yet children also connote the absence of freedom, as sexual reproduction is linked to social reproduction. Helen sees Jo's birth as the event that took away her own individual freedom, and the irony of the play is that Jo's desire to escape from her mother and assert her inde-pendence, through her brief relationship with a sailor, leaves her preg-nant and in the same position as her mother. The processes of social reproduction are therefore linked to the body, and not just through the motif of sexual reproduction: for example, at the beginning of Act I, Helen has a cold, and by the end of the act Jo has caught the cold. The play is therefore driven by the tension between the assertion of life as the desire for change, escape, and transformation, on the one hand, and the fear that life is cyclical and repetitive, on the other.

In its treatment of life as an ambivalent force, rather than as a synonym for individual freedom or for the affirmative, productive energies of the body, *A Taste of Honey* differs considerably from other angry texts. It also differs from them in refusing the notion of an affective elite. Angry texts with male protagonists are, without exception, organized around a distinction between 'us' and 'them', understood not as Hoggart's class antagonism but as an antagonism between those who are feeling, honest, and authentic, and those who are unfeeling, shallow, or hypocritical (and often feminine or feminized). This distinction is absent in *A Taste of Honey*, which is instead organized around an alternative and radically unstable series of oppositions. These oppositions structure the complex relationship between Helen and Jo, who constantly switch roles – at different times each of them is the one who wants to escape, and the one who impedes the other's escape; the one who cares, and the one who is cared for; the mother and the daughter; the one who hurts, and the one who is hurt. Jo, for example, says to Helen that she can't wait to be independent – 'The sooner the better. I'm sick of you' (15) – but then later turns around and tells her 'You should prepare my meals like a proper mother' (35). By the end of the play Jo says to Helen 'I feel as though I could take care of the world. I even feel as though I could take care of you, too!' (81), while Helen remembers her own childhood: 'You know when I was young we used to play all day long at this time of the year' (85). The identities of both characters are unstable, as they each move between the roles of mother and daughter, and adult and child.

This instability of these roles points to the way in which emotion can work to reproduce social and familial relations, as Jo's desire for love leads to her pregnancy and the repetition of her mother's life – when Helen finds out Jo has a boyfriend she tells her, somewhat cruelly, 'Why don't you learn from my mistakes?' (41). But emotion also opens up the possibility for new affective alliances that cross the boundaries of gender, race, and sexuality. In *The L-Shaped Room*, Jane's sexual shame leads not only to her liminal class position, but also to her friendships within the boarding house with John, who is black and gay, and Toby, who is Jewish: all three characters are linked not only by friendship but also by shame, and by the consequent fear of exposure. Similarly, Jo's marginal status as an itinerant working-class girl leads to her friendship with characters whose outsider status is figured in terms of race and sexuality, including her boyfriend and Geof. In this respect, both texts emphasize the capacity for feeling to disrupt and disturb identity categories as well as to define or to shape identity. This capacity is also visible in angry narratives, as angry protagonists mark their woundedness and their capacity for feeling through fleeting identifications with black or gay men, or through taking up a feminized subject position. Yet in angry texts such identifications, which cross various lines of difference, are undercut by the reinscription of a new form of difference: the distinction between the nonfeeling and the feeling. Neither Banks nor Delaney rely on such a distinction – which is not to romanticize the representation of sexuality or race in either text: the depiction of John is deeply problematic, as Jane frequently expresses her fear of him and describes him in animalistic terms, and Jo's attitude to Geof is frequently mocking. Nonetheless, in their refusal of a notion of the affective elite, both texts emphasize instead the unstable subject positions of their protagonists, and the shifting and open nature of affective affiliations. Affect in both texts is therefore both residual and emergent, to use Raymond Williams's terms: it is linked to the reproduction of the existing social order, but also offers new ways for this order to be reconfigured.

Doris Lessing and the New Left

Doris Lessing's *The Golden Notebook* (1962) is the final text I examine that both draws on and destabilizes the dominant discourse of affect, and it is also the most self-conscious about its relationship to contemporary literature and to New Left critical discourse. Lessing was one of the few women active in the New Left, as well as being perhaps the most explicitly political writer of her generation. She had been involved in anti-colonial communist politics as a young woman in Rhodesia, and after she moved to Britain in 1949, she was on the board not only of her friend Edward Thompson's journal the *New Reasoner* (Dworkin 53), but also, subsequently, of *New Left Review*.[15] Her authoritative position made her relatively anomalous amongst women in the New Left, in contrast to what Jean McCrindle subsequently described as the 'pathological absence of women, silencing of women, in those days' (Archer 105). Jenny Taylor argues that Lessing's colonial background and her involvement in politics in Rhodesia gave her the authority to speak both inside the New Left and outside it 'with both a "public" and a "personal" voice, which differentiated her within the dominant discourse of femininity – that of passivity – in Britain in the 1950s' (25). She was effectively a fresh new voice from the colonies, as Osborne and Sillitoe were the new voices of an unheard class, and she was the only female contributor included alongside such writers in the edited volume *Declaration* (1957). In her autobiography, however, Lessing distances herself from angry writing, wryly pointing out that the editor Tom Maschler, who had been turned down by Iris Murdoch, 'had to have a woman in it: I could not let him down. This is how I became an angry young man' (208); she adds 'Women have ever been useful to ambitious young men' (210). This same ambivalence towards angry literature marks her *Declaration* essay, in which she welcomes the 'injection of vitality into the withered arm of British literature' administered by the Angry Young Men, but criticizes the parochial quality of the same writers ('Small Personal Voice' 16).

Lessing's creative writing from the late 1950s also reveals her complicated relationship to angry literature. She was critical enough of the movement to write an unpublished parody of an angry novel called 'Excuse Me While I'm Sick', whose mood, she wrote in a 1957 letter to Thompson, 'is right out of key with what a very large number of people are feeling who would be its natural readers' (*Walking* 193). However, her 1958 play, *Each His Own Wilderness*, displays a combination of sympathy for and distance from angry concerns. The central character is Myra, a communist in her forties, who is criticized by her non-political son Tony, an angry young man figure who, like Jimmy Porter, believes that he has no causes to die for; but when Myra finally rejects politics, Tony becomes extremely political. The play interrogates the motivations for and the consequences of political affiliations, taking an ironic stance towards both the disaffected angry young man's egotism, and the political fervour of young socialists. While Tony Richardson liked the play, and wanted to put it on at the Royal Court, its run was delayed. Lessing discovered that Lindsay Anderson had taken over from Tony Richardson, who 'did not approve' of the play, with the result that it was only performed once (*Walking* 206).

As this incident suggests, when Lessing stepped out of her role as 'voice from the colonies', the reception of her work was uncertain.[16] She was frustrated at the New Left's response to *A Ripple from the Storm* (1958) – part of the Children of Violence sequence centred on Martha Quest, a young Rhodesian woman – and complained to Edward Thompson that the novel's commentary on left politics had been ignored:

> Seriously – I wrote a book all about the kind of politics which the *New Reasoner* has been theoretical about for the last two years. As the reviews came out, I was more and more cross, though not surprised, at the way no one said what this book was about – either, that enigmatic

girl, Martha Quest, at her antics again, or another jab at the colour bar. But no one could have deduced from the reviews that the book was about Stalinist attitudes of mind etc. Therefore, since the people I wanted to reach were obviously the *New Reasoner* and *The New Left Review* readers, I naturally hoped that either or both magazines would at least put in a paragraph saying that this novel was about current topics. But not a word. Not a bloody word.

(*Walking* 229)[17]

The Golden Notebook, which engaged explicitly with the relationship of the 'committed' writer to left and communist politics, was also ignored by the New Left. Janet Hase, the business manager of the *New Left Review*, told Lessing, 'the men of this new revolutionary movement treated the women as dogsbodies and she was sick of it. She had wanted to review *The Golden Notebook* for them, but they wouldn't let her' (*Walking* 272). Even Lessing's friend Thompson criticized the novel; Lessing wrote back to him: 'I don't understand how anyone could describe the G.N. as subjective – subjective attitudes are objectivized and related to society – or that is what I tried to do ....It was a novel about the kind of intellectual and emotional attitudes produced now, that people have now, and their relation to each other' (*Walking* 313). Ironically, this problem – the difficulty of women writers in being taken seriously as political writers – is addressed within *The Golden Notebook* itself, when Anna Wulf, the protagonist, attacks the way in which her own novel has been received by film and television producers, who want to adapt a novel about racial politics and the colour bar in Southern Africa into a kind of 'a simple moving love story ... a *Brief Encounter With Wings*' (285), turning it into a romantic drama set in an air force base in England.

Feeling, metafiction, and pastiche in *The Golden Notebook*

While Lessing was frustrated at the New Left's failure to take her work seriously, her comments to Thompson also indicate the extent to which *The Golden Notebook* shared the concern of the New Left and of angry writing with feeling. The novel is centred on Anna Wulf, and the crises she faces in three areas: her disillusionment with communism, her difficult personal relationships with men, and the writer's block which hampers her attempts to write a novel 'powered with an intellectual or moral passion strong enough to create order, to create a new way of looking at life' (61). Unable to understand the relationships between these different aspects of her life, and – more fundamentally – between the public world of politics and the private world of feeling, she divides her experience between four different notebooks: the red notebook records her political life; the black notebook looks at her past in Africa and her professional life as a writer; her emotional life and the therapy with Mother Sugar are documented in the diary-like blue notebook; and her attempts to write a novel are contained in the yellow notebook. *The Golden Notebook* portrays the uncertainties of a postwar, postnuclear, postcolonial world, and like angry literature and New Left critical writing, it posits feeling and emotion as a symptom of this social crisis: Anna tells Mother Sugar 'I'm living the kind of life women never lived before .... They didn't feel as I do. How could they? I don't want to be told when I wake up, terri-fied by a dream of total annihilation, because of the H-bomb exploding, that people felt that way about the crossbow. It isn't true. There is some-thing new in the world' (472). Anna realizes that she is more interested in '[f]ive lonely women going mad quietly by themselves, in spite of husband and children or rather because of them' than in the election canvassing (167), because their emotions point to a crisis that the language of party politics cannot describe or understand. Like New Left critical writing, *the Golden Notebook* suggests feeling and the language of feeling provide insight into social change in a way that conventional political language does not; when Anna's friend Molly praises her for not writing 'little nov-els about the emotions', Anna responds 'If marxism means anything, it means that a little novel about the emotions should reflect 'what's real' since the emotions are a function and a product of a society' (42).

However, *The Golden Notebook* destabilizes New Left and angry concerns by dislodging the feeling male body from its privileged place, and by focusing on the unhappy woman as both the symptom and the solution for the social and cultural crisis of the 1950s, rather than on the feeling male body. Anna herself is such an unhappy woman, and her alienation eventually leads to her breakdown, during which she obsessively papers walls with newspaper cuttings, an indication that her personal breakdown is related to a larger global crisis.[18] But the breakdown produced by alien-ation and unhappiness leads to the possibility of personal renewal and social change, as Anna explains to Mother Sugar: 'sometimes I meet peo-ple, and it seems to me the fact they are cracked across, they're split, means they are keeping themselves open for something' (473). Anna's own breakdown is not just the symptom of crisis but the solution to it, as it leads to the final golden notebook, co-written by Anna and her lover Saul, in which the former divisions and boundaries she has set up between the different facets of her life are broken down in a chaotic formlessness which is also a form of regeneration, so that she emerges from the break-down ready to write her novel, her writer's block over.

The character of Saul can be seen as a metafictional reference to the way in which *The Golden Notebook* draws on and reworks angry and New Left concerns by mixing them with a new narrative focused on a mid-dle-class woman and on the process of writing itself.[19] Saul is an American communist and a writer, and Anna is both seduced by him and profoundly critical of his sexualized romantic individualism:

> And Saul stood lecturing me about the pressures of society to con-form, while he used the sexy pose .... There were two languages being spoken to me at the same time .... I nearly challenged him in his turn, saying something like: What the hell do you mean by using that grown-up language to me, and then standing there like a hero-ic cowboy with invisible revolvers stuck all over your hips?
>
> (553–54)

Anna both recognizes and challenges the link between new left radical-ism and a pose of aggressive heterosexual masculinity, rejecting the 'language' of seduction implicit in this performance of masculinity and separating it from the 'grown-up language' of politics. *The Golden Note-book* parodies Saul, as Anna herself parodies the figure of the rebellious male writer, writing a satirical journal of a disaffected young American who is part Hemingway, part Kerouac, part Osborne – 'June 22nd. *Café de Flore*. Time is the river on which the leaves of our thoughts are called into oblivion. My father says I must come home. Will he never under-stand me?' (435). To Anna's horror, the desire for authentic new voices means that when she sends this piece to a journal its parodic quality is not recognized, since parody relies on a stable linguistic norm which has disappeared from the postwar world: 'something had happened in the world which made parody impossible' (440). This recalls Jameson's well-known (and much later) characterization of postmodern pastiche as a 'neutral practice of ... mimicry, without any of parody's ulterior motives, amputated of the satiric impulse, devoid of laughter and of any convic-tion that alongside the abnormal tongue you have momentarily bor-rowed, some healthy linguistic normality still exists' (*Postmodernism* 17). Anna initially sees the disappearance of parody in similar terms, lament-ing the fact that parodies are read as sincere, and that sincerely produced socialist realism reads like parody: 'It seems to me that this fact is another expression of the fragmentation of everything, the painful disintegration of something that is linked with what I feel to be true about language, the thinning of language against the density of our experience' (302).

However, both *The Golden Notebook* and the golden notebook ultimately welcome the new possibilities provided by linguistic breakdown, and therefore challenge Jameson's description of the politically neutral quality of pastiche, as they use pastiche to refuse a distinction between male and female writing, and to challenge the notions of wholeness and authenticity that dominated New Left and angry writing. Saul is incorporated in the novel not just as the object of parody, but as an author figure associated with pastiche. In the co-written golden notebook, the distinction between Saul and Anna is blurred: Anna dreams that both she and Saul are 'male-female' (594), and this dream is realized through the notebook's use of pastiche, in which Saul and Anna appropriate and ventriloquize the other's voice without satirical motives. Anna writes the first sentence of Saul's novel which deals with the Algerian resistance movement, and Saul writes the first sentence of 'Free Women', the realist narrative which starts *The Golden Notebook* – 'The two women were alone in the London flat' (639, 3). In this way the novel self-consciously stages its own relationship to angry and New Left writing as mimicry and as pastiche, and at the same time reveals that writing itself to be mimicry, a linguistic performance rather than the expression of an underlying stable, true self. In other words, Anna's ability to produce Saul's voice disrupts its authenticity and its connection to the feeling male body, so that the 'angry' male voice of Saul is aligned with performance and with the textual fragment, rather than with authenticity and wholeness.

In *The Golden Notebook*, therefore, the nature of crisis is registered and explored through form as well as through content. Pastiche is the formal equivalent of the thematic content of emotion, acting within the novel both as the symptom of a social crisis and as the solution to that crisis, insofar as both pastiche and emotion break open and disrupt the monadic, isolated, individual subject. In her use of postmodern techniques such as pastiche and self-reflexivity, and in her self-conscious interrogation of realism, Lessing draws on but also destabilizes the aesthetics of angry writing and of the New Left. Angry writing links realism and transparency with the qualities of openness and authenticity, associating performance and linguistic instability with dissimulation and dishonesty. As we have seen, New Left critical writing also privileges realist form.[20] In contrast, while Lessing defends realism in 'A Small Personal Voice', mounting a Lukácsian defence of realism's ability to represent the totality of social life, *The Golden Notebook* challenges the power of traditional realist form to adequately represent reality, suggesting that verisimilitude may not be the best way to represent the confusion of twentieth-century experience. In this respect it is closer to Brecht's criticism of Lukács in their famous exchange in the 1930s, in which he argued that the task of the writer was to expose reality by exposing contradictions, which could be done through a variety of forms: 'Realism is not a mere question of form .... Reality changes; in order to represent it, modes of representation must also change' (qtd. in Bloch et al. 82).

The Golden Notebook questions traditional realism both thematically and formally. The novel incorporates realist form in its framing narrative 'Free Women' (the novel written by Anna), but the novel reveals the gap between this fictionalized version of Anna's life and the versions that appear in her notebooks, which depart from realism to include different kinds of forms, from newspaper headlines to plot synopses. Moreover, Anna's breakdown is closely linked to her disillusionment with the versions of wholeness offered by both communism and realism, which seem either to fail or to deny the complexity and chaos of the world. She grows increasingly convinced that the social whirlwind of mid-twentieth-century life entails a crisis in representation, in which words are unmoored from a stable, shared meaning. She tells a Russian writer: 'We used the same language – the communist language. Yet our experience was so different that each phrase meant something different to each of us' (294), and she is worried by Stalin's pamphlet on linguistics for a similar reason: 'I find myself listening to a sentence, a phrase, a group of words, as if they are in a foreign language – the gap between what they are supposed to mean, and what in fact they say seems unbridgeable. I have been thinking of the novels about the breakdown of language, like *Finnegans Wake*' (300). If modern life is characterized by a crisis in language, a realist novel that asserts a transparent connection between signifiers and signifieds will inevitably fail to grasp the totality of modern life.

The question that both Anna and *The Golden Notebook* grapple with is how to represent the chaos and complexity of modern life without falsifying it, on the one hand, or falling into gibberish, on the other hand. In 'Free Women', Molly's son Tommy reads Anna's separate notebooks and asks her: 'What would happen if you had one big book without all those divisions and brackets and special writing?' Anna's response is 'chaos' (274). But during her breakdown, which she experiences as a breakdown in language – 'Words mean nothing. They have become ... not the form into which experience is shaped, but a series of meaningless sounds, like nursery talk, and away to one side of experience' (476) – she encounters the creative as well as the destructive potential of formlessness. She has an epiphanic, dream-like experience in which she is shown films which recount the stories of her notebooks: they are 'Directed by Anna Wulf' (619), and are 'conventionally well-made films, as if they had been made in a studio ... every scene glossy with untruth, false and stupid' (619). Later she is shown the same films, only this time 'they had another quality, which in the dream I named "realistic"; they had a rough, crude, rather jerky quality of an early Russian or German film' (634). In this dream, reality is portrayed not through traditional verisimilitude, synonymous in film with Hollywood's seamless classic realism, but through the jolts of montage (a term also favoured by Brecht), which uses cuts and gaps to show the discontinuous nature of reality.[21] This dream ends Anna's writer's block, as she is freed from the confines of verisimilitude to explore new ways of depicting and shaping the world, and is at the same time reconciled to the fact that 'the real experience can't be described' (633), as well as to the gap between experience and any literary form. Similarly, *The Golden Notebook* uses a montage-like technique, suturing together different forms, including traditional realism, but emphasizing the gaps and contradictions within any literary form.

The *Golden Notebook* goes beyond both *The L-Shaped Room* and *A Taste of Honey* by mimicking and destabilizing the form as well as the content of angry literature. In the angry text the protagonist's authenticity is mirrored through the realist form of the text, which refuses to acknowledge a gap between language and identity, or between representation and reality. It is this gap that Lessing highlights, in the name of a commitment to realism rather than a departure from it – as Lorna Sage argues, realism 'had always implied for her a set of values, an ideology' (45) rather than a specific form. *The Golden Notebook* is not only self-reflexive about its status as a text which mimics and destabilizes angry narratives, but more fundamentally it suggests that *all* texts are mimic texts insofar as they produce reality rather than reflecting it in an uncomplicated way. In its content, too, the novel rewrites the angry narrative, presenting feeling as a symptom of cultural crisis and also as its cure, but inserting the unhappiness and breakdown of a middle-class woman in place of the feeling male body. Lessing's novel shows the capacity of feeling to problematize subjectivity and to open the self out to others, and it uses pastiche to figure this process on the level of form.

Yet *A Taste of Honey* and *The L-Shaped Room*, which draw more closely on elements of 'angry' novels and plays, also rewrite the affective map of angry literature. Both texts refuse the link between feeling and freedom or authenticity (a link *The Golden Notebook* arguably reproduces in its depiction of breakdown as the source of Anna's renewal and regeneration). *The L-Shaped Room*'s concern with shame shows the way in which feelings can reinforce social norms, as it exposes and challenges the assumptions about femininity that produce Jane's sexual shame; *A Taste of Honey* suggests that 'life' is linked to restriction and to the body's capacity for negation, as much as to life-affirming energy. More positively, both texts emphasize the capacity for affective bonds to create affiliations that cut across race, gender, sexuality, and ethnicity – a capacity represented in angry texts, but always closed down by their distinction between an affective elite and this elite's inauthentic enemies. Whether implicitly or self-consciously 'the same but not quite', all three texts dislodge the connections between masculinity, authenticity, and feeling established in angry texts and in New Left criticism.

5
From Motorbikes to Male Strippers: The Persistence of the Feeling Male Body

The feeling male body that features so prominently in the literature and cultural criticism of the late 1950s and early 1960s has had an afterlife beyond this period. In this chapter, I argue that the trope has continued to be important in later twentieth-century British cultural criticism and literature, where it has still been invoked both as a sign of cultural and social crisis, and as the solution to that crisis. The chapter traces the feeling male body through the cultural criticism of the Birmingham Centre for Contemporary Cultural Studies, specifically in the work of Paul Willis and Dick Hebdige on subcultures in the 1970s, before turning to three incarnations of this body in the literature and film of the 1980s and 1990s: Martin Amis's *Money* (1984), Irvine Welsh's *Trainspotting* (1994), and *The Full Monty* (1997, dir. Peter Cattaneo). In all these texts, the feeling male body is socially peripheral but symbolically central, registering the deleterious effects of social changes and transitions, including the seismic shifts ushered in by Thatcherism, but at the same time embodying some hope for resistance, escape or transformation.[1]

I argue that there are significant continuities between the symbolic functions of the feeling male body in the 1950s and of its subsequent manifestations. These include the way in which the feeling male body is linked to anxieties around consumption, as later texts also emphasize style and a reworked form of consumption as a way of asserting masculinity in the face of the feminizing effects of mainstream consumption. In addition, the feeling male body continues to express and to displace class identity. In the texts I examine in this chapter, the affluent working-class labourers and lower-middle-class junior university lecturers have disappeared, but in their place are other figures who embody social changes and whose class positions are unstable or transitional. These include the subcultural motorbike boys and punks of the 1970s, who both express and reject their parent working-class culture, in Willis and Hebdige; the Thatcherite entrepreneurial yuppie of working-class origins in *Money*; the underclass who are members of a subcultural elite, in *Trainspotting*; and the paradoxical figure of the unemployed worker in *The Full Monty*. The feeling male body is therefore aligned with what could broadly be described as marginalized class positions, yet I will show that it also blurs or transcends class distinctions, as it did in the 1950s.

However, just as the feeling male body was articulated differently across cultural and literary texts in the 1950s, expressing contradictory fears and desires, so too are there important differences between the 1950s feeling male body and its later versions. One of these differences is the increasingly spectacular nature of the feeling male body, which is marked through subcultural style in Hebdige, Willis, and in *Trainspotting*, and is associated with excess and with vulnerability, becoming both grotesque and abject, in *Money*, *Trainspotting*, and *The Full Monty*. Another difference is that the distinction between masculinity and femininity in these texts becomes increasingly unstable, as the vulnerability of the feeling male body is explicitly and frequently expressed in terms of feminization. Similarly, the relationship between consumption and resistance to consumption is blurred, as consumption is parodied in a complicitous critique (as Hebdige suggests happens with punk, and as we see in *Trainspotting* and *The Full Monty*), or rejected partially and ironically (in *Money*). The assertion of active, masculine consumption therefore becomes progressively more difficult to separate from its feminized, passive counterpart, though the texts still attempt to make such distinctions. Finally, although the feeling male body is still associated with revitalization, whether of the individual or of a community, the nature of this renewal is often ambivalent or uncertain, particularly in *Money* and *Trainspotting*, where the narrative of renewal is invoked but also undercut. Like angry texts and New Left criticism, these texts associate a version of masculinity with social critique. But in the examples I examine, the distinction between the feeling male body as the symptom of crisis and as the solution to that crisis becomes increasingly unstable, as the utopian potential the feeling male body offers is fleeting or ironic, and as the fragility of the category of masculinity is made clear.

Subcultural bodies: Paul Willis's *Profane Culture* and Dick Hebdige's *Subculture*

The feeling male body as it emerges in the work on subcultures by Paul Willis and Dick Hebdige has obvious connections to the feeling male body of the New Left critics of the 1950s. Willis and Hebdige both studied at the Centre for Contemporary Cultural Studies (CCCS) at the University of Birmingham, which had direct links with the New Left and the *ULR*: Richard Hoggart was its first director, followed by Stuart Hall.[2] The continuities with earlier New Left interests are apparent in the Centre's focus on the intersection of youth culture and working-class culture, and on emergent popular cultural forms.[3] The Centre's most influential work on the intersection of youth and working-class culture came in its publications on subcultures, in *Resistance Through Rituals* (1976), Willis's *Learning to Labour* (1977) and *Profane Culture* (1978), and Hebdige's *Subculture: The Meaning of Style* (1979). Chris Jenks points out that in contrast to earlier American work on subcultures associated with the Chicago School, which focused on the deviant, the minority, and the delinquent, the CCCS concentrated instead on 'mostly white, male, working-class youth' (121), again illustrating a continuity with New Left preoccupations.

In this section, I concentrate on *Profane Culture* and *Subculture* as the best examples of the continuing fascination with the feeling male body among British left cultural critics well beyond the 1950s.[4] The emphasis on masculinity in the Centre's work on subcultures was noted early on, most famously by Angela McRobbie in 'Settling Accounts with Subcultures' (1981). In this article, McRobbie points out that the emphasis on music and drug-taking in both the critical literature on subcultures and in the subcultures themselves draw on discourses which have historically been mediated through masculinity, and argues that style, for Hebdige, is an implicitly male attribute: 'That is not to say that women are denied style, rather that the style of a subculture is primarily that of its men' (116).[5] Yet McRobbie's critique, like those of contemporary feminist scholars such as Sarah Thornton, primarily concentrates on the presence and absence of women in subcultures, rather than analysing subcultural theory's investment in masculinity. It is this investment that I explore here, as I argue that Hebdige and Willis represent the members of subcultures in ways that recall the symbolic function of the feeling male body in New Left criticism. For both Hebdige and Willis, subcultures represent, express, or encode certain conditions of working-class life and of postwar British society in general. Like the postwar working class, subcultures are the fragmented shards of a ruptured social whole, incarnating postwar social change and instability, yet at the same time subcultures open up the possibility of transforming that society. In this respect, the members of subcultures play a similar role for Hebdige and Willis as Jim Dixon and Jimmy Porter did for an earlier generation of left critics. First, they cater both for nostalgia and for the desire for change, embodying the possibility of an organic, whole community, and also the energies that could disrupt the status quo. Second, they provide an alternative to mainstream consumer culture by exemplifying an *active*, masculine appropriation and transformation of commodities. Third, in the very limits of their rebellion (limits wistfully recognized by both Hebdige and Willis), as well as in their bodies marked by piercing or wounded through accidents, the punks and the motorbike boys express a crisis in postwar (working-class) masculinity, but also hold out the possibility of social renewal.

Profane Culture, based on Paul Willis's PhD thesis, is an ethnographic study of two kinds of youth subculture: motorbike boys and hippies, the former from working-class backgrounds, the latter from middle-class. Willis sees the lifestyles of both groups as acts of resistance to the 'bourgeoisie' (5); he is aware of the 'tragic limit' of these acts of resistance, as these cultures 'penetrated, exposed and partially resolved [the larger contradictions of society], but only in a special disconnected and informal way which left their basic structures unaltered' (177). Nonetheless, he concludes that both groups 'scaled off the pretences and illusions of the bourgeois order' and showed 'the possibility of the revolutionary in the small, detailed and everyday' (182). Despite his dual focus on working-class and middle-class subcultures, Willis clearly sympathizes more closely with what he perceives to be the emphasis on visceral immediacy in the world of the motorbike boys, in contrast to the '*cerebral* hedonism' (173) and intellectual tendencies of the hippies. The motorbike boys are characterized by their physicality and their desire for immediacy: 'At a simple physical level ... the motor-bike boys were rough and tough' (18). When they ride, they reject helmet and goggles because 'the *experience* and the *image* of motor-cycling would have been muffled and blocked' (55). They are also characterized by their capacity for feeling, linked to their robust corporeality: the boys' language is peppered with 'concrete images' and 'vigorous use of swear-words' which produces a 'muscularity of style that made for a distinctive and incontrovertible expression of feelings' (42–43). Willis sees feeling in the most unlikely places, such as one boy's claim that the situation in Northern Ireland should be resolved by both sides being given guns and left to fight it out. Willis argues that this apparently callous attitude is in fact marked by 'real human feeling' (35), as it refuses the dilution of feeling encouraged by the daily depiction of brutality on the television. It is in fact the middle-class liberal whose lightly felt compassion indicates that 'he is dissociating his sensibility .... This is the kind of bloodless humanism, cerebralized compassion, that in the end can be more insulting, and less humanly relevant, than an apparently spontaneous rejection, which at least springs from a secure human base' (35).

In rejecting this bloodless humanism, Willis also seeks to mirror the visceral immediacy of the motorbike boys through his methodology of ethnography (although the Leavisite echoes reveals his undergraduate training in Cambridge English): 'Life is the thing. Ethnography is not simply description, it's about capturing that' (2).[6] The language of embodiment pervades Willis's own claims for the primacy of experience over theory: 'The sheer surprise of a living culture is a *slap* to reverie. Real, bustling, startling cultures *move*' (1; my emphasis). For Willis, it is precisely in the body rather than in the mind that the significance of any subculture lies, as the actions of subcultural participants stem from 'knots of feeling, contradiction, frustration', and their 'specificity … means we can learn from them. We learn from the culture, not from its explicit consciousness' (5).

The motorbike boy provides a model for the intellectual not just in his corporeality, but also in his connection to wholeness and unity. Everything links together in the world of the motorbike boy, in contrast to the dissociated 'schizophrenia' Willis laments in many intellectuals (34). According to Willis, the motorbike boys make a 'direct connection between rock music and fast bike-riding', because both these activities expressed a similar 'articulation of feeling' (72), allowing them to express the desire for speed, movement, and aggression. Willis notes that the boys anthropomorphize their bikes – 'mechanical qualities were recognized, appreciated, extended and transformed into human qualities' (61) – and he argues that the impulse to anthropomorphize is a rejection of the alienating and fragmenting effects of capitalism and industrialism. In their rejection of a 'cybernetic model of the relationship between experience and technology where machines condition and over-ride specifically human qualities', the boys' relationships with their bikes show 'a form of man's domination of the machine' (61), because they exemplify the capacity of humans to construct meanings for inorganic objects and incorporate them into the human world of culture. Again, Willis seeks to mirror the boys in his methodology, seeing a homology between the 'roughness and intimidation of the bike' with its 'aggressive thumping of the unbaffled exhaust' and the boys' own 'masculine assertiveness' (53). He thereby transforms the technology of the bike into an image of organic humanity.

We can see this depiction of the relationship between man and machine as a way in which Willis departs from an earlier condemnation of consumer culture by writers like Hoggart (his initial PhD supervisor), as he emphasizes the power of the boys to actively transform and rework the meaning of commodities such as motorbikes. The emphasis on agency characterizes the CCCS work on subcultures. Both Graeme Turner and Richard E. Lee point out that the Centre's emphasis on agency and creativity amongst subcultures must be seen in the context of the other influential disseminator of post-structuralist theory in Britain in the 1970s: that is, *Screen* criticism. This term refers to the work of critics such as Colin McCabe, Catherine Belsey, and Laura Mulvey, which was published in the well-known film journal *Screen*. Put simply, *Screen* criticism took a formalist approach to textual criticism, emphasizing the way in which particular formal techniques interpellated the viewer or reader in specific ways, producing subject positions. In contrast to this position, in which the political and social significance of a text was to be found in its internal formal structures, the Centre's work on subcultures emphasized the power of the reader, viewer, or participant to actively shape a 'text' (understood in a broad sense as a system of signification) and to resist the ideology of the dominant culture. The active reworking of commodities such as motorbikes from random objects to culturally symbolic objects illustrates the power of people to create their own meanings rather than just be helplessly interpellated by dominant systems of signification.

However, Willis's emphasis on the motorbike boys' creative transformation of the commodity also suggests that they offer the possibility of an *active*, and therefore masculine, relationship to consumer goods. The motorbike boys reject the 'plastic ersatz and the detritus of the bourgeoisie' (5), and transform degraded commodities into something authentic and real as these are 'taken out of context, claimed in a particular way, developed and repossessed to express something deeply and thereby to change somewhat the very feelings which are their product' (6). Here commodities are anthropomorphized, made capable of deep expression, and linked to the affective vitality of the boys themselves. But they are also aligned with change, metamorphosis, and with (masculine) activity rather than (feminine) passivity. Willis therefore often associates authenticity and feeling with the consumer goods that many in the early New Left saw as the enemy of these qualities: 'a bedizened, solid motor-bike, an embroidered sheepskin coat, an outrageous rock 'n' roll record .... show us the real movement of experience in the concrete world' (2). Consumer goods and the act of consumption are redeemed insofar as they provide the raw material for creative action and customizing.

While the feeling male body may help to masculinize consumption and to combat the tawdry, ersatz, fragmented world of industrial capitalism, its acts of resistance are only partially successful. Yet Willis sees triumph even in this failure. He notes the fighting, violence, and frequent deaths of the motorbike boys, commenting that the 'forces of life spoke strangely through death in the culture. This ambience tragically sealed the bike culture off and abnegated any role it might have had in the larger development of the working class, and the struggle for change' (178). The self-destructive tendency amongst both the hippies and the motorbike boys is a tragedy, as the potential to enact change on a broader collective level is wasted, and 'the power of finality and solution is turned back on to forms of desperate personal transformation and even destruction of the self ... as in the bike or drug death' (181). Yet this wounded body not only marks the failure of the subcultural project, but also, paradoxically, drives it. Using the language of Greek tragedy, Willis enthuses that 'this fatal flaw also provides the energy and eyes of the gods. It motors a creativity and vitality which is far from fatalism and pessimism' (181). It is precisely the 'suffering and destruction' (181) of the feeling male body that illustrates the 'burning creative pressure' with which the subcultures reject the 'bourgeois order' (182). The motorbike boys' suffering illustrates their status as cultural symptom, as they display the wounds that the bourgeois order inflicts on the working classes, but it also becomes the means of fighting that social order.

Dick Hebdige's *Subculture* has a different relationship to the feeling male body than *Profane Culture*. The romanticization and politicization of the feeling male body in Willis or indeed in earlier New Left work was implicitly based on an assumption of homology between signifier and signified: there seemed to be a necessary, rather than an arbitrary relationship between such a body and class-based acts of refusal and resistance to the dominant culture. In such work, the body bears an inherent relationship to the signified (whether this is political change or 'working-class values'); it is metonymic rather than metaphoric. Hebdige, by contrast, explicitly distances himself from the assumption that the style and the symbolic gestures of a subculture such as punk have a homologous relationship to an underlying class-based identity. Drawing on Kristeva and Barthes, he emphasizes instead the way in which a subculture like punk is expressed with reference to a set of signs which bear an arbitrary rather than a necessary relationship to any underlying signified.

Hebdige emphasizes the way in which the subcultural body signifies through surface and style. Such a body is therefore unnatural: he writes that the transformations of style 'go "against nature," interrupting the process of "normalization"' (18). Subcultures highlight the ideological nature of the signifying systems with which we are surrounded by drawing attention to the 'deceptive "innocence" of appearances' (19) and by denaturalizing the everyday world (they therefore bear a certain similarity to a semiotician such as Hebdige). Hebdige suggests that this manipulation of signs is an implicitly political act, one that 'challenges the principle of unity and cohesion, which contradicts the myth of consensus' (18). He sees a relation between subcultures and their 'parent' culture – working-class culture – in terms of their shared subordination in relation to power and 'ruling ideas', as a refusal of hegemony and 'a movement away from the consensus' (132). Nonetheless, he argues that subcultures bear only an oblique relationship to their parent working-class culture, just as their relationship to black Caribbean immigrant culture (which Hebdige sees as a repressed yet influential force on white working-class subcultures) is also mediated and oblique.[7]

As a result, subcultural symbols, such as the swastika, cannot be 'read' in any easy manner either as signs of racism or as parodic anti-racism. Rather, the swastika's meaning is precisely in the 'communicated absence of … identifiable values' (117), or in the way in which it resists and explodes interpretation. Punk style and symbols not only denaturalize the sign, but disrupt the very process of signification, so that punk style is 'in a constant state of assemblage, of flux' and is 'cut adrift from meaning' (126). Punk refers to working-class identity (through accent, in particular), and mirrors the experience of class domination – of 'inequality, powerlessness, alienation' (121) – but it does so through *representing* social contradictions rather than magically resolving these contradictions through a utopian alternative lifestyle.[8]

Punk style is based on parody and blankness rather than on the spontaneous expression of underlying feelings Willis had seen in the lifestyle of the motorbike boys. How then does Hebdige's account of punk illustrate the centrality of the feeling male body to subcultural theory? To start with, Hebdige continually focuses on the body as a locus of signification. Hebdige is not primarily interested in punk as musical practice or as a movement in art and design (there is no discussion of Vivian Westwood and Malcolm McLaren, for example). Instead, he returns to the body, whether clad in bondage gear, dancing the pogo or the robot, or subverting conventions of musical performance. As a successful subculture, punk is able to 'embody a sensibility' (122), and its style is corporeal: 'a gesture of defiance or contempt … a smile or a sneer' (3). For Hebdige, the stylized punk body, clad in safety pins and rubbish bags, disrupts, refuses, fractures, and subverts. Like previously encountered versions of the feeling male body, Hebdige's punk body disrupts and breaks apart the status quo.

Moreover, although Hebdige emphasizes the stylized and unnatural quality of the punk body, he nevertheless sees punk style as the expression – however oblique – of an underlying emotional content. The punk body is therefore also a feeling body. Subcultures like punk are partly 'representations of representations' (86): that is, they mediate and rework images of working-class life perpetuated from within and from outside working-class communities. But punk style also articulates *emotion*, albeit through the chaotic disruption of the process of signification and articulation itself, and it is this emotion that links punk style both with its working-class roots, and with its hidden shadow – black immigrant culture. Punk does not necessarily express the values widely held to be those of working-class culture (such as community or solidarity), and may in fact challenge these values, but it shares the same emotional content as working-class protest: 'the various stylistic ensembles adopted by the punks were undoubtedly expressive of genuine aggression, frustration and anxiety' (87). Similarly, Hebdige sees the connection between punk and blackness as emotional. Punks borrowed 'the feel' as well as the look of black style, turning to reggae 'in order to find a music which reflected more adequately their sense of frustration and oppression' (69). Paradoxically, then, the 'petrified quality' and the 'paralysed look' of punk hides at its 'heart' (69) – note the corporeal image – an emotional relationship to black dread and soul, as well as to white working-class culture. The blank face reworks the anger of these groups, becoming a gesture of refusal and resistance: 'beneath the clownish make-up there lurked the unaccepted and disfigured face of capitalism' (115).

Hebdige's punk body is not only a feeling body, but it is also implicitly male. Throughout *Subculture* Hebdige draws on male images and icons almost exclusively, from the made-up male face on the now iconic cover, to the numerous references to punk's high cultural equivalents such as William Burroughs and Jean Genet – who 'embodies our object' (138). This is a deviant form of masculinity that flirts with feminine style and homosexuality, in contrast to the rugged heterosexuality of the motorbike boys. But nonetheless, it is definitively male: in order for femininity to be coded as deviance rather than conformity, a male body is required. In addition, Hebdige explicitly associates subcultural resistance with male sexuality, albeit an illicit sexuality. He begins the book with the image of a tube of vaseline the police confiscate from Genet when he is arrested, which for him illustrates subcultural style, as the vaseline 'takes on a symbolic dimension' (2). Vaseline, like the punk's safety pin or bin bag, is a commodity that is made to mean differently by the body with which it is associated, and therefore becomes a token of refusal and subversion. This illustrates a persistent theme in Hebdige's work, which is the potential for commodities to be used and reworked by a subculture in a way that refuses the meaning attributed to the commodity by the dominant culture. Here we can see, as in Willis, an attempt to render consumption an active process, rather than a passive one, and thereby potentially to masculinize it. Moreover, Hebdige implicitly associates the act of giving meanings to commodities such as vaseline with the penetrating force of the male body, as he describes Genet's relationship to language as entering it 'by a back passage violently' (138), an image which links Genet's disruptive use of language with his rebellious use of vaseline.

The vaseline becomes a 'stigmata' (2) for Genet, an image both of his humiliation but also of his triumph. Salvation inevitably entails cruci-fixion, and it is through the pain of humiliation and through the sym-bol of the stigmatized body that Genet paradoxically proclaims his defeat of the police force. Similarly, for Hebdige, punk also claims vic-tory through woundedness, through a 'deformity' (138) that is both 'impotence and a kind of power' (3). Hebdige explicitly associates the (male) punk body with cultural crisis, arguing that it displays 'signs of the highly publicized decay' (87) of late 1970s Britain, beset with unem-ployment, oil crises, and rancorous labour relations. However, he also suggests that it also provides a potential cure for that crisis, as its refusal of the myth of social consensus and its rejection of dominant ideologies points towards the possibility of political change and of a more equal and less divided society. Symptomatically, Hebdige describes himself as an anthropologist, a mere 'student of deviance', and an 'amputee' (168) in implicit contrast to the members of the subcultures he studies. These members thus paradoxically become aligned with wholeness in contrast to the disabled, cerebral intellectual who is a mere onlooker, recalling Willis's description of himself as 'grey and detached' (*Profane Culture* 12) in comparison to the motorbike boys.

Both Hebdige and Willis therefore associate their subcultural subjects with the possibility of social change achieved through the violent ener-gies of the feeling male body. Both theorists see the deformed body of the (implicitly male) punk or the suffering body of the (explicitly male) motorbike boy as the symptom of underlying social inequality, but at the same time they see in these bodies gestures of refusal and creative forces that could lead to social transformation. They identify this potential for transformation with their subjects' corporeality, their expression of emotion, and their masculinity. The style of punk and the style of the motorbike boy obliquely express a working-class identity, but at the same time the punk and the motorbike boy reject the language and the semiotics of class in order to express their resistance to the status quo through the semiotics of their respective subcultures, a semiotics which expresses the disruptive creativity of the feeling male body.

Money, bodies, and Thatcherism

Willis and Hebdige both wrote at the end of the 1970s, when the possibility of counter-cultural revolution still hung headily in the air. Such a possibility seemed laughably unlikely by the 1980s, during which Margaret Thatcher's Conservative government, with its policy of denationalizing government-owned industries, its support for private industry and the entrepreneur, and its monetarist economics, fundamentally changed the political, economic, and social landscape of Britain. The effect of Thatcherism on traditional working-class communities was profound, as industries shut down and strikes paralysed communities across the north of England. Britain encountered large-scale unemployment on a scale not seen since the depression: whereas in 1954 the number of unemployed was 260,000, by 1982, this had risen to 3,400,000 (Kirk 78). One result of Thatcher's policies was the emergence of a generation of young people from working-class backgrounds who had never been employed, a category increasingly referred to as the 'underclass'. Along with the underclass, a new image of working-class men appeared: the socially mobile entrepreneur who left his working-class community behind and became socially mobile not through education but through entrepreneurial skills, by apparent dint of sheer will and force of character. The working-class entrepreneur, the underclass, and the unemployed industrial labourer came to embody the social changes associated with Thatcherism, and in the rest of this chapter, I look at the symbolic significance of these figures in *Money*, *Trainspotting* and *The Full Monty*, arguing that in all three texts they emerge as feeling male bodies who are associated with renewal and revitalization as well as with crisis and fragmentation.

The central character and narrator of Martin Amis's *Money* (1984), John Self, embodies the archetypal Thatcherite success story. He is a socially mobile entrepreneur from a working-class background (his father owns a pub) who has risen to the top of that quintessentially 1980s industry, advertising, making huge amounts of money.[9] At the same time, he is an everyman (at 35, he is the same age as the narrator of *The Divine Comedy*) whose task is to negotiate the purgatorial worlds of London and New York transformed by 1980s free-market capitalism, by an obsession with wealth creation, and by the rise of individualism. Self is therefore an ambivalent deep figure, at once the grotesque symptom of Thatcherite greed and the object of Amis's satire, and at the same time a hapless naïf attempting to make his way in a confusing and dangerous world. The novel follows Self as, flush from his success at selling 'smoking, drinking, junk food and nude magazines' (78), he embarks on a career as a film producer. But this move goes disastrously, spectacularly wrong, as he realizes by the end of the novel that he has been the victim of two confidence tricks, one engineered within the novel's fictional world by the corrupt producer Fielding Goodney, and the other metafictional, set up by Martin Amis the author who has controlled his fate from the start.

The novel satirizes a society obsessed with consumption and greed, but Amis's satire is ambiguous and ambivalent, like his attitude towards Self. On the one hand, the novel is a morality tale about the perils of consumption. It links the metaphorical consumption of commodities with literal forms of consumption such as eating and drinking, showing Self's consumption as excessive in both respects. Not only does he spend money with reckless abandon, encouraged by Fielding Goodney, but his ravaged body bears the signs of too much food, drink and pornography, as his face is described as being 'full of ... cheap food and junk money, the face of a fat snake, bearing all the signs of its sins' (9). Self declares: 'I am made of – junk, I'm just junk' (265). On the other hand, while Self may embody the worst excesses of the 1980s, his ebullient, immoderate appetites – mirrored by the extravagance of his language – stand in refreshing contrast to the stiff world of bourgeois propriety, exemplified by the middle-aged couple who 'retract slightly and lower their heads over their food' when Self and his friends effectively take over a restaurant: 'I suppose it must have been cool for people like them in places like this before people like us started coming here also' (82). Similarly, Self's shameless physical appetites are used for satirical purposes as a foil to the restrained, cerebral milieu of Martina Twain, the patrician New York art critic whose world is as fuelled by money as Self's. Self responds to a reproduction of Goya's *La Maja Desneuda* by masturbating, thereby flouting the supposed distinction between high art which demands distanced appreciation, and pornography which is basely physical. Like his father's creation, Jim Dixon, Martin Amis's John Self reveals the hypocrisy between such aesthetic divisions, as his actions suggest that 'money is always in the picture' (315), and that both art and porn are enmeshed in the venal and base circuits of money and of the body. Moreover, John Self and Martin Amis the character (in postmodern style, Amis writes himself into the novel) share appetites, both ordering the same full English breakfast in a greasy corner café.

The satire therefore cuts both ways. Amis skewers Self, but also casts a satirical eye on his educated, middle-class characters (and, potentially, the readers of the novel), with the result that the basis from which we might judge Self's excesses is less secure. From this perspective, John Self's consuming body functions as a kind of Bakhtinian grotesque realism, satirizing the neat order of a bourgeois world. But whereas Bakhtin contrasted the transgressive energies of the grotesque body with the stable hierarchies of the dominant order, Amis depicts a world in which the dominant order is characterized by excess. As a result, any transgressive potential of Self's body is undercut by the way in which it simultaneously incarnates the excesses of postmodernity and of late capitalism.

Self's body is the symptom of cultural crisis not just in its excessive appetites, but also in its weakness and vulnerability. Self tells us he is addicted to the twentieth century and, as James Diedrick notes, 'during his narrative the reader vicariously experiences the damage this addiction inflicts on Self's physical body – and the larger social body he also inhabits' (70). Constantly hungover, and struggling with physical disorders from gastric problems to impotence, both Self and his body are in a bad way. His tinnitus, a constant buzzing of different voices in his head, indicates the way his Self is a discursive construct, produced from the words of others (he is also, of course, literally a linguistic construct, and Amis's novel works simultaneously on the level of social commentary and of metafictional mise-en-abîme). Self sees his body as a blank canvas that can be transformed by enough money: 'What's the deal? Can money fix it? I need my whole body drilled down and repaired, replaced. I need my body capped is what I need. I'm going to do it too, the minute I hit the money' (5–6). Yet his body is not as malleable as he thinks, and throughout the novel his body functions not only as the casualty of late capitalism but also as its limit, and as a site of social critique.

As the casualty of Thatcherism and of late capitalism as well as its perpetrator, Self recalls Jameson's claim that 'history is what hurts' (*Political Unconscious* 102). He is emptied out of classic interiority – 'I feel invaded, duped, fucked around. I hear strange voices and speak in strange tongues' (66) – but his body feels the existential pain his mind cannot or will not: 'Happiness is the relief of pain, they say, and so I guess I'm a pretty happy guy. The relief of pain happens to me pretty frequently. But then so does pain.' (74) James Diedrick points out that 'Self's language is visceral, elemental; even his abstruse musings are experienced as sensations' (80). Self's constant tooth pain is a symptom of a broader social malaise, and although he cannot make such a critique directly, he recognizes that 'Pain is nature's way of telling us that something is wrong' (357). Through his physical pain Self's feeling male body is linked to a larger social body, illustrated in his response to a newspaper article about inner-city riots sparked by unemployment: '*I feel how you feel*. I haven't got that much to do all day myself. I sit here defencelessly, my mind full of earache and riot' (66). Here Amis links Self's individual pain to an expression of social pain, the riot, although he ironizes this comparison at the same time, as Self's expression of solidarity with the unemployed, 'I haven't got that much to do all day myself', is hilariously inappropriate.

Self's feeling body is an index of the postmodern condition, and of the social effects of late capitalism, but it also expresses a crisis in masculinity: not the vaguely amorphous crisis invoked as a commonplace in gender studies, but a crisis explicitly connected to consumption. The novel links consumption to the increased power of the working-class male, as John Self typifies the link between masculinity and consumption Frank Mort identifies as a key feature of the 1980s, exemplified by the rise of male style magazines. Yet Self's increasingly excessive consumption is also linked to his progressive feminization. Over the course of the novel Self becomes dependent on Fielding Goodney, the co-producer who encourages Self to spend vast amounts of money in pre-production for his film. Unbeknownst to Self, this is a confidence trick: the money is not there. Self is equally unaware that Goodney is 'Frank the Phone', a knowing, Satanic voice who calls constantly, and that he is also (dressed in drag) the mysterious ginger-haired woman who shadows Self; Goodney's gender identity is further complicated by the revelation that he sleeps with Doris Arthur, a lesbian, because 'In bed he's a woman' (353). The novel not only personifies the imperative to consume in the ambiguously gendered figure of Goodney, but also shows Self's masculinity becoming increasingly unstable as he consumes more and more frantically. He is given a once-over by two men as he enters Goodney's apartment: 'Christ, is this how you chicks feel?' (195); meeting the actor Spunk Davis in a gay bar, he muses: 'Maybe I have a big faggot future' (202). His sexuality is further questioned when Fielding Goodney, in his guise as the ginger-haired woman, leaves him a note written in lipstick: 'Frankie and Johnny were lovers' (219).

Self's feminization signifies the way he is controlled by Goodney and by consumption. Similarly, Self feels feminized in his relationship with Martina – 'I'm getting chicked' (331) – because that relationship also undermines his control: 'I don't know if I ever was in control. But I know I'm not now' (332). Love, including Self's love for Martina, is like consumption because it is fuelled by a desire that makes one powerless, thereby feminizing the masculine subject, a connection that Self makes when he muses: 'I've probably been deeply in love with Fielding Goodney from the moment we met' (326).

Self is also controlled by Martin Amis, though for most of the novel Self is blissfully unaware of his status as a character in Amis's plot, just as he is unaware that he is the victim of Goodney's plot. The character Martin Amis describes his control in terms of sadism, explaining to Self that 'The author is not free of sadistic impulses' (247), although Self ignores him because he is distracted by the pain from poking a pretzel into his tooth. In this ironic juxtaposition, Self's tooth pain illustrates Amis's sadistic control over his character, but it also functions satirically as a visceral riposte to Amis's lengthy and rather pompous abstract theorizing about the role of the author. Self's pain helps to deflate this pomposity and it also gives him a certain moral superiority over Amis, so that his physical vulnerability paradoxically becomes a sign of authenticity and strength.

For, if the novel anxiously records Self's vulnerability with respect to Goodney in terms of femininization, it recuperates his vulnerability with respect to Amis as a sign of strength. If Amis is a sadist, Self is a masochist, because although controlled by Amis the author he also chooses his own fate, sleeping with Selina and thereby wrecking his future with Martina, and ignoring the various warnings about his situation given to him by Frank and the ginger-haired woman. As he recognizes by the end of the novel, '*The confidence trick would have ended in five minutes if it hadn't been for John Self. I was the key. I was the needing, the hurting artist. I was the wanting artist. I wanted to believe*' (393). Self's masochism is illustrated most dramatically during his chess game with Martin Amis, when he realizes he has been manipulated and duped by both Goodney and Amis. He recognizes his own status as character, crying '*I'm the joke. I'm it!*' (379), and attempts to punch Amis, but since he is a character who cannot escape his fictional world to attack the author who exists outside as well as inside that world, he ends up, masochistically, indirectly hitting himself instead: 'I hurled myself round that room like a big ape in a small cage. But I could never connect. Oh Christ, he just isn't here, he just isn't there. My last shot upended me by the rhino-hide sofa, which kicked me full in the face with its square steel boot. The boil in my head now broke or burst' (379).

Self's masochism, like his tooth pain, is a sign of his vulnerability but also a source of strength that leads to his escape from Amis's control. His masochism expresses his feminization, but his capacity for pain also revitalizes him and remasculinizes him as he is freed from the control of the author.[10] Discussing their film script earlier in the novel, Self tells Amis that 'heroes don't lose fights' (247). Self is an anti-hero, whose failure to beat up Amis is followed by his suicide attempt, the ultimate act of masochistic, self-inflicted wounding. However, Self survives this attempt, since Martina's tranquilizers are placebos, and from this point he escapes the clutches of Martin Amis the author. He has bankrupted himself, and beaten himself up both literally and metaphorically, yet this fall also brings about his redemption. He is free from the clutches of money, and by the end of the novel, he has also escaped the sadistic control of Martin Amis the author. The final chapter of the novel is marked off from the rest by italics. In it, Self tells us that he has told Martin Amis to 'Fuck *off out of it*' (389), and describes his freedom from the author's mystical control: '*the pentagrams of shape and purpose have no power to harm or delight me now*' (384). He is an '*escape artist*' (393) who now writes his own story. By implication, Self's masochism and his vulnerability revitalize his masculinity, since by the end of the novel he is free from the external control that has contributed to his earlier feminization. This revitalization is tentative and ironic, rather than romantic: while he is free from Amis's sadism and from tooth pain in the novel's final section, his tooth is 'dead but still viable' (389) rather than miraculously regenerated. He is, moreover, beaten up by his girlfriend Georgina (a fitting reversal of the own violence he has previously meted out to women). But nonetheless, Self is alive and free from Amis's plots, as he asserts his own voice against that of Amis. Moreover, the linguistic blockage that characterizes Self's narrative – 'What happened out there ....? Ay, keep it away! Don't let it touch me. I can't give it headroom' (52) – disappears in this final section, as he reveals to us plot details that are earlier registered as gaps or blockages in his narrative.[11]

The novel links Self's individual revitalization with the possibility of social revitalization, as Self gains an insight into a potentially different future for society as a whole: '*If we all downed tools and joined hands for ten minutes and stopped believing in money, then money would no longer exist.*' Amis, ever the ironist, immediately undercuts this with the following line: '*We never will, of course*' (384). In this postmodern novel, the possibility of individual and social revitalization is partial, ironic, and under erasure, but it still remains. Gavin Keulks suggests a way of under-standing this unstable revitalization, arguing that Amis draws on the genre of Menippean satire, a dynamic form that inverts hierarchical distinctions and unleashes energies which destabilize moral and episte-mological frameworks, but which are 'phoenician and restorative', as Menippean satire destroys a character's wholeness and integrity, but reveals in him 'the possibilities of another man and another life' (153).[12] These possibilities are indicated in the novel's final paragraph, where Self is taken for a tramp, and receives a coin from a passer-by in his cap. Self has spent the novel recoiling from tramps, yet here the figure of the tramp suggests the possibility of a new life free from the demands of consumption. Self here receives money unexpectedly, rather than seek-ing it; it is significant that the money is in the form of a coin, a material object which contrasts with the unreal, simulacral forms of money (credit and cheques) he deals with earlier in the novel. Amis has spoken of the way he is drawn to people characterized by 'a lack of luck, con-spicuous disadvantage. I have a huge amount of sympathy for them: I think the plain are the real livers of life, the real receivers; they have great vividness. My feelings are always the opposite of dismissal of those people' (Haffenden 83). In light of these comments, Self's rebirth as a tramp can also be seen as the triumph of vividness over the simulacral, and of the man of feeling his father portrayed in Jim Dixon, reincar-nated for the 1980s.[13]

Trainspotting, the underclass, and subcultural rebellion

If *Money* captured the Zeitgeist of the 1980s, Irvine Welsh's *Trainspotting* (1993) did something similar for the 1990s, as the cult novel and film adaptation (1996, dir. Danny Boyle) were hugely successful worldwide. Andrew Spicer argues that its main character, Mark Renton, is an 'inverted Everyman' (194); as in other films of the 1990s, Renton is a representa-tive figure because of his social marginality rather than his typicality (188).[14] In both the film and the novel, the marginalized community of a group of unemployed Edinburgh drug users illustrates the effects of years of Thatcherism. These effects are both destructive and creative: for example, when the drug dealer Johnny Swan, who has lost his leg to drug-related gangrene, passes himself off as a Falkland's veteran, he is positioned both as a victim of Thatcher, but also as a parodic mirror-image of the Thatcherite entrepreneur. Yet the social marginality of Renton and his friends Sick Boy, Begbie, and Spud, is linked not just to their status as members of the underclass, but also to their subcultural affiliations. Renton and his friends exemplify the subcultural rebellion of Generation X, the generation who rejected conventional career structures and lifestyles, choosing in their place not the romantic rebellion of punk and the motorbike boys, nor the idealism of the hippies, but the ironic parody of consumer culture, as slackers worked at 'McJobs' and spending long hours watching MTV, where Nirvana's grunge anthem 'Smells Like Teen Spirit' referenced a well-known deodorant brand. The lifestyle of Renton and his friends reflects the anomie and boredom of this generation, as their drug taking similarly rejects and parodically mirrors mainstream consumer culture.

Like *Money*, *Trainspotting* also represents the feeling male body as both the symptom of cultural and social crisis and – to a limited extent – its cure. This crisis is linked to 'mainstream' consumer culture, as it was in *Money*. Renton's famous 'choose life' passage, adapted as iconic advertising in the film poster, describes the drug user's refusal of a life fuelled by consumption:

> Suppose that ah ken aw the pros and cons, know that ah'm gaunnae huv a short life, am ay sound mind etcetera, etcetera, but still want tae use smack? They won't let ye dae it.... Choose us. Choose life. Choose mortgage payments; choose washing machines; choose cars; choose sitting oan a couch watching mind-numbing and spirit-crushing game shows, stuffing fuckin junk food intae yir mooth. Choose rotting away, pishing and shiteing yersel in a home, a total fucking embarrassment tae the selfish, fucked-up brats ye've produced. Choose life.
>
> (187)

Consumption here is associated with the lack of true choice, with passivity and domesticity, with the loss of sensation ('mind-numbing and spirit-crushing game shows'), and with the breakdown of meaningful affective connections, leading to a lonely death in an institution. This passage suggests that the boredom, anomie, and physical degradation that many might associate with heroin addiction in fact lie at the heart of the 'mainstream'. The novel further suggests that mainstream consumption leads to death in a passage that juxtaposes the blaring sound of a television game show with Renton's father's discussion of HIV. The two voices blend together in Renton's head, woozy from rehab: *'first game's called "Shoot to Kill"* ... but it isnae an antomatic death sentence'

(194), as his stream-of consciousness interpretation of these voices links mainstream consumption with death and disease:

    AN AUTOMATIC DEATH SENTENCE DESTROY
    REHABILITATE
    FASCISM
    NICE WIFE
    NICE BAIRNS
    NICE HOOSE
    NICE JOAB
    NICE
    NICE TA SEE YA, TA SEE YA ....
    NICE NICE NICE

                                    BRAIN DISORDER (195)

Consumer culture also provides destructive representations of masculinity. Sick Boy is obsessed by Sean Connery as James Bond, using him as the model for his womanizing – he fantastizes '*I admire your rampant individualishm, Shimon. I shee parallelsh wish myshelf ash a young man*' (30) – while Begbie's tough, violent machismo is modelled on action heroes like Jean-Claude van Damme. With these references to film and television, the novel aligns hypermasculinity with the hyperreal; masculinity is a series of performances of performances. The novel is critical of such performances, as it is of the machismo associated with the army, exemplified by Renton's brother Billy; with Billy's friends, whose gambling cabal turns sour when one member escapes with the money and another's girlfriend; and with sectarian football fans – Stevie hears such fans singing with a desperate edge, and thinks: 'It was as if by singing loudly enough, they would weld themselves into a powerful brotherhood' (46). The novel suggests, in contrast, that traditional homosocial sites of bonding are both fragile and violent, far removed from any real sense of community.

In contrast, the heroin subculture to which Renton and his friends belong create a community which rejects both the hypermasculine activity and the numb passivity associated with mainstream consumer culture. The feeling, drug-taking body is associated with sensation and with the blurring of gender boundaries. Renton describes the effects of heroin in terms of physical intensity: 'When it came, ah savoured the hit.... Take your best fucking orgasm, multiply the feeling by twenty, and you're still fuckin miles of the pace' (11). Taking drugs allows for the expression of emotions that are otherwise censored, as Spud tells

Renton: 'It's jist thit ye git called aw the poofs under the sun if ye tell other guys how ye feel aboot them if yir no wrecked' (161). When they are shooting up together, the rivalry and antagonism between members of the group disappear: 'Sick Boy hugged Swanney tightly, then eased off, keeping his airms around him .... The adversaries ay a few minutes ago were now soul-mates' (10). As well as dissolving rivalries, the shooting-up ritual breaks down binary demarcations between masculine and feminine, and homosexual and heterosexual, as the penis becomes an organ of reception rather insertion. 'Ah shoot intae ma nob for the second consecutive day .... This is nice' (87). Both penetrated, and graphically expelling its fluids and waste, the male body in *Trainspotting* resembles David Savran's description of bodies in William Burroughs, another famous chronicler of drug-taking: 'the body-in-pieces is always porous, always ejecting or being penetrated by a myriad of tumescent objects and bodily fluids' (89). Not only do such bodies undermine the distinction between active inserter and passive receiver, but they also, as Savran argues, exaggerate and thereby parody the consumption process of the 'straight' world.

The heroin subculture marks the male bodies of users through track marks, bruises, or the loss of a gangrenous leg, just as the male characters are marked linguistically through pseudonyms and nicknames. This marking is both a sign of wounded working-class masculinity, rendering visible the class injuries inflicted by Thatcherism, and a way of marking out a subcultural identity. Whether through language or physicality, the male characters are defined against the mainstream – in contrast, as Robert Morace points out, the female characters have normal names and work or go to school or university (53). Indeed, the novel links language and the body by emphasizing the materiality of language in its transliteration of Scottish dialect, and in its typographic experimentation. Renton and his friends refuse to submit to the normalizing processes of society that attempt to control their bodies and to channel their search for pleasure into socially acceptable avenues. Throughout the novel, the excreting, grotesque body is used to expose the harsh realities glossed over by 'mainstream' culture, which hides pissing and shitting bodies in retirement homes, and as a riposte to southern middle-class English hegemony, most graphically when Kelly serves up menstrual blood and urine in her English customers' food.

Yet this subculture also shares the failings of mainstream culture, and in the end, it offers no real alternative to mainstream culture. It too is linked to death, as heroin is both a 'life-giving and life-taking elixir' (10), and the novel charts a series of graphic drug-related deaths, including those of Dawn, Tommy, and Venters. While shooting up might bring some release from hegemonic masculinity, this alternative form of consumption also mirrors the feminized passivity of consumer culture, generating feelings of impotence and anxiety. As they shoot up, Ali gasps 'that beats any fuckin cock in the world', which unnerves Renton 'tae the extent that ah feel ma ain genitals through ma troosers tae see if they're still thair' (9). The scene also reveals insecurities on the part of Johnny Swan, who fantasizes about going to Thailand 'whair the women knew how tae treat a gadge' (12), and on the part of Renton: 'Ah didnae really know much aboot women. Ah didnae really know much aboot women' (13). Inducing impotence and crippling users both literally and metaphorically, drug consumption ultimately shares in the problems associated with mainstream consumption, leading to passivity and the waning of sensation: the intense sensation of the high is always followed by depression, and the novel's episodic form reflects the pulsations and flow of this uneven affect.

The feeling body of the drug user therefore offers only limited possibilities for personal or social revitalization, and the novel turns instead to another model of the feeling male body: Renton as existentialist. One of the problems shared by both drug culture and consumer culture is, the novel suggests, their restriction of individual choice and freedom. The novel's representation of community is ambivalent. On the one hand, it mourns the loss of community, dissatisfied with a world where 'we are all acquaintances' (11) but not friends, but on the other hand, the novel represents groups – football teams, the army, the family, the users – as mechanisms of control and conformity that repress individual needs and desires. As *Trainspotting* proceeds, the emphasis is less on the sensation-driven feeling male drug users as a group, and more on Renton as an individual, who refuses attempts by counsellors and social workers to control and define him, and instead insists on the importance of subjective feeling as the basis for action. Here Renton looks to Kierkegaard, whose books he not only shoplifts but also reads. Kierkegaard offers Renton an ethics premised on the possibility of individual freedom and on the assertion of subjectivity rather than objectivity: for Kierkegaard, subjectivity is truth. Kierkegaard also links freedom with emotion and feeling, especially the feeling of angst; in Renton's paraphrase, 'genuine choice is made out of doubt and uncertainty' (165–66). One could argue that Renton's actions are a postmodern parody of Kierkegaardian ethics, which attempted to bring together the subjectivity of the aesthete with the religious follower's concern with morality. Instead, Renton tends to substitute the aesthetic for the ethical, and to flout social norms for hedonistic reasons rather than deep-held personal convictions. Nonetheless, the novel links this reworked form of existentialism with the possibility of revitalization. By the end of the novel, Renton decides he must leave the group, and he double-crosses them on a drug deal, before preparing to leave the country: 'Now, free from them all, for good, he would be what he wanted to be. He'd stand and fall alone. This thought both terrified and excited him as he contemplated life in Amsterdam' (344).

The novel therefore ends with the revitalization of the individual, 'terrified and excited', rather than of the nation or of other communities.[15] Renton's revitalization contrasts with the dead-end future he associates with Scotland and with Britain: 'Fuckin failures in a country ay failures' (78). Renton, no longer impotent and passive, is transformed into an active subject, and the shift of the narrative voice to the third person and to Standard English emphasizes the change that has occurred in him. *Trainspotting* asserts individuality as the only possible escape from mindless conformity, even if it ironically mirrors aspects of 'mainstream' individualism, and even if the novel ironizes the possibility of escape. Not only is Renton off to Amsterdam, hardly the most auspicious start to his new life, but in stealing from his friends he becomes a heartless entrepreneur. The similarities between Renton and mainstream entrepreneurs are emphasized in the film version, in which his escape with the money is dubbed over with the 'Choose life' riff. Here Sarah Thornton's arguments about subcultures are relevant. Thornton draws on Bourdieu to argue that subcultures operate according to the logic of what she describes as 'subcultural capital,' in which distinctions are constantly being made on the basis of taste. The emphasis on difference that characterizes the postindustrial world is also found in the world of subcultures, which ironically mirror the logic of distinction and status they critique in its mainstream form (which, Thornton also argues, is consistently gendered as feminine, even by female members of subcultures). According to this argument, Renton's desire for individuality, whether as a part of a subculture, or as the existentialist man alone, is as much a product of late capitalism as the conformity he resists. However, the novel asserts Renton's escape as a moment of rupture that will break the cycle of the monotonous routine of mainstream consumer culture and of the drug subculture, which are compared to the pointlessly repetitive activity of trainspotting. Renton's escape is parodic and ironized, but it nonetheless holds out the possibility of individual renewal associated with the feeling male body.

Affect and bricolage in *The Full Monty*

The Full Monty (1997) is, of all the films and novels I have discussed, the most self-conscious about its preoccupation with masculinity. It tells the story of a group of unemployed steelworkers from Sheffield who, following the closure of their factory, turn to stripping as a way of earning extra cash. As strippers, the men are placed in a potentially feminized position, and even they themselves refer to the professional strippers whose example has inspired them, the Chippendales, as 'poofs'. As many critics have noticed, the film self-consciously interrogates and reverses the male gaze, as Gaz and Dave move from rating the attractiveness of passing women, or commenting on the size of the tits in a girlie magazine, to themselves being the object of scrutiny in front of a female audience. Clare Monk suggests that *The Full Monty*'s preoccupation with men and masculinity is new and distinctive in 'its self-conciousness, its confessional and therapeutic impulses (its admission of male neediness and pain) and its attentiveness to men and masculinity as subjects-in-themselves' (157). We are certainly a long way here from the taken for granted, vigorous masculinity of Arthur Seaton or Joe Lampton, and yet there is a clear line of continuity between the 1950s films and texts that focused on the feeling male body and this film. The film shares with many of the texts discussed thus far three familiar concerns: it is centred on the feeling male body; it registers anxieties about the relationship between masculinity and consumption; and it turns apparent weakness – emotional and physical vulnerability – into a means of revitalization, both of the individual and of the community.

The Full Monty's opening scenes set up an implicit comparison between Dave and Gaz, the two central characters, and the scrap metal they are trying to salvage from the empty steelworks as a way of earning some money. Their plans go awry when the girders they take sink into the river, rather than providing them with a bridge to the other side, a phallic symbol gone wrong, rendered as uselessly impotent as the men themselves. Gaz and Dave flail about in the river while Gaz's son Nathan stands safely on the bank, the sense of separation between two generations of males emphasized by the use of shot-reverse shot. Gaz later makes the message of this scene explicit: 'We're scrap, we're obsolete, we're dinosaurs'. As Judith Halberstam points out, throughout the film steel is 'a metaphor for past models of masculinity' (437). Importantly, the opening scenes connect the men not only with lifeless, obsolete, scrap metal, but also with emotional impassivity: as a passer-by inquires whether the two stranded men are 'all right', Gaz replies, 'Not so bad'; as Dave points out, 'That's not much of a chuffing S.O.S'.

The film therefore links the failure to be emotionally open with the men's economic and social crisis. As a corollary, however, it suggests that their crisis can be resolved through emotional expressiveness, which becomes the means of creating new social and homosocial bonds. Throughout the film, the expression of emotion is associated with life and vitality, and with the refusal to accept the status quo. For example, one of the film's central concerns is the relationship between Gaz and Nathan, an affective bond that is threatened by Gaz's ex-wife, who threatens to stop contact between the two after Gaz falls behind in his child support payments. We see a close-up of actor Robert Carlyle's face working, on the verge of tears, as Gaz protests to his ex-wife 'it's all wrong'. Gaz's position is threatened by his ex-wife's new husband, who is clearly middle class, as well as smarmy and impassive; Gaz cries that the 'triple bloody glazing' of their suburban house blocks his impas-sioned appeals to Nathan. But Gaz eventually cements his bond with Nathan in a moment of reconciliation after Nathan walks off in disgust at his father's stripping. Gaz tells him, teary-eyed: 'I'm your Dad ... I like you. I love you, you bugger', and the two hug. In the triangulated rela-tionship between Gaz, his ex-wife's new husband, and Nathan, class antagonism is mapped out in terms of affect, as Gaz's emotional open-ness and intensity contrast with middle-class impassive masculinity; symptomatically, the new husband is the only character absent from the final stripping scene, which otherwise brings the community together.

Class antagonism is also registered as an affective antagonism in the initial relationship between Gerald, the lower-middle-class ex-foreman, and his former employees. This antagonism is played out as Gaz, Dave, and Lomper distract Gerald during a job interview by parading his gar-den gnomes in front of the window. Gerald subsequently explodes, exhibiting not just anger but also tears as he explains to the men that his wife thinks he is still employed. Dave and Gaz's regret is shown through close-ups of their faces as they too are brought close to tears. This emotional scene brings the men together, and Gerald subsequent-ly becomes the chief choreographer as well as a participant in the strip-show. Affect therefore has the capacity to resolve and transcend class distinctions, uniting the former foreman and former labourers.

Affect is communicated in the film not just through face and voice, but also through music. Throughout the film, music is the basis for communal affective bonds, from the Donna Summers song playing in the dole queue which provides the basis for an unconscious rehearsal of dance moves on the part of the men, as they are linked by shared bodily action, to the brass band playing at Lomper's mother's funeral. The band is a recurring trope, first appearing as they practice in the deserted factory in what might be seen as both a lament and an act of defiance. The factory may have closed, but working-class culture and affectivity persist in the form of the all-male band. This older, traditional form of affectivity provides a link to the new form of affectivity embodied in the male strippers, thereby emphasizing the continuities between traditional working-class masculinity and the new masculinity being worked out in a postindustrial epoch. The links are emphasized through Lomper, who plays in the band as well as being a stripper, and through the fact that both brass band and strippers practice in the old factory. When, in the film's final scene, the brass band accompany the strippers, an affective link is established between the past and the present, as the band play the 1960s soul music that the strippers favour (which itself could be seen as an attempt to hook into authenticity and the suffering associated with this genre, and with black affect more broadly).

Emotion and emotional expression form the basis for new bonds between men in the first instance. But the film suggests that emotional openness is also the precondition for successful relationships between men and women, and for communities that unite men and women.[16] Gerald eventually has to tell his wife that he has lost his job; but it is his failure to be open with her over the preceding six months that wounds her more than the loss of the job. Dave, struggling with intense vulnerability about his body, also finally tells Jean about the stripping plan; far from rejecting him, she is delighted, and her encouragement spurs him on to participate in the show. The display of the men's naked bodies is thus paralleled by their increasing ability to be open and honest about their feelings, and it is this emotional as well as physical 'full monty' that enables the final scene of social reconciliation, where men and women are brought together into the former working-men's club to watch the strippers. Moreover, the film does not just represent emotion, but encourages an emotional response from the audience. It juxtaposes emotional registers, following humour with pathos, as when Dave's earlier rejection of a slimming plan based on clingfilm – 'I'm not a chicken drumstick' – is later followed by a moving scene in which he sits alone in the garden shed, wrapped in film, eating a chocolate bar, the pathos emphasized by non-diegetic music as the film's theme plays in a rueful minor key. By appealing to its viewers' emotions, the film interpellates us as part of the inclusive affective community it represents on screen.

The Full Monty displays the plight of working-class men in a postindustrial era in which old manual skills are no longer needed, and even the industries remaining are feminized – such as the clothing factory in which Gaz's ex-wife is an overseer. Production has been replaced by consumption, as Dave's only opportunity for work is in a supermarket rather than a factory. Masculine inadequacy is indicated by men's exclusion from the sphere of consumption as well as the sphere of production. Gaz looks anguished when he tells Nathan he cannot afford a ticket to watch Manchester United. When Gaz, Nathan, and Dave go to the supermarket to try and buy a copy of *Flashdance*, they discover they have a grand total of twenty-seven pence in cash, and their abjection in the supermarket contrasts with Jean's confidence, as she laughs and jokes with a fellow (male) employee. Gerald's sense of failure is amplified when the bailiffs come to repossess his television and home gym equipment.

Yet it is unconvincing to suggest, as Moya Luckett does, that the film represents consumption as corrupt and linked with 'the inauthenticity of female culture' (95). Rather, it distinguishes between two different kinds of consumption, one that is associated with passivity, regulation, restriction, and surveillance, and another that is associated with activity, flow, libidinal pleasure and freedom, and with the feeling male body. If the first form of consumption is feminized, the latter form is connected to the revitalization of masculinity that occurs throughout the film. Part of the men's triumph at the end of the film lies in the way in which they have been able to forge a new relationship to the sphere of consumption, establishing themselves as renegade entrepreneurs in the sphere of the entertainment industry.

The first form of consumption is associated with the recurring image of the security guard. Dave chooses unemployment rather than a job as a security guard at the supermarket, and when he finally takes up the job, it is a sign of his plummeting self-esteem and lack of self-confidence. The task of a supermarket security guard is to regulate and police consumers, just as Lomper's task as a security guard involves policing and guarding the empty factory. Security guards are agents of restriction and enclosure, as when Lomper (unwittingly) locks Dave and Gary into the factory at the beginning of the film.[17] However, the men are able to subvert the factory's security equipment, turning it from a means of surveillance and restriction into technology of leisure and pleasure. They use the bank of security cameras to watch *Flashdance*, and the sound system to play music as they practice their stripping. The same thing happens when the security tape is brought in as evidence after the police find the men practicing and arrest them for indecent exposure.

The police and the men are united as they start to critique the performance caught on tape, and the tape becomes an aesthetic object associated with pleasure rather than a means of social control.

In these examples the men escape the surveillance and restriction
associated with one kind of consumption. Another kind of consumption, associated with freedom and pleasure, is illustrated when the men
engage in more and less legal forms of entrepreneurial activity. The film
suggests that consumer goods acquired through rule-breaking, daring,
entrepreneurial acts, and associated with pleasure and freedom, are
compatible with masculinity. At the beginning of the film Gaz and Dave
are 'liberating' girders in order to sell them and earn money. Later, Gaz
encourages Dave to shoplift the copy of *Flashdance*, and himself goads
Dave (in his role as security guard) into chasing him out of the shop by
flagrantly taking two jackets. In these acts of bricolage, the men practice
a different kind of consumption, associated with the freedom of the
body, which is expressed in the way in which they run out of the shop,
setting off alarms, as well as in the goods they take, which enable them
to become strippers. The men parody and rework the figure of the
Thatcherite entrepreneur, most notably in their entrepreneurial strip-
show itself, in which they enter the marketplace and provide services
for consumers and are simultaneously remasculinized. Significantly, in
the show the men are dressed in the costumes of security guards, and
they parody this role as they take off their clothes, thereby transforming the costumes from signs of control and surveillance to signs of libidinal pleasure. In the strip show the gaze of the security guard is reversed,
as the men are watched rather than watching, and as watching itself is
transformed from an act of control and policing to an act of pleasure.
The strip show therefore reconciles consumer goods and the marketplace with the pleasures of the body and with masculinity, rather than
showing consumption as antithetical to freedom. As Roger Bromley
points out, the men are 'defined through their "commodifiable" bodies'
(66), but I argue that this is a means to their revitalization rather than a
symbol of decline.

The strip show also reconciles vulnerability and strength. Critics have
variously interpreted the film as attempting to reinstate a lost male
camaraderie and to recuperate a lost sense of working-class masculinity
(Monk), or as mourning the passing of this masculinity, when Luckett
argues that the skinny body of Robert Carlyle, in contrast with Arthur
Finney's muscles, 'articulates a loss of authenticity and the demise of
a social order' (95). I argue instead that the bodies of the strippers in
The Full Monty both mark a lack or wound – the demise of traditional

working-class masculinity associated with manual labour – but also, through their very vulnerability, help to constitute a new, revitalized masculinity, which differs significantly from traditional working-class masculinity. The men's emotional vulnerability and openness is mapped onto their physical vulnerability, and vice versa. Their sense of unworthiness because of their lack of employment is mirrored by, and increasingly supplanted by, their insecurity about their bodies. Dave is convinced he is a 'fat bastard'; Lomper is self-conscious about his 'saggy tits'; Horse invests in a penis-inflater; while Gerald is terrified of an involuntary erection on stage. And yet their weakness and vulnerability also enables a sort of empowerment. When the men undress to their underpants for the first time in Gerald's living room, many of their physical anxieties come to the fore. But this scene is also the moment where the bailiffs, who arrive to repossess Gerald's television, turn tail and leave when they are confronted with the sight of the naked men. Rather than a weakness, nakedness therefore becomes a sign of strength. However, the paradoxical relationship between vulnerability and empowerment, and weakness and strength, is best shown in the final stripping scene, where the men decide to do the 'full monty'. The difficulty here lies in how to interpret the display of the naked male body and of the penis (which is displayed to the audience in the working-men's club rather than to the viewer).[18] Do the men here illustrate what Susan Faludi has called 'ornamental masculinity', and submit themselves to being objectified by a female gaze? Or do they assert the power of the phallus? I argue that the naked bodies are simultaneously a display of vulnerability and an assertion of strength. It is through opening themselves up to vulnerability, a potentially masochistic act, that the men are affirmed; for example, when Dave confesses his vulnerability about his body and says to Jean 'Who wants to see this dance', she replies 'I do'.

The vulnerable male body brings about not just the re-empowerment of the individual, but also the reconciliation of the community, as the space of the working-men's club, previously taken over by a women-only audience when the Chippendales visit, becomes finally the place where men and women meet together to affirm the strippers, responding with appreciative laughter rather than salacious arousal or hooting derision. In bringing together the community, these renegade entrepreneurs use feeling to heal the wounds of Thatcherism, both the wounds inflicted to working-class masculinity and to the notion of 'society'. Feeling, vulnerable male bodies are both the symptom of a broader social crisis, and its cure. Cora Kaplan argues that the 'men of feeling' in

The Full Monty use an affective register to express class, and react against a New Labour government which has tried to excise both affect and class in its neoliberal description of contemporary society. In contrast, however, I would point out that the cross-class nature of the strippers is important, and that this complicates the link Kaplan draws between affect and class. Male affect may recall older working-class masculinity, but here it transcends class barriers and heals class antagonisms. The group brings together black and white, gay and straight, middle class and working class, as masculinity trumps other identity categories, albeit a new form of masculinity 'welded together from a collectivity of minority masculinities' (Halberstam 440). In this fantasmatic, magical narrative, wounded masculinity makes a divided community whole again.[19]

In the trajectory traced in this chapter, the feeling male body becomes increasingly postmodern – fragmented, unstable, and in pieces. The feeling male body is always liminal and implicitly unstable, as it is associated with class transition with an ambivalent attitude to consumption, and with crisis and renewal. But by the late twentieth century, the feeling male body's instability is emphasized to the extent that the very categories of 'male' and 'body' start to come undone in spectacular ways. We see this in the contrast between Willis – who celebrates masculinity and corporeality – and Hebdige – where the feeling male body is linked to androgyny, and to the notion of the body as a text. *Money*, *Trainspotting*, and *The Full Monty* further undo these categories by blurring the boundaries between the inside and outside of the body, and between feminine bodies and masculine bodies, just as they complicate the distinction between dominant culture and subculture on which Willis and Hebdige rely.

Yet the unstable, grotesque, vulnerable male body of the late twentieth century is still invested with the potential for escape, resistance, or renewal, however complicit, parodic, or ironic. Despite their differences, all the texts in this chapter depict the feeling male body as oppositional – even if the opposition it mounts to mainstream society or the dominant culture is tentative or failed. John Self's pain signals his body's rejection of the solipsistic greed of the 1980s; Mark Renton's parody of Kierkegaardian ethics rejects mainstream society's definition of choice; the strippers in *The Full Monty* reject individualism and social fragmentation. The feeling male body romanticized and celebrated by Paul Willis is still present, but as a trace: *Money*, *Trainspotting*, and *The Full Monty* invoke the disruptive or recuperative force of this body wistfully or ironically, its oppositional force undercut yet simultaneously lingering on.

6
Conclusion: In Search of the Real

The feeling male bodies in *Money*, *Trainspotting*, and *The Full Monty* are radically unstable, blurring the boundaries between inside and outside, between complicity with and resistance to consumer culture, and between femininity and masculinity. Their instability makes visible – in spectacular, often grotesque fashion – the volatility of the feeling male body throughout postwar cultural criticism and literature: volatile because it is both the symptom of cultural crisis and its cure. The feeling male body is linked to the emergence of postmodernity, with the shift from national economies based on production to transnational consumer economies, and the breakdown of stable identity categories: it embodies the new order's possibilities, yet also registers its deleterious effects through bodily and emotional pain. The writing and cultural criticism of the 1950s is Janus-faced, welcoming the new order while mourning the passing of an older order. Feeling, sensation, and immediacy are frequently linked to the possibilities of social change opened up in the modern world, yet they are also associated with the reconciliation of a fragmented community, and with the revitalization of the authentic individual. The feeling male body of New Left cultural criticism and angry writing is connected with fragmentation, disruption, and the breakdown of the self, but also – and often simultaneously – with wholeness, reconciliation, and the assertion of the authentic self. The protagonists of 'angry' texts are feminized in many respects – relatively powerless and victimized – although this feminization becomes a means to re-establish masculine power. The feeling male body is therefore a precarious and unsteady trope, although it is frequently used to mark out a putatively stable category, such as the affective elite, authenticity, or vital masculinity.

The trope's volatility and ambiguity helps to explain how and why it was taken up and reworked by women writers in the 1950s and early 1960s. Writers such as Banks, Delaney, and Lessing also represent the feeling body as the site that registers social wounds, and – especially in the case of Banks and Lessing – as the site of the potential renewal of the individual or of society. The feeling bodies of the female protagonists in these texts occupy transitional or liminal positions in society, like their male counterparts. In detaching feeling from masculinity, however, these writers explore the way in which emotion and affect are linked to social reproduction, as well as opening up means to question social norms. Yet as I have shown, these texts failed to have the cultural impact of angry writing, as influential critics and film-makers were fascinated by the masculinity of the feeling male body in angry novels and plays, which they in turn romanticized.

Why then is the feeling *male* body such a key figure in postwar British culture? This book has argued that it both expresses and assuages a range of anxieties about class and consumption in postwar Britain. The 1950s is an important transitional moment when the feeling male body invokes the iconography of working-class masculinity, yet is simultaneously detached from any stable class position. Instead, the feeling male body is synonymous with class transition and instability, whether such transition is the change in the lived experience of working-class life – as we see in New Left criticism and in Sillitoe's writing – or the social mobility of Jim Dixon, Jimmy Porter, or Joe Lampton. Throughout New Left criticism, angry literature, and New Wave films, as well as in more recent cultural criticism and literature, masculinity based on style – the style of the feeling male body – both expresses and displaces class identity. I have also argued that masculinity provided a way of managing and defusing the potential threat of consumer culture. While consumer culture is at times treated with suspicion, it is also linked to the assertion of male power: *Saturday Night and Sunday Morning* and *Room at the Top* suggest that sharp suits help to display and enhance the male body's power, and Sillitoe's novel uses images of flow and release to link the potent male body with the consumption of alcohol. In *Money* and *Trainspotting*, consumer culture is resisted in complicitous fashion through the excessive, parodic consumption of the male bodies of Mark Renton and John Self. Like *The Full Monty*, these texts imagine a masculinized form of consumption, associated with the libidinal flows of the body, which counters and parodies the potentially feminizing effects of consumer culture.

Yet we can also look outside of a specific national context to help explain the centrality of the feeling male body in postwar Britain. This story about a particular time and place – Britain in the 1950s and early 1960s – is connected to a broader narrative about white masculinity in crisis, analysed in a postwar American context, and in skeptical fashion, by David Savran and Sally Robinson. I have argued that class complicates the argument that representations of white masculinity in crisis respond to the loss of male power during this period. The expression of powerlessness and vulnerability that we see in angry texts is not simply the disavowal of white male privilege, but also the expression of the relative powerlessness and marginality of the (implicitly) working-class or lower-middle-class protagonist which, in being mapped onto the vulnerable male body, is symbolically assuaged when this body is renewed and revitalized. In other words, the case studies in this book suggest that the rhetoric of 'masculinity in crisis' risks covering up and hypostasizing the complex ways in which masculinity is inflected by class, as well as by the more commonly recognized categories of race and sexuality. Nonetheless, the postwar fascination with masculinity – a fascination this book participates in as well as analyses – must be seen as part of a broader cultural attempt to understand the relationship between masculinity and power in the contemporary world.

Finally, we can understand the fascination with the feeling body – if not with masculinity – in the context of a broader fascination with the real. In all the texts I have discussed, the distinction between the natural and the performative breaks down, even when it is asserted. Similarly, although the realism of angry texts presents linguistic style as the transparent expression of the body's underlying energies, this anti-style is always haunted by and attracted to the destabilizing energies of performance and of figural language. Even in realist texts, the desire for authenticity and transparency is complicated by metaphor and performance. This tension between the desire for the real and the fear of its disappearance marks the postwar period more broadly. Postmodernity has long been identified with representation, mediation, and simulacra; more recently, however, critics have suggested that the second half of the twentieth century is also characterized by a concern with the body, affect, and the real. We are fascinated by the real and the immediate at the same time as the real seems to have disappeared. This description or understanding of postmodernity challenges Jameson's more famous description of postmodernism as the 'waning of affect' (10). First, it characterizes postmodern aesthetics: in *The Return of the Real*, Hal

Foster argues that the art world of the 1990s was dominated not just by mediated self-referentiality, but also by the resurgence of the abject body, which Foster identifies as a shift from 'reality as the effect of representation to the real as a thing of trauma' (Foster 146). Second, this description of postmodernity – as it emerges in the work of critics from Mark Seltzer to Slavoj Žižek – forms part of a broader account of theoretical and cultural concerns in the second part of the twentieth century. Seltzer suggests that late twentieth-century America is a 'wound culture', in which 'the very notion of sociality is bound to the excitations of the torn and opened body, the torn and exposed individual, as public spectacle' (3). The fascination with the wound, he argues, is also a fascination with the site where the line between the public and the private, and between the collective and the individual, becomes murky and unclear. Moreover, Seltzer argues that the wound is the switchpoint between the real and the virtual, or the event and the representation, illustrated in the anxiety around 'copycat' violence sparked off by media representations. Like Foster, Seltzer points to the continuing concern with affect and materiality in the era of mediation, rather than suggesting that the former has replaced the latter. Working within a very different theoretical framework from Seltzer, Slavoj Žižek nonetheless also challenges an account of postmodern culture in which the real and the material are assumed to have been replaced by the simulacral and the hyperreal. Žižek argues that postmodern culture is instead marked by the constant desire for the Real, understood in Lacanian terms as the realm of flux and disorder outside the Symbolic order. He reads the desire for such a Real in phenomena ranging from self-cutting to the paranoia of a film like *The Truman Show*, arguing that such paranoia is based on the desire for the Real that exists beyond the Symbolic order (or Big Other, in Žižek's terms), an order which no longer explains the world as once it used to. More generally, Žižek argues that the Real appears in postmodern film and literature as a stain or a disruption of the normal order of things: it is 'a detail which "sticks out" from the frame of symbolic reality' (236).

This narrative about postmodernism provides a way to understand the British concern with the feeling body from the 1950s to the 1990s as a symptom of the desire for the real and the immediate, and in the context of a broader cultural fascination with affect and with the body as means of both evoking and problematizing the real. This claim might seem counter-intuitive because British postmodernism is usually defined aesthetically, and identified with the experimental style of writers like John Fowles, J. G. Ballard, and Angela Carter. Yet if we understand postmodernity as an epoch, rather than simply in terms of aesthetic style, an analysis of the relationship between postmodernity and the desire for the real also helps explain the emergence of the 1950s feeling body, as well as the later manifestations of the feeling body in more obviously postmodern writers such as Doris Lessing, Martin Amis, and Irvine Welsh. Here it is worth remembering that British visual art of the 1950s encompasses Francis Bacon's bloody, wounded bodies as well as Richard Hamilton's early postmodern pastiche 'Just What Is It That Makes Today's Homes So Different, So Appealing?' (1956). The fascination with the feeling male body may ultimately therefore lie in the way it both indicates and putatively reverses the loss of the real, expressing the fear that the immediate and the authentic have disappeared, while simultaneously offering the fantasy of access to these qualities.

Notes

Introduction: The Feeling Male Body

1. The letter is dated 11 August 1952. 'I think perhaps the title had better be changed into *The man of feeling*; D. has more to feel about than he had before ...' (*Letters* 289).
2. Janet Todd explains that the novel of sentiment – understood as thought influenced by emotion – characterized the 1740s and 1750s, but thAat in the 1760s and 1770s the novel of sensibility concentrated on pure feeling. See Todd for a helpful discussion of the figure of the Man of Feeling in the novel of sensibility.
3. Eliot uses the term in his 1921 essay 'The Metaphysical Poets'. It is worth noting another influence on the modernist conception of feeling: Henri Bergson, a key influence, saw a form of feeling, 'élan vital', as the driving motor of evolution.
4. I discuss these changes in more detail in Chapters 1 and 2.
5. These superheroes with alter egos, such as Batman, were invented during the late 1930s, but their popularity in comics and television programmes was a postwar phenomenon.
6. Michael Davidson argues that Beat poets saw language as sacramental and physical, and therefore poetry was – like sex – the expression of emotion in physical terms (*San Francisco*).
7. Recent work on affect and emotion includes Brian Massumi, *Parables for the Virtual: Movement, Affect, Sensation* (Durham, NC: Duke UP, 2002); Eve Sedgwick, *Touching Feeling: Affect, Performativity, Pedagogy* (Durham, NC: Duke UP, 2003); Rei Terada, *Feeling in Theory: Emotion After the Death of the Subject* (Cambridge, MA: Harvard UP, 2003); Sara Ahmed, *The Cultural Politics of Emotion* (London: Routledge, 2004); Teresa Brennan, *The Transmission of Affect* (Ithaca: Cornell UP, 2004); Sianne Ngai, *Ugly Feelings* (Cambridge, MA: Harvard UP, 2005); Elspeth Probyn, *Blush: The Faces of Shame* (Minneapolis: U of Minnesota P, 2005); and Denise Riley, *Impersonal Passions: Language as Affect* (Durham, NC: Duke UP, 2005).
8. In 'The Quest for Primary Motives' Tomkins criticizes Shachter's theory of emotions in which cognition controlled emotion, on the grounds that it: 'offered a neurophysiologically respectable id, tamed and led by the cognitive soul, in the Platonic image of horse and rider' (Tomkins 37).
9. See here the work of historian Peter Stearns, who argues that America in the early to mid-twentieth century was characterized by the dampening of emotion, which he suggests stems from the needs of a retooled service sector economy; and of Arlie Russell Hochschild, who analyses the desire of this service sector to manage and control affect (the smiling air-hostess) in her classic work of sociology *The Managed Heart*.

1 From Dream Boy to Scholarship Boy: The New Left, Richard Hoggart, and Raymond Williams

1. Thompson and other members of the board of the *New Reasoner* resigned from the British Communist party after it had failed either to denounce the invasion of Hungary, or to adequately address Khrushchev's 1956 speech acknowledging the extent of Stalin's terror (Dworkin 45–46).
2. Stuart Hall resigned as editor in 1961, at which stage a collective took over the editorial role until Perry Anderson bought the journal in 1963, bailing it out after financial problems.
3. It also had close links with the Campaign for Nuclear Disarmament (CND), founded in 1958 by dissident intellectuals and political activists including Bertrand Russell and Michael Foot.
4. This description can be found in an advertisement for a public meeting in ULR 1 (1957), p. 3. The editorial team of *ULR* moved from Oxford to London in 1958, buoyed by the success of its initial issues, including the first issue which sold 8000 copies after an initial run of only 2000 (Chun 14).
5. Thompson was on the board of the *New Reasoner*; Williams contributed to *ULR* and was subsequently on the board of *New Left Review*; Hoggart's work was eagerly discussed in the pages of *ULR*, and he subsequently founded the Centre for Contemporary Cultural Studies at the University of Birmingham, along with Stuart Hall.
6. The welfare state was recommended by the Beveridge report of 1942, implemented under the Labour government that came to power in 1945 led by Attlee, and continued after 1951 by the Tory government, under Churchill, Eden, and Macmillan. The apparent political consensus produced by the crisis of war was translated into postwar policy agreements between the Labour and Tory parties about the desirability of redistributing the country's resources and improving overall standards of living: namely, making sure that everyone had free access to health care, education, and superannuation. This consensus (named 'Butskellism' after Tory chancellor R. A. B. Butler and Labour chancellor Hugh Gaitskell) preserved the results of Labour reforms, such as the National Health Service, universal national insurance, universal secondary education, and the nationalization of key sectors of the industrial infrastructure. See Chapter 2 for a more detailed discussion of the impact of postwar educational policy, including the Butler Education Act.
7. McKibbin also describes the way in which the middle class changed from being a class of landowners and employers before World War I to a class of homeowners and employees after the War (67–68).
8. Esty distinguishes between 'British' universalism and 'English' particularism (21).
9. In this respect, my argument is similar to Sally Robinson's description of the marking and visibility of white masculinity in postwar American culture. However, while Robinson suggests such bodies are invariably middle class, I argue that the feeling male body both expresses and displaces class identity including working-class identity. See Chapter 3 for a further discussion of Robinson's argument and my departure from her conclusions.

10. Francis essay is from *Moments of Modernity*, a volume that uses the terms modernity, postmodernity, and late modernity interchangeably. See Alan O'Shea, 'English Subjects of Modernity' in Mica Nava and Alan O'Shea (eds), *Modern Times: Reflections on a Century of English Modernity* (London: Routledge, 1996), pp. 7–37, for a further elaboration of the argument that postwar modernity – in this broad sense – was associated with immediacy and sensation. In fact, some of the evidence Francis uses to illustrate Labour's earlier restraint suggests that what was at stake was in fact styles of expression, rather than the value of emotion. Hugh Gaitskell, for example, was praised by a contemporary for the way in which his 'unadorned rational argument ... produced a more emotional conviction than rhetoric could ever achieve' (cit. 162), suggesting that the Labour government sought to marry working-class emotionality with middle-class restraint. As in the realm of literature, a pared-down style that rejected overt performance was linked to emotional authenticity.

11. Hoggart had to refer to an imaginary gangster novel whose quotations he himself wrote, for fear of legal action if he had quoted an actual novel.

12. Siegfried Kracauer, 'The Mass Ornament'. See Petro for a helpful discussion of the gendering of mass culture in Kracauer and other Frankfurt School critics.

13. However, the Partisan Coffee House (initially called the *ULR* Coffee House) distanced itself from fashion by describing itself as an 'Anti-Espresso Bar' (Ellis 240), illustrating the New Left's complicated relationship to modern culture. Alongside fashionable coffee drinks, the menu of the coffee house evinced a distinct nostalgia for a passing way of life, a nostalgia that was mobilized as a critique against the alienation and superficiality of modernity. The Partisan coffee house served Surrey fowl, Breconshire mutton, Whitechapel cheesecake, Yorkshire Ham, frankfurters, and borscht – a rather odd combination of the traditional English and the heartily Eastern European, implying a return to an organic English community alongside utopian notions of the socialist community to come in Eastern Europe (*ULR* 5: 66). In any case, the menu options lacked the fashionable and 'modern' cachet of the Mediterranean food which writers like Elizabeth David were then popularizing.

14. For important analyses of the role of masculinity in Beat writing, see David Savran (especially pp. 41–103) and Michael Davidson, *Guys Like Us*. Beat writing also emphasizes the masculine body and feeling, although there are differences between the American Beats, and the British New Left and Angry Young Men, as I briefly discuss in the Introduction.

15. See Higgins for a detailed account of the evolution of the term in Williams's work.

16. Eagleton, for example, asserts 'What this concept designates, in effect, is ideology' (*Criticism* 33)

17. Williams's understanding of experience as an unmediated category offering more or less direct access to the world was of course heavily criticised in the wake of structuralism and post-structuralism, which emphasized instead the mediating structures of language and ideology as themselves constitutive of experience. See Terry Eagleton's *Criticism and Ideology* (1976) for the best-known attack on this aspect of Williams's work. Further criticism is found in Joan W. Scott. See also David Simpson's insightful discussion of the relationship between ideology and structure of feeling.

18. Jane Miller argues that throughout the novel Williams associates women with mysterious and animal qualities which 'puts them outside the community's everyday values and, more importantly still, beyond the deep moral and political convictions, and the stamina and endurance, available to their husbands as part of those everyday values' (56–57).
19. Eagleton notes that Williams's next novel, *Second Generation* (1964), also begins and ends with images of 'the *essential* oneness of what it has shown to be a fissured, fractured society' (*Criticism* 30).
20. F. R. Leavis, 'Joyce and the Revolution of the Word', *Scrutiny* 2.2 (September 1933), p. 199. Leavis himself is quoting the philologist Logan Pearsall Smith.
21. In 'Components of the National Culture' Perry Anderson claims that the field of cultural criticism pioneered by Leavis in the 1930s, and associated with the journal *Scrutiny*, offered the only real example of engaged analysis of contemporary society in the university, so that literary studies was somewhat paradoxically the most obvious avenue for intellectuals wanting to study society.
22. Williams makes this claim in *Politics and Letters*, p. 78.
23. They take the term 'moral realism' from E. P. Thompson, who applies it to the work of William Morris.

2 Affect and Politics in *Lucky Jim* and *Look Back in Anger*

1. The 1944 Butler Education Act was introduced by the Conservative R. A. Butler, the minister of education in Churchill's coalition government; it brought in universal secondary education up to the age of 15, and abolished fees in state schools. Waugh was basing his description here on John Wain and Kingsley Amis, both in fact born before the war and therefore too old in fact to have benefited from the Butler Education Act.
2. In his review, Maugham actually conflates Jim's actions with the sneaking behaviour of one of Jim's enemies, Johns.
3. See Osborne, 'They Call it Cricket'.
4. This foreword is in the 1956 edition of the play, published by Samuel French. I have been unable to find a copy of this edition of the play; the quotation I use was included in the programme for the 1999 National Theatre production.
5. Osborne attended public school, though he was expelled; Braine was of lower-middle-class origin, and had not gone to university (Hewison, *In Anger* 135); and Sillitoe was working class, working in a factory, before writing full-time on his disability benefit after the war (Laing, *Representations* 66).
6. With the concept of habitus, Bourdieu suggests that bodily categories such as taste and deportment bypass the cognitive and the discursive, but that nonetheless, our unconscious, instinctive bodily behaviour displays the way in which social categories such as class and gender are ingrained on us all – from the way a teacup is held to the way in which legs are crossed. Here the body does not *represent* class – for that would imply that class exists entirely elsewhere, outside the body; instead, the body is one of the ways in which class is produced and reinforced.
7. See the previous chapter for a fuller discussion of Leavis's position.
8. His taste for jazz also, as Sinfield points out, 'helps to define an oppositional identity' (263).

9. T. C. Worsley in the *New Statesman*. This model of the individual pitted against a phoney, inauthentic world has resonances with other 1950s novels from America and France – from J. D. Salinger's *Catcher in the Rye* (1951) to Françoise Sagan's *Bonjour Tristesse* (1954) to Jack Kerouac's *On The Road* (1957). The concern with authenticity also shows the influence of existentialism, which can be seen most obviously in Britain in the work of Colin Wilson (whose 1956 book *The Outsider* quoted liberally from Sartre, Camus, and Heidegger) and in the novels of Iris Murdoch, who published an early English study of Sartre, *Sartre: Romantic Rationalist* (1953). In his 1991 autobiography *Almost a Gentleman*, John Osborne described how he had sniffed at those wanting 'a dollop of the gynaecological metaphysic of Simone de Beauvoir, a trilogy from Sartre, and a slice of melodrama from Camus' (qtd. in Rebellato 147). However, it is clear that existentialist concerns of honesty and individual freedom – 'existentialism lite' – resonated in 1950s Britain.
10. The Movement, like the Angry Young Man, was also invented by a newspaper article, in this case a review in the Spectator by J. D. Scott of recent writing, entitled 'In the Movement'. Blake Morrison argues that despite the lack of a formal grouping, Movement writing shares certain characteristics.
11. In Section 7 of *Critique of Judgment* Kant says that the taste of sense is subjective but argues that the taste of reflection makes a claim to objectivity or universality: 'As regards the *agreeable* everyone acknowledges that his judgment, which he bases on a private feeling and by which he says that he likes some object, is by the same token confined to his own person .... Hence about the agreeable the following principle holds: *Everyone has his own taste* (of sense).' A note qualifies the last word: '[As distinguished from taste of reflection]' (55). The taste of reflection is the taste provoked by the aesthetic.
12. It is widely believed that Margaret is a satirical portrait of Philip Larkin's girlfriend, Monica Jones, an English lecturer at Hull, for whom Amis had little time. Monica was undoubtedly Amis's rival for Larkin's time and affection; it is interesting that her fictional counterpart, Margaret, no longer disturbs men's relationships but bonds them together.
13. I explore the gendered dynamics of sadism and masochism more fully in the following chapter. There is a fascinating intertext between the play and the first volume of Osborne's autobiography, *A Better Class of Person*, where we find the same distinction between the unfeeling woman and the feeling man. In the autobiography, Osborne explains that the character of Alison was modelled after his first wife, Pamela Lane, an actress. Osborne describes Pamela's decision to have two abortions, and emphasizes her lack of emotion: 'Pamela soon declared herself pregnant. No, she didn't declare it, she mentioned it like a passing comment. Mention seemed all we could offer each other .... If she was relieved, she never expressed it, nor I my disappointment' (246–47). It is clear that Lane is doing better in her career than Osborne, and she tells him that she is finding it hard to combine marriage and career (252). Eventually, she begins an affair with a local dentist, and leaves him. Osborne's response is 'She's a very cold woman, my wife, my wife' (255). It is tempting to see the relationship between Jimmy and Alison as Osborne's fantasy rewriting of his own marriage; in his play, the wife's lack of feeling is punished, and she regrets the loss of her child, as well as returning to her husband – who has been unfaithful to her with an affair, rather

than the other way around. My thanks to Sandra Courtman for directing me to this episode in Osborne's biography.

14. Bourdieu gives the example of Jacques Duclos, the French Communist Party's candidate in the presidential elections of 1969 – the first election to be properly televised in France. Bourdieu argues that it was Duclos's working-class mannerisms, modes of speech, and bodily hexis which appealed to French working-class voters (the French Communist Party's leadership was peculiar in France for being almost exclusively drawn from the French working class, unlike the liberal professions who dominated the Socialists). See Bourdieu, 'Questions de politique' (my thanks to Jeremy Lane for this reference).

15. The film of *Look Back in Anger* came out in 1958, with a screenplay written by Osborne; it starred Richard Burton and Mary Ure in the main roles. It is interesting to note that the 1957 film version of *Lucky Jim*, which could not be considered New Wave (it was directed by the Boulting Brothers as a slapstick caper), was a box-office failure.

16. 'Articulation' is a term used by Ernesto Laclau and Stuart Hall to explain 'how ideological elements come, under certain conditions, to cohere together within a discourse' (Hall, 'On Postmodernism and Articulation' 141–42). We see here, though, in the records of critics' emotional responses to novels and plays, that the link between feeling and masculinity is not just discursive but also felt and embodied.

17. See Rebellato, 140–42, for an alternative reading of the text's nostalgia for the certainties of Empire.

18. Surveys of 'angry' drama (Lacey) and of New Wave film (Hill) point out that the importance in this period of the attempt to capture reality in a way that went beyond the reproduction of surface realities according to theatrical and filmic conventions of verisimilitude. Rather, the goal was poetic realism: in their filming and staging, both Free Cinema directors and theatrical directors concentrated on images and visual tropes which communicated not just surface truth but some deeper reality (Lacey 110–15; Hill 127–36). Both Osborne and Amis produced a less stylized aesthetics than a film and stage director such as Lindsay Anderson, yet what they had in common with Anderson is the desire to concentrate on fundamental truths rather than on the construction of verisimilitude.

19. This quotation is from Chapter 12 of *Ulysses*.

3 Consumption and Masochism in *Saturday Night and Sunday Morning* and *Room at the Top*

1. See Dominic Sandbrook for the most recent version of this argument.

2. John Kirk, for example, points out the 'scenes of communal culture and solidarity which contradict the individualistic emphasis and override commodification' (73). John Brannigan similarly argues that Arthur 'seems to represent the mind of a 1930s communist trapped in the body of a 1950s consumer' (57), and argues that the persistence of a 'resistant' Arthur, the 1930s communist, undercuts the narrative of progress associated with affluence.

3. Malcolm Bradbury notes the delight in consumption throughout *Room at the Top*, but concludes the novel is 'grossly material fiction, its best energies being spent on descriptions of very expensive cars and suits, a fiction of commodification. It is just saved from being a male version of female popular romance ... by the self-conscious relevance of the theme' (324). Bradbury here rehearses a familiar fear of both femininity and consumption that this novel complicates by connecting consumption to masculinity.

4. Macmillan used this phrase during a speech in Bedford, July 20 1957 (Jefferys 64).

5. See Brooke and Jefferys (154–75) for discussions of the parameters of these debates.

6. John Kirk, who wants to argue the novel is unambiguously critical of affluence, argues that the descriptions of the Thompsons' house 'constitute a comment upon "taste" and symbolic capital rather than a discourse upon relative affluence' (66). But such a reading overlooks the novel's keen awareness that symbolic capital and economic capital are inextricably intertwined: it is precisely Joe's desire for the former that encourages him to seek the latter.

7. Joe's physical hunger is frequently associated with his sexual drive: as one character comments, 'Joe has a huge appetite for everything' (129).

8. Like *Room at the Top* and *Look Back in Anger*, the novel was made into a successful film, directed by Karel Reisz, and starring Albert Finney. As with *Room at the Top*, the paperback sales of *Saturday Night and Sunday Morning* rocketed after the film adaptation, with one million copies sold in the following year (Hewison, *Culture* 105).

9. Here I am influenced by the work of Sally Robinson, who in *Marked Men* analyses images of physical flow in recent American literature and film as expressions both of emotional release and of masculinity.

10. In an analysis of the novel's film adaptation, Lovell points out that consumerism is associated with female domesticity through the depiction of the inside of Doreen's mother's house, which 'bears all the marks of Hoggart's working-class consumerism' ('Landscapes' 367), with modern furniture and fittings in contrast to the décor of Arthur's own traditional two-up two-down terraced house. Lowell argues that Arthur's household with two working men must be more affluent than Doreen's; but modern households filled with consumer goods are coded as female 'despite the anomaly that the working-class aspirations they represent could only be realized by women through access to a male wage' (367).

11. The sexualized anxiety about the instability of language here recalls Rebellato's argument that, in 1950s theatre, realism and the display of emotion was an endorsement and assertion of 'straight' masculinity, unperverted by artifice. In *Room at the Top*, masculinity is also linked to anxieties about aesthetics, as the novel constantly attempts to distinguish its own realist form from inauthentic theatricality. Joe experiences Warley 'as if I were watching myself take part in a documentary film – a really well produced one, accurate, sharp, with none of the more obvious camera tricks' (26). However, the text's putative distinction between authentic realism and inauthentic theatricality cannot be maintained in a work which is, after all, fiction (and therefore artifice); when Joe uses the simile of the documentary film, his dismissal of 'the more obvious camera tricks' also invokes the

problem that a good documentary is one in which those tricks are not absent, merely imperceptible. Verisimilitude demands artifice or performance. The novel exhibits moments of anxiety about its own status as representation rather than reality, expressed in gendered terms: Mr Thompson, an English teacher, tells Joe *'theatregoing's* all right. It's reading that you should beware of. Healthy young men shouldn't read. They finish by becoming broken-winded ushers' (20).

12. Harvey was nominated for an Academy Award for his portrayal of Joe, and the popularity of the film boosted the sales of the novel: although the novel had already sold very well in its first year, the Penguin edition of the text issued in 1959 was reprinted eight times in its first year, and throughout the 1960s the novel became one of all-time Penguin's best-sellers (Laing, *'Room'* 158).

13. His position is, however, similar to Nick Mansfield, who argues that '[the masochist male subject] consolidates and fragments himself at one and the same time. As well as this, he remains a consistent narrating core, able to produce his experience as literature throughout. Contrary to the post-structuralist logic of the dispersal of the subject the masochist never decentres himself without simultaneously centering and strengthening himself' (10).

14. Braine was a working-class scholarship boy who worked as a librarian, while Sillitoe was also from a working-class background, and began to write only after being wounded in the war, and receiving a disability pension.

15. Another example of such identification with a racial other comes in the previous chapter of the novel, when Arthur has spent Christmas with his cousin's friend Sam, a young West Indian soldier temporarily stationed in England. Sam can also be seen as another potential outsider figure with whom Arthur identifies, and even a kind of double for Arthur. This could be compared with Jimmy Porter's identification with the Indian stall-holder in the film of *Look Back in Anger*.

16. According to Andrew Spicer, the director Karel Reisz saw it as futile (153).

17. Joe portrays himself as literally wounded after hearing such news: 'I bit my lip sharply, drawing blood .... It was as if I were being attacked by an invisible enemy' (121). In contrast, the film depicts Joe as sadist rather than masochist at this moment, as he puts his hands round Alice's neck and snarls, 'I understand what makes men kill women like you.'

4   Angry Young Women?: *The L-Shaped Room, A Taste of Honey,* and *The Golden Notebook*

1. Exceptions can be found in Martin McQuillan's edited collection, *Theorising Muriel Spark* (2001).

2. Ian Haywood and Deborah Philips' account of popular women's writing and Niamh Baker's *Happily Ever After* survey of postwar women's literature map out some recurring themes. However, neither of these books attempt a really sustained analysis of the significance of gender in the period. The most useful work is contained in articles by Alison Light and the Birmingham Feminist History Group, and in the edited collection by Jane Dowson.

3. Nonetheless, the identification persisted, so that Murdoch was approached to be in the *Declaration* anthology along with writers like Osborne and Colin Wilson (Lessing, *Walking in the Shade* 208), and was subsequently included (the only woman) in the anthology of opinion pieces *Conviction*, alongside Williams and Hoggart.

4. Other women who began to write in the 1950s and who received fairly short shrift from the dominant taste-makers of the period include Barbara Pym, Penelope Mortimer, and Elizabeth Taylor. Symptomatically, Pym's gentle (though rebarbative) satire, and her focus on a feminized, suburban milieu were seen to be out of step with the times: she found it increasingly difficult to get her novels published in the 1960s, the archetypal example of a woman who was neither angry young man nor unequivocally feminist, and who fell between two literary fashions. In 1963, her novel *An Unsuitable Attachment* was rejected by her publishers, who explained that they could not sell enough copies to cover costs. Robert Long explains that Pym was told her fiction was 'too "mild" or was not the kind of fiction "to which the public is now turning"' (18), and her later novels were also rejected, until her career was revived in 1977 following a defence by Philip Larkin in the *Sunday Times*.

5. Writing in the 1990s, Byatt comments: 'He would have been the hero of any male version of this story, l'homme moyen sensuel, suspicious of Henry's wilder edges, guilty about his wife and the girl, but essentially "decent." This novel doesn't see him quite that way. It is afraid of him, though I only understand now how much' (xi). Alan Sinfield misreads the gendered anxieties at play here when he interprets the novel purely in terms of class: 'the upper-middle-class people dislike [Oliver], and the novel abets them by making him the only character not presented through his own self-perceptions and not shown in any of his own milieux' (241).

6. Toril Moi's critique of Irigaray in *Sexual/Textual Politics* makes the point that mimicry's subversive character must be assessed in a given context: 'Mimicry or impersonation clearly cannot be rejected as unsuitable for feminist purposes, but neither is it the panacea Irigaray occasionally takes it to be .... For what she seems not to see is that sometimes a woman imitating male discourse *is* just a woman speaking like a man: Margaret Thatcher is a case in point. It is the *political context* of such mimicry that is surely always decisive' (142–43).

7. The novel was not reviewed in major literary journals, nor in *ULR*. It did have some commercial success on its publication, however, and was picked as a choice for the Book of the Month Club in 1960 (unpublished correspondence in the archive of the University of Reading). This may have had a negative impact on its critical reception, however, placing it within the category of middlebrow literature.

8. In this respect it shares something with John Wain's 1953 novel *Hurry On Down*, whose middle-class narrator also explores working-class life. Yet Wain's novel is a picaresque, whereas the tone of Banks's novel is very different.

9. Fox rejects psychoanalytic models of shame as being too ahistorical, and anthropological accounts as having a troubling ethnocentric history. Eve Sedgwick finds Silvan Tomkins's account of shame perhaps the most interesting aspect of his theory of affect, yet Tomkins's account of shame is also notably ahistorical.

10. It is interesting to speculate about Banks's personal investment in rewriting the 'angry' paradigm. Banks worked as an actress before she turned to writing; John Osborne's autobiography reveals that she was good friends with his wife, Pamela Lane, also an actress, and suggests that Banks herself may have been the model for Helena in *Look Back in Anger*.

11. The play was first performed by Joan Littlewood's Theatre Workshop which had a 'communitarian, working-class tradition' (Hewison, *In Anger* 148). As with all the plays Littlewood staged, it was workshopped in rehearsal, so that the final version was to some extent a collaborative venture between Delaney, Littlewood, and the actors.

12. These reviews are cited by Samantha Ellis.

13. Lovell points out that this gives Jo, who became pregnant at Christmas, a ten-and-half month pregnancy – a lack of realist detail which appeared not to strike Richardson ('Landscape' 372).

14. The activities in the Heinemann edition focus above all on plot, and on connecting this to the present day. One activity asks students to: 'Imagine that there is to be a "case conference" involving a district nurse and social workers about Jo and her baby and that, following the conference, recommendations are to be made about the baby's future' (95). There is no mention at all in this edition of imagery, symbolism, or narrative structure.

15. Lessing, like Thompson, had been a member of the Communist Party of Great Britain, before leaving in 1957 in the wake of Hungary and revelations about Stalinist death camps.

16. Louise Yelin argues that Lessing's writing in the late 1950s and early 1960s, including her 1960 semi-autobiographical narrative *In Pursuit of the English* as well as *The Golden Notebook* itself, displays her attempt to 'English' herself, a move that depended on her unexamined race privileges as a white colonial. A similar move, however, was arguably made by Stuart Hall who, although a black Jamaican, was virtually silent on issues of race and colonialism during his involvement with the New Left. The more accurate conclusion might be that it was difficult, if not impossible, to be seen simultaneously both as a commentator on British culture and on colonial politics – especially if one's relationship to Britishness was marginal to begin with.

17. This letter is undated. *A Ripple from the Storm* was published in 1958; therefore it is probable that here Lessing is referring to *ULR*, as *New Left Review* subsumed both *New Reasoner* and *ULR*.

18. In connecting psychic breakdown and social crisis, Lessing is similar to her friend R. D. Laing, who argued in his 1960 book *The Divided Self* that the classification of madness was ideological, and that alienation, depression, and breakdown could be seen as valid responses to an alienated world: 'In the context of our present pervasive madness that we call normality, sanity, freedom, all our frames of reference are ambiguous and equivocal. A man who prefers to be dead rather than Red is normal. A man who says he has lost is soul is mad' (12).

19. The character of Saul was based on Lessing's own lover, Clancy Sigal, an American novelist and author of *Weekend in Dinlock* (1960), and a New Left activist. Lessing writes that Sigal 'was a mirror of everything I was beginning to be uneasy about in myself .... What I was beginning to be unhappy about was left-wing romanticism, not to say sentimentality ...] it permeates the left

wing' (*Walking* 152). Sigal, in turn, wrote about a figure like Lessing in his 1979 novel *Zone of the Interior*, which features 'a young American radical named Sid Bell [...] [who] lives in London with an African-born British writer called Coral' (Leonard 275) as well as in his 1992 *The Secret Defector*, in which Gus Black lives with the African-born British novelist Rose, who 'had once written about him in a novel called *Loose Leaves from a Random Life* in which his name was Paul Blue' (Leonard 275).

20. See, for example, Raymond Williams's defence of realism: 'We need this recovery of wholeness, for the most ordinary business of living, yet the necessary learning and adjustment in experience can only take place in ways which the realistic novel alone can record' ('Realism' 25).

21. 'Montage' was a key concept in the debates in the 1930s between Lukács, Brecht, and Bloch about realism and the nature of society under capitalism (and whether such a society was fragmented or unitary). Bloch argued that 'Montage can now work wonders .... Surrealism is nothing if not montage ... it is an account of the chaos of reality as actually experienced' (Bloch et al. 34–35). Brecht similarly suggested that montage could accurately reflect new social relations which were themselves montages: 'these new institutions which undoubtedly shape individuals today are precisely – compared to the family – the products of montage, quite literally "assembled".' (Bloch et al. 79). Lessing may have known of the German debates through her Communist Party contacts, including her husband, Gottfried Lessing, a German Communist.

5 From Motorbikes to Male Strippers: The Persistence of the Feeling Male Body

1. The argument that what is 'socially peripheral is so frequently symbolically central' is made by Peter Stallybrass and Allon White, and undergirds their analyses in *The Politics and Poetics of Transgression* (5).

2. Now seen as the birthplace of British cultural studies, the Centre was established in 1963, with partial funding from the publisher Allen Lane, in gratitude for Richard Hoggart's testimony at the trial of *Lady Chatterley's Lover*, which allowed Hoggart to employ Hall. The Centre's links with the earlier New Left tradition were complicated. Particularly after the departure of Richard Hoggart to a UNESCO post in 1969, Stuart Hall and the graduate students at the Centre engaged with a wide range of European Marxist and post-structuralist theory, most notably the work of Antonio Gramsci and Louis Althusser, which complicated earlier New Left appeals to untheorized notions of experience (as did *New Left Review* under the editorship of Perry Anderson). Similarly, in many of the students' work, a more methodologically rigorous ethnography replaced Hoggart's own quasi-anecdotal evidence in *The Uses of Literacy* (see, for example, both McRobbie and Willis).

3. Like many of the articles in *ULR*, much of the Centre's work reveals an ambivalent attitude to such culture and forms, which are alternately celebrated for their ability to 'resist' or 'transform' the 'dominant culture', and viewed more suspiciously or critically as misguided and ultimately futile expressions of such resistance. See Stanley Cohen for an analysis of the terms

Hebdige, Willis, and others use to express these underlying perceptions of either resistance or transformation.

4. Willis's *Learning to Labour*, written after *Profane Culture*, though published a year earlier, is more self-reflexive about the masculinity of its subjects, a group of alienated, rebellious working-class secondary school boys. This influential book draws on Gramsci's concept of hegemony to argue that the very acts through which these boys expressed their rejection of school culture and dominant ideology enabled the reproduction of the dominant order. In their refusal of the opportunities for social mobility afforded to them by education, the boys unwittingly collude with and give their consent to a system that works through naturalizing and legitimating a distinction between the intelligent middle classes and the stupid working classes; this is why 'working-class kids get working-class jobs'. However, despite Willis's explicit discussion of the relationship between masculinity and manual labour, Beverley Skeggs argues that the book is still dogged by a romantic attitude which sees in its subjects 'the revolutionary potential of the working class' ('Paul Willis' 188), an interpretation contested by Madeleine Arnot, and, perhaps unsurprisingly, by Willis himself (see Mills and Gibb).

5. McRobbie had first made this critique five years previously, in her co-authored chapter on girls' subcultures in *Resistance to Rituals*, which begins 'The absence of girls from the whole literature in this area is quite striking, and demands explanation' (McRobbie and Garber 209).

6. For Willis's discussion of his undergraduate years see Mills and Gibb.

7. On the latter topic, Hebdige identifies a connection between reggae and punk, arguing that the former was 'an alien essence, a foreign body which implicitly threatened mainstream British culture from within and as such it resonated with punk's adopted values – "anarchy," "surrender" and "decline"' (64).

8. In rejecting the notion that punk was magically resolving the contradictions of bourgeois society, Hebdige was not just describing a shift within subcultures themselves, but arguing for a new approach to decoding the semiotics of subcultures, rejecting the methodology used by Phil Cohen and by Willis in *Profane Culture*.

9. In a plot twist – this being a Martin Amis novel – John Self discovers at the end of the novel that Barry Self, the owner of the Shakespeare pub, is in fact not his father, who is in fact Fat Vince, one of Barry's employees.

10. See Chapter 3 for a discussion of this dynamic in relation to *Saturday Night and Sunday Morning* and *Room at the Top*. The gendering of sadism as masculine and masochism as feminism is further reinforced by the contrast between Amis and his female double, Martina Twain, who tries to help Self by trying to teach him how to read, in contrast to Martin, who deliberately plays with his character. Martin is the masculine sadist and the ludic author in comparison with female Martina, the moral author whose relationship with John Self is both selfless and masochistic.

11. As Sally Robinson argues, 'the language of crisis carries with it a vocabulary of blockage and release' (12). A comparison could be made between John Self and Jim Dixon, whose freedom from Welch's clutches is also signalled by the ability to speak in his own voice.

12. Keulks bases his analysis on Bakhtin's discussion of Menippean satire in *Problems in Dostoevsky's Poetics* (Ann Arbor: U of Michigan P, 1973), pp. 94–96, and 103–11. As Diedrick points out, Amis almost certainly was aware of this book as it was reviewed in the *Times Literary Supplement* while he was working there (33).
13. See also, though, Amis's comments on tramps in his memoir *Experience*; 'There was still the suspicion, despite all the current evidence, that you would not only fail but actually go under. Perhaps everybody has this. Christopher Hitchens had it: we called it "tramp dread"'. (35)
14. Spicer sees the underclass male as everyman in a number of 1990s films, including Ken Loach's *Riff-Raff* (1991) and *My Name is Joe* (1998), as well as *The Full Monty*.
15. Grant Farred reads the ending of the novel differently, suggesting it turns to the possibility of community offered by the European Union, which 'for all its flaws and uncertainties, enables itinerant Scottish figures such as Renton to find or construct communities beyond the local or the (suffocating) nation' ('Wankerdom' 224). This reading, however, seems overly idealistic in its attempt to find a desire for community in Renton's escape to Amsterdam.
16. Here I disagree Claire Monk's claim that the film shows the way in which 'male social and emotional bonds once associated with the workplace and the working-man's club are threatened, mourned, struggled for – and finally restored' (162). The emotional bonds formed amongst the strippers cross barriers of class that would in fact have been enforced in the workplace. Moreover, the emotional bonds between men do not lead to an exclusive male community but bring together the community across divisions of gender and class in an inclusive comic vision.
17. This is the first of the many images of enclosure and restriction in the film, from the men's toilet in which Gaz and Dave hide, to the children's crèche from which Dave, Gaz, and Lomper spy on Gerald, to the garden shed in which Dave sits, depressed and bingeing.
18. This fact is key for Judith Halberstam, who argues that the film thereby 'refuses to make the visibility of the phallus into the totality of maleness' (440).
19. Kelly Farrell points that the men in the film were appropriated by both Prince Charles and Tony Blair as symbolic representatives of national wholeness and revitalization.

WORKS CITED

'Editorial.' *Universities and Left Review* 7 (1959): 1.

Adorno, Theodor, and Max Horkheimer. *Dialectic of Enlightenment*. 1947. Palo Alto: Stanford UP, 2002.

Allcorn, K. 'The Unnoticed Generation.' *Universities and Left Review* 4 (1958): 54–58.

Amis, Kingsley. *Lucky Jim*. 1954. London: Penguin, 1992.

———. 'Socialism and the Intellectuals.' London: The Fabian Society, 1957.

———. *The Letters of Kingsley Amis*. Ed. Zachary Leader. 2000. New York: Miramax, 2001.

Amis, Martin. *Money*. 1984. New York: Penguin, 1986.

———. *Experience*. London: Vintage, 2000.

Anderson, Lindsay. 'Commitment in Cinema Criticism.' *Universities and Left Review* 1 (1957): 44–48.

———. 'Free Cinema.' *Universities and Left Review* 2 (1957): 51–52.

Anderson, Perry. 'Components of the National Culture.' *English Questions*. London: Verso, 1992. 48–104.

Archer, Robin, et al., eds. *Out of Apathy: Voices of the New Left Thirty Years On*. London: Verso, 1989.

Armstrong, Michael. 'Commitment in Criticism.' *Universities and Left Review* 2 (1957): 65–66.

Arnott, Madeleine. 'Male Working-Class Identities and Social Justice: A Reconsideration of Paul Willis's *Learning to Labor* in Light of Contemporary Research.' Dolby 17–40.

Baker, Niamh. *Happily Ever After? Women's Fiction in Postwar Britain 1945–1960*. London: Macmillan, 1989.

Baldick, Chris. *The Social Mission of English Criticism 1848–1932*. Oxford: Clarendon Press, 1983.

Banks, Lynne Reid. *The L-Shaped Room*. 1960 London: Penguin, 1962.

Baucom, Ian. *Out of Place: Englishness, Empire, and the Locations of Identity*. Princeton: Princeton UP, 1999.

Bhabha, Homi. *The Location of Culture*. London: Routledge, 1994.

Billington, Michael. 'The Angry Generation.' *Guardian* 17 July 1999. Saturday Review: 5.

Birmingham Feminist History Group. 'Feminism as Femininity in the Nineteen-Fifties?' *Feminist Review* 3 (1979): 48–65.

Bloch, Ernst, et al. *Aesthetics and Politics*. 1977. London: Verso, 1980.

Bourdieu, Pierre. *Distinction: A Social Critique of the Judgement of Taste*. Trans. Richard Nice. London: Routledge, 1984.

———. 'Questions de politique.' *Actes de la recherche en sciences socials* 16 (1977): 55–89.

Bradbury, Malcolm. *The Modern British Novel*. London: Secker & Warburg, 1993.

Braine, John. *Room at the Top*. 1957. London: Arrow, 1989.

Brannigan, John. *Orwell to the Present: Literature in England, 1945–2000.* London: Palgrave, 2003.

Bromley, Roger. 'The Theme That Dare Not Speak Its Name: Class and Recent British Film.' *Cultural Studies and the Working Class.* Ed. Sally R. Munt. London: Cassell, 2000.

Brooke, Stephen. 'Gender and Working Class Identity in Britain during the 1950s.' *Journal of Social History* 34.4 (2001): 773–95.

Byatt, A. S., and intr. *The Shadow of the Sun.* 1964. London: Vintage, 1991.

———. *Still Life.* New York: Charles Scribner's, 1985.

Cairns, David, and Shaun Richards. 'No Good Brave Causes? The Alienated Intellectual and the End of Empire.' *Literature and History* 14:2 (1988): 194–206.

Carpenter, Humphrey. 'Behind the Fringe.' *Sunday Times* 2 July 2000: B1–2.

Carr, W. I. 'Mr Osborne and an Indifferent society.' *Universities and Left Review,* 4 (1958): 32–33.

Chapman, Mary, and Glenn Hendler. *Sentimental Men: Masculinity and the Politics of Affect in American Culture.* Berkeley: U of California P, 1999.

Chun, Lin. *The British New Left.* Edinburgh: Edinburgh UP, 1993.

Cohen, Stanley. 'Symbols of Trouble.' *The Subcultures Reader.* Eds Ken Gelder and Sarah Thornton. London: Routledge, 1997. 149–62.

Colebrook, Claire. 'The Politics and Potential of Everyday Life: On the Very Concept of Everyday Life.' *New Literary History* 33.4 (2002): 687–706.

Coleman, John. 'All Sorts.' *New Statesman* 23 November 1962, 752.

Conekin, Becky, Frank Mort and Chris Waters. *Moments of Modernity: Reconstructing Britain 1945–1964.* London: Rivers Oram P, 1999.

Connell, R. W. *Masculinities.* Berkeley: U of California P, 1995.

Cunningham, Valentine. *British Writers of the Thirties.* Oxford: Oxford UP, 1988.

Davidson, Michael. *The San Francisco Renaissance: Poetics and Community at Mid-Century.* Cambridge: Cambridge UP, 2000.

———. *Guys Like Us: Citing Masculinity in Cold War Poetics.* Chicago: U of Chicago P, 2004.

Davies, Ioan. *Cultural Studies and Beyond: Fragments of Empire.* London: Routledge, 1995.

Day, Gary. *Re-reading Leavis.* London: Macmillan, 1996.

Delaney, Shelagh. *A Taste of Honey.* 1959. Oxford: Heinemann, 1989.

Diedrick, James. *Understanding Martin Amis.* Columbia: U of South Carolina P, 1995.

Dolby, Nadine, and Greg Dimitriadis, eds. *Learning to Labor in New Times.* New York: Routledge, 2004.

Dowson, Jane, ed. *Women's Writing 1945–1960: After the Deluge.* London: Palgrave, 2003.

Dworkin, Dennis. *Cultural Marxism in Postwar Britain: History, the New Left and the Origins of Cultural Studies.* Durham: Duke UP, 1997.

Eagleton, Terry. *Criticism and Ideology: A Study in Marxist Literary Theory.* 1976 London: Verso, 1978.

———. *Literary Theory: An Introduction.* Oxford: Blackwell, 1983.

Ellis, Markman. *The Coffee-House: A Cultural History.* London: Weidenfeld and Nicholson, 2005.

Ellis, Samantha. 'A Taste of Honey, London, May 1958.' *The Guardian.* 10 September 2003. April 2 2006. http://arts.guardian.co.uk/curtainup/story/0,,1040110,00.html.

English, James F. *Comic Transactions: Literature, Humor, and the Politics of Community in Twentieth-Century Britain*. Ithaca: Cornell UP, 1994.

Esty, Jed. *A Shrinking Island: Modernism and National Culture in England*. Princeton, NJ: Princeton UP, 1994.

Faludi, Susan. *Stiffed: The Betrayal of the American Man*. New York: Harper, 2000.

Farred, Grant. 'Endgame Identity? Mapping the New Left Roots of Identity Politics.' *New Literary History* 31.4 (2000): 627–48.

———. 'Wankerdom: *Trainspotting* as a Rejection of the Postcolonial?' *South Atlantic Quarterly* 103.1 (2004): 215–26.

Farrell, Kelly. 'Naked Nation: *The Full Monty*, Working-Class Masculinity, and the British Image. *Men And Masculinities* 6.2 (2003): 119–35.

Fleming, Ian. *Doctor No*. New York: Macmillan, 1958.

Foster, Hal. *The Return of the Real: Art and Theory at the End of the Century*. Cambridge: MIT P, 1996.

Fox, Pamela. *Class Fictions: Shame and Resistance in the British Working-Class Novel, 1890–1945*. Durham: Duke UP, 1994.

Francis, Martin. 'The Labour Party: Modernisation and the Politics of Restraint.' Conekin, Mort and Waters 152–71.

Genette, Gerard. *Narrative Discourse*. Trans. Jane E. Lewin. Oxford: Blackwell, 1980.

Geraghty, Christine. 'Albert Finney—a Working-Class Hero.' *Me Jane: Masculinity, Movies and Women*. Eds Pat Kirkham and Janet Thumin. London: Lawrence and Wishart, 1995. 62–72.

Gilroy, Paul. *Postcolonial Melancholia*. New York: Columbia UP, 2005.

Gosling, Ray. 'Dream Boy.' *New Left Review* 3 (1960): 30–34.

Grossberg, Lawrence. *We Gotta Get Out of This Place*. London: Routledge, 1992.

Haffenden, John. *Novelists in Interview*. London: Methuen, 1985.

Halberstam, Judith. 'Oh Behave! Austin Powers and the Drag Kings.' *GLQ* 7.3 (2001): 425–52.

Hall, Stuart. 'In the No Man's land.' *Universities and Left Review* 3 (1958): 86–87.

———. 'The Politics of Adolescence.' *Universities and Left Review* 6 (1959): 2–4.

———. 'Absolute Beginnings.' *Universities and Left Review* 7 (1959): 17–25.

——— and Tony Jefferson, eds. *Resistance Through Rituals: Youth Subcultures in Post-war Britain*. London: Hutchinson, 1976.

——— et al. eds. *Policing the Crisis: Mugging, the State, and Law and Order*. London: Macmillan, 1978.

———. 'The "First" New Left.' Archer 11–38.

———. 'On Postmodernism and Articulation: An Interview with Stuart Hall.' Ed. Larry Grossberg. *Stuart Hall: Critical Dialogues in Cultural Studies*. Eds David Morley and Kuan-Hsing Chen. London: Routledge, 1996. 131–50.

Haywood, Ian. *Working-Class Fiction: from Chartism to Trainspotting*. Plymouth: Northcote House, 1997.

——— and Deborah Philips. *Brave New Causes: Literature and Gender in Post-war Britain*. Leicester: Leicester UP, 1998.

Hebdige, Dick. *Subculture: The Meaning of Style*. London: Methuen, 1979.

Hewison, Robert. *In Anger: British Culture in the Cold War 1945–60*. New York: Oxford UP, 1981.

———. *Culture and Consensus: England, Art and Politics Since 1940*. London: Methuen, 1995.

Higgins, John. *Raymond Williams: Literature, Marxism and Cultural Materialism*. London: Routledge, 1999.

Hill, John. *Sex, Class and Realism; British Cinema 1956-1963*. London: British Film Institute, 1986.

Hitchcock, Peter. *Working-Class Fiction in Theory and Practice: A Reading of Alan Sillitoe*. Ann Arbor: UMI P, 1989.

Hitchens, Christopher. 'The Man of Feeling.' *The Atlantic Monthly* 289.5 (May 2002): 103–108.

Hochschild, Arlie Russell. *The Managed Heart: Commercialization of Human Feeling*. Berkeley: California UP, 1983.

Hoggart, Richard. *The Uses of Literacy*. London: Chatto & Windus, 1957. London: Penguin, 1958.

——— and Raymond Williams. 'Working Class Attitudes.' Discussion. *New Left Review* 1 (1960): 26–30.

Jameson, Fredric. *The Political Unconscious: Narrative as a Socially Symbolic Act*. Ithaca: Cornell UP, 1982.

———. *Postmodernism: or, the cultural logic of late capitalism*. Durham, NC: Duke UP, 1991.

Jardine, Lisa, and Julia Swindells. *What's Left?: Women in Culture and the Labour Movement*. London: Routledge, 1990.

Jay, Martin, Anton Kaes, and Edmund Dimendberg, eds. *The Weimar Republic Sourcebook*. Berkeley: U of California P, 1995.

Jefferys, Kevin. *Retreat From New Jerusalem: British Politics, 1951–64*. London: Macmillan, 1997.

Jenks, Chris. *Subculture: The Fragmentation of the Social*. London: Sage, 2005.

Kalliney, Peter. 'Cities of Affluence: Masculinity, Class, and the Angry Young Men.' *Modern Fiction Studies* 47.1 (2001): 92–117.

Kant, Immanuel. *Critique of Judgment*. Ed. Werner S. Pluhar. Cambridge: Hackett, 1987.

Kaplan, Cora. 'The Death of the Working-Class Hero.' *New Formations* 52 (2004): 94–110.

Kaye, Michael. 'The New Drama.' *New Left Review* 5 (1960): 64–66.

Kenny, Michael. *The First New Left: British Intellectuals After Stalin*. London: Lawrence and Wishart, 1995.

Keulks, Gavin. *Father and Son: Kingsley Amis, Martin Amis, and the British Novel Since 1950*. Madison: U of Wisconsin P, 2003.

Kirk, John. *Twentieth-Century Writing and the British Working Class*. Cardiff: U of Wales P, 2003.

Koch, Adolf. 'The Truth about the Berlin Nudist Groups.' Jay, Kaes and Dimendberg 676.

Kracauer, Siegfried. 'The Mass Ornament.' Trans. Barbara Correll and Jack Zipes. *New German Critique* 5 (Spring 1975): 67–76.

Kullman, M. 'The Anti-culture Born of Despair.' *Universities and Left Review* 4 (1958): 51–54.

Lacey, Stephen. *British Realist Drama: The New Wave in its Context, 1956–1965*. London: Routledge, 1995.

Laing, R. D. *The Divided Self*. 1960. London: Penguin, 1965.

Laing, Stuart. '*Room at the Top*: The Morality of Affluence.' *Popular Fiction and Social Change*. Ed. Chris Pawling. London: Macmillan, 1984. 157–84.

——. *Representations of Working-Class Life 1957–64*. London: Macmillan, 1986.

Lawrence, D. H. *The Rainbow*. 1915. Harmondsworth: Penguin, 1949.

Leavis, F. R. *Mass Civilization and Minority Culture*. Cambridge: Minority P, 1930.

—— and Denys Thompson. *Culture and Environment: The Training of Critical Awareness*. 1933. London: Chatto and Windus, 1964.

——. *English Literature in the University*. Cambridge: Cambridge UP, 1969.

Lee, Richard E. *Life and Times of Cultural Studies: The Politics and Transformation of the Structures of Knowledge*. Durham: Duke UP, 2003.

Leonard, John. *When the Kissing Had to Stop*. New York: The New Press, 1999.

Lessing, Doris. *Each His Own Wilderness*. *New English Dramatists*. Ed. E. Martin Browne. London: Penguin, 1959. 11–95.

——. *The Golden Notebook*. 1962. New York: Bantam, 1973.

——. *A Small Personal Voice: Essays, Reviews, Interviews*. Ed. Paul Schlueter. London: Flamingo, 1994.

——. 'The Small Personal Voice.' *Declaration*. Ed. Tom Maschler. London: McGibbon & Kee, 1957. 3–21.

——. *Walking in the Shade: Volume Two of My Autobiography, 1949–1962*. 1997. London: Flamingo, 1998.

Light, Alison. 'Writing Fictions: Femininity and the 1950s.' *The Progress of Romance*. Ed. Jean Radford. London: Routledge, 1985: 139–65.

Lodge, David. Introduction. *Lucky Jim*. London: Penguin, 1992. v–xvii.

Long, Robert Emmett. *Barbara Pym*. New York: Unger, 1987.

Lovell, Terry. 'Landscapes and Stories in 1960s British Realism.' *Screen* 31:4 (1990): 357–76.

——. 'Resisting With Authority: Historical Specificity, Agency, and the performative Self.' *Theory, Culture and Society* 20.1 (2003): 1–18.

Luckett, Moya. 'Image and Nation in 1990s British Cinema.' Murphy 88–99.

MacInnes, Colin. *England, Half English*. London: Chatto and Windus, 1986.

Mackenzie, Norman, ed. *Conviction*. London: MacGibbon & Kee, 1958.

McClure, Michael. *Scratching the Beat Surface*. San Francisco: North Point, 1982.

McKibbin, Ross. *Classes and Cultures: England 1918–1951*. Oxford: Oxford UP, 1998.

McQuillan, Martin, ed. *Theorising Muriel Spark*. London: Palgrave, 2001.

McRobbie, Angela. 'Settling Accounts with Subcultures.' 1980. *Culture, Ideology and Social Process*. Eds Tony Bennett et al. London: Batsford, 1981. 111–24.

—— and Jenny Garber. 'Girls and Subculture.' Eds Hall et al., *Resistance to Rituals* 209–22.

Mansfield, Nick. *Masochism: The Art of Power*. London: Praeger, 1997.

Marquand, David. 'Lucky Jim and the Labour Party.' *Universities and Left Review* 1 (1957): 57–60.

——. 'The New Left at Oxford.' *The Guardian* 18 August 1958: 4.

Martin, Graham. 'A Look Back at Osborne.' *Universities and Left Review* 7 (1959): 37–40.

Maschler, Tom, ed. *Declaration*. London: McGibbon & Kee, 1957.

Massumi, Brian. 'The Autonomy of Affect.' *Cultural Critique* 31 (Fall 1995): 83–109.

Maugham, Somerset. 'Books of the Year.' *Sunday Times* 25 December 1955: 4.

Miller, Jane. *Seductions: Studies in Reading and Culture*. Cambridge, MA: Harvard UP, 1991.

Mills, David, and Robert Gibb. '"Centre" and Periphery—An Interview with Paul Willis.' Dolby 197–226.

Moi, Toril. *Sexual/Textual Politics*. London: Methuen, 1985.

Monk, Claire. 'Men in the 90s.' Murphy 156–66.

Morace, Robert. *Irvine Welsh's Trainspotting: A Reader's Guide*. London: Continuum, 2001.

Morrison, Blake. *The Movement: English Poetry and Fiction of the 1950s*. Oxford: Oxford UP, 1980.

Mort, Frank. *Cultures of Consumption: Masculinities and Social Space in Late Twentieth-Century Britain*. London: Routledge, 1996.

Mulhern, Francis. *The Moment of 'Scrutiny'*. 1979. London: Verso, 1981.

Murdoch, Iris. *Under the Net*. London: Chatto & Windus, 1954.

Murphy, Robert, ed. *British Cinema of the 1990s*. London: British Film Institute, 2000.

Orwell, George. *The Road to Wigan Pier*. 1937. Harmondsworth: Penguin, 2001.

Osborne, John. *Look Back in Anger*. London: Faber, 1960.

———. 'They Call it Cricket.' Maschler 61–84.

———. *A Better Class of Person: An Autobiography, 1929–56*. London: Faber, 1981.

Pearson, Gabriel. Review of *Room at the Top*. *Universities and Left Review* 2 (1957): 72–73.

Pease, Alison. *Modernism, Mass Culture, and the Aesthetics of Obscenity*. Cambridge: Cambridge UP, 2000.

Petro, Patrice. *Joyless Streets: Women and Melodramatic Representation in Weimar Germany*. Princeton, NJ: Princeton UP, 1989.

Rebellato, Dan. *1956 And All That*. London: Routledge, 1999.

Reich, Wilhelm. *Listen, Little Man!* 1948. Trans. Ralph Manheim. New York: Noonday P, 1974.

Robinson, Sally. *Marked Men: White Masculinity in Crisis*. New York: Columbia UP, 2000.

Samuel, Raphael. 'Born-again Socialism.' Archer 39–58.

Sandbrook, Dominic. *Never Had it So Good: A History of Britain from Suez to the Beatles*. London: Little Brown, 2005.

Savran, David. *Taking it Like a Man: White Masculinity, Maochism, and Contemporary American Culture*. Princeton: Princeton UP, 1997.

Schoene-Harwood, Berthold. *Writing Men: Literary Masculinities from Frankenstein to the New Man*. Edinburgh: Edinburgh UP, 2000.

Schwartz, Bill. 'Reveries of Race: The Closing of the Imperial Moment.' Conekin, Mort and Waters 189–207.

Scott, Joan W. 'The Evidence of Experience.' *Critical Inquiry* 17 (Summer 1991): 733–97.

Sedgwick, Eve Kosofsky. *Between Men: English Literature and Male Homosocial Desire*. New York: Columbia UP, 1985.

——— and Adam Frank, eds. *Shame and Its Sisters: A Silvan Tomkins Reader*. Durham: Duke UP, 1995.

Segal, Lynne. 'Look Back in Anger: Men in the Fifties.' *Male Order: UnWrapping Masculinity*. Eds Rowena Chapman and Jonathan Rutherford. London: Lawrence and Wishart, 1988. 68–96.

———. *Slow Motion: Changing Masculinities, Changing Men*. London: Virago, 1990.

Seltzer, Mark. 'Wound Culture: Trauma in the Pathological Public Sphere.' *October* 80 (Spring 1997): 3–26.

Sigal, Clancy. 'Nihilism's Organization Man.' *Universities and Left Review* 4 (1958): 59–65.

Sillitoe, Alan. *Saturday Night and Sunday Morning*. 1958. London: Flamingo, 1994.

Silverman, Kaja. 'Masochism and Male Subjectivity.' *Male Trouble*. Eds Constance Penley and Sharon Willis. Minneapolis: U of Minnesota P, 1993. 33–66.

Simpson, David. 'Raymond Williams: Feeling for Structures, Voicing "History".' *On Raymond Williams*. Ed. Christopher Prendergast. Minneapolis: U of Minnesota P, 1995. 29–50.

Sinfield, Alan. *Literature, Politics and Culture in Postwar Britain*. Oxford: Basil Blackwell, 1989.

Skeggs, Beverley. 'Paul Willis, *Learning to Labour*.' *Reading into Cultural Studies*. Eds M. Narker and A. Beezer. London: Routledge, 1992. 181–96.

Speakman, Ray. Introduction to *A Taste of Honey*. Oxford: Heinemann, 1989. v–vi.

Stallybrass, Peter, and Allon White. *The Politics and Poetics of Transgression*. London: Methuen, 1986.

Stearns, Peter. *American Cool: Constructing a Twentieth-Century Emotional Style*. New York: New York UP, 1994.

Steedman, Carolyn. *Landscape for a Good Woman*. London: Virago, 1986.

Taylor, Jenny, ed. and intr. *Notebooks/memoirs/archives: Reading and Rereading Doris Lessing*. London: Routledge, 1982.

Taylor, John Russell, ed. *John Osborne, Look Back in Anger; A Casebook*. London: Macmillan, 1968.

———. *Anger and After: A Guide to the New British Drama*. London: Methuen, 1969.

Thompson, E. P. 'The Long Revolution.' Part 1. *New Left Review* 9 (1961): 24-33.

———. *The Making of the English Working Class*. 1963. Harmondsworth: Penguin, 1980.

Thornton, Sarah. *Club Cultures: Music, Media, and Subcultural Capital*. Hanover: Wesleyan UP, 1996.

Todd, Janet. *Sensibility: An Introduction*. London: Methuen, 1986.

Tomkins, Silvan. *Exploring Affect: The Selected Writings of Silvan S. Thomas*. Ed. E. Virginia Demos. Cambridge: Cambridge UP, 1995.

Turner, Graeme. *British Cultural Studies: An Introduction*. Second Edition. London: Routledge, 1996.

Tynan, Kenneth. *A View of the English Stage 1944–65*. London: Methuen, 1984.

Waugh, Evelyn. 'An open letter to the Hon. Mrs Peter Rodd (Nancy Mitford) on a very serious subject.' *Encounter*, December 1955: 11–21.

Welsh, Irvine. *Trainspotting*. 1993 London: Vintage, 1994.

Wildung, Fritz. 'Sport is the Will to Culture.' Jay, Kaes and Edmund Dimendberg 681–82.

Williams, Raymond. *Culture and Society: Coleridge to Orwell*. London: Chatto & Windus, 1958. London: The Hogarth Press, 1990.

———. 'Realism and the Contemporary Novel.' *Universities and Left Review* 4 (1958): 22–25.

———. *Border Country*. 1960. Harmondsworth: Penguin, 1964.

———. *The Long Revolution*. 1961. London: The Hogarth Press, 1992.

————. *Politics and Letters: Interviews with New Left Review.* London: New Left Books, 1979.

————. 'Film and the Dramatic Tradition.' *The Raymond Williams Reader.* Ed. John Higgins. Oxford: Blackwell, 2001. 25–41.

Willis, Paul. *Learning to Labour: How Working-Class Kids Get Working-Class Jobs.* Aldershot: Gower, 1977.

————. *Profane Culture.* London: Routledge, 1978.

Wilson, Elizabeth. *Only Halfway to Paradise: Women in Postwar Britain 1945–68.* London: Tavistock, 1980.

Yelin, Louise. *From the Margins of Empire: Christina Stead, Doris Lessing, Nadine Gordimer.* Ithaca: Cornell UP, 1998.

Young, Robert J. C. *Postcolonialism: An Historical Introduction.* Oxford: Blackwell, 2001.

Žižek, Slavoj. *Everything You Always Wanted to Know About Lacan (But Were Afraid To Ask Hitchcock).* London: Verso, 1992.

Index